FABLES OF WIT
AND
ELEGANCE

FABLES OF WIT
AND
ELEGANCE

Edited and with an Introduction by

❊ LOUIS AUCHINCLOSS ❊

CHARLES SCRIBNER'S SONS ❊ NEW YORK

ACKNOWLEDGMENTS

"Autres Temps . . ." (Copyright 1911 The Century Company; renewal copyright 1939 D. Appleton-Century Co., Inc.) is reprinted by permission of Charles Scribner's Sons from THE COLLECTED SHORT STORIES OF EDITH WHARTON.

"Hilary Maltby and Stephen Braxton" reprinted by permission of William Heinemann Ltd. from SEVEN MEN AND TWO OTHERS by Max Beerbohm.

"Thirty Clocks Strike the Hour" (Copyright 1929, 1930, 1931, 1932 by V. Sackeville-West) is reprinted by permission of John Cushman Associates, Inc., from THIRTY CLOCKS STRIKE THE HOUR by V. Sackeville-West.

"Lambert Orme" (First published in the USA 1926) is reprinted by permission of John Cushman Associates, Inc., from SOME PEOPLE by Harold Nicolson.

"Incident in Azania" (Copyright 1936 by Evelyn Waugh) is reprinted by permission of Little, Brown and Co., and A. D. Peters & Company from MR. LOVEDAY'S LITTLE OUTING AND OTHER SAD STORIES by Evelyn Waugh.

"Glory in the Daytime" from THE PORTABLE DOROTHY PARKER. Copyright 1933, copyright © renewed 1961 by Dorothy Parker. Reprinted by permission of The Viking Press, Inc.

"The Eternal Moment" from THE ETERNAL MOMENT AND OTHER STORIES by E. M. Forster, copyright 1928 by Harcourt Brace Jovanovich, Inc.; copyright 1956 by E. M. Forster. Reprinted by permission of the publisher.

"The Echo and the Nemesis" is reprinted with the permission of Farrar, Straus & Giroux, Inc., from THE COLLECTED STORIES OF JEAN STAFFORD, copyright © 1950, 1969 by Jean Stafford.

"The Friend of the Family" copyright 1947 by Mary McCarthy. Reprinted from her volume CAST A COLD EYE by permission of Harcourt Brace Jovanovich, Inc.

"The Tillotson Banquet" from COLLECTED SHORT STORIES by Aldous Huxley. Copyright 1921 by Aldous Huxley. Reprinted by permission of Harper & Row, Publishers, Inc., Chatto & Windus Ltd. and Mrs. Laura Huxley.

"In the Absence of Angels" copyright 1951 by Hortense Calisher, from IN THE ABSENCE OF ANGELS by Hortense Calisher. Reprinted by permission of Little, Brown and Co.

Printed in the United States of America
Library of Congress Catalog Card Number 73–37198
SBN 684–12745–8 (Trade cloth)

CONTENTS

(v)

INTRODUCTION

IN selecting these stories I have tried to make the volume "irrelevant"—as the term is used by young people today—because, where literary subjects are concerned, I find a definite link between the relevant and the boring. Lord knows, there is trouble enough on our plundered, polluted planet, but the puritanical impulse, so much abroad in our times, to confine the arts to a consideration of local or current agony does very little for the arts and even less, I fear, for the agony. It is interesting, on the other hand, to look back and consider how many of the great nineteenth century novels are set in a period twenty-five years or more prior to their dates of publication and to contemporary agonies: *Vanity Fair, Wuthering Heights, War and Peace, Middlemarch,* to name but a few. Even the great Zola wrote his entire *Rougon-Macquart* series about an earlier generation. Yet in our day a novel set in the 1920s would be classified by many critics as escapist trash, fit only for the lending library trade.

In the years immediately following World War II, I used to frequent a literary group that had its origins in a series of Sunday afternoons at a Greenwich Village bar called the White Horse Tavern. The group was largely made up by Vance Bourjaily, and he had a discerning eye, for among the new writers who made their appearance there I recall Norman Mailer, Calder Willingham, Gore Vidal, Hortense Calisher, Chandler Brossard and Herman Wouk. And there were many others. What I remember particularly about the discussions was how little interest the writers seemed to have in the literary past. There was a great deal of emphasis on craft—one's own craft. They were mostly individualists who did not consider themselves heirs or even debtors of any particular literary tradition. And very rarely—with the exceptions of Vidal and Calisher—was there the smallest emphasis on elegance or wit. A considerable body of first class writing emanated from that group, but one could see in it the break with the past that has been carried so far by the colleges today.

I decided in this anthology to go back to our immediate literary forebears, from the nineties to the great depression, and to pick out examples of "literary" writers, writers, that is, who cared as much about reading as writing, writers who were sophisticated, cultivated and possessed of a knowledge of the world, writers, in short, who represented some of the grace and beauty of a way of life in England and America that has pretty well ceased to exist. And then I would bring the collection almost but not quite down to date. My idea was that the project would pay off in terms of sheer entertainment, a quality too often neglected by writers in the past thirty years. Whether or not it does must be decided by each reader of the anthology.

In some of these stories the borderline between fiction and the literary essay is hazy. The characters, once created, can be released to play such parts as they find in the rich cultural background of the artist. This is particularly true, of course, of *The Portrait of Mr W. H.,* but it is also true of *Hilary Maltby and Stephen Braxton,* a lampoon of contemporary best sellers, of *Lambert Orme,* which contains a bit of searching and profound autobiography, and of *The Friend of the Family,* a deeply penetrating essay on the plight of the single man and woman in a society that makes a fetish of marriage—or marriages. *The Tillotson Banquet* moves almost into the area of art criticism; it contains a delightful survey of early nineteenth century British art of the minor school of Haydon. I find a kind of exhilaration in this crossing and recrossing of fictional borderlines. It requires, like Thackeray's, a firm hand to hold two reins, but it can be done, and I see no reason that it should not be.

The master, Henry James, would, of course, have passionately disagreed, and it is with the master that we start. James laid down as a cardinal principle that the author must keep himself strictly out of his fiction, and he could not abide Thackeray's habit of asides. His rules worked too well in his own case to be criticized, but he went too far in applying them to others. I selected *The Abasement of the Northmores* because it was written just as he was entering the final and perfect stage of his novel writing career. The unhappy, abortive period of his play writing was over, and he was already at work on the great trio of novels that was to be his finest monument: *The Ambassadors, The Golden Bowl* and *The Wings of the Dove. The*

Abasement is a sad, muted, charming tale, with its wonderful contrast of two lives, one all brass and tinkling cymbals, the other all depth and gentleness and sympathy, against their common background of a seemingly fooled but ultimately unfooled public. The letters of the two men, which we never read, are so vividly described that in the end they take the place of their writers. It is a perfectly balanced fable.

Autres Temps, in a similar fashion, represents Edith Wharton at her peak. The story is a kind of capsule *House of Mirth.* New York society has changed since 1905, the year of that novel's publication, but it has changed as any reader of Lily Bart's tragedy could have easily predicted: it is even looser, even less disciplined, even greedier, even more worldly. The simple lesson that Mrs. Wharton teaches us (although when was it taught before?) is that society is always too busy to revise its judgments. Mrs. Lidcote remains condemned for abandoning her husband twenty years before, although her daughter, championed by her mother's old judges, can abandon hers with impunity. There is no generation gap in the modern sense of the term, because mother and daughter both perfectly comprehend what is happening to them and both accept the double standard by which they are judged. The story has some of the chill of a tale of aborigines. The condemned accept the voodoo just as reverently as do the condemners.

I assume that Oscar Wilde put *The Portrait of Mr W. H.* in the form of a story because his theory of the identity of the young man of Shakespeare's sonnets was more a flight of the imagination than a proposition to be taken literally. In fictional guise it could not be torn to slivers by the scholars. Yet to me Wilde's essay-story comes closer to the emotional message of the sonnets than much of the massive literature that has grown up about them. We know that the beautiful youth played a great role in the poet's heart, and it makes a kind of crazy sense that he should have played the principal female roles in the plays as well. Stern critics have scolded readers for generations for allowing their fancies to play with the scanty but tantalizing autobiographical tidbits of the sonnets, but how is one to resist? The master poet of history, in some of his greatest verse, seems to be admitting one to the most intimate chapter of his heart. It is almost impossible not to probe. Wilde's characters vividly illustrate this difficulty, and the theory which they concoct is enough to give one a heady moment of satisfaction before it falls to pieces. At any rate, the story acts as a kind of catharsis of the detective spirit, and one may be better able after it to return to the sonnets as poetry alone.

I submit that *Hilary Maltby and Stephen Braxton* is one of the funniest stories in the language. I never cease to roar at the hilarious and terrible retribution of the dinner party where Hilary Maltby, his face bandaged from shaving cuts, spills bortsch down his white shirt front at table. And to Max Beerbohm's farce I offer the contrast of the austere grandeur of V. Sackeville-West's old lady in her Paris palace. Few writers have caught the splendor of the Edwardian age as the author of *The Edwardians,* and in *Thirty Clocks Strike the Hour* she evokes the earlier lavishness of the mid-nineteenth century with her great, empty, silent house (in fact, the one that housed what is now the Wallace Collection of London) standing in the heart of a noisy modern city.

Harold Nicolson in *Lambert Orme* composed an important chapter of his own biography in describing the effect upon a basically conventional, aristocratic, pre-World War I Oxford dilettante of an utterly uninhibited aesthete. It is Harold Nicolson and Lambert Orme, or Harold Nicolson and (as he has admitted) Ronald Firbank. Nicolson is at once repulsed and intrigued by Orme-Firbank, but in the end he comes down on the side of the British upper-class world and rejects the too mauve poet. The latter has a double revenge. He dies bravely in the war while Nicolson is tucked away safely in the Foreign Office, and he achieves a posthumous fame, becoming a light in the Bloomsbury firmament which has no place for the too square Nicolson. Nicolson endowed Firbank with a fictional love affair and a fictional war death, neither of which seems quite convincing, but the presentation of the ancient choice between the life of the artist and the life of the philistine is very fairly presented, for the philistines are moderate and attractive and the artist is screamingly absurd— and yet a real artist. Or is he? Is there an intended double irony that Lambert Orme is, after all, a bad poet? Nicolson's excerpt from Orme's poem *Thera,* which is Nicolson's own parody of T. S. Eliot, may have been intended to cast ridicule on the Bloomsbury admirers. Or it may simply be that it is a bad parody—of which Nicolson was presumably unaware. I suspect the latter, for the deeper feeling in the story is that Orme is a true artist.

Evelyn Waugh's *Black Mischief* can be fairly sampled in *Incident in Azania*. It is also a comic miniature of E. M. Forster's *Passage to India*. Nowhere does the snobbishness and prejudice of the English bureaucrat show up more vividly than in the tropics, where he seems like Tolstoy's Napoleon in the coach, pulling straps and turning handles in the illusion that he is causing its forward motion. In this story, however, it is not, as with Forster, the natives and the native scene which triumph over the alien intruder, but one of the intruders themselves, or rather two of them, the resourceful Prunella Brooks with the help of the despised remittance man from Kenya.

The Eternal Moment is my favorite of all of E. M. Forster's work. It seems to me that here he catches most poignantly the yearning of the individual to establish some resistance, no matter how small— one good, valid moment—against the huge glacier of vulgarity and self-interest, known as civilization, that ineluctably flows down over every square inch of nineteenth century Europe. One of the greatnesses of Forster is that he is never angry, only sad. He has an unusual understanding of mean little people, for he knows that they cannot much help being mean or little. But his compassion (if that is the word—tolerance might be better) for such people does not mean that he recognizes any particular salvation for them. They are what they are, and that seems to be that. There may, however, be an opportunity for more sensitive souls to find some attunement with the universe and a deep inner (even if brief) satisfaction. That is what Mrs. Moore finds (and loses) in *A Passage to India* and what Miss Raby finds, perhaps more permanently, in *The Eternal Moment*. For she has the courage to speak out about her love, long dead, for the Italian guide, once romantic, now grown fat and vulgar. It does not matter that she alienates her shocked audience. What she has gained is something more than friendship, more even than love.

Glory in the Daytime is to me the supreme moment of Dorothy Parker, her funniest and most beautifully plotted tale. I do not know where the ancient comedy of the disillusionment of the clown is carried to more disastrous, more shattering limits. Mrs. Murdock is spared nothing. It is not enough that Lily Wynton should prove drunken, obscene, old, Lesbian, coarse. When Mrs. Murdock hurries home to the husband whom now she wildly romanticizes, he, of course, must reject her too.

The Tillotson Banquet is in the tradition of *The Waste Land*. Aldous Huxley contrasts the aridity of the cultural present against the richer colors of the past, and he does it with a particular twist by selecting not the rich past of a Titian or a Michelangelo but that of a minor British painter, Robert Haydon. What Huxley makes one feel was superior in the past, was not so much the difference in quality of the art but the difference in the public's veneration of it. Tillotson is full of an antiquated passion for his god, Haydon; he seems lost and quaint and pathetic in the multitude of modern fashionable critics and society collectors who throng to meet him.

It is no coincidence that I end with the stories of three contemporaries, all women, for women in our time have manifested a much livelier concern for clarity, elegance and wit than have men. Mary McCarthy is deeply read in Latin literature, which shows in the high lucidity and order of her style. She is saturated in French, English, Italian and American culture, and she is not, thank heavens, ashamed of it. She wears her learning with a grace, and when she uses it against the tawdriness of the present, she can be devastating indeed. She is probably the most intelligent writer of fiction living today. Some feel that her mind is more that of the critic than the novelist, but I believe that our fiction writers could do with more of her critical faculty. *The Friend of the Family*, at any rate, could pass for either an essay or a short story. What does it serve to classify it?

Jean Stafford has the feeling for words of a poet and a philologist; like Emily Dickinson she finds profit and delight in reading dictionaries. Although her stories are perfect entities, one can break off chunks of them, for independent reading, in anthologies of prose. She is, however, whimsical, vivid, exact and terrifying. Ramona Dunn, the compulsive eater of *The Echo and the Nemesis*, whose fantasy is that her lost thin self is an absent, mocking twin, is a characteristic and fascinating creation.

I have ended the collection with *In the Absence of Angels*, partly because of my belief that Hortense Calisher belongs with the authors herein represented and partly because I could not resist the fantasy that its sombre note pulls down an appropriate dark curtain on the decorative era of elegance and wit that I have tried to evoke. There are, alas, plenty of Hilda Kantrowitzes today ready to tear out and destroy, so long as hunger exists, every rose that occupies in a garden the potential place of a bean. The Hildas of 1971 are more affluent than the Hildas of 1950; they make bombs and supply prisoners with firearms, but they are still Hildas. Miss Calisher's nightmare could yet become real.

FABLES OF WIT
AND
ELEGANCE

The Abasement of the Northmores

✳ HENRY JAMES ✳

HENRY JAMES (1843–1916), although one of the acknowledged masters of the American novel, spent his adult years in Europe and became an English subject during World War I. He dedicated his life to the art of fiction, producing twenty novels and more than a hundred tales in a progressive scheme of literary experimentation. It was his objective to attain reality and unity by admitting into his fiction, insofar as practicable, only what could be shown through the feelings or experience of his characters. In this respect he changed fiction as probably no other author has before or since. To some today (including this writer) he has achieved the ultimate in literary art. To others he is attenuated and wordy. *The Abasement of the Northmores* first appeared in *The Soft Side* (1900).

I

WHEN Lord Northmore died public reference to the event took for the most part rather a ponderous and embarrassed form. A great political figure had passed away. A great light of our time had been quenched in mid-career. A great usefulness had somewhat anticipated its term, though a great part, none the less, had been signally played. The note of greatness, all along the line, kept sounding, in short, by a force of its own, and the image of the departed evidently lent itself with ease to figures and flourishes, the poetry of the daily press. The newspapers and their purchasers equally did their duty by it—arranged it neatly and impressively, though perhaps with a hand a little violently expeditious, upon the funeral-car, saw the conveyance properly down the avenue and then, finding the subject suddenly quite exhausted, proceeded to the next item on their list. His lordship had been a person in connexion with whom—that was it—there was almost nothing but the fine monotony of his success to mention. This success had been his profession, his means as well as his end; so that his career admitted of no other description and demanded, indeed suffered, no further analysis. He had made politics, he had made literature, he had made land, he had made a bad manner and a great many mistakes, he had made a gaunt foolish wife, two extravagant sons and four awkward daughters—he had made everything, as he *could* have made almost anything, thoroughly pay. There had been something deep down in him that did it, and his old friend Warren Hope, the person knowing him earliest and probably on the whole best, had never, even to the last, for curiosity, quite made out what it was. The secret was one that this distinctly distanced competitor had in fact mastered as little for intellectual relief as for emulous use; and there was a virtual tribute to it in the way that, the night before the obsequies and addressing himself to his wife, he said after some silent thought: "Hang it, you know, I must see the old boy through. I must go to the grave."

Mrs. Hope at first looked at her husband but in anxious silence. "I've no patience with you. You're much more ill than *he* ever was."

"Ah but if that qualifies me only for the funerals of others!"

"It qualifies you to break my heart by your exaggerated chivalry, your renewed refusal to consider your interests. You sacrificed them to him, for thirty years, again and again, and from this supreme sacrifice—possibly that of your life—you might, in your condition, I think, be absolved." She indeed lost patience. "To the grave—in this weather—after his treatment of you?"

"My dear girl," Hope replied, "his treatment of me is a figment of your ingenious mind—your too-passionate, your beautiful loyalty. Loyalty, I mean, to *me*."

"I certainly leave it to you," she declared, "to have any to *him!*"

"Well, he was after all one's oldest, one's earliest friend. I'm not in such bad case—I do go out; and I want to do the decent thing. The fact remains that we never broke—we always kept together."

"Yes indeed," she laughed in her bitterness, "he always took care of that! He never recognised you, but he never let you go. You kept him up, and he kept you down. He used you, to the last drop he could squeeze, and left you the only one to wonder, in your incredible idealism and your incorrigible modesty, how on earth such an idiot made his way. He made his way on your back. You put it candidly to others—'What in the world was his gift?' And others are such gaping idiots that they too haven't the least idea. *You* were his gift!"

"And you're mine, my dear!" her husband, pressing her to him, more gaily and resignedly cried. He went down the next day by "special" to the interment, which took place on the great man's own property and in the great man's own church. But he went alone— that is in a numerous and distinguished party, the flower of the unanimous gregarious demonstration; his wife had no wish to accompany him, though she was anxious while he travelled. She passed the time uneasily, watching the weather and fearing the cold; she roamed from room to room, pausing vaguely at dull windows, and before he came back she had thought of many things. It was as if, while he saw the great man buried, she also, by herself, in the contracted home of their later years, stood before an open grave. She lowered into it with her weak hands the heavy past and all their common dead dreams and accumulated ashes. The pomp surrounding Lord Northmore's extinction made her feel more than ever that it was not Warren who had made anything pay. He had been always what he was still, the cleverest man and the hardest worker she knew; but what was there, at fifty-seven, as the vulgar said, to "show" for it all but his wasted genius, his ruined health and his paltry pension? It was the term of comparison conveniently given her by his happy rival's now foreshortened splendour that set these things in her eye. It was as happy rivals to their own flat union that she always had thought of the Northmore pair; the two men at least having started together, after the University, shoulder to shoulder and with—superficially speaking—much the same outfit of preparation, ambition and opportunity. They had begun at the same point and wanting the same things—only wanting them in such different ways. Well, the dead man had wanted them in the way that got them; but got too, in his peerage for instance, those Warren had never wanted: there was nothing else to be said. There was nothing else, and yet, in her sombre, her strangely apprehensive solitude at this hour, she said much more than I can tell. It all came to this—that there had been somewhere and somehow a wrong. Warren was the one who should have succeeded. But she was the one person who knew it now, the single other person having descended, with *his* knowledge, to the tomb.

She sat there, she roamed there, in the waiting greyness of her small London house, with a deepened sense of the several odd knowledges that had flourished in their company of three. Warren had always known everything and, with his easy power—in nothing so high as for indifference—had never cared. John Northmore had known, for he had, years and years before, told her so; and thus had had a reason the more—in addition to not believing her stupid—for guessing at her view. She lived back; she lived it over; she had it all there in her hand. John Northmore had known her first, and how he had wanted to marry her the fat little bundle of his love-letters still survived to tell. He had introduced Warren Hope to her—quite by accident and because, at the time they had chambers together, he couldn't help it: that was the one thing he *had* done for them. Thinking of it now she perhaps saw how much he might conscientiously have considered that it disburdened him of more. Six months later she had accepted Warren, and just for the reason the absence of which had determined her treatment of his friend. She had believed in his future. She held that John Northmore had never afterwards remitted the effort to ascertain the degree in which she felt herself "sold." But, thank God, she had never shown him.

Her husband came home with a chill and she put him straight to bed. For a week, as she hovered near him, they only looked deep things at each other; the point was too quickly passed at which she could bearably have said "I told you so!" That his late patron should never have had difficulty in making *him* pay was certainly no marvel. But it was indeed a little too much, after all, that he should have made him pay with his life. This was what it had come to—she was now sure from the first. Congestion of the lungs declared itself that night and on the morrow, sickeningly, she was face to face with pneumonia. It was more than—with all that had gone before—they could meet. Ten days later Warren Hope succumbed. Tenderly, divinely as he loved her, she felt his surrender, through all the anguish, as an unspeakable part of the sublimity of indifference into which his hapless history had finally flowered. "His easy power, his easy power!"—her passion had never yet found such relief in that simple secret phrase for him. He was so proud, so fine and so flexible that to fail a little had been as bad for him as to fail much; therefore he had opened the flood-gates wide—had thrown, as the saying was, the helve after the hatchet. He had amused himself with seeing what the devouring world would take. Well, it had taken all.

II

But it was after he had gone that his name showed as written in water. What had he left? He had only left *her* and her grey desolation, her lonely piety and her sore unresting rebellion. When a man died it sometimes did for him what life hadn't done; people after a little, on one side or the other, discovered and named him, claiming him for their party, annexing him to their flag. But the sense of having lost Warren Hope appeared not in the least to have quickened the world's wit; the sharper pang for his widow indeed sprang just from the commonplace way in which he was spoken of as known. She received letters enough, when it came to that, for personally of course he had been liked; the newspapers were fairly copious and perfectly stupid; the three or four societies, "learned" and other, to which he had belonged, passed resolutions of regret and condolence, and the three or four colleagues about whom he himself used to be most amusing stammered eulogies; but almost anything really would have been better for her than the general understanding that the occasion had been met. Two or three solemn noodles in "administrative circles" wrote her that she must have been gratified at the unanimity of regret, the implication being quite that she was else of the last absurdity. Meanwhile what she felt was that she could have borne well enough his not being noticed at all; what she couldn't bear was this treatment of him as a minor celebrity. He was, in economics, in the higher politics, in philosophic history, a splendid unestimated genius or he was nothing. He wasn't at any rate—heaven forbid!—a "notable figure." The waters, none the less, closed over him as over Lord Northmore; which was precisely, as time went on, the fact she found it hardest to accept. That personage, the week after his death, without an hour of reprieve, the place swept as clean of him as a hall lent for charity, of the tables and booths of a three-days' bazaar—that personage had gone straight to the bottom, dropped like a crumpled circular into the waste-basket. Where then was the difference?—if the end *was* the end for each alike? For Warren it should have been properly the beginning.

During the first six months she wondered what she could herself do, and had much of the time the sense of walking by some swift stream on which an object dear to her was floating out to sea. All her instinct was to keep up with it, not to lose sight of it, to hurry along the bank and reach in advance some point from which she could stretch forth and catch and save it. Alas it only floated and floated; she held it in sight, for the stream was long, but no gentle promontory offered itself to the rescue. She ran, she watched, she lived with her great fear; and all the while, as the distance to the sea diminished, the current visibly increased. To do anything at the last she must hurry. She went into his papers, she ransacked his drawers; something of that sort at least she might do. But there were difficulties, the case was special; she lost herself in the labyrinth and her competence was challenged; two or three friends to whose judgement she appealed struck her as tepid, even as cold, and publishers, when sounded— most of all in fact the house through which his three or four impor- tant volumes had been given to the world—showed an absence of eagerness for a collection of literary remains. It was only now she fully understood how remarkably little the three or four important volumes had "done." He had successfully kept that from her, as he had kept other things she might have ached at: to handle his notes and memoranda was to come at every turn, amid the sands of her be- reavement, upon the footsteps of some noble reason. But she had at last to accept the truth that it was only for herself, her own relief, that she must follow him. His work, unencouraged and interrupted, failed of a final form: there would have been nothing to offer but fragments of fragments. She felt, all the same, in recognising this, that she abandoned him: he died for her at that hour over again.

The hour moreover happened to coincide with another hour, so that the two mingled their bitterness. She received from Lady North- more a note announcing a desire to gather in and publish his late lordship's letters, so numerous and so interesting, and inviting Mrs. Hope, as a more than probable depositary, to be so good as to enrich the scheme with those addressed to her husband. This gave her a start of more kinds than one. The long comedy of his late lordship's greatness was *not* then over? The monument was to be built to him that she had but now schooled herself to regard as impossible for his defeated friend? Everything was to break out afresh, the comparisons, the contrasts, the conclusions so invidiously in his favour?—the business all cleverly managed to place him in the light and keep every one else in the shade? Letters?—had John Northmore indited three lines that could at that time of day be of the smallest consequence? Whose inept idea was such a publication, and what infatuated editorial patronage could the family have secured? She of course didn't know, but she should be surprised if there were material. Then it came to her, on reflexion, that editors and publishers must of course have flocked—his star would still rule. Why shouldn't he make his letters pay in death as he had made them pay in life? Such as they were they *had* paid. They would be a tremendous hit. She thought again of her husband's rich confused relics—thought of the loose blocks of marble that could only lie now where they had fallen; after which, with one of her deep and frequent sighs, she took up anew Lady Northmore's communication.

His letters to Warren, kept or not kept, had never so much as occurred to her. Those to herself were buried and safe—she knew where her hand would find them; but those to herself her correspondent had carefully not asked for and was probably unaware of the existence of. They belonged moreover to that phase of the great man's career that was distinctly—as it could only be called—previous: previous to the greatness, to the proper subject of the volume, previous above all to Lady Northmore. The faded fat packet lurked still where it had lurked for years; but she could no more to-day have said why she had kept it than why—though he knew of the early episode—she had never mentioned her preservation of it to Warren. This last maintained reserve certainly absolved her from mentioning it to Lady Northmore, who probably knew of the episode too. The odd part of the matter was at any rate that her retention of these documents had not been an accident. She had obeyed a dim instinct or a vague calculation. A calculation of what? She couldn't have told: it had operated, at the back of her head, simply as a sense that, not destroyed, the complete little collection made for safety. But for whose, just heaven?

Perhaps she should still see; though nothing, she trusted, would occur requiring her to touch the things or to read them over. She wouldn't have touched them or read them over for the world.

She had not as yet, in any case, overhauled those receptacles in which the letters Warren kept would have accumulated; and she had her doubts of their containing any of Lord Northmore's. Why should he have kept any? Even she herself had had more reasons. Was his lordship's later epistolary manner supposed to be good, or of the kind that, on any grounds, prohibited the waste-basket or the glowing embers? Warren had lived in a deluge of documents, but these perhaps he might have regarded as contributions to contemporary history. None the less, surely, he wouldn't have stored up many. She began a search in cupboards, boxes, drawers yet unvisited, and she had her surprises both at what he had kept and at what he hadn't. Every word of her own was there—every note that in occasional absence he had ever had from her. Well, that matched happily enough her knowing just where to put her finger on every note that, on such occasions, she herself had received. *Their* correspondence at least was complete. But so, in fine, on one side, it gradually appeared, was Lord Northmore's. The superabundance of these missives hadn't been sacrificed by her husband, evidently, to any passing convenience; she judged more and more that he had preserved every scrap; and she was unable to conceal from herself that she was—she scarce knew why—a trifle disappointed. She hadn't quite unhopefully, even though vaguely, seen herself informing Lady Northmore that, to her great regret and after a general hunt, she could find nothing at all.

She in fact, alas, found everything. She was conscientious and she rummaged to the end, by which time one of the tables quite groaned with the fruits of her quest. The letters appeared moreover to have been cared for and roughly classified—she should be able to consign them to the family in excellent order. She made sure at the last that she had overlooked nothing, and then, fatigued and distinctly irritated, she prepared to answer in a sense so different from the answer she had, as might have been said, planned. Face to face with her note, however, she found she could not write it; and, not to be alone longer with the pile on the table, she presently went out of the room. Late in the evening—just before going to bed—she came back almost as if hoping there might have been since the afternoon some pleasant intervention in the interest of her distaste. Mightn't it have magically happened that her discovery was a mistake?—that the letters either weren't there or were after all somebody else's? Ah they *were* there, and as she raised her lighted candle in the dusk the pile on the table squared itself with insolence. On this, poor lady, she had for an hour her temptation.

It was obscure, it was absurd; all that could be said of it was that it was for the moment extreme. She saw herself, as she circled round the table, writing with perfect impunity: "Dear Lady Northmore, I've hunted high and low and have found nothing whatever. My husband evidently, before his death, destroyed everything. I'm *so* sorry—I should have liked so much to help you. Yours most truly." She should have only on the morrow privately and resolutely to annihilate the heap, and those words would remain an account of the matter that nobody was in a position to challenge. What good it would do her?—was *that* the question? It would do her the good that it would make poor Warren seem to have been just a little less used and duped. This, in her mood, would ease her off. Well, the temptation was real; but so, she after a while felt, were other things. She sat down at midnight to her note. "Dear Lady Northmore, I'm happy to say I've found a great deal—my husband appears to have been so careful to keep everything. I've a mass at your disposition if you can conveniently send. So glad to be able to help your work. Yours most truly." She stepped out as she was and dropped the letter into the nearest pillar-box. By noon the next day the table had, to her relief, been cleared. Her ladyship sent a responsible servant—her butler—in a four-wheeler and with a large japanned box.

III

After this, for a twelvemonth, there were frequent announcements and allusions. They came to her from every side, and there were hours at which the air, to her imagination, contained almost nothing else. There had been, at an early stage, immediately after Lady Northmore's communication to her, an official appeal, a circular *urbi et orbi*, reproduced, applauded, commented in every newspaper, desiring all possessors of letters to remit them without delay to the family. The family, to do it justice, rewarded the sacrifice freely—so far as it was a reward to keep the world informed of the rapid progress of the work. Material had shown itself more copious than was to have been conceived. Interesting as the imminent volumes had naturally been expected to prove, those who had been favoured with a glimpse of their contents already felt warranted in promising the public an unprecedented treat. They would throw upon certain sides of the writer's mind and career lights hitherto unsuspected. Lady Northmore, deeply indebted for favours received, begged to renew her solicitation; gratifying as the response had been it was believed that, particularly in connexion with several dates now specified, a residuum of buried treasure might still be looked for.

Mrs. Hope saw, she could but recognise, fewer and fewer people; yet her circle was even now not too narrow for her to hear it blown about that Thompson and Johnson had "been asked." Conversation in the London world struck her for a time as almost confined to such questions and answers. "Have *you* been asked?" "Oh yes—rather. Months ago. And you?" With the whole place under contribution the striking thing seemed that being asked had been attended in every case by the ability to respond. The spring had but to be touched—millions of letters flew out. Ten volumes at such a rate, Mrs. Hope brooded, wouldn't exhaust the supply. She brooded a great deal, did nothing but brood; and, strange as this may at first appear, one of the final results of her brooding was the growth of a germ of doubt. It could only seem possible, in view of such unanimity, that she should have been stupidly mistaken. The great departed's reputation *was* then to the general sense a sound safe thing. Not he, immortal, had been at fault, but just her silly self, still burdened with the fallibility of Being. He had thus been a giant, and the letters would triumphantly show it. She had looked only at the envelopes of those she had surrendered, but she was prepared for anything. There was the fact, not to be blinked, of Warren's own marked testimony. The attitude of others was but *his* attitude; and she sighed as she found him in this case for the only time in his life on the side of the chattering crowd.

She was perfectly aware that her obsession had run away with her, but as Lady Northmore's publication really loomed into view—it was now definitely announced for March, and they were in January—her pulses quickened so that she found herself, in the long nights, mostly lying awake. It was in one of these vigils that suddenly, in the cold darkness, she felt the brush of almost the only thought that for many a month hadn't made her wince; the effect of which was that she bounded out of bed with a new felicity. Her impatience flashed on the spot up to its maximum—she could scarce wait for day to give herself to action. Her idea was neither more nor less than immediately to collect and put forth the letters of *her* hero. She would publish her husband's own—glory be to God!—and she even wasted none of her time in wondering why she had waited. She *had* waited—all too long; yet it was perhaps no more than natural that, for eyes sealed with tears and a heart heavy with injustice, there shouldn't have been an instant vision of where her remedy lay. She thought of it already as her remedy—though she would probably have found an awkwardness in giving a name publicly to her wrong. It was a wrong to feel, but doubtless not to talk about. And lo, straightway, the balm had begun to drop: the balance would so soon be even. She spent all that day in reading over her own old letters, too intimate and too sacred—oh unluckily!—to figure in her project, but pouring wind nevertheless into its sails and adding greatness to her presumption. She had of course, with separation, all their years, never frequent and never prolonged, known her husband as a correspondent much less than others; still, these relics constituted a property—she was surprised at their number—and testified hugely to his inimitable gift.

He was a letter-writer if you liked—natural witty various vivid, playing with the idlest lightest hand up and down the whole scale. His easy power—his easy power: everything that brought him back brought back that. The most numerous were of course the earlier and the series of those during their engagement, witnesses of their long probation, which were rich and unbroken; so full indeed and so wonderful that she fairly groaned at having to defer to the common measure of married modesty. There was discretion, there was usage, there was taste; but she would fain have flown in their face. If many were pages too intimate to publish, most others were too rare to suppress. Perhaps after her death—! It not only pulled her up, the happy thought of that liberation alike for herself and for her treasure, making her promise herself straightway to arrange: it quite re-emphasised her impatience for the term of her mortality, which would leave a free field to the justice she invoked. Her great resource, however, clearly, would be the friends, the colleagues, the private admirers to whom he had written for years, to whom she had known him to write, and many of whose own letters, by no means remarkable, she had come upon in her recent sortings and siftings. She drew up a list of these persons and immediately wrote to them or, in cases in which they had passed away, to their widows, children, representatives; reminding herself in the process not disagreeably, in fact quite inspiringly, of Lady Northmore in person. It had struck her that Lady Northmore in person took somehow a good deal for granted; but this idea failed, oddly enough, to occur to her in regard to Mrs. Hope. It was indeed with her ladyship she began, addressing her exactly in the terms of the noble widow's own appeal, every word of which she recalled.

Then she waited, but she had not, in connexion with that quarter, to wait long. "Dear Mrs. Hope, I have hunted high and low and have found nothing whatever. My husband evidently before his death destroyed everything. I'm so sorry—I should have liked so much to help you. Yours most truly." This was all Lady Northmore wrote, without the grace of an allusion to the assistance she herself had received; though even in the first flush of amazement and resentment our friend recognised the odd identity of form between her note and another that had never been written. She was answered as she had, in the like case and in her one evil hour, dreamed of answering. But the answer wasn't over with this—it had still to flow in, day after day, from every other source reached by her question. And day after day, while amazement and resentment deepened, it consisted simply of three lines of regret. Everybody had looked, and everybody had looked in vain. Everybody would have been so glad, but everybody was reduced to being, like Lady Northmore, so sorry. Nobody could find anything, and nothing, it was therefore to be gathered, had been kept. Some of these informants were more prompt than others, but all replied in time, and the business went on for a month, at the end of which the poor woman, stricken, chilled to the heart, accepted perforce her situation and turned her face to the wall. In this position, as it were, she remained for days, taking heed of nothing and only feeling and nursing her wound. It was a wound the more cruel for having found her so unguarded. From the moment her remedy had glimmered to her she hadn't had an hour of doubt, and the beautiful side of it had seemed that it was just so easy. The strangeness of the issue was even greater than the pain. Truly it was a world *pour rire,* the world in which John Northmore's letters were classed and labelled for posterity and Warren Hope's helped housemaids to light fires. All sense, all measure of anything, could only leave one—leave one indifferent and dumb. There was nothing to be done—the show was upside-down. John Northmore was immortal and Warren Hope was damned. For herself, therefore, she was finished. She was beaten. She leaned thus, motionless, muffled, for a time of which, as I say, she took no account; then at last she was reached by a great sound that made her turn her veiled head. It was the report of the appearance of Lady Northmore's volumes.

IV

This filled the air indeed, and all the papers that day were particularly loud with it. It met the reader on the threshold and then within, the work everywhere the subject of a "leader" as well as of a review. The reviews moreover, she saw at a glance, overflowed with quotation; to look at two or three sheets was to judge fairly of the raptures. Mrs. Hope looked at the two or three that, for confirmation of the single one she habitually received, she caused, while at breakfast, to be purchased; but her attention failed to penetrate further: she couldn't, she found, face the contrast between the pride of the Northmores on such a morning and her own humiliation. The papers brought it too sharply home; she pushed them away and, to get rid of them, not to feel their presence, left the house early. She found pretexts for remaining out; there had been a cup prescribed for her to drain, yet she could put off the hour of the ordeal. She filled the time as she might; bought things, in shops, for which she had no use, and called on friends for whom she had no taste. Most of her friends at present were reduced to that category, and she had to choose for visits the houses guiltless, as she might have said, of her husband's blood. She couldn't speak to the people who had answered in such dreadful terms her later circular; on the other hand the people out of its range were such as would also be stolidly unconscious of Lady Northmore's publication and from whom the sop of sympathy could be but circuitously extracted. As she had lunched at a pastry-cook's so she stopped out to tea, and the March dusk had fallen when she got home. The first thing she then saw in her lighted hall was a large neat package on the table; whereupon she knew before approaching it that Lady Northmore had sent her the book. It had arrived, she learned, just after her going out; so that, had she not done this, she might have spent the day with it. She now quite understood her prompt instinct of flight. Well, flight had helped her, and the touch of the great indifferent general life. She would at last face the music.

She faced it, after dinner, in her little closed drawing-room, unwrapping the two volumes—*The Public and Private Correspondence of the Right Honourable &c., &c.*—and looking well, first, at the great escutcheon on the purple cover and at the various portraits within, so numerous that wherever she opened she came on one. It hadn't been present to her before that he was so perpetually "sitting," but he figured in every phase and in every style, while the gallery was further enriched with views of his successive residences, each one a little grander than the last. She had ever, in general, found that in portraits, whether of the known or the obscure, the eyes seemed to seek and to meet her own; but John Northmore everywhere looked straight away from her, quite as if he had been in the room and were unconscious of acquaintance. The effect of this was, oddly enough, so sharp that at the end of ten minutes she felt herself sink into his text as if she had been a stranger beholden, vulgarly and accidentally, to one of the libraries. She had been afraid to plunge, but from the moment she got in she was—to do every one all round justice—thoroughly held. Sitting there late she made so many reflexions and discoveries that—as the only way to put it—she passed from mystification to stupefaction. Her own offered series figured practically entire; she had counted Warren's letters before sending them and noted now that scarce a dozen were absent—a circumstance explaining to her Lady Northmore's courtesy. It was to these pages she had turned first, and it was as she hung over them that her stupefaction dawned. It took in truth at the outset a particular form—the form of a sharpened wonder at Warren's unnatural piety. Her original surprise had been keen—when she had tried to take reasons for granted; but her original surprise was as nothing to her actual bewilderment. The letters to

Warren had been virtually, she judged, for the family, the great card; yet if the great card made only that figure what on earth was one to think of the rest of the pack?

She pressed on at random and with a sense of rising fever; she trembled, almost panting, not to be sure too soon; but wherever she turned she found the prodigy spread. The letters to Warren were an abyss of inanity; the others followed suit as they could; the book was surely then a gaping void, the publication a theme for mirth. She so lost herself in uplifting visions as her perception of the scale of the mistake deepened that toward eleven o'clock, when her parlour-maid opened the door, she almost gave the start of guilt surprised. The girl, withdrawing for the night, had come but to mention that, and her mistress, supremely wide awake and with remembrance kindled, appealed to her, after a blank stare, with intensity. "What have you done with the papers?"

"The papers, ma'am?"

"All those of this morning—don't tell me you've destroyed them! Quick, quick—bring them back."

The young woman, by a rare chance, hadn't destroyed the public prints; she presently reappeared with them neatly folded; and Mrs. Hope, dismissing her with benedictions, had at last in a few minutes taken the time of day. She saw her impression portentously reflected in the long grey columns. It wasn't then the illusion of her jealousy —it was the triumph, unhoped for, of her justice. The reviewers observed a decorum, but frankly, when one came to look, their stupefaction matched her own. What she had taken in the morning for enthusiasm proved mere perfunctory attention, unwarned in advance and seeking an issue for its mystification. The question was, if one liked, asked civilly, yet asked none the less all round: "What *could* have made Lord Northmore's family take him for a letter-writer?" Pompous and ponderous and at the same time loose and obscure, he managed by a trick of his own to be both slipshod and stiff. Who in such a case had been primarily responsible and under what strangely belated advice had a group of persons destitute of wit themselves been thus deplorably led astray? With fewer accomplices in the preparation it might almost have been assumed that they had been designedly befooled, been elaborately trapped.

They had at all events committed an error of which the most merci-

ful thing to say was that, as founded on loyalty, it was touching. These
things, in the welcome offered, lay perhaps not quite on the face,
but they peeped between the lines and would force their way through
on the morrow. The long quotations given were quotations marked
Why?—"Why," in other words, as interpreted by Mrs. Hope, "drag
to light such helplessness of expression? why give the text of his
dulness and the proof of his fatuity?" The victim of the error had
certainly been, in his way and day, a useful and remarkable person,
but almost any other evidence of the fact might more happily have
been adduced. It rolled over her, as she paced her room in the small
hours, that the wheel had come full circle. There was after all a rough
justice. The monument that had overdarkened her was reared, but
it would be within a week the opportunity of every humourist, the
derision of intelligent London. Her husband's strange share in it continued, that night, between dreams and vigils, to puzzle her, but
light broke with her final waking, which was comfortably late. She
opened her eyes to it and, on its staring straight into them, greeted
it with the first laugh that had for a long time passed her lips. How
could she idiotically not have guessed? Warren, playing insidiously
the part of a guardian, had done what he had done on purpose! He
had acted to an end long foretasted, and the end—the full taste—had
come.

V

It was after this, none the less—after the other organs of criticism,
including the smoking-rooms of the clubs, the lobbies of the House
and the dinner-tables of everywhere, had duly embodied their reserves
and vented their irreverence, and the unfortunate two volumes had
ranged themselves, beyond appeal, as a novelty insufficiently curious
and prematurely stale—it was when this had come to pass that she
really felt how beautiful her own chance would now have been and
how sweet her revenge. The success of *her* volumes, for the inevitability of which nobody had had an instinct, would have been as
great as the failure of Lady Northmore's, for the inevitability of
which everybody had had one. She read over and over her letters and
asked herself afresh if the confidence that had preserved *them* mightn't,

at such a crisis, in spite of everything, justify itself. Didn't the discredit to English wit, as it were, proceeding from the uncorrected attribution to an established public character of such mediocrity of thought and form, really demand, for that matter, some such redemptive stroke as the appearance of a collection of masterpieces gathered from a similar walk? To have such a collection under one's hand and yet sit and see one's self not use it was a torment through which she might well have feared to break down.

But there was another thing she might do, not redemptive indeed, but perhaps after all, as matters were going, relevant. She fished out of their nook, after long years, the packet of John Northmore's epistles to herself and, reading them over in the light of his later style, judged them to contain to the full the promise of that inimitability; felt how they would deepen the impression and how, in the way of the *inédit*, they constituted her supreme treasure. There was accordingly a terrible week for her in which she itched to put them forth. She composed mentally the preface, brief, sweet, ironic, presenting her as prompted by an anxious sense of duty to a great reputation and acting upon the sight of laurels so lately gathered. There would naturally be difficulties; the documents were her own, but the family, bewildered, scared, suspicious, figured to her fancy as a dog with a dust-pan tied to its tail and ready for any dash to cover at the sound of the clatter of tin. They would have, she surmised, to be consulted, or, if not consulted, would put in an injunction; yet, of the two courses, that of scandal braved for the man she had rejected drew her on, while the charm of this vision worked, still further than that of delicacy overridden for the man she had married.

The vision closed round her and she lingered on the idea—fed, as she handled again her faded fat packet, by re-perusals more richly convinced. She even took opinions as to the interference open to her old friend's relatives; took in fact, from this time on, many opinions; went out anew, picked up old threads, repaired old ruptures, resumed, as it was called, her place in society. She had not been for years so seen of men as during the few weeks that followed the abasement of the Northmores. She called in particular on every one she had cast out after the failure of her appeal. Many of these persons figured as Lady Northmore's contributors, the unwitting agents of the cruel exposure; they having, it was sufficiently clear, acted in dense good faith. Warren, foreseeing and calculating, might have the benefit of such subtlety, but it wasn't for any one else. With every one else—for they did, on facing her, as she said to herself, look like fools—she made inordinately free; putting right and left the question of what in the past years they or their progenitors could have been thinking of. "What on earth had you in mind and where among you were the rudiments of intelligence when you burnt up my husband's priceless letters and clung as for salvation to Lord Northmore's? You see how you've been saved!" The weak explanations, the imbecility, as she judged it, of the reasons given, were so much balm to her wound. The great balm, however, she kept to the last: she would go to see Lady Northmore only when she had exhausted all other comfort. That resource would be as supreme as the treasure of the fat packet. She finally went and, by a happy chance, if chance could ever be happy in such a house, was received. She remained half an hour—there were other persons present; and on rising to go knew herself satisfied. She had taken in what she desired, had sounded to the bottom what she saw; only, unexpectedly, something had overtaken her more absolute than the hard need she had obeyed or the vindictive advantage she had cherished. She had counted on herself for anything rather than pity of these people, yet it was in pity that at the end of ten minutes she felt everything else dissolve.

They were suddenly, on the spot, transformed for her by the depth of their misfortune, and she saw them, the great Northmores, as—of all things—consciously weak and flat. She neither made nor encountered an allusion to volumes published or frustrated; and so let her arranged enquiry die away that when on separation she kissed her wan sister in widowhood it was not with the kiss of Judas. She had meant to ask lightly if she mightn't have *her* turn at editing; but the renunciation with which she re-entered her house had formed itself before she left the room. When she got home indeed she at first only wept—wept for the commonness of failure and the strangeness of life. Her tears perhaps brought her a sense of philosophy; it was all as broad as it was long. When they were spent, at all events, she took out for the last time the faded fat packet. Sitting down by a receptacle daily emptied for the benefit of the dustman, she destroyed one by one the gems of the collection in which each piece had been a gem. She tore up to the last scrap Lord Northmore's letters. It would never be known now, as regards this series, either that they had been hoarded or that they had been sacrificed. And she was content so to let it rest. On the following day she began another task. She took out her husband's and attacked the business of transcription. She copied them piously, tenderly, and, for the purpose to which she now found herself settled, judged almost no omissions imperative. By the time they should be published—! She shook her head, both knowingly and resignedly, as to criticism so remote. When her transcript was finished she sent it to a printer to set up, and then, after receiving and correcting proof, and with every precaution for secrecy, had a single copy struck off and the type dispersed under her eyes. Her last act but one—or rather perhaps but two—was to put these sheets, which, she was pleased to find, would form a volume of three hundred pages, carefully away. Her next was to add to her testamentary instrument a definite provision for the issue, after her death, of such a volume. Her last was to hope that death would come in time.

The Portrait of Mr W. H.

❊ OSCAR WILDE ❊

OSCAR WILDE (1854–1900) was born in Ireland and graduated from Oxford. In London he became the leader of the aesthetic movement: "Art for Art's Sake," and the author of the most popular parlor comedies of the 'nineties, including *Lady Windemere's Fan* and *The Importance of Being Earnest*. His brilliant career, marked by a megalomaniacal self-exhibitionism, ended in his conviction for sodomy and a term at hard labor after which, a broken man, he emigrated to France. *The Portrait of Mr W. H.* first appeared in 1889 in *Blackwood's Magazine* in the form in which it is here printed. Wilde later expanded it, but in this writer's opinion he overembroidered his theme.

I

I HAD been dining with Erskine in his pretty little house in Bird-cage Walk, and we were sitting in the library over our coffee and cigarettes, when the question of literary forgeries happened to turn up in conversation. I cannot at present remember how it was that we struck upon this somewhat curious topic, as it was at that time, but I know that we had a long discussion about Macpherson, Ireland, and Chatterton, and that with regard to the last I insisted that his so-called forgeries were merely the result of an artistic desire for perfect representation; that we had no right to quarrel with an artist for the conditions under which he chooses to present his work; and that all Art being to a certain degree a mode of acting, an attempt to realise one's own personality on some imaginative plane out of reach of the trammelling accidents and limitations of real life, to censure an artist for a forgery was to confuse an ethical with an æsthetical problem.

Erskine, who was a good deal older than I was, and had been listening to me with the amused deference of a man of forty, suddenly put his hand upon my shoulder and said to me, "What would you say about a young man who had a strange theory about a certain work of art, believed in his theory, and committed a forgery in order to prove it?"

"Ah! that is quite a different matter," I answered.

Erskine remained silent for a few moments, looking at the thin grey threads of smoke that were rising from his cigarette. "Yes," he said, after a pause, "quite different."

There was something in the tone of his voice, a slight touch of bitterness perhaps, that excited my curiosity. "Did you ever know anybody who did that?" I cried.

"Yes," he answered, throwing his cigarette into the fire,—"a great friend of mine, Cyril Graham. He was very fascinating, and very foolish, and very heartless. However, he left me the only legacy I ever received in my life."

"What was that?" I exclaimed. Erskine rose from his seat, and going over to a tall inlaid cabinet that stood between the two windows, unlocked it, and came back to where I was sitting, holding in his hand a small panel picture set in an old and somewhat tarnished Elizabethan frame.

It was a full-length portrait of a young man in late sixteenth-century costume, standing by a table, with his right hand resting on an open book. He seemed about seventeen years of age, and was of quite extraordinary personal beauty, though evidently somewhat effeminate. Indeed, had it not been for the dress and the closely cropped hair, one would have said that the face, with its dreamy wistful eyes, and its delicate scarlet lips, was the face of a girl. In manner, and especially in the treatment of the hands, the picture reminded one of François Clouet's later work. The black velvet doublet with its fantastically gilded points, and the peacock-blue background against which it showed up so pleasantly, and from which it gained such luminous value of colour, were quite in Clouet's style; and the two masks of Tragedy and Comedy that hung somewhat formally from the marble pedestal had that hard severity of touch—so different from the facile grace of the Italians—which even at the Court of France the great Flemish master never completely lost, and which in itself has always been a characteristic of the northern temper.

"It is a charming thing," I cried; "but who is this wonderful young man, whose beauty Art has so happily preserved for us?"

"This is the portrait of Mr W. H.," said Erskine, with a sad smile. It might have been a chance effect of light, but it seemed to me that his eyes were quite bright with tears.

"Mr W. H.!" I exclaimed; "who was Mr W. H.?"

"Don't you remember?" he answered; "look at the book on which his hand is resting."

"I see there is some writing there, but I cannot make it out," I replied.

"Take this magnifying-glass and try," said Erskine, with the same sad smile still playing about his mouth.

I took the glass, and moving the lamp a little nearer, I began to spell out the crabbed sixteenth-century handwriting. "To the onlie begetter of these insuing sonnets." . . . "Good heavens!" I cried, "is this Shakespeare's Mr W. H.?"

"Cyril Graham used to say so," muttered Erskine.

"But it is not a bit like Lord Pembroke," I answered. "I know the Penshurst portraits very well. I was staying near there a few weeks ago."

"Do you really believe then that the Sonnets are addressed to Lord Pembroke?" he asked.

"I am sure of it," I answered. "Pembroke, Shakespeare, and Mrs Mary Fitton are the three personages of the Sonnets; there is no doubt at all about it."

"Well, I agree with you," said Erskine, "but I did not always think so. I used to believe—well, I suppose I used to believe in Cyril Graham and his theory."

"And what was that?" I asked, looking at the wonderful portrait, which had already begun to have a strange fascination for me.

"It is a long story," said Erskine, taking the picture away from me —rather abruptly I thought at the time—"a very long story; but if you care to hear it, I will tell it to you."

"I love theories about the Sonnets," I cried; "but I don't think I am likely to be converted to any new idea. The matter has ceased to be a mystery to any one. Indeed, I wonder that it ever was a mystery."

"As I don't believe in the theory, I am not likely to convert you to it," said Erskine, laughing; "but it may interest you."

"Tell it to me, of course," I answered. "If it is half as delightful as the picture, I shall be more than satisfied."

"Well," said Erskine, lighting a cigarette, "I must begin by telling you about Cyril Graham himself. He and I were at the same house at Eton. I was a year or two older than he was, but we were immense friends, and did all our work and all our play together. There was, of course, a good deal more play than work, but I cannot say that I am sorry for that. It is always an advantage not to have received a sound commercial education, and what I learned in the playing fields at Eton has been quite as useful to me as anything I was taught at Cambridge. I should tell you that Cyril's father and mother were both dead. They had been drowned in a horrible yachting accident off the Isle of Wight. His father had been in the diplomatic service, and had married a daughter, the only daughter, in fact, of old Lord Crediton, who became Cyril's guardian after the death of his parents. I don't think that Lord Credition cared very much for Cyril. He had never really forgiven his daughter for marrying a man who had no title. He was an extraordinary old aristocrat, who swore like a costermonger, and had the manners of a farmer. I remember seeing him once on Speech-day. He growled at me, gave me a sovereign, and told me not to grow up 'a damned Radical' like my father. Cyril had very little affection for him, and was only too glad to spend most of his holidays with us in Scotland. They never really got on together at all. Cyril thought him a bear, and he thought Cyril effeminate. He was effeminate, I suppose, in some things, though he was a very good rider and a capital fencer. In fact he got the foils before he left Eton. But he was very languid in his manner, and not a little vain of his good looks, and had a strong objection to football. The two things that really gave him pleasure were poetry and acting. At Eton he was always dressing up and reciting Shakespeare, and when we went up to Trinity he became a member of the A.D.C. his first term. I remember I was always very jealous of his acting. I was absurdly devoted to him; I suppose because we were so different in some things. I was a rather awkward, weakly lad, with huge feet, and horribly freckled. Freckles run in Scotch families just as gout does in English families. Cyril used to say that of the two he preferred the gout; but he always set an absurdly high value on personal appearance, and once read a paper before our debating society to prove that it was better to be good-looking than to be good. He certainly was wonderfully handsome. People who did not like him, Philistines and college tutors, and young men reading for the Church, used to say that he was merely pretty; but there was a great deal more in his face than mere prettiness. I think he was the most splendid creature I ever saw, and nothing could exceed the grace of his movements, the charm of his manner. He fascinated everybody who was worth fascinating, and a great many people who were not. He was often wilful and petulant, and I used to think him dreadfully insincere. It was due, I think, chiefly to his inordinate desire to please. Poor Cyril! I told him once that he was contented with very cheap triumphs, but he only laughed. He was horribly spoiled. All charming people, I fancy, are spoiled. It is the secret of their attraction.

"However, I must tell you about Cyril's acting. You know that no actresses are allowed to play at the A.D.C. At least they were not in my time. I don't know how it is now. Well, of course Cyril was always cast for the girls' parts, and when 'As You Like It' was produced he played Rosalind. It was a marvellous performance. In fact, Cyril Graham was the only perfect Rosalind I have ever seen. It would be impossible to describe to you the beauty, the delicacy, the refinement of the whole thing. It made an immense sensation, and the horrid little theatre, as it was then, was crowded every night. Even when I read the play now I can't help thinking of Cyril. It might have been written for him. The next term he took his degree, and came to London to read for the diplomatic. But he never did any work. He spent his days in reading Shakespeare's Sonnets, and his evenings at the theatre. He was, of course, wild to go on the stage. It was all that I and Lord Credition could do to prevent him. Perhaps if he had gone on the stage he would be alive now. It is always a silly thing to give advice, but to give good advice is absolutely fatal. I hope you will never fall into that error. If you do, you will be sorry for it.

"Well, to come to the real point of the story, one day I got a letter from Cyril asking me to come round to his rooms that evening. He had charming chambers in Piccadilly overlooking the Green Park, and as I used to go to see him every day, I was rather surprised at his taking the trouble to write. Of course I went, and when I arrived I found him in a state of great excitement. He told me that he had at last discovered the true secret of Shakespeare's Sonnets; that all the scholars and critics had been entirely on the wrong tack; and that he was the first who, working purely by internal evidence, had found out who Mr W. H. really was. He was perfectly wild with delight, and for a long time would not tell me his theory. Finally, he produced a bundle of notes, took his copy of the Sonnets off the mantelpiece, and sat down and gave me a long lecture on the whole subject.

"He began by pointing out that the young man to whom Shakespeare addressed these strangely passionate poems must have been somebody who was a really vital factor in the development of his dramatic art, and that this could not be said either of Lord Pembroke or Lord Southampton. Indeed, whoever he was, he could not have been anybody of high birth, as was shown very clearly by the 25th Sonnet, in which Shakespeare contrasts himself with those who are 'great princes' favourites'; says quite frankly—

> " 'Let those who are in favour with their stars
> Of public honour and proud titles boast,
> Whilst I, whom fortune of such triumph bars,
> Unlooked for joy in that I honour most;'

and ends the sonnet by congratulating himself on the mean state of him he so adored:

> " 'Then happy I, that loved and am beloved
> Where I may not remove nor be removed.'

This sonnet Cyril declared would be quite unintelligible if we fancied that it was addressed to either the Earl of Pembroke or the Earl of Southampton, both of whom were men of the highest position in England and fully entitled to be called 'great princes'; and he in corroboration of his view read me Sonnets cxxiv. and cxxv., in which Shakespeare tells us that his love is not 'the child of state,' that it 'suffers not in smiling pomp,' but is 'builded far from accident.' I listened with a good deal of interest, for I don't think the point had ever been made before; but what followed was still more curious, and seemed to me at the time to entirely dispose of Pembroke's claim. We know from Meres that the Sonnets had been written before 1598, and Sonnet civ. informs us that Shakespeare's friendship for Mr W. H. had been already in existence for three years. Now Lord Pembroke, who was born in 1580, did not come to London till he was eighteen years of age, that is to say till 1598, and Shakespeare's acquaintance with Mr W. H. must have begun in 1594, or at the latest in 1595. Shakespeare, accordingly, could not have known Lord Pembroke till after the Sonnets had been written.

"Cyril pointed out also that Pembroke's father did not die till 1601; whereas it was evident from the line,

'You had a father, let your son say so,'

that the father of Mr W. H. was dead in 1598. Besides, it was absurd to imagine that any publisher of the time, and the preface is from the publisher's hand, would have ventured to address William Herbert, Earl of Pembroke, as Mr W. H.; the case of Lord Buckhurst being spoken of as Mr Sackville being not really a parallel instance, as Lord Buckhurst was not a peer, but merely the younger son of a peer, with a courtesy title, and the passage in 'England's Parnassus,' where he is so spoken of, is not a formal and stately dedication, but simply a casual allusion. So far for Lord Pembroke, whose supposed claims Cyril easily demolished while I sat by in wonder. With Lord Southampton Cyril had even less difficulty. Southampton became at a very early age the lover of Elizabeth Vernon, so he needed no en-treaties to marry; he was not beautiful; he did not resemble his mother, as Mr W. H. did—

"'Thou art thy mother's glass, and she in thee
Calls back the lovely April of her prime;'

and, above all, his Christian name was Henry, whereas the punning sonnets (cxxxv. and cxliii.) show that the Christian name of Shake-speare's friend was the same as his own—*Will*.

"As for the other suggestions of unfortunate commentators, that

Mr W. H. is a misprint for Mr W. S., meaning Mr William Shake-speare; that 'Mr W. H. all' should be read 'Mr W. Hall'; that Mr W. H. is Mr William Hathaway; and that a full stop should be placed after 'wisheth,' making Mr W. H. the writer and not the subject of the dedication,—Cyril got rid of them in a very short time; and it is not worth while to mention his reasons, though I remember he sent me off into a fit of laughter by reading to me, I am glad to say not in the original, some extracts from a German commentator called Barn-storff, who insisted that Mr W. H. was no less a person than 'Mr Williams Himself.' Nor would he allow for a moment that the Sonnets are mere satires on the work of Drayton and John Davies of Hereford. To him, as indeed to me, they were poems of serious and tragic im-port, wrung out of the bitterness of Shakespeare's heart, and made sweet by the honey of his lips. Still less would he admit that they were merely a philosophical allegory, and that in them Shakespeare is addressing his Ideal Self, or Ideal Manhood, or the Spirit of Beauty, or the Reason, or the Divine Logos, or the Catholic Church. He felt, as indeed I think we all must feel, that the Sonnets are addressed to an individual,—to a particular young man whose personality for some reason seems to have filled the soul of Shakespeare with terrible joy and no less terrible despair.

"Having in this manner cleared the way as it were, Cyril asked me to dismiss from my mind any preconceived ideas I might have formed on the subject, and to give a fair and unbiassed hearing to his own theory. The problem he pointed out was this: Who was that young man of Shakespeare's day who, without being of noble birth or even of noble nature, was addressed by him in terms of such pas-sionate adoration that we can but wonder at the strange worship, and are almost afraid to turn the key that unlocks the mystery of the poet's heart? Who was he whose physical beauty was such that it became the very cornerstone of Shakespeare's art; the very source of Shake-speare's inspiration; the very incarnation of Shakespeare's dreams? To look upon him as simply the object of certain love-poems is to miss the whole meaning of the poems: for the art of which Shakespeare talks in the Sonnets is not the art of the Sonnets themselves, which in-deed were to him but slight and secret things—it is the art of the dramatist to which he is always alluding; and he to whom Shakespeare said—

> " 'Thou art all my art, and dost advance
> As high as learning my rude ignorance,'—

he to whom he promised immortality,

> " 'Where breath most breathes, even in the mouth of men,'—

was surely none other than the boy-actor for whom he created Viola and Imogen, Juliet and Rosalind, Portia and Desdemona, and Cleopatra herself. This was Cyril Graham's theory, evolved as you see purely from the Sonnets themselves, and depending for its acceptance not so much on demonstrable proof or formal evidence, but on a kind of spiritual and artistic sense, by which alone he claimed could the true meaning of the poems be discerned. I remember his reading to me that fine sonnet—

> " 'How can my Muse want subject to invent,
> While thou dost breathe, that pour'st into my verse
> Thine own sweet argument, too excellent
> For every vulgar paper to rehearse?
> O, give thyself the thanks, if aught in me
> Worthy perusal stand against thy sight;
> For who's so dumb that cannot write to thee,
> When thou thyself dost give invention light?
> Be thou the tenth Muse, ten times more in worth
> Than those old nine which rhymers invocate;
> And he that calls on thee, let him bring forth
> Eternal numbers to outlive long date'

—and pointing out how completely it corroborated his theory; and indeed he went through all the Sonnets carefully, and showed, or fancied that he showed, that, according to his new explanation of their meaning, things that had seemed obscure, or evil, or exaggerated, became clear and rational, and of high artistic import, illustrating Shakespeare's conception of the true relations between the art of the actor and the art of the dramatist.

"It is of course evident that there must have been in Shakespeare's company some wonderful boy-actor of great beauty, to whom he intrusted the presentation of his noble heroines; for Shakespeare was a practical theatrical manager as well as an imaginative poet, and Cyril Graham had actually discovered the boy-actor's name. He was Will, or, as he preferred to call him, Willie Hughes. The Christian name he found of course in the punning sonnets, cxxxv. and cxliii.; the surname was, according to him, hidden in the eighth line of the 20th Sonnet, where Mr W. H. is described as—

" 'A man in hew, all *Hews* in his controwling.'

"In the original edition of the Sonnets "Hews" is printed with a capital letter and in italics, and this, he claimed, showed clearly that a play on words was intended, his view receiving a good deal of corroboration from those sonnets in which curious puns are made on the words 'use' and 'usury.' Of course I was converted at once, and Willie Hughes became to me as real a person as Shakespeare. The only objection I made to the theory was that the name of Willie Hughes does not occur in the list of the actors of Shakespeare's company as it is printed in the first folio. Cyril, however, pointed out that the absence of Willie Hughes's name from this list really corroborated the theory, as it was evident from Sonnet lxxxvi. that Willie Hughes had abandoned Shakespeare's company to play at a rival theatre, probably in some of Chapman's plays. It is in reference to this that in the great sonnet on Chapman Shakespeare said to Willie Hughes—

" 'But when your countenance filled up his line,
Then lacked I matter; that enfeebled mine'—

the expression 'when your countenance filled up his line' referring obviously to the beauty of the young actor giving life and reality and added charm to Chapman's verse, the same idea being also put forward in the 79th Sonnet—

" 'Whilst I alone did call upon thy aid,
My verse alone had all thy gentle grace,
But now my gracious numbers are decayed,
And my sick Muse does give another place;'

and in the immediately preceding sonnet, where Shakespeare says,

> " 'Every alien pen has got my *use*
> And under thee their poesy disperse,'

the play upon words (use = Hughes) being of course obvious, and
the phrase 'under thee their poesy disperse,' meaning 'by your assistance as an actor bring their plays before the people.'

"It was a wonderful evening, and we sat up almost till dawn reading and re-reading the Sonnets. After some time, however, I began
to see that before the theory could be placed before the world in a
really perfected form, it was necessary to get some independent
evidence about the existence of this young actor Willie Hughes. If
this could be once established, there could be no possible doubt about
his identity with Mr W. H.; but otherwise the theory would fall to
the ground. I put this forward very strongly to Cyril, who was a good
deal annoyed at what he called my Philistine tone of mind, and indeed was rather bitter upon the subject. However, I made him promise
that in his own interest he would not publish his discovery till he had
put the whole matter beyond the reach of doubt; and for weeks and
weeks we searched the registers of City churches, the Alleyn MSS.
at Dulwich, the Record Office, the papers of the Lord Chamberlain—
everything, in fact, that we thought might contain some allusion to
Willie Hughes. We discovered nothing, of course, and every day the
existence of Willie Hughes seemed to me to become more problemati-
cal. Cyril was in a dreadful state, and used to go over the whole
question day after day, entreating me to believe; but I saw the one
flaw in the theory, and I refused to be convinced till the actual
existence of Willie Hughes, a boy-actor of Elizabethan days, had
been placed beyond the reach of doubt or cavil.

"One day Cyril left town to stay with his grandfather, I thought at
the time, but I afterwards heard from Lord Crediton that this was not
the case; and about a fortnight afterwards I received a telegram from
him, handed in at Warwick, asking me to be sure to come and dine
with him that evening at eight o'clock. When I arrived, he said to me,
'The only apostle who did not deserve proof was S. Thomas, and S.
Thomas was the only apostle who got it.' I asked him what he meant.
He answered that he had not merely been able to establish the

existence in the sixteenth century of a boy-actor of the name of Willie Hughes, but to prove by the most conclusive evidence that he was the Mr W. H. of the Sonnets. He would not tell me anything more at the time; but after dinner he solemnly produced the picture I showed you, and told me that he had discovered it by the merest chance nailed to the side of an old chest that he had bought at a farm-house in Warwickshire. The chest itself, which was a very fine example of Elizabethan work, he had, of course, brought with him, and in the centre of the front panel the initials W. H. were undoubtedly carved. It was this monogram that had attracted his attention, and he told me that it was not till he had had the chest in his possession for several days that he had thought of making any careful examination of the inside. One morning, however, he saw that one of the sides of the chest was much thicker than the other, and looking more closely, he discovered that a framed panel picture was clamped against it. On taking it out, he found it was the picture that is now lying on the sofa. It was very dirty, and covered with mould; but he managed to clean it, and, to his great joy, saw that he had fallen by mere chance on the one thing for which he had been looking. Here was an authentic portrait of Mr W. H., with his hand resting on the dedicatory page of the Sonnets, and on the frame itself could be faintly seen the name of the young man written in black uncial letters on a faded gold ground, 'Master Will. Hews.'

"Well, what was I to say? It never occurred to me for a moment that Cyril Graham was playing a trick on me, or that he was trying to prove his theory by means of a forgery."

"But is it a forgery?" I asked.

"Of course it is," said Erskine. "It is a very good forgery; but it is a forgery none the less. I thought at the time that Cyril was rather calm about the whole matter; but I remember he more than once told me that he himself required no proof of the kind, and that he thought the theory complete without it. I laughed at him, and told him that without it the theory would fall to the ground, and I warmly congratulated him on the marvellous discovery. We then arranged that the picture should be etched or facsimiled, and placed as the frontispiece to Cyril's edition of the Sonnets; and for three months we did nothing but go over each poem line by line, till we had settled every difficulty of text or meaning. One unlucky day I was in a print-shop in Holborn, when

I saw upon the counter some extremely beautiful drawings in silver-point. I was so attracted by them that I bought them; and the proprietor of the place, a man called Rawlings, told me that they were done by a young painter of the name of Edward Merton, who was very clever, but as poor as a church mouse. I went to see Merton some days afterwards, having got his address from the print-seller, and found a pale, interesting young man, with a rather common-looking wife—his model, as I subsequently learned. I told him how much I admired his drawings, at which he seemed very pleased, and I asked him if he would show me some of his other work. As we were looking over a portfolio, full of really very lovely things,—for Merton had a most delicate and delightful touch,—I suddenly caught sight of a draw-ing of the picture of Mr W. H. There was no doubt whatever about it. It was almost a facsimile—the only difference being that the two masks of Tragedy and Comedy were not suspended from the marble table as they are in the picture, but were lying on the floor at the young man's feet. 'Where on earth did you get that?' I said. He grew rather confused, and said—'Oh, that is nothing. I did not know it was in this portfolio. It is not a thing of any value.' 'It is what you did for Mr Cyril Graham,' exclaimed his wife; 'and if this gentleman wishes to buy it, let him have it.' 'For Mr Cyril Graham?' I repeated. 'Did you paint the picture of Mr W. H.?' 'I don't understand what you mean,' he answered, growing very red. Well, the whole thing was quite dreadful. The wife let it all out. I gave her five pounds when I was going away. I can't bear to think of it now; but of course I was furious. I went off at once to Cyril's chambers, waited there for three hours before he came in, with that horrid lie staring me in the face, and told him I had discovered his forgery. He grew very pale, and said—'I did it purely for your sake. You would not be convinced in any other way. It does not affect the truth of the theory.' 'The truth of the theory!' I exclaimed; 'the less we talk about that the better. You never even believed in it yourself. If you had, you would not have committed a forgery to prove it.' High words passed between us; we had a fearful quarrel. I daresay I was unjust. The next morning he was dead."

"Dead!" I cried.

"Yes; he shot himself with a revolver. Some of the blood splashed upon the frame of the picture, just where the name had been painted.

By the time I arrived—his servant had sent for me at once—the police were already there. He had left a letter for me, evidently written in the greatest agitation and distress of mind."

"What was in it?" I asked.

"Oh, that he believed absolutely in Willie Hughes; that the forgery of the picture had been done simply as a concession to me, and did not in the slightest degree invalidate the truth of the theory; and that in order to show me how firm and flawless his faith in the whole thing was, he was going to offer his life as a sacrifice to the secret of the Sonnets. It was a foolish, mad letter. I remember he ended by saying that he intrusted to me the Willie Hughes theory, and that it was for me to present it to the world, and to unlock the secret of Shakespeare's heart."

"It is a most tragic story," I cried; "but why have you not carried out his wishes?"

Erskine shrugged his shoulders. "Because it is a perfectly unsound theory from beginning to end," he answered.

"My dear Esrskine," I said, getting up from my seat, "you are entirely wrong about the whole matter. It is the only perfect key to Shakespeare's Sonnets that has ever been made. It is complete in every detail. I believe in Willie Hughes."

"Don't say that," said Erskine, gravely; "I believe there is something fatal about the idea, and intellectually there is nothing to be said for it. I have gone into the whole matter, and I assure you the theory is entirely fallacious. It is plausible up to a certain point. Then it stops. For heaven's sake, my dear boy, don't take up the subject of Willie Hughes. You will break your heart over it."

"Erskine," I answered, "it is your duty to give this theory to the world. If you will not do it, I will. By keeping it back you wrong the memory of Cyril Graham, the youngest and the most splendid of all the martyrs of literature. I entreat you to do him justice. He died for this thing—don't let his death be in vain."

Erskine looked at me in amazement. "You are carried away by the sentiment of the whole story," he said. "You forget that a thing is not necessarily true because a man dies for it. I was devoted to Cyril Graham. His death was a horrible blow to me. I did not recover it for years. I don't think I have ever recovered it. But Willie Hughes? There is nothing in the idea of Willie Hughes. No such person ever existed. As for bringing the whole thing before the world—the world thinks that Cyril Graham shot himself by accident. The only proof of his suicide was contained in the letter to me, and of this letter the public never heard anything. To the present day Lord Crediton thinks that the whole thing was accidental."

"Cyril Graham sacrificed his life to a great idea," I answered; "and if you will not tell of his martyrdom, tell at least of his faith."

"His faith," said Erskine, "was fixed in a thing that was false, in a thing that was unsound, in a thing that no Shakespearian scholar would accept for a moment. The theory would be laughed at. Don't make a fool of yourself, and don't follow a trail that leads nowhere. You start by assuming the existence of the very person whose existence is the thing to be proved. Besides, everybody knows that the Sonnets were addressed to Lord Pembroke. The matter is settled once for all."

"The matter is not settled!" I exclaimed. "I will take up the theory where Cyril Graham left it, and I will prove to the world that he was right."

"Silly boy!" said Erskine. "Go home: it is after two, and don't think about Willie Hughes any more. I am sorry I told you anything about it, and very sorry indeed that I should have converted you to a thing in which I don't believe."

"You have given me the key to the greatest mystery of modern literature," I answered; "and I shall not rest till I have made you recognise, till I have made everybody recognise, that Cyril Graham was the most subtle Shakespearian critic of our day."

As I walked home through St. James's Park the dawn was just breaking over London. The white swans were lying asleep on the polished lake, and the gaunt Palace looked purple against the pale-green sky. I thought of Cyril Graham, and my eyes filled with tears.

II

It was past twelve o'clock when I awoke, and the sun was streaming in through the curtains of my room in long slanting beams of dusty gold. I told my servant that I would be at home to no one; and after I had had a cup of chocolate and a *petit-pain*, I took down from

the book-shelf my copy of Shakespeare's Sonnets, and began to go carefully through them. Every poem seemed to me to corroborate Cyril
Graham's theory. I felt as if I had my hand upon Shakespeare's
heart, and was counting each separate throb and pulse of passion. I
thought of the wonderful boy-actor, and saw his face in every line.

Two sonnets, I remember, struck me particularly: they were the
53d and the 67th. In the first of these, Shakespeare, complimenting
Willie Hughes on the versatility of his acting, on his wide range of
parts, a range extending from Rosalind to Juliet, and from Beatrice to
Ophelia, says to him—

> "What is your substance, whereof are you made,
> That millions of strange shadows on you tend?
> Since every one hath, every one, one shade,
> And you, but one, can every shadow lend"—

lines that would be unintelligible if they were not addressed to an
actor, for the word "shadow" had in Shakespeare's day a technical
meaning connected with the stage. "The best in this kind are but
shadows," says Theseus of the actors in the "Midsummer Night's
Dream," and there are many similar allusions in the literature of the
day. These sonnets evidently belonged to the series in which Shakespeare discusses the nature of the actor's art, and of the strange and
rare temperament that is essential to the perfect stage-player. "How
is it," says Shakespeare to Willie Hughes, "that you have so many
personalities?" and then he goes on to point out that his beauty is such
that it seems to realise every form and phase of fancy, to embody each
dream of the creative imagination—an idea that is still further expanded in the sonnet that immediately follows, where, beginning
with the fine thought,

> "O, how much more doth beauty beauteous seem
> By that sweet ornament which *truth* doth give!"

Shakespeare invites us to notice how the truth of acting, the truth of
visible presentation on the stage, adds to the wonder of poetry, giving
life to its loveliness, and actual reality to its ideal form. And yet, in
the 67th Sonnet, Shakespeare calls upon Willie Hughes to abandon

the stage with its artificiality, it false mimic life of painted face and unreal costume, its immoral influences and suggestions, its remoteness from the true world of noble action and sincere utterance.

> "Ah! wherefore with infection should he live,
> And with his presence grace impiety,
> That sin by him advantage should achieve,
> And lace itself with his society?
> Why should false painting imitate his cheek
> And steal dead seeming of his living hue?
> Why should poor beauty indirectly seek
> Roses of shadow, since his rose is true?"

It may seem strange that so great a dramatist as Shakespeare, who realised his own perfection as an artist and his humanity as a man on the ideal plane of stage-writing and stage-playing, should have written in these terms about the theatre; but we must remember that in Sonnets cx. and cxi. Shakespeare shows us that he too was wearied of the world of puppets, and full of shame at having made himself "a motley to the view." The 111th Sonnet is especially bitter:—

> "O, for my sake do you with Fortune chide
> The guilty goddess of my harmful deeds,
> That did not better for my life provide
> Than public means which public manners breeds.
> Thence comes it that my name receives a brand,
> And almost thence my nature is subdued
> To what it works in, like the dyer's hand:
> Pity me, then, and wish I were renewed"—

and there are many signs elsewhere of the same feeling, signs familiar to all real students of Shakespeare.

One point puzzled me immensely as I read the Sonnets, and it was days before I struck on the true interpretation, which indeed Cyril Graham himself seems to have missed. I could not understand how it was that Shakespeare set so high a value on his young friend marrying. He himself had married young, and the result had been unhappiness, and it was not likely that he would have asked Willie

Hughes to commit the same error. The boy-player of Rosalind had nothing to gain from marriage, or from the passions of real life. The early sonnets, with their strange entreaties to have children, seemed to me a jarring note. The explanation of the mystery came on me quite suddenly, and I found it in the curious dedication. It will be remembered that the dedication runs as follows:—

"TO · THE · ONLIE · BEGETTER · OF ·

THESE · INSUING · SONNETS ·

MR W. H. · ALL · HAPPINESSE ·

AND · THAT · ETERNITIE ·

PROMISED · BY ·

OUR · EVER-LIVING · POET ·

WISHETH ·

THE · WELL-WISHING ·

ADVENTURER · IN ·

SETTING ·

FORTH.

T. T."

Some scholars have supposed that the word "begetter" in this dedication means simply the procurer of the Sonnets for Thomas Thorpe the publisher; but this view is now generally abandoned, and the highest authorities are quite agreed that it is to be taken in the sense of inspirer, the metaphor being drawn from the analogy of physical life. Now I saw that the same metaphor was used by Shakespeare himself all through the poems, and this set me on the right track. Finally I made my great discovery. The marriage that Shakespeare proposes for Willie Hughes is the "marriage with his Muse," an expression which is definitely put forward in the 82d Sonnet, where, in the bitterness of his heart at the defection of the boy-actor for whom he had written his greatest parts, and whose beauty had indeed suggested them, he opens his complaint by saying—

"I'll grant thou wert not married to my Muse."

The children he begs him to beget are no children of flesh and blood, but more immortal children of undying fame. The whole cycle of the early sonnets is simply Shakespeare's invitation to Willie Hughes to go upon the stage and become a player. How barren and profitless a thing, he says, is this beauty of yours if it be not used:

> "When forty winters shall besiege thy brow,
> And dig deep trenches in thy beauty's field,
> Thy youth's proud livery, so gazed on now,
> Will be a tattered weed, of small worth held:
> Then being asked where all thy beauty lies,
> Where all the treasure of thy lusty days,
> To say, within thine own deep-sunken eyes,
> Were an all-eating shame and thriftless praise."

You must create something in art: my verse "is thine, and *born* of thee;" only listen to me, and I will *"bring forth* eternal numbers to outlive long date," and you shall people with forms of your own image the imaginary world of the stage. These children that you beget, he continues, will not wither away, as mortal children do, but you shall live in them and in my plays: do but

> "Make thee another self, for love of me,
> That beauty still may live in thine or thee!"

I collected all the passages that seemed to me to corroborate this view, and they produced a strong impression on me, and showed me how complete Cyril Graham's theory really was. I also saw that it was quite easy to separate those lines in which he speaks of the Sonnets themselves from those in which he speaks of his great dramatic work. This was a point that had been entirely overlooked by all critics up to Cyril Graham's day. And yet it was one of the most important points in the whole series of poems. To the Sonnets Shakespeare was more or less indifferent. He did not wish to rest his fame on them. They were to him his "slight Muse," as he calls them, and intended, as Meres tells us, for private circulation only among a few, a very few, friends. Upon the other hand he was extremely conscious of the high artistic value of his plays, and shows a noble self-reliance upon his dramatic genius. When he says to Willie Hughes:

"But thy eternal summer shall not fade,
Nor lose possession of that fair thou owest;
Nor shall Death brag thou wander'st in his shade,
When in *eternal lines* to time thou growest;
   So long as men can breathe or eyes can see,
   So long lives this and this gives life to thee;"—

the expression "eternal lines" clearly alludes to one of his plays that he was sending him at the time, just as the concluding couplet points to his confidence in the probability of his plays being always acted. In his address to the Dramatic Muse (Sonnets c. and ci.), we find the same feeling.

"Where art thou, Muse, that thou forget'st so long
To speak of that which gives thee all thy might?
Spends thou thy fury on some worthless song,
Darkening thy power to lend base subjects light?"

he cries, and he then proceeds to reproach the mistress of Tragedy and Comedy for her "neglect of Truth in Beauty dyed," and says—

"Because he needs no praise, wilt thou be dumb?
Excuse not silence so; for 't lies in thee
To make him much outlive a gilded tomb,
And to be praised of ages yet to be.
   Then do thy office, Muse; I teach thee how
   To make him seem long hence as he shows now."

It is, however, perhaps in the 55th Sonnet that Shakespeare gives to this idea its fullest expression. To imagine that the "powerful rhyme" of the second line refers to the sonnet itself, is to entirely mistake Shakespeare's meaning. It seemed to me that it was extremely likely, from the general character of the sonnet, that a particular play was meant, and that the play was none other but "Romeo and Juliet."

"Not marble, nor the gilded monuments
Of princes, shall outlive this powerful rhyme;

But you shall shine more bright in these contents
Than unswept stone besmeared with sluttish time.
When wasteful wars shall statues overturn,
And broils root out the work of masonry,
Not Mars his sword nor war's quick fire shall burn
The living record of your memory.
'Gainst death and all-oblivious enmity
Shall you pace forth; your praise shall still find room
Even in the eyes of all posterity
That wear this world out to the ending doom.
 So, till the judgment that yourself arise,
 You live in this, and dwell in lovers' eyes."

It was also extremely suggestive to note how here as elsewhere Shakespeare promised Willie Hughes immortality in a form that appealed to men's eyes—that is to say, in a spectacular form, in a play that is to be looked at.

For two weeks I worked hard at the Sonnets, hardly ever going out, and refusing all invitations. Every day I seemed to be discovering something new, and Willie Hughes became to me a kind of spiritual presence, an ever-dominant personality. I could almost fancy that I saw him standing in the shadow of my room, so well had Shakespeare drawn him, with his golden hair, his tender flower-like grace, his dreamy deep-sunken eyes, his delicate mobile limbs, and his white lily hands. His very name fascinated me. Willie Hughes! Willie Hughes! How musically it sounded! Yes; who else but he could have been the master-mistress of Shakespeare's passion,[1] the lord of his love to whom he was bound in vassalage,[2] the delicate minion of pleasure,[3] the rose of the whole world,[4] the herald of the spring[5] decked in the proud livery of youth,[6] the lovely boy whom it was sweet music to hear,[7] and whose beauty was the very raiment of Shakespeare's heart,[8] as it was the keystone of his dramatic power? How bitter now seemed the whole tragedy of his desertion and his shame!—shame

[1] Sonnet xx. 2.
[2] Sonnet xxvi. 1.
[3] Sonnet cxxvi. 9.
[4] Sonnet cix. 14.
[5] Sonnet i. 10.
[6] Sonnet ii. 3.
[7] Sonnet viii. 1.
[8] Sonnet xxii. 6.

that he made sweet and lovely[9] by the mere magic of his personality, but that was none the less shame. Yet as Shakespeare forgave him, should not we forgive him also? I did not care to pry into the mystery of his sin.

His abandonment of Shakespeare's theatre was a different matter, and I investigated it at great length. Finally I came to the conclusion that Cyril Graham had been wrong in regarding the rival dramatist of the 80th Sonnet as Chapman. It was obviously Marlowe who was alluded to. At the time the Sonnets were written, such an expression as "the proud full sail of his great verse" could not have been used of Chapman's work, however applicable it might have been to the style of his later Jacobean plays. No: Marlowe was clearly the rival dramatist of whom Shakespeare spoke in such laudatory terms; and that

> "Affable familiar ghost
> Which nightly gulls him with intelligence,"

was the Mephistopheles of his Doctor Faustus. No doubt, Marlowe was fascinated by the beauty and grace of the boy-actor, and lured him away from the Blackfriars' Theatre, that he might play the Gaveston of his "Edward II." That Shakespeare had the legal right to retain Willie Hughes in his own company is evident from Sonnet lxxxvii., where he says:—

> "Farewell! thou art too dear for my possessing,
> And like enough thou know'st thy estimate:
> The *charter of thy worth* gives thee releasing;
> My *bonds* in thee are all determinate.
> For how do I hold thee but by thy granting?
> And for that riches where is my deserving?
> The cause of this fair gift in me is wanting,
> *And so my patent back again is swerving.*
> Thyself thou gavest, thy own work then not knowing,
> Or me, to whom thou gavest it, else mistaking;

[9] Sonnet xcv. 1.

So thy great gift, upon misprision growing,
Comes none again, on better judgment making.
This have I had thee, as a dream doth flatter,
In sleep a king, but waking no such matter."

But him whom he could not hold by love, he would not hold by force. Willie Hughes became a member of Lord Pembroke's company, and, perhaps in the open yard of the Red Bull Tavern, played the part of King Edward's delicate minion. On Marlowe's death, he seems to have returned to Shakespeare, who, whatever his fellow-partners may have thought of the matter, was not slow to forgive the wilfulness and treachery of the young actor.

How well, too, had Shakespeare drawn the temperament of the stage-player! Willie Hughes was one of those

"That do not do the thing they most do show,
Who, moving others, are themselves as stone."

He could act love, but could not feel it, could mimic passion without realising it.

"In many's looks the false heart's history
Is writ in moods and frowns and wrinkles strange,"

but with Willie Hughes it was not so. "Heaven," says Shakespeare, in a sonnet of mad idolatry—

"Heaven in thy creation did decree
That in thy face sweet love should ever dwell;
Whate'er thy thoughts or thy heart's workings be,
Thy looks should nothing thence but sweetness tell."

In his "inconstant mind" and his "false heart," it was easy to recognise the insincerity and treachery that somehow seem inseparable from the artistic nature, as in his love of praise, that desire for immediate recognition that characterises all actors. And yet, more fortunate in this than other actors, Willie Hughes was to know something

of immortality. Inseparably connected with Shakespeare's plays, he
was to live in them.

> "Your name from hence immortal life shall have,
> Though I, once gone, to all the world must die:
> The earth can yield me but a common grave,
> When you entombed in men's eyes shall lie.
> Your monument shall be my gentle verse,
> Which eyes not yet created shall o'er-read,
> And tongues to be your being shall rehearse
> When all the breathers of this world are dead."

There were endless allusions, also, to Willie Hughes's power over his
audience,—the "gazers," as Shakespeare calls them; but perhaps the
most perfect description of his wonderful mastery over dramatic art
was in "The Lover's Complaint," where Shakespeare says of him:—

> "In him a plentitude of subtle matter,
> Applied to cautels, all strange forms receives,
> Of burning blushes, or of weeping water,
> Or swooning paleness; and he takes and leaves,
> In either's aptness, as it best deceives,
> To blush at speeches rank, to weep at woes,
> Or to turn white and swoon at tragic shows.
>
> .   .   .   .
>
> So on the tip of his subduing tongue,
> All kind of arguments and questions deep,
> All replication prompt and reason strong,
> For his advantage still did wake and sleep,
> To make the weeper laugh, the laugher weep.
>   He had the dialect and the different skill,
>   Catching all passions in his craft of will."

Once I thought that I had really found Willie Hughes in Elizabethan literature. In a wonderfully graphic account of the last days
of the great Earl of Essex, his chaplain, Thomas Knell, tells us that
the night before the Earl died, "he called William Hewes, which was
his musician, to play upon the virginals and to sing. 'Play,' said he,

'my song, Will Hewes, and I will sing it myself.' So he did it most joyfully, not as the howling swan, which, still looking down, waileth her end, but as a sweet lark, lifting up his hands and casting up his eyes to his God, with this mounted the crystal skies, and reached with his unwearied tongue the top of highest heavens." Surely the boy who played on the virginals to the dying father of Sidney's Stella was none other but the Will Hews to whom Shakespeare dedicated the Sonnets, and whom he tells us was himself sweet "music to hear." Yet Lord Essex died in 1576, when Shakespeare himself was but twelve years of age. It was impossible that his musician could have been the Mr W. H. of the Sonnets. Perhaps Shakespeare's young friend was the son of the player upon the virginals? It was at least something to have discovered that Will Hews was an Elizabethan name. Indeed the name Hews seemed to have been closely connected with music and the stage. The first English actress was the lovely Margaret Hews, whom Prince Rupert so madly loved. What more probable than that between her and Lord Essex's musician had come the boy-actor of Shakespeare's plays? But the proofs, the links—where were they? Alas! I could not find them. It seemed to me that I was always on the brink of absolute verification, but that I could never really attain to it.

From Willie Hughes's life I soon passed to thoughts of his death. I used to wonder what had been his end.

Perhaps he had been one of those English actors who in 1604 went across sea to Germany and played before the great Duke Henry Julius of Brunswick, himself a dramatist of no mean order, and at the Court of that strange Elector of Brandenburg, who was so enamoured of beauty that he was said to have bought for his weight in amber the young son of a travelling Greek merchant, and to have given pageants in honour of his slave all through that dreadful famine year of 1606–7, when the people died of hunger in the very streets of the town, and for the space of seven months there was no rain. We know at any rate that "Romeo and Juliet" was brought out at Dresden in 1613, along with "Hamlet" and "King Lear," and it was surely to none other than Willie Hughes that in 1615 the death-mask of Shakespeare was brought by the hand of one of the suite of the English ambassador, pale token of the passing away of the great poet who had

so dearly loved him. Indeed there would have been something peculiarly fitting in the idea that the boy-actor, whose beauty had been so
vital an element in the realism and romance of Shakespeare's art,
should have been the first to have brought to Germany the seed of
the new culture, and was in his way the precursor of that *Aufklarung*
or Illumination of the eighteenth century, that splendid movement
which, though begun by Lessing and Herder, and brought to its full
and perfect issue by Goethe, was in no small part helped on by another actor—Friedrich Schroeder—who awoke the popular consciousness, and by means of the feigned passions and mimetic methods of
the stage showed the intimate, the vital, connection between life and
literature. If this was so,—and there was certainly no evidence against
it,—it was not improbable that Willie Hughes was one of those
English comedians (*mimæ quidam ex Britannia,* as the old chronicle
calls them), who were slain at Nuremberg in a sudden uprising of
the people, and were secretly buried in a little vineyard outside the
city by some young men "who had found pleasure in their performances, and of whom some had sought to be instructed in the mysteries
of the new art." Certainly no more fitting place could there be for
him to whom Shakespeare said, "thou art all my art," than this little
vineyard outside the city walls. For was it not from the sorrows of
Dionysos that Tragedy sprang? Was not the light laughter of Comedy, with its careless merriment and quick replies, first heard on the
lips of the Sicilian vine-dressers? Nay, did not the purple and red
stain of the wine-froth on face and limbs give the first suggestion of
the charm and fascination of disguise—the desire for self-concealment,
the sense of the value of objectivity thus showing itself in the rude
beginnings of the art? At any rate, wherever he lay—whether in the
little vineyard at the gate of the Gothic town, or in some dim London
churchyard amidst the roar and bustle of our great city—no gorgeous
monument marked his resting-place. His true tomb, as Shakespeare
saw, was the poet's verse, his true monument the permanence of the
drama. So had it been with others whose beauty had given a new
creative impulse to their age. The ivory body of the Bithynian slave
rots in the green ooze of the Nile, and on the yellow hills of the
Cerameicus is strewn the dust of the young Athenian; but Antinous
lives in sculpture, and Charmides in philosophy.

III

After three weeks had elapsed, I determined to make a strong appeal to Erskine to do justice to the memory of Cyril Graham, and to give to the world his marvellous interpretation of the Sonnets—the only interpretation that thoroughly explained the problem. I have not any copy of my letter, I regret to say, nor have I been able to lay my hand upon the original; but I remember that I went over the whole ground, and covered sheets of paper with passionate reiteration of the arguments and proofs that my study had suggested to me. It seemed to me that I was not merely restoring Cyril Graham to his proper place in literary history, but rescuing the honour of Shakespeare himself from the tedious memory of a commonplace intrigue. I put into the letter all my enthusiasm. I put into the letter all my faith.

No sooner, in fact, had I sent it off than a curious reaction came over me. It seemed to me that I had given away my capacity for belief in the Willie Hughes theory of the Sonnets, that something had gone out of me, as it were, and that I was perfectly indifferent to the whole subject. What was it that had happened? It is difficult to say. Perhaps, by finding perfect expression for a passion, I had exhausted the passion itself. Emotional forces, like the forces of physical life, have their positive limitations. Perhaps the mere effort to convert any one to a theory involves some form of renunciation of the power of credence. Perhaps I was simply tired of the whole thing, and, my enthusiasm having burnt out, my reason was left to its own unimpassioned judgment. However it came about, and I cannot pretend to explain it, there was no doubt that Willie Hughes suddenly became to me a mere myth, an idle dream, the boyish fancy of a young man who, like most ardent spirits, was more anxious to convince others than to be himself convinced.

As I had said some very unjust and bitter things to Erskine in my letter, I determined to go and see him at once, and to make my apologies to him for my behaviour. Accordingly, the next morning I drove down to Birdcage Walk, and found Erskine sitting in his library, with the forged picture of Willie Hughes in front of him.

"My dear Erskine!" I cried, "I have come to apologise to you."

"To apologise to me?" he said. "What for?"

"For my letter," I answered.

"You have nothing to regret in your letter," he said. "On the contrary, you have done me the greatest service in your power. You have shown me that Cyril Graham's theory is perfectly sound."

"You don't mean to say that you believe in Willie Hughes?" I exclaimed.

"Why not?" he rejoined. "You have proved the thing to me. Do you think I cannot estimate the value of evidence?"

"But there is no evidence at all," I groaned, sinking into a chair. "When I wrote to you I was under the influence of a perfectly silly enthusiasm. I had been touched by the story of Cyril Graham's death, fascinated by his romantic theory, enthralled by the wonder and novelty of the whole idea. I see now that the theory is based on a delusion. The only evidence for the existence of Willie Hughes is that picture in front of you, and the picture is a forgery. Don't be carried away by mere sentiment in this matter. Whatever romance may have to say about the Willie Hughes theory, reason is dead against it."

"I don't understand you," said Erskine, looking at me in amazement. "Why, you yourself have convinced me by your letter that Willie Hughes is an absolute reality. Why have you changed your mind? Or is all that you have been saying to me merely a joke?"

"I cannot explain it to you," I rejoined, "but I see now that there is really nothing to be said in favour of Cyril Graham's interpretation. The Sonnets are addressed to Lord Pembroke. For heaven's sake don't waste your time in a foolish attempt to discover a young Elizabethan actor who never existed, and to make a phantom puppet the centre of the great cycle of Shakespeare's Sonnets."

"I see that you don't understand the theory," he replied.

"My dear Erskine," I cried, "not understand it! Why, I feel as if I had invented it. Surely my letter shows you that I not merely went into the whole matter, but that I contributed proofs of every kind. The one flaw in the theory is that it presupposes the existence of the person whose existence is the subject of dispute. If we grant that there was in Shakespeare's company a young actor of the name of Willie

Hughes, it is not difficult to make him the object of the Sonnets. But as we know that there was no actor of this name in the company of the Globe Theatre, it is idle to pursue the investigation further."

"But that is exactly what we don't know," said Erskine. "It is quite true that his name does not occur in the list given in the first folio; but, as Cyril pointed out, that is rather a proof in favour of the existence of Willie Hughes than against it, if we remember his treacherous desertion of Shakespeare for a rival dramatist."

We argued the matter over for hours, but nothing that I could say could make Erskine surrender his faith in Cyril Graham's interpretation. He told me that he intended to devote his life to proving the theory, and that he was determined to do justice to Cyril Graham's memory. I entreated him, laughed at him, begged of him, but it was of no use. Finally we parted, not exactly in anger, but certainly with a shadow between us. He thought me shallow, I thought him foolish. When I called on him again, his servant told me that he had gone to Germany.

Two years afterwards, as I was going into my club, the hall-porter handed me a letter with a foreign postmark. It was from Erskine, and written at the Hotel d'Angleterre, Cannes. When I had read it I was filled with horror, though I did not quite believe that he would be so mad as to carry his resolve into execution. The gist of the letter was that he had tried in every way to verify the Willie Hughes theory, and had failed, and that as Cyril Graham had given his life for his theory, he himself had determined to give his own life also to the same cause. The concluding words of the letter were these: "I still believe in Willie Hughes; and by the time you receive this, I shall have died by my own hand for Willie Hughes's sake: for his sake, and for the sake of Cyril Graham, whom I drove to his death by my shallow scepticism and ignorant lack of faith. The truth was once revealed to you, and you rejected it. It comes to you now stained with the blood of two lives,—do not turn away from it."

It was a horrible moment. I felt sick with misery, and yet I could not believe it. To die for one's theological beliefs is the worst use a man can make of his life, but to die for a literary theory! It seemed impossible.

I looked at the date. The letter was a week old. Some unfortunate chance had prevented my going to the club for several days, or I might have got it in time to save him. Perhaps it was not too late. I drove off to my rooms, packed up my things, and started by the night-mail from Charing Cross. The journey was intolerable. I thought I would never arrive.

As soon as I did I drove to the Hotel d'Angleterre. They told me that Erskine had been buried two days before, in the English cemetery. There was something horribly grotesque about the whole tragedy. I said all kinds of wild things, and the people in the hall looked curiously at me.

Suddenly Lady Erskine, in deep mourning, passed across the vestibule. When she saw me she came up to me, murmured something about her poor son, and burst into tears. I led her into her sitting-room. An elderly gentleman was there waiting for her. It was the English doctor.

We talked a great deal about Erskine, but I said nothing about his motive for committing suicide. It was evident that he had not told his mother anything about the reason that had driven him to so fatal, so mad an act. Finally Lady Erskine rose and said, "George left you something as a memento. It was a thing he prized very much. I will get it for you."

As soon as she had left the room I turned to the doctor and said, "What a dreadful shock it must have been to Lady Erskine! I wonder that she bears it as well as she does."

"Oh, she knew for months past that it was coming," he answered.

"Knew it for months past!" I cried. "But why didn't she stop him? Why didn't she have him watched? He must have been mad."

The doctor stared at me. "I don't know what you mean," he said.

"Well," I cried, "if a mother knows that her son is going to commit suicide——"

"Suicide!" he answered. "Poor Erskine did not commit suicide. He died of consumption. He came here to die. The moment I saw him I knew that there was no hope. One lung was almost gone, and the other was very much affected. Three days before he died he asked me was there any hope. I told him frankly that there was none, and that he had only a few days to live. He wrote some letters, and was quite resigned, retaining his senses to the last."

At that moment Lady Erskine entered the room with the fatal picture of Willie Hughes in her hand. "When George was dying he begged me to give you this," she said. As I took it from her, her tears fell on my hand.

The picture hangs now in my library, where it is very much admired by my artistic friends. They have decided that it is not a Clouet, but an Ouvry. I have never cared to tell them its true history. But sometimes, when I look at it, I think that there is really a great deal to be said for the Willie Hughes theory of Shakespeare's Sonnets.

Autres Temps . . .

EDITH WHARTON

EDITH WHARTON (1862–1937) grew up in Newport, and for many years led the life of a society matron. Brilliantly cultivated (though she had had largely to educate herself) and incompatibly married, she turned her great energies to fiction in middle life. *The House of Mirth* (1905) was a great best seller, and thereafter she continued to turn out novels, short stories, essays, travel books and poems steadily for the rest of a long life, publishing in all forty-seven volumes. She settled in Paris and eventually lost touch with her American source material, but her early and middle work, with its brilliant style and vivid pictures of New York fashionable life, ensure her a permanent place in American letters. *Autres Temps* appeared in *Xingu* in 1916.

I

MRS. LIDCOTE, as the huge menacing mass of New York defined itself far off across the waters, shrank back into her corner of the deck and sat listening with a kind of unreasoning terror to the steady onward drive of the screws.

She had set out on the voyage quietly enough—in what she called her "reasonable" mood—but the week at sea had given her too much time to think of things and had left her too long alone with the past.

When she was alone, it was always the past that occupied her. She couldn't get away from it, and she didn't any longer care to. During her long years of exile she had made her terms with it, had learned to accept the fact that it would always be there, huge, obstructing, encumbering, bigger and more dominant than anything the future could ever conjure up. And, at any rate, she was sure of it, she understood it, knew how to reckon with it; she had learned to screen and manage and protect it as one does an afflicted member of one's family.

There had never been any danger of her being allowed to forget the past. It looked out at her from the face of every acquaintance, it appeared suddenly in the eyes of strangers when a word enlightened them: "Yes, *the* Mrs. Lidcote, don't you know?" It had sprung at her the first day out, when, across the dining room, from the captain's table, she had seen Mrs. Lorin Boulger's revolving eyeglass pause and the eye behind it grow as blank as a dropped blind. The next day, of course, the captain had asked: "You know your ambassadress, Mrs. Boulger?" and she had replied that, No, she seldom left Florence, and hadn't been to Rome for more than a day since the Boulgers had been sent to Italy. She was so used to these phrases that it cost her no effort to repeat them. And the captain had promptly changed the subject.

No, she didn't, as a rule, mind the past, because she was used to it and understood it. It was a great concrete fact in her path that she had to walk around every time she moved in any direction. But now, in the light of the unhappy event that had summoned her from Italy,— the sudden unanticipated news of her daughter's divorce from Horace Pursh and remarriage with Wilbour Barkley—the past, her own poor miserable past, started up at her with eyes of accusation, became, to her disordered fancy, like the afflicted relative suddenly breaking away from nurses and keepers and publicly parading the horror and misery she had, all the long years, so patiently screened and secluded.

Yes, there it had stood before her through the agitated weeks since the news had come—during her interminable journey from India, where Leila's letter had overtaken her, and the feverish halt in her apartment in Florence, where she had had to stop and gather up her possessions for a fresh start—there it had stood grinning at her with a new balefulness which seemed to say: "Oh, but you've got to look at me *now*, because I'm not only your own past but Leila's present."

Certainly it was a master stroke of those arch-ironists of the shears and spindle to duplicate her own story in her daughter's. Mrs. Lidcote had always somewhat grimly fancied that, having so signally failed to be of use to Leila in other ways, she would at least serve her as a warning. She had even abstained from defending herself, from making the best of her case, had stoically refused to plead extenuating circumstances, lest Leila's impulsive sympathy should lead to deductions that might react disastrously on her own life. And now that very thing had happened, and Mrs. Lidcote could hear the whole of New York saying with one voice: "Yes, Leila's done just what her mother did. With such an example what could you expect?"

Yet if she had been an example, poor woman, she had been an awful one; she had been, she would have supposed, of more use as a deterrent than a hundred blameless mothers as incentives. For how could anyone who had seen anything of her life in the last eighteen years have had the courage to repeat so disastrous an experiment?

Well, logic in such cases didn't count, example didn't count, nothing probably counted but having the same impulses in the blood; and that was the dark inheritance she had bestowed upon her daughter. Leila hadn't consciously copied her; she had simply "taken after" her, had been a projection of her own long-past rebellion.

Mrs. Lidcote had deplored, when she started, that the "Utopia" was a slow steamer, and would take eight full days to bring her to her unhappy daughter; but now, as the moment of reunion approached, she would willingly have turned the boat about and fled back to the high seas. It was not only because she felt still so unprepared to face what New York had in store for her, but because she needed more time to dispose of what the "Utopia" had already given her. The past was bad enough, but the present and future were worse, because they were less comprehensible, and because, as she grew older, surprises and inconsequences troubled her more than the worst certainties.

There was Mrs. Boulger, for instance. In the light, or rather the darkness, of new developments, it might really be that Mrs. Boulger had not meant to cut her, but had simply failed to recognize her. Mrs. Lidcote had arrived at this hypothesis simply by listening to the conversation of the persons sitting next to her on deck—two lively young women with the latest Paris hats on their heads and the latest New York ideas in them. These ladies, as to whom it would have been impossible for a person with Mrs. Lidcote's old-fashioned categories to determine whether they were married or unmarried, "nice" or "horrid," or any one or other of the definite things which young women, in her youth and her society, were conveniently assumed to be, had revealed a familiarity with the world of New York that, again according to Mrs. Lidcote's traditions, should have implied a recognized place in it. But in the present fluid state of manners what did anything imply except what their hats implied—that no one could tell what was coming next?

They seemed, at any rate, to frequent a group of idle and opulent people who executed the same gestures and revolved on the same pivots as Mrs. Lidcote's daughter and her friends: their Coras, Matties and Mabels seemed at any moment likely to reveal familiar patronymics, and once one of the speakers, summing up a discussion of which Mrs. Lidcote had missed the beginning, had affirmed with headlong confidence: "Leila? Oh, *Leila's* all right."

Could it be *her* Leila, the mother had wondered, with a sharp thrill of apprehension? If only they would mention surnames! But their talk leaped elliptically from allusion to allusion, their unfinished sentences dangled over bottomless pits of conjecture, and they gave their bewildered hearer the impression not so much of talking only of their intimates, as of being intimate with everyone alive.

Her old friend Franklin Ide could have told her, perhaps; but here was the last day of the voyage, and she hadn't yet found courage to ask him. Great as had been the joy of discovering his name on the passenger list and seeing his friendly bearded face in the throng against the taffrail at Cherbourg, she had as yet said nothing to him except, when they had met: "Of course I'm going out to Leila."

She had said nothing to Franklin Ide because she had always instinctively shrunk from taking him into her confidence. She was sure he felt sorry for her, sorrier perhaps than anyone had ever felt; but he had always paid her the supreme tribute of not showing it. His attitude allowed her to imagine that compassion was not the basis of his feeling for her, and it was part of her joy in his friendship that it was the one relation seemingly unconditioned by her state, the only one in which she could think and feel and behave like any other woman.

Now, however, as the problem of New York loomed nearer, she began to regret that she had not spoken, had not at least questioned him about the hints she had gathered on the way. He did not know the two ladies next to her, he did not even, as it chanced, know Mrs. Lorin Boulger; but he knew New York, and New York was the sphinx whose riddle she must read or perish.

Almost as the thought passed through her mind his stooping shoulders and grizzled head detached themselves against the blaze of light in the west, and he sauntered down the empty deck and dropped into the chair at her side.

"You're expecting the Barkleys to meet you, I suppose?" he asked.

It was the first time she had heard any one pronounce her daughter's new name, and it occurred to her that her friend, who was shy and inarticulate, had been trying to say it all the way over and had at last shot it out at her only because he felt it must be now or never.

"I don't know. I cabled, of course. But I believe she's at—they're at—*his* place somewhere."

"Oh, Barkley's; yes, near Lenox, isn't it? But she's sure to come to town to meet you."

He said it so easily and naturally that her own constraint was relieved, and suddenly, before she knew what she meant to do, she had burst out: "She may dislike the idea of seeing people."

Ide, whose absent shortsighted gaze had been fixed on the slowly gliding water, turned in his seat to stare at his companion.

"Who? Leila?" he said with an incredulous laugh.

Mrs. Lidcote flushed to her faded hair and grew pale again. "It took *me* a long time—to get used to it," she said.

His look grew gently commiserating. "I think you'll find"—he paused for a word—"that things are different now—altogether easier."

"That's what I've been wondering—ever since we started." She was determined now to speak. She moved nearer, so that their arms touched, and she could drop her voice to a murmur. "You see, it all came on me in a flash. My going off to India and Siam on that long trip kept me away from letters for weeks at a time; and she didn't want to tell me beforehand—oh, I understand *that,* poor child! You know how good she's always been to me; how she's tried to spare me. And she knew, of course, what a state of horror I'd be in. She knew I'd rush off to her at once and try to stop it. So she never gave me a hint of anything, and she even managed to muzzle Susy Suffern—you know Susy is the one of the family who keeps me informed about things at home. I don't yet see how she prevented Susy's telling me; but she did. And her first letter, the one I got up at Bangkok, simply said the thing was over—the divorce, I mean—and that the very next day she'd—well, I suppose there was no use waiting; and *he* seems to have behaved as well as possible, to have wanted to marry her as much as—"

"Who? Barkley?" he helped her out. "I should say so! Why what do you suppose—" He interrupted himself. "He'll be devoted to her, I assure you."

"Oh, of course; I'm sure he will. He's written me—really beautifully. But it's a terrible strain on a man's devotion. I'm not sure that Leila realizes—"

Ide sounded again his little reassuring laugh. "I'm not sure that you realize. *They're* all right."

It was the very phrase that the young lady in the next seat had applied to the unknown "Leila," and its recurrence on Ide's lips flushed Mrs. Lidcote with fresh courage.

"I wish I knew just what you mean. The two young women next to me—the ones with the wonderful hats—have been talking in the same way."

"What? About Leila?"

"About *a* Leila; I fancied it might be mine. And about society in general. All their friends seem to be divorced; some of them seem to announce their engagements before they get their decree. One of them—*her* name was Mabel—as far as I could make out, her husband found out that she meant to divorce him by noticing that she wore a new engagement ring."

"Well, you see Leila did everything 'regularly,' as the French say," Ide rejoined.

"Yes; but are these people in society? The people my neighbors talk about?"

He shrugged his shoulders. "It would take an arbitration commission a good many sittings to define the boundaries of society nowadays. But at any rate they're in New York; and I assure you you're *not*; you're farther and farther from it."

"But I've been back there several times to see Leila." She hesitated and looked away from him. Then she brought out slowly: "And I've never noticed—the least change—in—in my own case—"

"Oh," he sounded deprecatingly, and she trembled with the fear of having gone too far. But the hour was past when such scruples could restrain her. She must know where she was and where Leila was. "Mrs. Boulger still cuts me," she brought out with an embarrassed laugh.

"Are you sure? You've probably cut *her;* if not now, at least in the past. And in a cut if you're not first you're nowhere. That's what keeps up so many quarrels."

The word roused Mrs. Lidcote to a renewed sense of realities. "But the Purshes," she said—"the Purshes are so strong! There are so many of them, and they all back each other up, just as my husband's family did. I know what it means to have a clan against one. They're stronger than any number of separate friends. The Purshes will *never* forgive Leila for leaving Horace. Why, his mother opposed his marrying her because of—of me. She tried to get Leila to promise that she wouldn't see me when they went to Europe on their honeymoon. And now she'll say it was my example."

Her companion, vaguely stroking his beard, mused a moment upon this; then he asked, with seeming irrelevance, "What did Leila say when you wrote that you were coming?"

"She said it wasn't the least necessary, but that I'd better come, because it was the only way to convince me that it wasn't."

"Well, then, that proves she's not afraid of the Purshes."

She breathed a long sigh of remembrance. "Oh, just at first, you know—one never is."

He laid his hand on hers with a gesture of intelligence and pity. "You'll see, you'll see," he said.

A shadow lengthened down the deck before them, and a steward stood there, proffering a Marconigram.

"Oh, now I shall know!" she exclaimed.

She tore the message open, and then let it fall on her knees, dropping her hands on it in silence.

Ide's inquiry roused her: "It's all right?"

"Oh, quite right. Perfectly. She can't come; but she's sending Susy Suffern. She says Susy will explain." After another silence she added, with a sudden gush of bitterness: "As if I needed any explanation!"

She felt Ide's hesitating glance upon her. "She's in the country?"

"Yes. 'Prevented last moment. Longing for you, expecting you. Love from both.' Don't you *see*, the poor darling, that she couldn't face it?"

"No, I don't." He waited. "Do you mean to go to her immediately?"

"It will be too late to catch a train this evening; but I shall take the first tomorrow morning." She considered a moment. "Perhaps it's better. I need a talk with Susy first. She's to meet me at the dock, and I'll take her straight back to the hotel with me."

As she developed this plan, she had the sense that Ide was still thoughtfully, even gravely, considering her. When she ceased, he remained silent a moment; then he said almost ceremoniously: "If your talk with Miss Suffern doesn't last too late, may I come and see you when it's over? I shall be dining at my club, and I'll call you up at about ten, if I may. I'm off to Chicago on business tomorrow morning, and it would be a satisfaction to know, before I start, that your cousin's been able to reassure you, as I know she will."

He spoke with a shy deliberateness that, even to Mrs. Lidcote's troubled perceptions, sounded a long-silenced note of feeling. Perhaps the breaking down of the barrier of reticence between them had released unsuspected emotions in both. The tone of his appeal moved her curiously and loosened the tight strain of her fears.

"Oh, yes, come—do come," she said, rising. The huge threat of New York was imminent now, dwarfing, under long reaches of embattled masonry, the great deck she stood on and all the little specks of life it carried. One of them, drifting nearer, took the shape of her maid, followed by luggage-laden stewards, and signing to her that it was time to go below. As they descended to the main deck, the throng swept her against Mrs. Lorin Boulger's shoulder, and she heard the ambassadress call out to someone, over the vexed sea of hats: "So sorry! I should have been delighted, but I've promised to spend Sunday with some friends at Lenox."

II

Susy Suffern's explanation did not end till after ten o'clock, and she had just gone when Franklin Ide, who, complying with an old New York tradition, had caused himself to be preceded by a long white box of roses, was shown into Mrs. Lidcote's sitting room.

He came forward with his shy half-humorous smile and, taking her hand, looked at her for a moment without speaking.

"It's all right," he then pronounced.

Mrs. Lidcote returned his smile. "It's extraordinary. Everything's changed. Even Susy has changed; and you know the extent to which Susy used to represent the old New York. There's no old New York left, it seems. She talked in the most amazing way. She snaps her fingers at the Purshes. She told me—*me,* that every woman had a right to happiness and that self-expression was the highest duty. She accused me of misunderstanding Leila; she said my point of view was conventional! She was bursting with pride at having been in the secret, and wearing a brooch that Wilbour Barkley'd given her!"

Franklin Ide had seated himself in the armchair she had pushed forward for him under the electric chandelier. He threw back his head and laughed. "What did I tell you?"

"Yes; but I can't believe that Susy's not mistaken. Poor dear, she has the habit of lost causes; and she may feel that, having stuck to me, she can do no less than stick to Leila."

"But she didn't—did she—openly defy the world for you? She didn't snap her fingers at the Lidcotes?"

Mrs. Lidcote shook her head, still smiling. "No. It was enough to defy *my* family. It was doubtful at one time if they would tolerate her seeing me, and she almost had to disinfect herself after each visit. I believe that at first my sister-in-law wouldn't let the girls come down when Susy dined with her."

"Well, isn't your cousin's present attitude the best possible proof that times have changed?"

"Yes, yes; I know." She leaned forward from her sofa-corner, fixing her eyes on his thin kindly face, which gleamed on her indistinctly through her tears. "If it's true, it's—it's dazzling. She says Leila's perfectly happy. It's as if an angel had gone about lifting gravestones, and the buried people walked again, and the living didn't shrink from them."

"That's about it," he assented.

She drew a deep breath, and sat looking away from him down the long perspective of lamp-fringed streets over which her windows hung.

"I can understand how happy you must be," he began at length.

She turned to him impetuously. "Yes, yes; I'm happy. But I'm lonely, too—lonelier than ever. I didn't take up much room in the world before; but now—where is there a corner for me? Oh, since I've begun to confess myself, why shouldn't I go on? Telling you this lifts a gravestone from *me!* You see, before this, Leila needed me. She was unhappy, and I knew it, and though we hardly ever talked of it I felt that, in a way, the thought that I'd been through the same thing, and down to the dregs of it, helped her. And her needing me helped *me.* And when the news of her marriage came my first thought was that now she'd need me more than ever, that she'd have no one but me to turn to. Yes, under all my distress there was a fierce joy in that. It was so new and wonderful to feel again that there was one person who wouldn't be able to get on without me! And now what you and Susy tell me seems to have taken my child from me; and just at first that's all I can feel."

"Of course it's all you feel." He looked at her musingly. "Why didn't Leila come to meet you?"

"That was really my fault. You see, I'd cabled that I was not sure of being able to get off on the "Utopia," and apparently my second cable was delayed, and when she received it she'd already asked some people over Sunday—one or two of her old friends, Susy says. I'm so glad they should have wanted to go to her at once; but naturally I'd rather have been alone with her."

"You still mean to go, then?"

"Oh, I must. Susy wanted to drag me off to Ridgefield with her over Sunday, and Leila sent me word that of course I might go if I wanted to, and that I was not to think of her; but I know how disappointed she would be. Susy said she was afraid I might be upset at her having people to stay, and that, if I minded, she wouldn't urge me to come. But if *they* don't mind, why should I? And of course, if they're willing to go to Leila it must mean—"

"Of course. I'm glad you recognize that," Franklin Ide exclaimed abruptly. He stood up and went over to her, taking her hand with one of his quick gestures. "There's something I want to say to you," he began—

The next morning, in the train, through all the other contending thoughts in Mrs. Lidcote's mind there ran the warm undercurrent of what Franklin Ide had wanted to say to her.

He had wanted, she knew, to say it once before, when, nearly eight years earlier, the hazard of meeting at the end of a rainy autumn in a deserted Swiss hotel had thrown them for a fortnight into unwonted propinquity. They had walked and talked together, borrowed each other's books and newspapers, spent the long chill evenings over the fire in the dim lamplight of her little pitch-pine sitting room; and she had been wonderfully comforted by his presence, and hard frozen places in her had melted, and she had known that she would be desperately sorry when he went. And then, just at the end, in his odd indirect way, he had let her see that it rested with her to have him stay. She could still relive the sleepless night she had given to that discovery. It was preposterous, of course, to think of repaying his devotion by accepting such a sacrifice; but how find reasons to convince him? She could not bear to let him think her less touched, less inclined to him than she was: the generosity of his love deserved that she should repay it with the truth. Yet how let him see what she felt, and yet refuse what he offered? How confess to him what had been on her lips when he made the offer: "I've seen what it did to one man; and there must never, never be another"? The tacit ignoring of her past had been the element in which their friendship lived, and she could not suddenly, to him of all men, begin to talk of herself like a guilty woman in a play. Somehow, in the end, she had managed it, had averted a direct explanation, had made him understand that her life was over, that she existed only for her daughter, and that a more definite word from him would have been almost a breach of delicacy. She was so used to behaving as if her life were over! And, at any rate, he had taken her hint, and she had been able to spare her sensitiveness and his. The next year, when he came to Florence to see her, they met again in the old friendly way; and that till now had continued to be the tenor of their intimacy.

And now, suddenly and unexpectedly, he had brought up the question again, directly this time, and in such a form that she could not evade it: putting the renewal of his plea, after so long an interval, on the ground that, on her own showing, her chief argument against it no longer existed.

"You tell me Leila's happy. If she's happy, she doesn't need you—need you, that is, in the same way as before. You wanted, I know, to be always in reach, always free and available if she should suddenly call you to her or take refuge with you. I understood that—I respected it. I didn't urge my case because I saw it was useless. You couldn't, I understand well enough, have felt free to take such happiness as life with me might give you while she was unhappy, and, as you imagined, with no hope of release. Even then I didn't feel as you did about it; I understood better the trend of things here. But ten years ago the change hadn't really come; and I had no way of convincing you that it was coming. Still, I always fancied that Leila might not think her case was closed, and so I chose to think that ours wasn't either. Let me go on thinking so, at any rate, till you've seen her, and confirmed with your own eyes what Susy Suffern tells you."

III

All through what Susy Suffern told and retold her during their four-hours' flight to the hills this plea of Ide's kept coming back to Mrs. Lidcote. She did not yet know what she felt as to its bearing on her own fate, but it was something on which her confused thoughts could stay themselves amid the welter of new impressions, and she was inexpressibly glad that he had said what he had, and said it at that particular moment. It helped her to hold fast to her identity in the rush of strange names and new categories that her cousin's talk poured out on her.

With the progress of the journey Miss Suffern's communications grew more and more amazing. She was like a cicerone preparing the mind of an inexperienced traveler for the marvels about to burst on it.

"You won't know Leila. She's had her pearls reset. Sargent's to paint her. Oh, and I was to tell you that she hopes you won't mind being the least bit squeezed over Sunday. The house was built by Wilbour's father, you know, and it's rather old-fashioned—only ten spare bedrooms. Of course that's small for what they mean to do, and she'll show you the new plans they've had made. Their idea is to keep the present house as a wing. She told me to explain—she's so dreadfully sorry not to be able to give you a sitting room just at first. They're thinking of Egypt for next winter, unless, of course, Wilbour gets his appointment. Oh, didn't she write you about that? Why, he wants Rome, you know—the second secretaryship. Or, rather, he wanted England; but Leila insisted that if they went abroad she must be near you. And of course what she says is law. Oh, they quite hope they'll get it. You see Horace's uncle is in the Cabinet—one of the assistant secretaries—and I believe he has a good deal of pull—"

"Horace's uncle? You mean Wilbour's, I suppose," Mrs. Lidcote interjected, with a gasp of which a fraction was given to Miss Suffern's flippant use of the language.

"Wilbour's? No, I don't. I mean Horace's. There's no bad feeling between them, I assure you. Since Horace's engagement was announced—you didn't know Horace was engaged? Why, he's marrying one of Bishop Thorbury's girls: the red-haired one who wrote the novel that everyone's talking about. *This Flesh of Mine.* They're to be married in the cathedral. Of course Horace *can,* because it was Leila who—but, as I say, there's not the *least* feeling, and Horace wrote himself to his uncle about Wilbour."

Mrs. Lidcote's thoughts fled back to what she had said to Ide the day before on the deck of the "Utopia." "I didn't take up much room before, but now where is there a corner for me?" Where indeed in this crowded, topsy-turvy world, with its headlong changes and helter-skelter readjustments, its new tolerances and indifferences and accommodations, was there room for a character fashioned by slower sterner processes and a life broken under their inexorable pressure? And then, in a flash, she viewed the chaos from a new angle, and order seemed to move upon the void. If the old processes were changed, her case was changed with them; she, too, was a part of the general readjustment, a tiny fragment of the new pattern worked out in bolder freer harmonies. Since her daughter had no penalty to pay, was not she herself released by the same stroke? The rich arrears of youth and joy were gone; but was there not time enough left to accumulate new stores of happiness? That, of course, was what Franklin Ide had felt and had meant her to feel. He had seen at once what the change in her daughter's situation would make in her view of her own. It was almost—wondrously enough!—as if Leila's folly had been the means of vindicating hers.

Everything else for the moment faded for Mrs. Lidcote in the glow of her daughter's embrace. It was unnatural, it was almost terrifying, to find herself standing on a strange threshold, under an unknown roof, in a big hall full of pictures, flowers, firelight, and hurrying servants, and in this spacious unfamiliar confusion to discover Leila, bareheaded, laughing, authoritative, with a strange young man jovially echoing her welcome and transmitting her orders; but once Mrs. Lidcote had her child on her breast, and her child's "It's all right, you old darling!" in her ears, every other feeling was lost in the deep sense of well-being that only Leila's hug could give.

The sense was still with her, warming her veins and pleasantly fluttering her heart, as she went up to her room after luncheon. A little constrained by the presence of visitors, and not altogether sorry to defer for a few hours the "long talk" with her daughter for which she somehow felt herself tremulously unready, she had withdrawn, on the plea of fatigue, to the bright luxurious bedroom into which Leila had again and again apologized for having been obliged to squeeze her. The room was bigger and finer than any in her small apartment in Florence; but it was not the standard of affluence implied in her daughter's tone about it that chiefly struck her, nor yet the finish and complexity of its appointments. It was the look it shared with the rest of the house, and with the perspective of the gardens beneath its windows, of being part of an "establishment"—of something solid, avowed, founded on sacraments and precedents and principles. There was nothing about the place, or about Leila and Wilbour, that suggested either passion or peril: their relation seemed as comfortable as their furniture and as respectable as their balance at the bank.

This was, in the whole confusing experience, the thing that confused Mrs. Lidcote most, that gave her at once the deepest feeling of security for Leila and the strongest sense of apprehension for herself. Yes, there was something oppressive in the completeness and compactness of Leila's well-being. Ide had been right: her daughter did not need her. Leila, with her first embrace, had unconsciously attested the fact in the same phrase as Ide himself and as the two young women with the hats. "It's all right, you old darling!" she had said: and her mother sat alone, trying to fit herself into the new scheme of things which such a certainty betokened.

Her first distinct feeling was one of irrational resentment. If such a change was to come, why had it not come sooner? Here was she, a woman not yet old, who had paid with the best years of her life for the theft of the happiness that her daughter's contemporaries were taking as their due. There was no sense, no sequence, in it. She had had what she wanted, but she had had to pay too much for it. She had had to pay the last bitterest price of learning that love has a price: that it is worth so much and no more. She had known the anguish of watching the man she loved discover this first, and of reading the discovery in his eyes. It was a part of her history that she had not trusted herself to think of for a long time past: she always took a big turn about that haunted corner. But now, at the sight of the young man downstairs, so openly and jovially Leila's, she was overwhelmed at the senseless waste of her own adventure, and wrung with the irony of perceiving that the success or failure of the deepest human experiences may hang on a matter of chronology.

Then gradually the thought of Ide returned to her. "I chose to think that our case wasn't closed," he had said. She had been deeply touched by that. To everyone else her case had been closed so long! *Finis* was scrawled all over her. But here was one man who had believed and waited, and what if what he believed in and waited for were coming true? If Leila's "all right" should really foreshadow hers?

As yet, of course, it was impossible to tell. She had fancied, indeed, when she entered the drawing room before luncheon, that a too-sudden hush had fallen on the assembled group of Leila's friends, on the slender vociferous young women and the lounging golf-stockinged young men. They had all received her politely, with the kind of petrified politeness that may be either a tribute to age or a protest at laxity; but to them, of course, she must be an old woman because she was Leila's mother, and in a society so dominated by youth the mere presence of maturity was a constraint.

One of the young girls, however, had presently emerged from the group, and, attaching herself to Mrs. Lidcote, had listened to her with a blue gaze of admiration which gave the older woman a sudden happy consciousness of her long-forgotten social graces. It was agreeable to find herself attracting this young Charlotte Wynn, whose mother had been among her closest friends, and in whom something of the soberness and softness of the earlier manners had survived. But the little colloquy, broken up by the announcement of luncheon, could of course result in nothing more definite than this reminiscent emotion.

No, she could not yet tell how her own case was to be fitted into the new order of things; but there were more people—"older people" Leila had put it—arriving by the afternoon train, and that evening at dinner she would doubtless be able to judge. She began to wonder nervously who the newcomers might be. Probably she would be spared the embarrassment of finding old acquaintances among them; but it was odd that her daughter had mentioned no names.

Leila had proposed that, later in the afternoon, Wilbour should take her mother for a drive: she said she wanted them to have a "nice, quiet talk." But Mrs. Lidcote wished her talk with Leila to come first, and had, moreover, at luncheon, caught stray allusions to an impending tennis match in which her son-in-law was engaged. Her fatigue had been a sufficient pretext for declining the drive, and she had begged Leila to think of her as peacefully resting in her room till such time as they could snatch their quiet moment.

"Before tea, then, you duck!" Leila with a last kiss had decided; and presently Mrs. Lidcote, through her open window, had heard the fresh loud voices of her daughter's visitors chiming across the gardens from the tennis court.

IV

Leila had come and gone, and they had had their talk. It had not lasted as long as Mrs. Lidcote wished, for in the middle of it Leila had been summoned to the telephone to receive an important message from town, and had sent word to her mother that she couldn't come back just then, as one of the young ladies had been called away unexpectedly and arrangements had to be made for her departure. But the mother and daughter had had almost an hour together, and Mrs. Lidcote was happy. She had never seen Leila so tender, so solicitous. The only thing that troubled her was the very excess of this solicitude, the exaggerated expression of her daughter's annoyance that their first moments together should have been marred by the presence of strangers.

"Not strangers to me, darling, since they're friends of yours," her mother had assured her.

"Yes; but I know your feeling, you queer wild mother. I know how you've always hated people." (*Hated people!* Had Leila forgotten why?) "And that's why I told Susy that if you preferred to go with her to Ridgefield on Sunday I should perfectly understand, and patiently wait for our good hug. But you didn't really mind them at luncheon, did you, dearest?"

Mrs. Lidcote, at that, had suddenly thrown a startled look at her daughter. "I don't mind things of that kind any longer," she had simply answered.

"But that doesn't console me for having exposed you to the bother of it, for having let you come here when I ought to have *ordered* you off to Ridgefield with Susy. If Susy hadn't been stupid she'd have made you go there with her. I hate to think of you up here all alone."

Again Mrs. Lidcote tried to read something more than a rather obtuse devotion in her daughter's radiant gaze. "I'm glad to have had a rest this afternoon, dear; and later—"

"Oh, yes, later, when all this fuss is over, we'll more than make up for it, shan't we, you precious darling?" And at this point Leila had been summoned to the telephone, leaving Mrs. Lidcote to her conjectures.

These were still floating before her in cloudy uncertainty when Miss Suffern tapped at the door.

"You've come to take me down to tea? I'd forgotten how late it was," Mrs. Lidcote exclaimed.

Miss Suffern, a plump peering little woman, with prim hair and a conciliatory smile, nervously adjusted the pendent bugles of her elaborate black dress. Miss Suffern was always in mourning, and always commemorating the demise of distant relatives by wearing the discarded wardrobe of their next of kin. "It isn't *exactly* mourning," she would say; "but it's the only stitch of black poor Julia had—and of course George was only my mother's step-cousin."

As she came forward Mrs. Lidcote found herself humorously wondering whether she were mourning Horace Pursh's divorce in one of his mother's old black satins.

"Oh, *did* you mean to go down for tea?" Susy Suffern peered at her, a little fluttered. "Leila sent me up to keep you company. She thought it would be cozier for you to stay here. She was afraid you were feeling rather tired."

(67)

"I was; but I've had the whole afternoon to rest in. And this wonderful sofa to help me."

"Leila told me to tell you that she'd rush up for a minute before dinner, after everybody had arrived; but the train is always dreadfully late. She's in despair at not giving you a sitting room; she wanted to know if I thought you really minded."

"Of course I don't mind. It's not like Leila to think I should." Mrs. Lidcote drew aside to make way for the housemaid, who appeared in the doorway bearing a table spread with a bewildering variety of tea cakes.

"Leila saw to it herself," Miss Suffern murmured as the door closed. "Her one idea is that you should feel happy here."

It struck Mrs. Lidcote as one more mark of the subverted state of things that her daughter's solicitude should find expression in the multiplicity of sandwiches and the piping hotness of muffins; but then everything that had happened since her arrival seemed to increase her confusion.

The note of a motor horn down the drive gave another turn to her thoughts. "Are those the new arrivals already?" she asked.

"Oh, dear, no; they won't be here till after seven." Miss Suffern craned her head from the window to catch a glimpse of the motor. "It must be Charlotte leaving."

"Was it the little Wynn girl who was called away in a hurry? I hope it's not on account of illness."

"Oh, no; I believe there was some mistake about dates. Her mother telephoned her that she was expected at the Stepleys, at Fishkill, and she had to be rushed over to Albany to catch a train."

Mrs. Lidcote meditated. "I'm sorry. She's a charming young thing. I hoped I should have another talk with her this evening after dinner."

"Yes; it's too bad." Miss Suffern's gaze grew vague. "You *do* look tired, you know," she continued, seating herself at the tea table and preparing to dispense its delicacies. "You must go straight back to your sofa and let me wait on you. The excitement has told on you more than you think, and you mustn't fight against it any longer. Just stay quietly up here and let yourself go. You'll have Leila to yourself on Monday."

Mrs. Lidcote received the teacup which her cousin proffered, but showed no other disposition to obey her injunctions. For a moment she stirred her tea in silence; then she asked: "Is it your idea that I should stay quietly up here till Monday?"

Miss Suffern set down her cup with a gesture so sudden that it endangered an adjacent plate of scones. When she had assured herself of the safety of the scones she looked up with a fluttered laugh. "Perhaps, dear, by tomorrow you'll be feeling differently. The air here, you know—"

"Yes, I know." Mrs. Lidcote bent forward to help herself to a scone. "Who's arriving this evening?" she asked.

Miss Suffern frowned and peered. "You know my wretched head for names. Leila told me—but there are so many—"

"So many? She didn't tell me she expected a big party."

"Oh, not big: but rather outside of her little group. And of course, as it's the first time, she's a little excited at having the older set."

"The older set? Our contemporaries, you mean?"

"Why—yes." Miss Suffern paused as if to gather herself up for a leap. "The Ashton Gileses," she brought out.

"The Ashton Gileses? Really? I shall be glad to see Mary Giles again. It must be eighteen years," said Mrs. Lidcote steadily.

"Yes," Miss Suffern gasped, precipitately refilling her cup.

"The Ashton Gileses; and who else?"

"Well, the Sam Fresbies. But the most important person, of course, is Mrs. Lorin Boulger."

"Mrs. Boulger? Leila didn't tell me she was coming."

"Didn't she? I suppose she forgot everything when she saw you. But the party was got up for Mrs. Boulger. You see, it's very important that she should—well, take a fancy to Leila and Wilbour; his being appointed to Rome virtually depends on it. And you know Leila insists on Rome in order to be near you. So she asked Mary Giles, who's intimate with the Boulgers, if the visit couldn't possibly be arranged; and Mary's cable caught Mrs. Boulger at Cherbourg. She's to be only a fortnight in America; and getting her to come directly here was rather a triumph."

"Yes; I see it was," said Mrs. Lidcote.

"You know, she's rather—rather fussy; and Mary was a little doubtful if—"

"If she would, on account of Leila?" Mrs. Lidcote murmured.

"Well, yes. In her official position. But luckily she's a friend of the

Barkleys. And finding the Gileses and Fresbies here will make it all right. The times have changed!" Susy Suffern indulgently summed up.

Mrs. Lidcote smiled. "Yes; a few years ago it would have seemed improbable that I should ever again be dining with Mary Giles and Harriet Fresbie and Mrs. Lorin Boulger."

Miss Suffern did not at the moment seem disposed to enlarge upon this theme; and after an interval of silence Mrs. Lidcote suddenly resumed: "Do they know I'm here, by the way?"

The effect of her question was to produce in Miss Suffern an exaggerated access of peering and frowning. She twitched the tea things about, fingered her bugles, and, looking at the clock, exclaimed amazedly: "Mercy! Is it seven already?"

"Not that it can make any difference, I suppose," Mrs. Lidcote continued. "But did Leila tell them I was coming?"

Miss Suffern looked at her with pain. "Why, you don't suppose, dearest, that Leila would do anything—"

Mrs. Lidcote went on: "For, of course, it's of the first importance, as you say, that Mrs. Lorin Boulger should be favorably impressed, in order that Wilbour may have the best possible chance of getting Rome."

"I *told* Leila you'd feel that, dear. You see, it's actually on *your* account—so that they may get a post near you—that Leila invited Mrs. Boulger."

"Yes, I see that." Mrs. Lidcote, abruptly rising from her seat, turned her eyes to the clock. "But, as you say, it's getting late. Oughtn't we to dress for dinner?"

Miss Suffern, at the suggestion, stood up also, an agitated hand among her bugles. "I do wish I could persuade you to stay up here this evening. I'm sure Leila'd be happier if you would. Really, you're much too tired to come down."

"What nonsense, Susy!" Mrs. Lidcote spoke with a sudden sharpness, her hand stretched to the bell. "When do we dine? At half-past eight? Then I must really send you packing. At my age it takes time to dress."

Miss Suffern, thus projected toward the threshold, lingered there to repeat: "Leila'll never forgive herself if you make an effort you're not up to." But Mrs. Lidcote smiled on her without answering, and the icy light-wave propelled her through the door.

V

Mrs. Lidcote, though she had made the gesture of ringing for her maid, had not done so.

When the door closed, she continued to stand motionless in the middle of her soft spacious room. The fire which had been kindled at twilight danced on the brightness of silver and mirrors and sober gilding; and the sofa toward which she had been urged by Miss Suffern heaped up its cushions in inviting proximity to a table laden with new books and papers. She could not recall having ever been more luxuriously housed, or having ever had so strange a sense of being out alone, under the night, in a wind-beaten plain. She sat down by the fire and thought.

A knock on the door made her lift her head, and she saw her daughter on the threshold. The intricate ordering of Leila's fair hair and the flying folds of her dressing gown showed that she had interrupted her dressing to hasten to her mother; but once in the room she paused a moment, smiling uncertainly, as though she had forgotten the object of her haste.

Mrs. Lidcote rose to her feet. "Time to dress, dearest? Don't scold! I shan't be late.

"To dress?" Leila stood before her with a puzzled look. "Why, I thought, dear—I mean, I hoped you'd decided just to stay here quietly and rest."

Her mother smiled. "But I've been resting all the afternoon!"

"Yes, but—you know you *do* look tired. And when Susy told me just now that you meant to make the effort—"

"You came to stop me?"

"I came to tell you that you needn't feel in the least obliged—"

"Of course. I understand that."

There was a pause during which Leila, vaguely averting herself from her mother's scrutiny, drifted toward the dressing table and began to disturb the symmetry of the brushes and bottles laid out on it. "Do your visitors know that I'm here?" Mrs. Lidcote suddenly went on.

"Do they—of course—why, naturally," Leila rejoined, absorbed in trying to turn the stopper of a salts bottle.

"Then won't they think it odd if I don't appear?"

"Oh, not in the least, dearest. I assure you they'll *all* understand." Leila laid down the bottle and turned back to her mother, her face alight with reassurance.

Mrs. Lidcote stood motionless, her head erect, her smiling eyes on her daughter's. "Will they think it odd if I *do?*"

Leila stopped short, her lips half parted to reply. As she paused, the color stole over her bare neck, swept up to her throat, and burst into flame in her cheeks. Thence it sent its devastating crimson up to her very temples, to the lobes of her ears, to the edges of her eyelids, beating all over her in fiery waves, as if fanned by some imperceptible wind.

Mrs. Lidcote silently watched the conflagration; then she turned away her eyes with a slight laugh. "I only meant that I was afraid it might upset the arrangement of your dinner table if I didn't come down. If you can assure me that it won't, I believe I'll take you at your word and go back to this irresistible sofa." She paused, as if waiting for her daughter to speak; then she held out her arms. "Run off and dress, dearest; and don't have me on your mind." She clasped Leila close, pressing a long kiss on the last afterglow of her subsiding blush. "I do feel the least bit overdone, and if it won't inconvenience you to have me drop out of things, I believe I'll basely take to my bed and stay there till your party scatters. And now run off, or you'll be late; and make my excuses to them all."

VI

The Barkleys' visitors had dispersed, and Mrs. Lidcote, completely restored by her two days' rest, found herself, on the following Monday, alone with her children and Miss Suffern.

There was a note of jubilation in the air, for the party had "gone off" so extraordinarily well, and so completely, as it appeared, to the satisfaction of Mrs. Lorin Boulger, that Wilbour's early appointment to Rome was almost to be counted on. So certain did this seem that the prospect of a prompt reunion mitigated the distress with which Leila learned of her mother's decision to return almost immediately to Italy. No one understood this decision; it seemed to Leila absolutely unintelligible that Mrs. Lidcote should not stay on with them till their own fate was fixed, and Wilbour echoed her astonishment.

"Why shouldn't you, as Leila says, wait here till we can all pack up and go together?"

Mrs. Lidcote smiled her gratitude with her refusal. "After all, it's not yet sure that you'll be packing up."

"Oh, you ought to have seen Wilbour with Mrs. Boulger," Leila triumphed.

"No, you ought to have seen Leila with her," Leila's husband exulted.

Miss Suffern enthusiastically appended: "I *do* think inviting Harriet Fresbie was a stroke of genius!"

"Oh, we'll be with you soon," Leila laughed. "So soon that it's really foolish to separate."

But Mrs. Lidcote held out with the quiet firmness which her daughter knew it was useless to oppose. After her long months in India, it was really imperative, she declared, that she should get back to Florence and see what was happening to her little place there; and she had been so comfortable on the "Utopia" that she had a fancy to return by the same ship. There was nothing for it, therefore, but to acquiesce in her decision and keep her with them till the afternoon before the day of the "Utopia's" sailing. This arrangement fitted in with certain projects which, during her two days' seclusion, Mrs. Lidcote had silently matured. It had become to her of the first importance to get away as soon as she could, and the little place in Florence, which held her past in every fold of its curtains and between every page of its books, seemed now to her the one spot where that past would be endurable to look upon.

She was not unhappy during the intervening days. The sight of Leila's well-being, the sense of Leila's tenderness, were, after all, what she had come for; and of these she had had full measure. Leila had never been happier or more tender; and the contemplation of her bliss, and the enjoyment of her affection, were an absorbing occupation for her mother. But they were also a sharp strain on certain overtightened chords, and Mrs. Lidcote, when at last she found herself alone in the New York hotel to which she had returned the night before embarking, had the feeling that she had just escaped with her life from the clutch of a giant hand.

She had refused to let her daughter come to town with her; she had even rejected Susy Suffern's company. She wanted no viaticum but that of her own thoughts; and she let these come to her without shrinking from them as she sat in the same high-hung sitting room in which, just a week before, she and Franklin Ide had had their memorable talk.

She had promised her friend to let him hear from her, but she had not kept her promise. She knew that he had probably come back from Chicago, and that if he learned of her sudden decision to return to Italy it would be impossible for her not to see him before sailing; and as she wished above all things not to see him she had kept silent, intending to send him a letter from the steamer.

There was no reason why she should wait till then to write it. The actual moment was more favorable, and the task, though not agreeable, would at least bridge over an hour of her lonely evening. She went up to the writing table, drew out a sheet of paper and began to write his name. And as she did so, the door opened and he came in.

The words she met him with were the last she could have imagined herself saying when they had parted. "How in the world did you know that I was here?"

He caught her meaning in a flash. "You didn't want me to, then?" He stood looking at her. "I suppose I ought to have taken your silence as meaning that. But I happened to meet Mrs. Wynn, who is stopping here, and she asked me to dine with her and Charlotte, and Charlotte's young man. They told me they'd seen you arriving this afternoon, and I couldn't help coming up."

There was a pause between them, which Mrs. Lidcote at last surprisingly broke with the exclamation: "Ah, she *did* recognize me, then!"

"Recognize you?" He stared. "Why—"

"Oh, I saw she did, though she never moved an eyelid. I saw it by Charlotte's blush. The child has the prettiest blush. I saw that her mother wouldn't let her speak to me."

Ide put down his hat with an impatient laugh. "Hasn't Leila cured you of your delusions?"

She looked at him intently. "Then you don't think Margaret Wynn meant to cut me?"

"I think your ideas are absurd."

She paused for a perceptible moment without taking this up; then she said, at a tangent: "I'm sailing tomorrow early. I meant to write to you—there's the letter I'd begun."

Ide followed her gesture, and then turned his eyes back to her face. "You didn't mean to see me, then, or even to let me know that you were going till you'd left?"

"I felt it would be easier to explain to you in a letter—"

"What in God's name is there to explain?" She made no reply, and he pressed on: "It can't be that you're worried about Leila, for Charlotte Wynn told me she'd been there last week, and there was a big party arriving when she left: Fresbies and Gileses, and Mrs. Lorin Boulger—all the board of examiners! If Leila has passed *that,* she's got her degree."

Mrs. Lidcote had dropped down into a corner of the sofa where she had sat during their talk of the week before. "I was stupid," she began abruptly. "I ought to have gone to Ridgefield with Susy. I didn't see till afterward that I was expected to."

"You were expected to?"

"Yes. Oh, it wasn't Leila's fault. She suffered—poor darling; she was distracted. But she'd asked her party before she knew I was arriving."

"Oh, as to that—" Ide drew a deep breath of relief. "I can understand that it must have been a disappointment not to have you to herself just at first. But, after all, you were among old friends or their children: the Gileses and Fresbies—and little Charlotte Wynn." He paused a moment before the last name, and scrutinized her hesitatingly. "Even if they came at the wrong time, you must have been glad to see them all at Leila's."

She gave him back his look with a faint smile. "I didn't see them."

"You didn't see them?"

"No. That is, excepting little Charlotte Wynn. That child is exquisite. We had a talk before luncheon the day I arrived. But when her mother found out that I was staying in the house she telephoned her to leave immediately, and so I didn't see her again."

The color rushed to Ide's sallow face. "I don't know where you get such ideas!"

She pursued, as if she had not heard him: "Oh, and I saw Mary Giles for a minute too. Susy Suffern brought her up to my room the last evening, after dinner, when all the others were at bridge. She meant it kindly—but it wasn't much use."

"But what were you doing in your room in the evening after dinner?"

"Why, you see, when I found out my mistake in coming,—how embarrassing it was for Leila, I mean—I simply told her I was very tired, and preferred to stay upstairs till the party was over."

Ide, with a groan, struck his hand against the arm of his chair. "I wonder how much of all this you simply imagined!"

"I didn't imagine the fact of Harriet Fresbie's not even asking if she might see me when she knew I was in the house. Nor of Mary Giles's getting Susy, at the eleventh hour, to smuggle her up to my room when the others wouldn't know where she'd gone; nor poor Leila's ghastly fear lest Mrs. Lorin Boulger, for whom the party was given, should guess I was in the house, and prevent her husband's giving Wilbour the second secretaryship because she'd been obliged to spend a night under the same roof with his mother-in-law!"

Ide continued to drum on his chair arm with exasperated fingers. "You don't *know* that any of the acts you describe are due to the causes you suppose."

Mrs. Lidcote paused before replying, as if honestly trying to measure the weight of this argument. Then she said in a low tone: "I know that Leila was in an agony lest I should come down to dinner the first night. And it was for me she was afraid, not for herself. Leila is never afraid for herself."

"But the conclusions you draw are simply preposterous. There are narrow-minded women everywhere, but the women who were at Leila's knew perfectly well that their going there would give her a sort of social sanction, and if they were willing that she should have it, why on earth should they want to withhold it from you?"

"That's what I told myself a week ago, in this very room, after my first talk with Susy Suffern." She lifted a misty smile to his anxious eyes. "That's why I listened to what you said to me the same evening, and why your arguments half-convinced me, and made me think that what had been possible for Leila might not be impossible for me. If the new dispensation had come, why not for me as well as for the others? I can't tell you the flight my imagination took!"

Franklin Ide rose from his seat and crossed the room to a chair near her sofa-corner. "All I cared about was that it seemed—for the moment —to be carrying you toward me," he said.

"I cared about that, too. That's why I meant to go away without seeing you." They gave each other grave look for look. "Because, you see, I was mistaken," she went on. "We were both mistaken. You say it's preposterous that the women who didn't object to accepting Leila's hospitality should have objected to meeting me under her roof. And so it is; but I begin to understand why. It's simply that society is much too busy to revise its own judgments. Probably no one in the house with me stopped to consider that my case and Leila's were identical. They only remembered that I'd done something which, at the time I did it, was condemned by society. My case had been passed on and classified: I'm the woman who has been cut for nearly twenty years. The older people have half-forgotten why, and the younger ones have never really known: it's simply become a tradition to cut me. And traditions that have lost their meaning are the hardest of all to destroy."

Ide sat motionless while she spoke. As she ended, he stood up with a short laugh and walked across the room to the window. Outside, the immense black prospect of New York, strung with its myriad lines of light, stretched away into the smoky edges of the night. He showed it to her with a gesture.

"What do you suppose such words as you've been using—'society,' 'tradition,' and the rest—mean to all the life out there?"

She came and stood by him in the window. "Less than nothing, of course. But you and I are not out there. We're shut up in a little tight round of habit and association, just as we're shut up in this room. Remember, I thought I'd got out of it once; but what really happened was that the other people went out, and left me in the same little room. The only difference was that I was there alone. Oh, I've made it habitable now, I'm used to it; but I've lost any illusions I may have had as to an angel's opening the door."

Ide again laughed impatiently. "Well, if the door won't open, why not let another prisoner in? At least it would be less of a solitude—"

She turned from the dark window back into the vividly lighted room.

"It would be more of a prison. You forget that I know all about that. We're all imprisoned, of course—all of us middling people, who don't

carry our freedom in our brains. But we've accommodated ourselves
to our different cells, and if we're moved suddenly into the new ones
we're likely to find a stone wall where we thought there was thin air,
and to knock ourselves senseless against it. I saw a man do that once."

Ide, leaning with folded arms against the window frame, watched
her in silence as she moved restlessly about the room, gathering together some scattered books and tossing a handful of torn letters into
the paper basket. When she ceased, he rejoined: "All you say is based
on preconceived theories. Why didn't you put them to the test by
coming down to meet your old friends? Don't you see the inference
they would naturally draw from your hiding yourself when they
arrived? It looked as though you were afraid of them—or as though
you hadn't forgiven them. Either way, you put them in the wrong
instead of waiting to let them put you in the right. If Leila had
buried herself in a desert do you suppose society would have gone to
fetch her out? You say you were afraid for Leila and that she was
afraid for you. Don't you see what all these complications of feeling
mean? Simply that you were too nervous at the moment to let things
happen naturally, just as you're too nervous now to judge them ra-
tionally." He paused and turned his eyes to her face. "Don't try to
just yet. Give yourself a little more time. Give *me* a little more time.
I've always known it would take time."

He moved nearer, and she let him have her hand. With the grave
kindness of his face so close above her she felt like a child roused
out of frightened dreams and finding a light in the room.

"Perhaps you're right—" she heard herself begin; then something
within her clutched her back, and her hand fell away from him.

"I know I'm right: trust me," he urged. "We'll talk of this in
Florence soon."

She stood before him, feeling with despair his kindness, his patience and his unreality. Everything he said seemed like a painted
gauze let down between herself and the real facts of life; and a sudden
desire seized her to tear the gauze into shreds.

She drew back and looked at him with a smile of superficial reassurance. "You *are* right—about not talking any longer now. I'm
nervous and tired, and it would do no good. I brood over things too
much. As you say, I must try not to shrink from people." She turned
away and glanced at the clock. "Why, it's only ten! If I send you off

I shall begin to brood again; and if you stay we shall go on talking
about the same thing. Why shouldn't we go down and see Margaret
Wynn for half an hour?"

She spoke lightly and rapidly, her brilliant eyes on his face. As she
watched him, she saw it change, as if her smile had thrown a too
vivid light upon it.

"Oh, no—not tonight!" he exclaimed.

"Not tonight? Why, what other night have I, when I'm off at dawn?
Besides, I want to show you at once that I mean to be more sensible—
that I'm not going to be afraid of people any more. And I should
really like another glimpse of little Charlotte." He stood before her,
his hand in his beard, with the gesture he had in moments of perplexity. "Come!" she ordered him gaily, turning to the door.

He followed her and laid his hand on her arm. "Don't you think—
hadn't you better let me go first and see? They told me they'd had a
tiring day at the dressmaker's. I dare say they have gone to bed."

"But you said they'd a young man of Charlotte's dining with them.
Surely he wouldn't have left by ten? At any rate, I'll go down with
you and see. It takes so long if one sends a servant first." She put
him gently aside, and then paused as a new thought struck her. "Or
wait; my maid's in the next room. I'll tell her to go and ask if
Margaret will receive me. Yes, that's much the best way."

She turned back and went toward the door that led to her bedroom;
but before she could open it she felt Ide's quick touch again.

"I believe—I remember now—Charlotte's young man was suggesting that they should all go out—to a music hall or something of the
sort. I'm sure—I'm positively sure that you won't find them."

Her hand dropped from the door, his dropped from her arm, and
as they drew back and faced each other she saw the blood rise slowly
through his sallow skin, redden his neck and ears, encroach upon
the edges of his beard, and settle in dull patches under his kind
troubled eyes. She had seen the same blush on another face, and the
same impulse of compassion she had then felt made her turn her
gaze away again.

A knock on the door broke the silence, and a porter put his head
into the room.

"It's only just to know how many pieces there'll be to go down to
the steamer in the morning."

With the words she felt that the veil of painted gauze was torn in tatters, and that she was moving again among the grim edges of reality.

"Oh, dear," she exclaimed, "I never *can* remember! Wait a minute; I shall have to ask my maid."

She opened her bedroom door and called out: "Annette!"

Hilary Maltby and Stephen Braxton

☀ MAX BEERBOHM ☀

MAX BEERBOHM (1872–1956), novelist, essayist, dramatic reviewer and caricaturist, was a half-brother of the actor Sir Herbert Beerbohm-Tree and one of the brilliant young men of London's mauve decade. He survived into our own times to become, in his retreat in Rapallo, a legend of wit and satiric genius. *Hilary Maltby and Stephen Braxton* was published in *Seven Men* in 1919. For those less familiar with Edwardian politics it may be pointed out that Mr. Balfour, whom the unhappy Maltby is tricked into pointing to as the cause of his bicycle disaster, was the Prime Minister.

1917

PEOPLE still go on comparing Thackeray and Dickens, quite cheerfully. But the fashion of comparing Maltby and Braxton went out so long ago as 1795. No, I am wrong. But anything that happened in the bland old days before the War does seem to be a hundred more years ago than actually it is. The year I mean is the one in whose spring-time we all went bicycling (O thrill!) in Battersea Park, and ladies wore sleeves that billowed enormously out from their shoulders, and Lord Rosebery was Prime Minister.

In that Park, in that spring-time, in that sea of sleeves, there was almost as much talk about the respective merits of Braxton and Maltby as there was about those of Rudge and Humber. For the benefit of my younger readers, and perhaps, so feeble is human memory, for the benefit of their elders too, let me state that Rudge and Humber were rival makers of bicycles, that Hilary Maltby was the author of 'Ariel in Mayfair,' and Stephen Braxton of 'A Faun on the Cotswolds.'

'Which do you think is *really* the best—"Ariel" or "A Faun"?' Ladies were always asking one that question. 'Oh, well, you know, the two are so different. It's really very hard to compare them.' One was always giving that answer. One was not very brilliant perhaps.

The vogue of the two novels lasted throughout the summer. As both were 'firstlings,' and Great Britain had therefore nothing else of Braxton's or Maltby's to fall back on, the horizon was much scanned for what Maltby, and what Braxton, would give us next. In the autumn Braxton gave us his secondling. It was an instantaneous failure. No more was Braxton compared with Maltby. In the spring of '96 came Maltby's secondling. Its failure was instantaneous. Maltby might once more have been compared with Braxton. But Braxton was now forgotten. So was Maltby.

This was not kind. This was not just. Maltby's first novel, and Braxton's, had brought delight into many thousands of homes. People should have paused to say of Braxton 'Perhaps his third novel will be better than his second,' and to say as much for Maltby. I blame people for having given no sign of wanting a third from either; and I blame them with the more zest because neither 'A Faun on the Cotswolds' nor 'Ariel in Mayfair' was a merely popular book each, I maintain, was a good book. I don't go so far as to say that the one had 'more of natural magic, more of British woodland glamour, more of the sheer joy of life in it than anything since "As You Like It," ' though Higsby went so far as this in the *Daily Chronicle*; nor can I allow the claim made for the other by Grigsby in the *Globe* that 'for pungency of satire there has been nothing like it since Swift laid down his pen, and for sheer sweetness and tenderness of feeling—*ex forti dulcedo*—nothing to be mentioned in the same breath with it since the lute fell from the tired hand of Theocritus.' These were foolish exaggerations. But one must not condemn a thing because it has been over-praised. Maltby's 'Ariel' was a delicate, brilliant work; and Braxton's 'Faun,' crude through it was in many ways, had yet a genuine power and beauty. This is not a mere impression remembered from early youth. It is the reasoned and seasoned judgment of middle age. Both books have been out of print for many years; but I secured a second-hand copy of each not long ago, and found them well worth reading again.

From the time of Nathaniel Hawthorne to the outbreak of the War, current literature did not suffer from any lack of fauns. But when Braxton's first book appeared fauns had still an air of novelty about them. We had not yet tired of them and their hoofs and their slanting eyes and their way of coming suddenly out of woods to wean quiet English villages from respectability. We did tire later. But Braxton's faun, even now, seems to me an admirable specimen of his class—wild and weird, earthly, goat-like, almost convincing. And I find myself convinced altogether by Braxton's rustics. I admit that I do not know much about rustics, except from novels. But I plead that the little I do know about them by personal observation does not confirm much of what the many novelists have taught me. I plead also that Braxton may well have been right about the rustics of Gloucestershire because he was (as so many interviewers recorded of him in his brief heyday) the son of a yeoman farmer at Far Oakridge, and his boyhood had been divided between that village and the Grammar School at Stroud. Not long ago I happened to be staying in the neighbourhood, and came across several villagers who might, I assure you, have stepped straight out of Braxton's pages. For that matter, Braxton himself, whom I met often in the spring of '95, might have stepped straight out of his own pages.

I am guilty of having wished he would step straight back into them. He was a very surly fellow, very rugged and gruff. He was the antithesis of pleasant little Maltby. I used to think that perhaps he would have been less unamiable if success had come to him earlier. He was thirty years old when his book was published, and had had a very hard time since coming to London at the age of sixteen. Little Maltby was a year older, and so had waited a year longer; but then, he had waited under a comfortable roof at Twickenham, emerging into the metropolis for no grimmer purpose than to sit and watch the fashionable riders and walkers in Rotten Row, and then going home to write a little, or to play lawn-tennis with the young ladies of Twickenham. He had been the only child of his parents (neither of whom, alas, survived to take pleasure in their darling's sudden fame). He had now migrated from Twickenham and taken rooms in Ryder Street. Had he ever shared with Braxton the bread of adversity—but no, I think he would in any case have been pleasant. And conversely I cannot imagine that Braxton would in any case have been so.

No one seeing the two rivals together, no one meeting them at Mr. Hookworth's famous luncheon parties in the Authors' Club, or at Mrs.

Foster-Dugdale's not less famous garden parties in Greville Place, would have supposed off-hand that the pair had a single point in common. Dapper little Maltby—blond, bland, diminutive Maltby, with his monocle and his gardenia; big black Braxton, with his lanky hair and his square blue jaw and his square sallow forehead. Canary and crow. Maltby had a perpetual chirrup of amusing small-talk. Braxton was usually silent, but very well worth listening to whenever he did croak. He had distinction, I admit it; the distinction of one who steadfastly refuses to adapt himself to surroundings. He stood out. He awed Mr. Hookworth. Ladies were always asking one another, rather intently, what they thought of him. One could imagine that Mr. Foster-Dugdale, had he come home from the City to attend the garden parties, might have regarded him as one from whom Mrs. Foster-Dugdale should be shielded. But the casual observer of Braxton and Maltby at Mrs. Foster-Dugdale's or elsewhere was wrong in supposing that the two were totally unlike. He overlooked one simple and obvious point. This was that he had met them both at Mrs. Foster-Dugdale's or elsewhere. Wherever they were invited, there certainly, there punctually, they would be. They were both of them gluttons for the fruits and signs of their success.

Interviewers and photographers had as little reason as had hostesses to complain of two men so earnestly and assiduously 'on the make' as Maltby and Braxton. Maltby, for all his sparkle, was earnest; Braxton, for all his arrogance, assiduous.

'A Faun on the Cotswolds' had no more eager eulogist than the author of 'Ariel in Mayfair.' When any one praised his work, Maltby would lightly disparage it in comparison with Braxton's—'Ah, if I could write like *that!*' Maltby won golden opinions in this way. Braxton, on the other hand, would let slip no opportunity for sneering at Maltby's work—'gimcrack,' as he called it. This was not good for Maltby. Different men, different methods.

'The Rape of the Lock' was 'gimcrack,' if you care to call it so; but it was a delicate, brilliant work; and so, I repeat, was Maltby's 'Ariel.' Absurd to compare Maltby with Pope? I am not so sure. I have read 'Ariel,' but have never read 'The Rape of the Lock.' Braxton's opprobrious term for 'Ariel' may not, however, have been due to jealousy alone. Braxton had imagination, and his rival did not soar above fancy. But the point is that Maltby's fancifulness went far and well.

In telling how Ariel re-embodied himself from thin air, leased a small house in Chesterfield Street, was presented at a Levée, played the part of good fairy in a matter of true love not running smooth, and worked meanwhile all manner of amusing changes among the aristocracy before he vanished again, Maltby showed a very pretty range of ingenuity. In one respect, his work was a more surprising achievement than Braxton's. For, whereas Braxton had been born and bred among his rustics, Maltby knew his aristocrats only through Thackeray, through the photographs and paragraphs in the newspapers, and through those passionate excursions of his to Rotten Row. Yet I found his aristocrats as convincing as Braxton's rustics. It is true that I may have been convinced wrongly. That is a point which I could settle only by experience. I shift my ground, claiming for Maltby's aristocrats just this: that they pleased me very much.

Aristocrats, when they are presented solely through a novelist's sense of beauty, do not satisfy us. They may be as beautiful as all that, but, for fear of thinking ourselves snobbish, we won't believe it. We do believe it, however, and revel in it, when the novelist saves his face and ours by a pervading irony in the treatment of what he loves. The irony must, mark you, be pervading and obvious. Disraeli's great ladies and lords won't do, for his irony was but latent in his homage, and thus the reader feels himself called on to worship and in duty bound to scoff. All's well, though, when the homage is latent in the irony. Thackeray, inviting us to laugh and frown over the follies of Mayfair, enables us to reel with him in a secret orgy of veneration for those fools.

Maltby, too, in his measure, enabled us to reel thus. That is mainly why, before the end of April, his publisher was in a position to state that 'the Seventh Large Impression of "Ariel in Mayfair" is almost exhausted.' Let it be put to our credit, however, that at the same moment Braxton's publisher had 'the honour to inform the public that an Eighth Large Impression of "A Faun on the Cotswolds" is in instant preparation.'

Indeed, it seemed impossible for either author to outvie the other in success and glory. Week in, week out, you saw cancelled either's every momentary advantage. A neck-and-neck race. As thus:—Maltby appears as a Celebrity At Home in the *World* (Tuesday). Ha! No, *Vanity Fair* (Wednesday) has a perfect presentment of Braxton by

'Spy.' Neck-and-neck! No, *Vanity Fair* says 'the subject of next week's cartoon will be Mr. Hilary Maltby.' Maltby wins! No, next week Braxton's in the *World*.

Throughout May I kept, as it were, my eyes glued to my field-glasses. On the first Monday in June I saw that which drew from me a hoarse ejaculation.

Let me explain that always on Monday mornings at this time of year, when I opened my daily paper, I looked with respectful interest to see what bevy of the great world had been entertained since Saturday at Keeb Hall. The list was always august and inspiring. Statecraft and Diplomacy were well threaded there with mere Lineage and mere Beauty, with Royalty sometimes, with mere Wealth never, with privileged Genius now and then. A noble composition always. It was said that the Duke of Hertfordshire cared for nothing but his collection of birds' eggs, and that the collections of guests at Keeb were formed entirely by his young Duchess. It was said that he had climbed trees in every corner of every continent. The Duchess' hobby was easier. She sat aloft and beckoned desirable specimens up.

The list published on that first Monday in June began ordinarily enough, began with the Austro-Hungarian Ambassador and the Portuguese Minister. Then came the Duke and Duchess of Mull, followed by four lesser Peers (two of them Proconsuls, however) with their Peeresses, three Peers without their Peeresses, four Peeresses without their Peers, and a dozen bearers of courtesy-titles with or without their wives or husbands. The rear was brought up by 'Mr. A. J. Balfour, Mr. Henry Chaplin, and Mr. Hilary Maltby.'

Youth tends to look at the darker side of things. I confess that my first thought was for Braxton.

I forgave and forgot his faults of manner. Youth is generous. It does not criticise a strong man stricken.

And anon, so habituated was I to the parity of those two strivers, I conceived that there might be some mistake. Daily newspapers are printed in a hurry. Might not 'Henry Chaplin' be a typographical error for 'Steven Braxton'? I went out and bought another newspaper. But Mr. Chaplin's name was in that too.

'Patience!' I said to myself. 'Braxton crouches only to spring. He will be at Keeb Hall on Saturday next.'

My mind was free now to dwell with pleasure on Maltby's great achievement. I though of writing to congratulate him, but feared this might be in bad taste. I did, however, write asking him to lunch with me. He did not answer my letter. I was, therefore, all the more sorry, next Monday, at not finding 'and Mr. Stephen Braxton' in Keeb's week-end catalogue.

A few days later I met Mr. Hookworth. He mentioned that Stephen Braxton had left town. 'He has taken,' said Hookworth, 'a delightful bungalow on the east coast. He has gone there to *work*.' He added that he had a great liking for Braxton—'a man utterly *unspoilt*.' I inferred that he, too, had written to Maltby and received no answer.

That butterfly did not, however, appear to be hovering from flower to flower in the parterres of rank and fashion. In the daily lists of guests at dinners, reception, dances, balls, the name of Maltby figured never. Maltby had not caught on.

Presently I heard that he, too, had left town. I gathered that he had gone quite early in June—quite soon after Keeb. Nobody seemed to know where he was. My own theory was that he had taken a delightful bungalow on the west coast, to balance Braxton. Anyhow, the parity of the two strivers was now somewhat re-established.

In point of fact, the disparity had been less than I supposed. While Maltby was at Keeb, there Braxton was also—in a sense. . . . It was a strange story. I did not hear it at the time. Nobody did. I heard it seventeen years later. I heard it in Lucca.

Little Lucca I found so enchanting that, though I had only a day or two to spare, I stayed there a whole month. I formed the habit of walking, every morning, round that high-pitched path which girdles Lucca, that wide and tree-shaded path from which one looks down over the city wall at the fertile plains beneath Lucca. There were never many people there; but the few who did come came daily, so that I grew to like seeing them and took a mild personal interest in them.

One of them was an old lady in a wheeled chair. She was not less than seventy years old, and might or might not have once been beautiful. Her chair was slowly propelled by an Italian woman. She herself was obviously Italian. Not so, however, the little gentleman who walked assiduously beside her. Him I guessed to be English. He was a very stout little gentleman, with gleaming spectacles and a full blond beard, and he seemed to radiate cheerfulness. I thought at first that he might be the old lady's resident physician; but no, there was something subtly un-professional about him: I became sure that his constancy was gratuitous, and his radiance real. And one day, I know not how, there dawned on me a suspicion that he was—who?— some one I had known—some writer—what's-his-name—something with an M—Maltby—Hilary Maltby of the long-ago!

At sight of him on the morrow this suspicion hardened almost to certainty. I wished I could meet him alone and ask him if I were not right, and what he had been doing all these years, and why he had left England. He was always with the old lady. It was only on my last day in Lucca that my chance came.

I had just lunched, and was seated on a comfortable bench outside my hotel, with a cup of coffee on the table before me, gazing across the faded old sunny piazza and wondering what to do with my last afternoon. It was then that I espied yonder the back of the putative Maltby. I hastened forth to him. He was buying some pink roses, a great bunch of them, from a market-woman under an umbrella. He looked very blank, he flushed greatly, when I ventured to accost him. He admitted that his name was Hilary Maltby. I told him my own name, and by degrees he remembered me. He apologised for his con- fusion. He explained that he had not talked English, had not talked to an Englishman, 'for—oh, hundreds of years.' He said that he had, in the course of his long residence in Lucca, seen two or three people whom he had known in England, but that none of them had rec- ognised him. He accepted (but as though he were embarking on the oddest adventure in the world) my invitation that he should come and sit down and take coffee with me. He laughed with pleasure and surprise at finding that he could still speak his native tongue quite fluently and idiomatically. 'I know absolutely nothing,' he said, 'about England nowadays—except from stray references to it in the *Corriere della Sera*'; nor did he show the faintest desire that I should enlighten him. 'England,' he mused, '—how it all comes back to me!'

'But not you to it?'

'Ah, no indeed,' he said gravely, looking at the roses which he had laid carefully on the marble table. 'I am the happiest of men.'

He sipped his coffee, and stared out across the piazza, out beyond it into the past.

'I am the happiest of men,' he repeated. I plied him with the spur of silence.

'And I owe it all to having once yielded to a bad impulse. Absurd, the threads our destinies hang on!'

Again I plied him with that spur. As it seemed not to prick him, I repeated the words he had last spoken. 'For instance?' I added.

'Take,' he said, 'a certain evening in the spring of '95. Suppose the Duchess of Hertfordshire had had a bad cold that evening. If she had had that, or a headache, or if she had decided that it *wouldn't* be rather interesting to go on to that party—that Annual Soirée, I think it was—of the Inkwomen's Club; or again—to go a step further back—if she hadn't ever written that one little poem, and if it *hadn't* been printed in "The Gentlewoman," and if the Inkwomen's committee *hadn't* instantly and unanimously elected her an Honorary Vice-President because of that one little poem; or if—well, if a million-and-one utterly irrelevant things hadn't happened, don't-you-know, I shouldn't be here . . . I might be *there,*' he smiled, with a vague gesture indicating England.

'Suppose,' he went on, 'I hadn't been invited to that Annual Soirée; or suppose that other fellow,—'

'Braxton?' I suggested. I had remembered Braxton at the moment of recognising Maltby.

'Suppose *he* hadn't been asked. . . . But of course we both were. It happened that I was the first to be presented to the Duchess. . . . It was a great moment. I hoped I should keep my head. She wore a tiara. I had often seen women in tiaras, at the Opera. But I had never talked to a woman in a tiara. Tiaras were symbols to me. Eyes are just a human feature. I fixed mine on the Duchess's. I kept my head by not looking at hers. I behaved as one human being to another. She seemed very intelligent. We got on very well. Presently she asked whether I should think her *very* bold if she said how *perfectly* divine she thought my book. I said something about doing my best, and asked with animation whether she had read "A Faun on the Cotswolds." She had. She said it was *too* wonderful, she said it was *too* great. If she hadn't been a Duchess, I might have thought her slightly hysterical. Her innate good-sense quickly reasserted itself. She used her great power. With a wave of her magic wand she turned into a fact the glittering possibility that had haunted me. She asked me down to Keeb.

'She seemed very pleased that I would come. Was I, by any chance, free on Saturday week? She hoped there would be some amusing people to meet me. Could I come by the 3.30? It was only an hour-and-a-quarter from Victoria. On Saturday there were always compartments reserved for people coming to Keeb by the 3.30. She hoped I would bring my bicycle with me. She hoped I wouldn't find it very dull. She hoped I wouldn't forget to come. She said how lovely it must be to spend one's life among clever people. She supposed I knew everybody here tonight. She asked me to tell her who everybody was. She asked who was the tall, dark man, over there. I told her it was Stephen Braxton. She said they had promised to introduce her to him. She added that he looked rather wonderful. "Oh, he is, very," I assured her. She turned to me with a sudden appeal: "*Do* you think, if I took my courage in both hands and asked him, he'd care to come to Keeb?"

'I hesitated. It would be easy to say that Satan answered *for* me; easy but untrue; it was I that babbled: "Well—as a matter of fact— since you ask me—if I were you—really I think you'd better not. He's very odd in some ways. He has an extraordinary hatred of sleeping out of London. He has the real Gloucestershire *love* of London. At the same time, he's very shy; and if you asked him he wouldn't very well know how to refuse. I think it would be *kinder* not to ask him."

'At that moment, Mrs. Wilpham—the President—loomed up to us, bringing Braxton. He bore himself well. Rough dignity with a touch of mellowness. I daresay you never saw him smile. He smiled gravely down at the Duchess, while she talked in her pretty little quick humble way. He made a great impression.

'What I had done was not merely base: it was very dangerous. I was in terror that she might rally him on his devotion to London. I didn't dare to move away. I was immensely relieved when at length she said she must be going.

'Braxton seemed loth to relax his grip on her hand at parting. I feared she wouldn't escape without uttering that invitation. But all was well. . . . In saying good night to me, she added in a murmur,

"Don't forget Keeb—Saturday week—the 3.30." Merely an exquisite murmur. But Braxton heard it. I knew, by the diabolical look he gave me, that Braxton had heard it. . . . If he hadn't, I shouldn't be here.

'Was I a prey to remorse? Well, in the days between that Soirée and that Saturday, remorse often claimed me, but rapture wouldn't give me up. Arcady, Olympus, the right people, at last! I hadn't realised how good my book was—not till it got me this guerdon; not till I got it this huge advertisement. I foresaw how pleased my publisher would be. In some great houses, I had often heard, it was possible to stay without any one knowing you had been there. But the Duchess of Hertfordshire hid her light under no bushel. Exclusive she was, but not of publicity. Next to Windsor Castle, Keeb Hall was the most advertised house in all England.

'Meanwhile, I had plenty to do. I rather thought of engaging a valet, but decided that this wasn't necessary. On the other hand, I felt a need for three new summer suits, and a new evening suit, and some new white waistcoats. Also a smoking suit. And had any man ever stayed at Keeb without a dressing-case? Hitherto I had been content with a pair of wooden brushes, and so forth. I was afraid these would appal the footman who unpacked my things. I ordered, for his sake, a large dressing-case, with my initials engraved throughout it. It looked compromisingly new when it came to me from the shop. I had to kick it industriously, and throw it about and scratch it, so as to avert possible suspicion. The tailor did not send my things home till the Friday evening. I had to sit up late, wearing the new suits in rotation.

'Next day, at Victoria, I saw strolling on the platform many people, male and female, who looked as if they were going to Keeb—tall, cool, ornate people who hadn't packed their own things and had reached Victoria in broughams. I was ornate, but not tall nor cool. My porter was rather off-hand in his manner as he wheeled my things along to the 3.30. I asked severely if there were any compartments reserved for people going to stay with the Duke of Hertfordshire. This worked an instant change in him. Having set me in one of those shrines, he seemed almost loth to accept a tip. A snob, I am afraid.

'A selection of the tall, the cool, the ornate, the intimately acquainted with one another, soon filled the compartment. There I was, and I think they felt they ought to try to bring me into the conversation. As they were all talking about a cotillion of the previous night, I shouldn't have been able to shine. I gazed out the window, with middle-class aloofness. Presently the talk drifted on to the topic of bicycles. But by this time it was too late for me to come in.

'I gazed at the squalid outskirts of London as they flew by. I doubted, as I listened to my fellow-passengers, whether I should be able to shine at Keeb. I rather wished I were going to spend the week-end at one of those little houses with back-gardens beneath the rail-way-line. I was filled with fears.

'For shame! thought I. Was I nobody? Was the author of "Ariel in Mayfair" nobody?

'I reminded myself how glad Braxton would be if he knew of my faint-heartedness. I thought of Braxton sitting, at this moment, in his room in Clifford's Inn and glowering with envy of his hated rival in the 3.30. And after all, how enviable I was! My spirits rose. I would acquit myself well. . . .

'I much admired the scene at the little railway station where we alighted. It was like a *fête* by Lancret. I knew from the talk of my fellow-passengers that some people had been going down by an earlier train, and that others were coming by a later. But the 3.30 had brought a full score of us. Us! That was the final touch of beauty.

'Outside there were two broughams, a landau, dog-carts, a phaeton, a wagonette, I know not what. But almost everybody, it seemed, was going to bicycle. Lady Rodfitten said *she* was going to bicycle. Year after year, I had seen that famous Countess riding or driving in the Park. I had been told at fourth hand that she had a masculine in-tellect and could make and unmake Ministries. She was nearly sixty now, a trifle dyed and stout and weather-beaten, but still tremen-dously handsome, and hard as nails. One would not have said she had grown older, but merely that she belonged now to a rather later period of the Roman Empire. I had never dreamed of a time when one roof would shelter Lady Rodfitten and me. Somehow, she struck my imagination more than any of these others—more than Count Deym, more than Mr. Balfour, more than the lovely Lady Thisbe Crowborough.

'I might have had a ducal vehicle all to myself, and should have liked that; but it seemed more correct that I should use my bicycle. On the other hand, I didn't want to ride with all these people—a stranger in their midst. I lingered around the luggage till they were off, and then followed at a long distance.

'The sun had gone behind clouds. But I rode slowly, so as to be sure not to arrive hot. I passed, not without a thrill, through the massive open gates into the Duke's park. A massive man with a cock-ade saluted me—hearteningly—from the door of the lodge. The park seemed endless. I came, at length, to a long straight avenue of elms that were almost blatantly immemorial. At the end of it was—well, I felt like a gnat going to stay in a public building.

'If there had been turnstiles—IN and OUT—and a shilling to pay, I should have felt easier as I passed into that hall—that Palladio-Gargantuan hall. Some one, some butler or groom-of-the-chamber, murmured that her Grace was in the garden. I passed out through the great opposite doorway on to a wide spectacular terrace with lawns beyond. Tea was on the nearest of these lawns. In the central group of people—some standing, others sitting—I espied the Duchess. She sat pouring out tea, a deft and animated little figure. I advanced firmly down the steps from the terrace, feeling that all would be well so soon as I had reported myself to the Duchess.

'But I had a staggering surprise on my way to her. I espied in one of the smaller groups—whom d'you think? Braxton.

'I had no time to wonder how he had got there—time merely to grasp the black fact that he *was* there.

'The Duchess seemed really pleased to see me. She said it was *too* splendid of me to come. "You know Mr. Maltby?" she asked Lady Rodfitten, who exclaimed "Not Mr. *Hilary* Maltby?" with a vigorous grace that was overwhelming. Lady Rodfitten declared she was the greatest of my admirers; and I could well believe that in whatever she did she excelled all competitors. On the other hand, I found it hard to believe she was afraid of me. Yet I had her word for it that she was.

'Her womanly charm gave place now to her masculine grip. She eulogised me in the language of a seasoned reviewer on the staff of a long-established journal—wordy perhaps, but sound. I revered and loved her. I wished I could give her my undivided attention. But, whilst I sat there, teacup in hand, between her and the Duchess, part of my brain was fearfully concerned with that glimpse I had had of Braxton. It didn't so much matter that he was here to halve my triumph. But suppose he knew what I had told the Duchess? And suppose he had—no, surely if he *had* shown me up in all my meanness she wouldn't have received me so very cordially. I wondered where she could have met him since that evening of the Inkwomen. I heard Lady Rodfitten concluding her review of "Ariel" with two or three sentences that might have been framed specially to give the publisher an easy "quote." And then I heard myself asking mechanically whether she had read "A Faun on the Cotswolds." The Duchess heard me too. She turned from talking to other people and said "I did like Mr. Braxton so *very* much."

' "Yes," I threw out with a sickly smile, "I'm so glad you asked him to come."

' "But I didn't ask him. I didn't *dare*."

' "But—but—surely he wouldn't be—be *here* if—" We stared at each other blankly. "Here?" she echoed, glancing at the scattered little groups of people on the lawn. I glanced too. I was much embarrassed. I explained that I had seen Braxton "standing just over there" when I arrived, and had supposed he was one of the people who came by the earlier train. "Well," she said with a slightly irritated laugh, "you must have mistaken some one else for him." She dropped the subject, talked to other people, and presently moved away.

'Surely, thought I, she didn't suspect me of trying to make fun of her? On the other hand, surely she hadn't conspired with Braxton to make a fool of *me*? And yet, how could Braxton be here without an invitation, and without her knowledge? My brain whirled. One thing only was clear. I could *not* have mistaken anybody for Braxton. There Braxton had stood—Stephen Braxton, in that old pepper-and-salt suit of his, with his red tie all askew, and without a hat—his hair hanging over his forehead. All this I had seen sharp and clean-cut. There he had stood, just beside one of the women who travelled down in the same compartment as I; a very pretty woman in a pale blue dress; a tall woman—but I had noticed how small she looked beside Braxton. This woman was now walking to and fro, yonder, with M. de Soveral. I had seen Braxton beside her as clearly as I now saw M. de Soveral.

'Lady Rodfitten was talking about India to a recent Viceroy. She seemed to have as firm a grip of India as of "Ariel." I sat forgotten. I wanted to arise and wander off—in a vague search for Braxton. But I feared this might look as if I were angry at being ignored. Presently Lady Rodfitten herself arose, to have what she called her "annual look round." She bade me come too, and strode off between me and the recent Viceroy, noting improvements that had been made in the grounds, suggesting improvements that might be made, indicating improvements that *must* be made. She was great on landscape-gardening. The recent Viceroy was less great on it, but great enough. I don't say I walked forgotten: the eminent woman constantly asked my opinion; but my opinion, though of course it always coincided with hers, sounded quite worthless, somehow. I longed to shine. I could only bother about Braxton.

'Lady Rodfitten's voice was over-strong for the stillness of evening. The shadows lengthened. My spirits sank lower and lower, with the sun. I was a naturally cheerful person, but always, towards sunset, I had a vague sense of melancholy: I seemed always to have grown weaker; morbid misgivings would come to me. On this particular evening there was one such misgiving that crept in and out of me again and again . . . a very horrible misgiving as to the *nature* of what I had seen.

'Well, dressing for dinner is always great tonic. Especially if one shaves. My spirits rose as I lathered my face. I smiled to my reflection in the mirror. The afterglow of the sun came through the window behind the dressing-table, but I had switched on all the lights. My new silver-topped bottles and things made a fine array. To-night *I* was going to shine, too. I felt I might yet be the life and soul of the party. Anyway, my new evening suit was without a fault. And meanwhile this new razor was perfect. Having shaved "down," I lathered myself again and proceeded to shave "up." It was then that I uttered a sharp sound and swung round on my heel.

'No one was there. Yet this I knew: Stephen Braxton had just looked over my shoulder. I had seen the reflection of his face beside mine—craned forward to the mirror. I had met his eyes.

'He had been with me. This I knew.

'I turned to look again at that mirror. One of my cheeks was all covered with blood. I stanched it with a towel. Three long cuts where the razor had slipped and skipped. I plunged the towel into cold water and held it to my cheek. The bleeding went on—alarmingly. I rang the bell. No one came. I vowed I wouldn't bleed to death for Braxton. I rang again. At last a very tall powdered footman appeared— more reproachful-looking than sympathetic, as though I hadn't ordered that dressing-case specially on his behalf. He said he thought one of the housemaids would have some sticking-plaster. He was very sorry he was needed downstairs, but he would tell one of the house-maids. I continued to dab and to curse. The blood flowed less. I showed great spirit. I vowed Braxton should not prevent me from going down to dinner.

'But—a pretty sight I was when I did go down. Pale but determined, with three long strips of black sticking-plaster forming a sort of Z on my left cheek. Mr. Hilary Maltby at Keeb. Literature's Ambassador.

'I don't know how late I was. Dinner was in full swing. Some servant piloted me to my place. I sat down unobserved. The woman on either side of me was talking to her other neighbour. I was near the Duchess' end of the table. Soup was served to me—that dark-red soup that you pour cream into—Bortsch. I felt it would steady me. I raised the first spoonful to my lips, and—my hand gave a sudden jerk.

'I was aware of two separate horrors—a horror that had been, a horror that was. Braxton had vanished. Not for more than an instant had he stood scowling at me from behind the opposite diners. Not for more than the fraction of an instant. But he had left his mark on me. I gazed down with a frozen stare at my shirtfront, at my white waistcoat, both dark with Bortsch. I rubbed them with a napkin. I made them worse.

'I looked at my glass of champagne. I raised it carefully and drained it at one draught. It nerved me. But behind that shirtfront was a broken heart.

'The woman on my left was Lady Thisbe Crowborough. I don't know who was the woman on my right. She was the first to turn and see me. I thought it best to say something about my shirtfront at once. I said it to her sideways, without showing my left cheek. Her hand-some eyes rested on the splashes. She said, after a moment's thought, that they looked "rather gay." She said she thought the eternal black and white of men's evening clothes was "so very dreary." She did her best. . . . Lady Thisbe Crowborough did her best, too, I suppose; but breeding isn't proof against all possible shocks: she visibly started at sight of me and my Z. I explained that I had cut myself shaving. I said, with an attempt at lightness, that shy men ought always to cut themselves shaving: it made such a good conversational opening. "But

surely," she said after a pause, "you don't cut yourself on purpose?"
She was an abysmal fool. I didn't think so at the time. She was Lady
Thisbe Crowborough. This fact hallowed her. That we didn't get on
at all well was a misfortune for which I blamed only myself and my
repulsive appearance and—the unforgettable horror that distracted
me. Nor did I blame Lady Thisbe for turning rather soon to the man
on her other side.

'The woman on my right was talking to the man on *her* other side;
so that I was left a prey to secret memory and dread. I wasn't wondering, wasn't attempting to explain; I was merely remembering—and
dreading. And—how odd one is!—on the top-layer of my consciousness I hated to be seen talking to no one. Mr. Maltby at Keeb. I
caught the Duchess' eye once or twice, and she nodded encouragingly,
as who should say "You do look rather awful, and you do seem rather
out of it, but I don't for a moment regret having asked you to come."
Presently I had another chance of talking. I heard myself talk. My
feverish anxiety to please rather touched *me*. But I noticed that the
eyes of my listener wandered. And yet I was sorry when the ladies
went away. I had a sense of greater exposure. Men who hadn't seen
me saw me now. The Duke, as he came round to the Duchess' end
of the table, must have wondered who I was. But he shyly offered me
his hand as he passed, and said it was so good of me to come. I had
thought of slipping away to put on another shirt and waistcoat, but
had decided that this would make me the more ridiculous. I sat
drinking port—poison to me after champagne, but a lulling poison—
and listened to noblemen with unstained shirtfronts talking about
the Australian cricket match. . . .

'Is Rubicon Bézique still played in England? There was a mania
for it at that time. The floor of Keeb's Palladio-Gargantuan hall was
dotted with innumerable little tables. I didn't know how to play. My
hostess told me I must "come and amuse the dear old Duke and
Duchess of Mull," and led me to a remote sofa on which an old
gentleman had just sat down beside an old lady. They looked at me
with a dim kind interest. My hostess had set me and left me on a
small gilt chair in front of them. Before going she had conveyed to
them loudly—one of them was very deaf—that I was "the famous
writer." It was a long time before they understood that I was not a
political writer. The Duke asked me, after a troubled pause, whether

I had known "old Mr. Abraham Hayward." The Duchess said I was too young to have known Mr. Hayward, and asked if I knew her "clever friend Mr. Mallock." I said I had just been reading Mr. Mallock's new novel. I heard myself shouting a confused précis of the plot. The place where we were sitting was near the foot of the great marble staircase. I said how beautiful the staircase was. The Duchess of Mull said she had never cared very much for that staircase. The Duke, after a pause, said he had "often heard old Mr. Abraham Hayward hold a whole dinner table." There were long and frequent pauses—between which I heard myself talking loudly, frantically, sinking lower and lower in the esteem of my small audience. I felt like a man drowning under the eyes of an elderly couple who sit on the bank regretting that they can offer *no* assistance. Presently the Duke looked at his watch and said to the Duchess that it was "time to be thinking of bed."

'They rose, as it were from the bank, and left me, so to speak, under water. I watched them as they passed slowly out of sight up the marble staircase which I had mispraised. I turned and surveyed the brilliant, silent scene presented by the card-players.

'I wondered what old Mr. Abraham Hayward would have done in my place. Would he have just darted in among those tables and "held" them? I presumed that he would not have stolen silently away, quickly and cravenly away, up the marble staircase—as *I* did.

'I don't know which was the greater, the relief or the humiliation of finding myself in my bedroom. Perhaps the humiliation was the greater. There, on a chair, was my grand new smoking-suit, laid out for me—what a mockery! Once I had foreseen myself wearing it in the smoking-room at a late hour—the centre of a group of eminent men entranced by the brilliancy of my conversation. And now—! I was nothing but a small, dull, soup-stained, sticking-plastered, nerve-racked recluse. Nerves, yes. I assured myself that I had not seen—what I had seemed to see. All very odd, of course, and very unpleasant, but easily explained. Nerves. Excitement of coming to Keeb too much for me. A good night's rest: that was all I needed. To-morrow I should laugh at myself.

'I wondered that I wasn't tired physically. There my grand new silk pyjamas were, yet I felt no desire to go to bed . . . none while it was still possible for me to go. The little writing-table at the foot of my bed seemed to invite me. I had brought with me in my port-manteau a sheaf of letters, letters that I had purposely left unan-swered in order that I might answer them on KEEB HALL note-paper. These the footman had neatly laid beside the blotting-pad on that little writing-table at the foot of the bed. I regretted that the note-paper stacked there had no ducal coronet on it. What matter? The address sufficed. If I hadn't yet made a good impression on the people who were staying here, I could at any rate make one on the people who weren't. I sat down. I set to work. I wrote a prodigious number of fluent and graceful notes.

'Some of these were to strangers who wanted my autograph. I was always delighted to send my autograph, and never perfunctory in the manner of sending it. . . . "Dear Madam," I remember writing to somebody that night, "Were it not that you make your request for it so charmingly, I should hesitate to send you that which rarity alone can render valuable.—Yours truly, Hilary Maltby." I remember read-ing this over and wondering whether the word "render" looked rather commercial. It was in the act of wondering thus that I raised my eyes from the note-paper and saw, through the bars of the brass bed-stead, the naked sole of a large human foot—saw beyond it the calf of a great leg; a nightshirt; and the face of Stephen Braxton. I did not move.

'I thought of making a dash for the door, dashing out into the corridor, shouting at the top of my voice for help. I sat quite still.

'What kept me to my chair was the fear that if I tried to reach the door Braxton would spring off the bed to intercept me. If I sat quite still perhaps he wouldn't move. I felt that if he moved I should collapse utterly.

'I watched him, and he watched me. He lay there with his body half-raised, one elbow propped on the pillow, his jaw sunk on his breast; and from under his black brows he watched me steadily.

'No question of mere nerves now. That hope was gone. No mere optical delusion, this abiding presence. Here Braxton was. He and I were together in the bright, silent room. How long would he be con-tent to watch me?

'Eleven nights ago he had given me one horrible look. It was this look that I had to meet, in infinite prolongation, now, not daring to shift my eyes. He lay as motionless as I sat. I did not hear him breathing, but I knew, by the rise and fall of his chest under his nightshirt, that he was breathing heavily. Suddenly I started to my feet. For he had moved. He had raised one hand slowly. He was stroking his chin. And as he did so, and as he watched me, his mouth gradually slackened to a grin. It was worse, it was more malign, this grin, than the scowl that remained with it; and its immediate effect on me was an impulse that was as hard to resist as it was hateful. The window was open. It was nearer to me than the door. I could have reached it in time. . . .

'Well, I live to tell the tale. I stood my ground. And there dawned on me now a new fact in regard to my companion. I had all the while been conscious of something abnormal in his attitude— a lack of ease in his gross possessiveness. I saw now the reason for this effect. The pillow on which his elbow rested was still uniformly puffed and convex; like a pillow untouched. His elbow rested but on the very surface of it, not changing the shape of it at all. His body made not the least furrow along the bed. . . . He had no weight.

'I knew that if I leaned forward and thrust my hand between those brass rails, to clutch his foot, I should clutch—nothing. He wasn't tangible. He was realistic. He wasn't real. He was opaque. He wasn't solid.

'Odd as it may seem to you, these certainties took the edge off my horror. During that walk with Lady Rodfitten, I had been appalled by the doubt that haunted me. But now the very confirmation of that doubt gave me a sort of courage: I could cope better with anything to-night than with actual Braxton. And the measure of the relief I felt is that I sat down again on my chair.

'More than once there came to me a wild hope that the thing might be an optical delusion, after all. Then would I shut my eyes tightly, shaking my head sharply; but, when I looked again, there the presence was, of course. It—he—not actual Braxton but, roughly speaking, Braxton—had come to stay. I was conscious of intense fatigue, taut and alert though every particle of me was; so that I became, in the course of that ghastly night, conscious of a great envy also. For some time before the dawn came in through the window, Braxton's eyes had been closed; little by little now his head drooped sideways, then fell on his forearm and rested there. He was asleep.

'Cut off from sleep, I had a great longing for smoke. I had cigarettes on me, I had matches on me. But I didn't dare to strike a match. The sound might have waked Braxton up. In slumber he was less terrible, though perhaps more odious. I wasn't so much afraid now as indignant. "It's intolerable," I sat saying to myself, "utterly intolerable!"

'I had to bear it, nevertheless. I was aware that I had, in some degree, brought it on myself. If I hadn't interfered and lied, actual Braxton would have been here at Keeb, and I at this moment sleeping soundly. But this was no excuse for Braxton. Braxton didn't know what I had done. He was merely envious of me. And—wanly I puzzled it out in the dawn—by very force of the envy, hatred, and malice in him he had projected hither into my presence this simulacrum of himself. I had known that he would be thinking of me. I had known that the thought of me at Keeb Hall would be of the last bitterness to his most sacred feelings. But—I had reckoned without the passionate force and intensity of the man's nature.

'If by this same strength and intensity he had merely projected himself as an invisible guest under the Duchess' roof—if his feat had been wholly, as perhaps it was in part, a feat of mere wistfulness and longing—then I should have felt really sorry for him; and my conscience would have soundly rated me in his behalf. But no; if the wretched creature *had* been invisible to me, I shouldn't have thought of Braxton at all—except with gladness that he wasn't here. That he was visible to me, and to me alone, wasn't any sign of proper remorse within me. It was but the gauge of his incredible ill-will.

'Well, it seemed to me that he was avenged—with a vengeance. There I sat, hot-browed from sleeplessness, cold in the feet, stiff in the legs, cowed and indignant all through—sat there in the broadening daylight, and in that new evening suit of mine with the Braxtonised shirtfront and waistcoat that by day were more than ever loathsome. Literature's Ambassador at Keeb. . . . I rose gingerly from my chair, and caught sight of my face, of my Braxtonised cheek, in the mirror. I heard the twittering of birds in distant trees. I saw through my window the elaborate landscape of the Duke's grounds, all soft in the grey bloom of early morning. I think I was nearer to tears than I had ever been since I was a child. But the weakness passed. I turned towards the personage on my bed, and, summoning all such power as was in me, *willed* him to be gone. My effort was not without result—an inadequate result. Braxton turned in his sleep.

'I resumed my seat, and . . . and . . . sat up staring and blinking at a tall man with red hair. "I must have fallen asleep," I said. "Yessir," he replied; and his toneless voice touched in me one or two spring of memory: I was at Keeb; this was the footman who looked after me. But—why wasn't I in bed? Had I—no, surely it had been no nightmare. Surely I had *seen* Braxton on that white bed.

'The footman was impassively putting away my smoking-suit. I was too dazed to wonder what he thought of me. Nor did I attempt to stifle a cry when, a moment later, turning in my chair, I beheld Braxton leaning moodily against the mantelpiece. "Are you unwell-sir?" asked the footman. "No," I said faintly, "I'm quite well."— "Yessir. Will you wear the blue suit or the grey?"—"The grey."— "Yessir."—It seemed almost incredible that *he* didn't see Braxton; *he* didn't appear to me one wit more solid than the night-shirted brute who stood against the mantelpiece and watched him lay out my things.—"Shall I let your bath-water run nowsir?"—"Please, yes." —"Your bathroom's the second door to the leftsir."—He went out with my bath-towel and sponge, leaving me alone with Braxton.

'I rose to my feet, mustering once more all the strength that was in me. Hoping against hope, with set teeth and clenched hands, I faced him, thrust forth my will at him, with everything but words commanded him to vanish—to cease to be.

'Suddenly, utterly, he vanished. And you can imagine the truly exquisite sense of triumph that thrilled me and continued to thrill me till I went into the bathroom and found him in my bath.

'Quivering with rage, I returned to my bedroom. "Intolerable," I heard myself repeating like a parrot that knew no other word. A bath was just what I had needed. Could I have lain for a long time basking in very hot water, and then have sponged myself with cold water, I should have emerged calm and brave; comparatively so, at any rate. I should have looked less ghastly, and have had less of a headache, and something of an appetite, when I went down to breakfast. Also, I shouldn't have been the very first guest to appear on the scene. There were five or six round tables, instead of last night's long table. At the further end of the room the butler and two other servants were lighting the little lamps under the hot dishes. I didn't like to make myself ridiculous by running away. On the other hand, was it right for me to begin breakfast all by myself at one of these round tables? I supposed it was. But I dreaded to be found eating, alone in that vast room, by the first downcomer. I sat dallying with dry toast and watching the door. It occurred to me that Braxton might occur at any moment. Should I be able to ignore him?

'Some man and wife—a very handsome couple—were the first to appear. They nodded and said "good morning" when they noticed me on their way to the hot dishes. I rose—uncomfortably, guiltily— and sat down again. I rose again when the wife drifted to my table, followed by the husband with two steaming plates. She asked me if it wasn't a heavenly morning, and I replied with nervous enthusiasm that it was. She then ate kedgeree in silence. "You just finishing, what?" the husband asked, looking at my plate. "Oh, no—no— only just beginning," I assured him, and helped myself to butter. He then ate kedgeree in silence. He looked like some splendid bull, and she like some splendid cow, grazing. I envied them their eupeptic calm. I surmised that ten thousand Braxtons would not have prevented *them* from sleeping soundly by night and grazing steadily by day. Perhaps their stolidity infected me a little. Or perhaps what braced me was the great quantity of strong tea that I consumed. Anyhow, I had begun to feel that if Braxton came in now I shouldn't blench nor falter.

'Well, I wasn't put to the test. Plenty of people drifted in, but Braxton wasn't one of them. Lady Rodfitten—no, she didn't drift, she marched, in; and presently, at an adjacent table, she was drawing a comparison, in clarion tones, between Jean and Edouard de Reszke. It seemed to me that her own voice had much in common with Edouard's. Even more was it akin to a military band. I found myself beating time to it with my foot. Decidedly, my spirits had risen. I was in a mood to face and outface anything. When I rose from the table and made my way to the door, I walked with something of a swing— to the tune of Lady Rodfitten.

'My buoyancy didn't last long, though. There was no swing in my walk when, a little later, I passed out on to the spectacular terrace. I had seen my enemy elsewhere, and had beaten a furious retreat. No doubt I should see him yet again soon—here, perhaps, on this terrace. Two of the guests were bicycling slowly up and down the long paven expanse, both of them smiling with pride in the new delicious form of locomotion. There was a great array of bicycles propped neatly along the balustrade. I recognised my own among them. I wondered whether Braxton had projected from Clifford's Inn an image of *his* own bicycle. He may have done so; but I've no evidence that he did. I myself was bicycling when next I saw him; he, I remember, was on foot.

'This was a few minutes later. I was bicycling with dear Lady Rod-fitten. She seemed really to like me. She had come out and accosted me heartily on the terrace, asking me, because of my sticking-plaster, with whom I had fought a duel since yesterday. I did not tell her with whom, and she had already branched off on the subject of duelling in general. She regretted the extinction of duelling in England, and gave cogent reasons for her regret. Then she asked me what my next book was to be. I confided that I was writing a sort of sequel—"Ariel Returns to Mayfair." She shook her head, said with her usual soundness that sequels were very dangerous things, and asked me to tell her "briefly" the lines along which I was working. I did so. She pointed out two or three weak points in my scheme. She said she could judge better if I would let her see my manuscript. She asked me to come and lunch with her next Friday—"just our two selves"—at Rodfitten House, and to bring my manuscript with me. Need I say that I walked on air?

' "And now," she said strenuously, "let us take a turn on our bicycles." By this time there were a dozen riders on the terrace, all of them smiling with pride and rapture. We mounted and rode along together. The terrace ran round two sides of the house, and before we came to the end of it these words had provisionally marshalled themselves in my mind:

TO

ELEANOR

COUNTESS OF RODFITTEN

THIS BOOK WHICH OWES ALL

TO HER WISE COUNSEL

AND UNWEARYING SUPERVISION

IS GRATEFULLY DEDICATED

BY HER FRIEND

THE AUTHOR

'Smiled to masonically by the passing bicyclists, and smiling masonically to them in return, I began to feel that the rest of my visit would run smooth, if only——

' "Let's go a little faster. Let's race!" said Lady Rodfitten; and we did so—"just our two selves." I was on the side nearer to the balustrade, and it was on this side that Braxton suddenly appeared from nowhere, solid-looking as a rock, his arms akimbo, less than three yards ahead of me, so that I swerved involuntarily, sharply, striking broadside the front wheel of Lady Rodfitten and collapsing with her, and with a crash of machinery, to the ground.

'I wasn't hurt. She had broken my fall. I wished I was dead. She was furious. She sat speechless with fury. A crowd had quickly collected—just as in the case of a street accident. She accused me now to the crowd. She said I had done it on purpose. She said such terrible things of me that I think the crowd's sympathy must have veered towards me. She was assisted to her feet. I tried to be one of the assistants. "Don't let him come near me!" she thundered. I caught sight of Braxton on the fringe of the crowd, grinning at me. "It was all HIS fault," I madly cried, pointing at him. Everybody looked at Mr. Balfour, just behind whom Braxton was standing. There was a general murmur of surprise, in which I have no doubt Mr. Balfour joined. He gave a charming, blank, deprecating smile. "I mean—I can't explain what I mean," I groaned. Lady Rodfitten moved away, refusing support, limping terribly, towards the house. The crowd followed her, solicitous. I stood helplessly, desperately, where I was.

'I stood an outlaw, a speck on the now empty terrace. Mechanically I picked up my straw hat, and wheeled the two bent bicycles to the balustrade. I suppose Mr. Balfour has a charming nature. For he presently came out again—on purpose, I am sure, to alleviate my misery. He told me that Lady Rodfitten had suffered no harm. He took me for a stroll up and down the terrace, talking thoughtfully and enchantingly about things in general. Then, having done his deed of mercy, this Good Samaritan went back into the house. My eyes followed him with gratitude; but I was still bleeding from wounds beyond his skill. I escaped down into the gardens. I wanted to see no one. Still more did I want to be seen by no one. I dreaded in every nerve of me my reappearance among those people. I walked ever faster and faster, to stifle thought; but in vain. Why hadn't I simply ridden *through* Braxton? I was aware of being now in the park, among great trees and undulations of wild green ground. But Nature did not achieve the task that Mr. Balfour had attempted; and my anguish was unassuaged.

'I paused to lean against a tree in the huge avenue that led to the huge hateful house. I leaned wondering whether the thought of re-entering that house were the more hateful because I should have to face my fellow-guests or because I should probably have to face Braxton. A church bell began ringing somewhere. And anon I was aware of another sound—a twitter of voices. A consignment of hatted and parasoled ladies was coming fast down the avenue. My first impulse was to dodge behind my tree. But I feared that I had been observed; so that what was left to me of self-respect compelled me to meet these ladies.

'The Duchess was among them. I had seen her from afar at break-fast, but not since. She carried a prayer-book, which she waved to me as I approached. I was a disastrous guest, but still a guest, and nothing could have been prettier than her smile. "Most of my men this week," she said, "are Pagans, and all the others have dispatch-boxes to go through—except the dear old Duke of Mull, who's a member of the Free Kirk. You're Pagan, of course?"

'I said—and indeed it was a heart-cry—that I should like very much to come to church. "If I shan't be in the way," I rather abjectly added. It didn't strike me that Braxton would try to intercept me. I don't know why, but it never occurred to me, as I walked briskly along beside the Duchess, that I should meet him so far from the house. The church was in a corner of the park, and the way to˙it was by a side path that branched off from the end of the avenue. A little way along, casting its shadow across the path, was a large oak. It was from behind this tree, when we came to it, that Braxton sprang suddenly forth and tripped me up with his foot.

'Absurd to be tripped up by the mere semblance of a foot? But remember, I was walking quickly, and the whole thing happened in a flash of time. It was inevitable that I should throw out my hands and come down headlong—just as though the obstacle had been as real as it looked. Down I came on palms and knee-caps, and up I scrambled, very much hurt and shaken and apologetic. "*Poor* Mr. Maltby! *Really*—!" the Duchess wailed for me in this latest of my mishaps. Some other lady chased my straw hat, which had bowled far ahead. Two others helped to brush me. They were all very kind, with a quaver of mirth in their concern for me. I looked furtively around for Braxton, but he was gone. The palms of my hands were abraded with gravel. The Duchess said I must on no account come to church *now*. I was utterly determined to reach that sanctuary. I marched firmly on with the Duchess. Come what might on the way, I wasn't going to be left out here. I was utterly bent on winning at least one respite.

'Well, I reached the little church without further molestation. To be there seemed almost too good to be true. The organ, just as we entered, sounded its first notes. The ladies rustled into the front pew. I, being the one male of the party, sat at the end of the pew, beside the Duchess. I couldn't help feeling that my position was a proud one. But I had gone through too much to take instant pleasure in it, and was beset by thoughts of what new horror might await me on the way back to the house. I hoped the Service would not be brief. The swelling and dwindling strains of the "voluntary" on the small organ were strangely soothing. I turned to give an almost feudal glance to the simple villagers in the pews behind, and saw a sight that cowed my soul.

'Braxton was coming up the aisle. He came slowly, casting a tourist's eye at the stained-glass windows on either side. Walking heavily, yet with no sound of boots on the pavement, he reached our pew. There, towering and glowering, he halted, as though demanding that we should make room for him. A moment later he edged sullenly into the pew. Instinctively I had sat tight back, drawing my knees aside, in a shudder of revulsion against contact. But Braxton did not push past me. What he did was to sit slowly and fully down on me.

'No, not down *on* me. Down *through* me——and around me. What befell me was not mere ghastly contact with the intangible. It was inclusion, envelopment, eclipse. What Braxton sat down on was not I, but the seat of the pew; and what he sat back against was not my face and chest, but the back of the pew. I didn't realise this at the moment. All I knew was a sudden black blotting-out of all things; an infinite and impenetrable darkness. I dimly conjectured that I was dead. What was wrong with me, in point of fact, was that my eyes, with the rest of me, were inside Braxton. You remember what a great hulking fellow Braxton was. I calculate that as we sat there my eyes were just beneath the roof of his mouth. Horrible!

'Out of the unfathomable depths of that pitch darkness, I could yet hear the "voluntary" swelling and dwindling, just as before. It was by this I knew now that I wasn't dead. And I suppose I must have craned my head forward, for I had a sudden glimpse of things —a close quick downward glimpse of a pepper-and-salt waistcoat and of two great hairy hands clasped across it. Then darkness again. Either I had drawn back my head, or Braxton had thrust his forward; I don't know which. "Are you all right?" the Duchess' voice whispered, and no doubt my face was ashen. "Quite," whispered my voice. But this pathetic monosyllable was the last gasp of the social instinct in me. Suddenly, as the "voluntary" swelled to its close, there was a great sharp shuffling noise. The congregation had risen to its feet, at the entry of choir and vicar. Braxton had risen, leaving me in daylight. I beheld his towering back. The Duchess, beside him, glanced round at me. But I could not, dared not, stand up into that presented back, into that great waiting darkness. I did but clutch my hat from beneath the seat and hurry distraught down the aisle, out through the porch, into the open air.

'Whither? To what goal? I didn't reason. I merely fled—like Orestes; fled like an automaton along the path we had come by. And was followed? Yes, yes. Glancing back across my shoulder, I saw that brute some twenty yards behind me, gaining on me. I broke into a sharper run. A few sickening moments later, he was beside me, scowling down into my face.

'I swerved, dodged, doubled on my tracks, but he was always at me. Now and again, for lack of breath, I halted, and he halted with me. And then, when I had got my wind, I would start running again, in the insane hope of escaping him. We came, by what twisting and turning course I know not, to the great avenue, and as I stood there in an agony of panting I had a dazed vision of the distant Hall. Really I had quite forgotten I was staying at the Duke of Hertfordshire's. But Braxton hadn't forgotten. He planted himself in front of me. He stood between me and the house.

'Faint though I was, I could almost have laughed. Good heavens! was *that* all he wanted: that I shouldn't go back there? Did he suppose I wanted to go back there—with *him?* Was I the Duke's prisoner on parole? What was there to prevent me from just walking off to the railway station? I turned to do so.

'He accompanied me on my way. I thought that when once I had passed through the lodge gates he might vanish, satisfied. But no, he didn't vanish. It was as though he suspected that if he let me out of his sight I should sneak back to the house. He arrived with me, this quiet companion of mine, at the little railway station. Evidently he meant to see me off. I learned from an elderly and solitary porter that the next train to London was the 4.3.

'Well, Braxton saw me off by the 4.3. I reflected, as I stepped up into an empty compartment, that it wasn't yet twenty-four hours ago since I, or some one like me, had alighted at that station.

'The guard blew his whistle; the engine shrieked, and the train jolted forward and away; but I did not lean out of the window to see the last of my attentive friend.

'Really not twenty-four hours ago? Not twenty-four years?'

Maltby paused in his narrative. 'Well, well,' he said, 'I don't want you to think I overrate the ordeal of my visit to Keeb. A man of stronger nerve than mine, and of greater resourcefulness, might have coped successfully with Braxton from first to last—might have stayed on till Monday, making a very favourable impression on every one all the while. Even as it was, even after my manifold failures and sudden flight, I don't say my position was impossible. I only say it seemed so to me. A man less sensitive than I, and less vain, might have cheered up after writing a letter of apology to his hostess, and have resumed his normal existence as though nothing very terrible had happened after all. I wrote a few lines to the Duchess that night; but I wrote amidst the preparations for my departure from England: I crossed the Channel next morning. Throughout that Sunday afternoon with Braxton at the Keeb railway station, pacing the desolate platform with him, waiting in the desolating waiting-room with him, I was numb to regrets, and was thinking of nothing but the 4.3. On the way to Victoria my brain worked and my soul wilted. Every incident in my stay at Keeb stood out clear to me; a dreadful, a hideous pattern. I had done for myself, so far as *those* people were concerned. And now that I had sampled *them*, what cared I for others? "Too low for a hawk, too high for a buzzard." That homely old saying seemed to sum me up. And suppose I *could* still take pleasure in the company of my own old upper-middle class, how would that class regard me now? Gossip percolates. Little by little, I was sure, the story of my Keeb fiasco would leak down into the drawing-room of Mrs. Foster-Dugdale. I felt I could never hold up my head in any company where anything of that story was known. Are you quite sure you never heard anything?'

I assured Maltby that all I had known was the great bare fact of his having stayed at Keeb Hall.

'It's curious,' he reflected. 'It's a fine illustration of the loyalty of those people to one another. I suppose there was a general agreement for the Duchess' sake that nothing should be said about her queer guest. But even if I had dared hope to be so efficiently hushed up, I couldn't have not fled. I wanted to forget. I wanted to leap into some void, far away from all reminders. I leapt straight from Ryder Street into Vaule-la-Rochette, a place of which I had once heard that it was the least frequented seaside-resort in Europe. I leapt leaving no address—leapt telling my landlord that if a suit-case and a portmanteau arrived for me he could regard them, them and their contents, as his own for ever. I daresay the Duchess wrote me a kind little letter, forcing herself to express a vague hope that I would come again "some other time." I daresay Lady Rodfitten did *not* write reminding me of my promise to lunch on Friday and bring "Ariel Returns to Mayfair" with me. I left that manuscript at Ryder Street; in my bedroom grate; a shuffle of ashes. Not that I'd yet given up all thought of writing. But I certainly wasn't going to write now about the two things I most needed to forget. I wasn't going to write about the British aristocracy, nor about any kind of supernatural presence. . . . I did write a novel —my last—while I was at Vaule. "Mr. and Mrs. Robinson." Did you ever come across a copy of it?'

I nodded gravely.

'Ah; I wasn't sure,' said Maltby, 'whether it was ever published. A dreary affair, wasn't it? I knew a great deal about suburban life. But —well, I suppose one can't really understand what one doesn't love, and one can't make good fun without real understanding. Besides, what chance of virtue is there for a book written merely to distract the author's mind? I had hoped to be healed by sea and sunshine and solitude. These things were useless. The labour of "Mr. and Mrs. Robinson" did help, a little. When I had finished it, I thought I might as well send it off to my publisher. He had given me a large sum of money, down, after "Ariel," for my next book—so large that I was rather loth to disgorge. In the note I sent with the manuscript, I gave no address, and asked that the proofs should be read in the office. I didn't care whether the thing were published or not. I knew it would be a dead failure if it were. What mattered one more drop in the foaming cup of my humiliation? I knew Braxton would grin and gloat. I didn't mind even that.'

'Oh, well,' I said, 'Braxton was in no mood for grinning and gloating. "The Drones" had already appeared.'

Maltby had never heard of 'The Drones'—which I myself had remembered only in the course of his disclosures. I explained to him that it was Braxton's second novel, and was by way of being a savage indictment of the British aristocracy; that it was written in the worst possible taste, but was so very dull that it fell utterly flat; that Braxton had forthwith taken, with all of what Maltby had called 'the passionate force and intensity of his nature,' to drink, and had presently gone under and not re-emerged.

Maltby gave signs of genuine, though not deep, emotion, and cited two or three of the finest passages from 'A Faun on the Cotswolds.' He even expressed a conviction that 'The Drones' must have been misjudged. He said he blamed himself more than ever for yielding to that bad impulse at that Soirée.

'And yet,' he mused, 'and yet, honestly, I can't find it in my heart to regret that I did yield. I can only wish that all had turned out as well, in the end, for Braxton as for me. I wish he could have won out, as I did, into a great and lasting felicity. For about a year after I had finished "Mr. and Mrs. Robinson" I wandered from place to place, trying to kill memory, shunning all places frequented by the English. At last I found myself in Lucca. Here, if anywhere, I thought, might a bruised and tormented spirit find gradual peace. I determined to move out of my hotel into some permanent lodging. Not for felicity, not for any complete restoration of self-respect, was I hoping; only for peace. A "mezzano" conducted me to a noble and ancient house, of which, he told me, the owner was anxious to let the first floor. It was in much disrepair, but even so seemed to me very cheap. According to the simple Luccan standard, I am rich. I took that first floor for a year, had it furbished up, and engaged two servants. My "padrona" inhabited the ground floor. From time to time she allowed me to visit her there. She was the Contessa Adriano-Rizzoli, the last of her line. She is the Contessa Adriano-Rizzoli-Maltby. We have been married fifteen years.'

Maltby looked at his watch and, rising, took tenderly from the table his great bunch of roses. 'She is a lineal descendant,' he said, 'of the Emperor Hadrian.'

Thirty Clocks Strike the Hour

❋ V. SACKEVILLE-WEST ❋

V.[ICTORIA] SACKEVILLE-WEST (1892–1962) was a member of the ancient English family who received the historic house Knole from Elizabeth I. She married Sir Harold Nicolson. Her story of English aristocratic life at the turn of the century, *The Edwardians* (1930), is the best known of her novels. She states in *Thirty Clocks Strike the Hour* that it is not a story, but this may be a fiction within a fiction, for she had no great-grandmother who lived in any such house in Paris. The house is demonstrably that of Sir John Murray Scott, at the corner of the Rue Lafitte and the Boulevard des Italiens, for she describes it in the same terms in her life of her mother, *Pepita*.

I REMEMBER being taken to visit my great-grandmother.
This is no story. It is a recollection—a reconstruction. A wish to give shape to a fading impression at the back of my mind before that impression should become irrecoverable. It is not only a personal impression, it is an impression in a wider sense, of an age that I·saw in the act of passing.

She lived in Paris, in an unfashionable quarter. Hers was a vast corner house on the Boulevard des Italiens; I remember I used to count the row of windows, and there were twenty each way, twenty looking on the boulevard, and twenty on the narrow side street. There was a vast portecochère in the side street; one rang the bell, the concierge pulled a string, the door clicked on its latch, and one pushed one's way through, into the central courtyard, where a great business of washing carriages always seemed to be going on; a business of mops and immense quantities of water and grooms clacking round in wooden clogs; patches of sunlight, birdcages hanging in the windows, and girls arriving with parcels. All round the courtyard dwelt an indeterminate population, for portions of the upper floors were let out in flats, but these tenants were kept severely in their place, nor did I ever hear any save one, Mme Jacquemin, referred to by name. Consequently they existed for me in a cloud of alluring and tantalizing mystery, so that I spent hours inventing the inner drama of their families, and wondering what they did when they wanted to play the piano, and how they managed their exits and their entrances. I was sure that none of them would dare risk an encounter with my great-grandmother, their landlady, who occupied the whole of the first floor.

The staircase was very dark and grand. One arrived on the first-floor landing, already awed into a suitable frame of mind. Of course the bell was not electric; one pulled a cord, which produced a jangle within. The door was opened, with a miraculous promptitude, before the jangle had ceased, by either Jacques or Baptiste in white cotton gloves, white-whiskered and respectfully benevolent; at least, Baptiste was quite definitely benevolent, and often dandled me in secret on his knee, giving me meanwhile brandy cherries rolled in pink sugar, and murmuring confidences about his daughter, who had been guilty of some misdemeanour forever and perhaps fortunately enigmatic to me; but the benevolence of Jacques I had to take on trust, on the general principle that all the retainers in that house were benevolent. For Jacques was outwardly *grincheux*. In appearance he was like an old whiskered chimpanzee, and his hands, which I once saw denuded of their cotton gloves, were hairy. I never heard him make but one statement about his private life, but that statement he made with great frequency: *"Moi, j'ai mes cent sous par jour, et je me fiche du Pape."* Whence Jacques got his *"cent sous,"* and what the Pope had to do with it, I never discovered.

But I linger too long in the antechamber, where Jacques or Baptiste closed the door behind one and relieved one of one's parcels or one's umbrella.

Great-grandmother's apartment was on what in an Italian palace would be called the *"piano nobile."*

This meant that, standing in the last doorway, one could see right down the vista of rooms; that is to say, down the rooms represented by the twenty windows on the side street, until the flat turned the corner and took on a new lease of life represented by the twenty windows on the boulevard.

It was an impressive vista. Parquet floors, ivory woodwork, tarnished gilding—it seemed they must be reflected in a halfway mirror, so endlessly did they continue. I was irreverent, of course. Whenever I thought great-grandmother safe in her bedroom, I used to slide along the parquet, or, more irreverent still, get her wheeled chair out of the dining room and trundle myself down the vista. I shiver now to think of the bruised paint and dented ormolu that must have marked my progress—for, unlike great-grandmother's stately advance in the wheeled chair, my one idea was to go as fast as I could. But what did I know then of the privilege that was mine in being admitted to that beautiful house? Small and clean, with painfully frizzed hair, I would stand by, very bored, while visitors marvelled at the furniture under the direction of great-grandmother's stick. Louis Quatorze, Louis Quinze, Louis Seize, Directoire, Empire—all these were names, half meaningless, which I absorbed till they became as familiar as bread, milk, water, butter. Empire came last on the list; for the life of the house seemed to have stopped there. As the door of the ante-chamber closed behind you, the gulf of a century opened, and you stood on the further side.

True, there was the noise of Paris without, motors, and motor horns, and clanging bells; when you opened the window, the roar of the boulevard came in like a great sea; but within the flat, when the windows were shut, there were silence and silken walls, and a faint musty smell, and the shining golden floors, and the dimness of mirrors, and the curve of furniture, and the arabesques of the dull gilding on the ivory *boiserie*. There was an old stately peace never broken by the ring of a telephone; shadows never startled by the leap of electric light. It seemed that the flat itself, rather than its occupant, had refused to accept the modifications of a new century. It had en-shrined itself in the gravity and beauty of a courtly age, until the day when its very masonry should go down in ruin before the mattocks of the house-breakers.

Given up to its dream, in a sumptuous melancholy ennobled by the inexorable menace of its eventual end, few were aware of the exist-ence of this fragment intact in the heart of Paris. A little museum, said the connoisseurs; but they were wrong. It was no museum, for it had preserved its life; its appointments had never been deposed from their proper use to the humiliation of a display for the curious; chairs that should, said the connoisseurs, have stood ranged behind the safety of red ropes, carried the weight of the living as well as the ghosts of the dead; the sconces and the chandeliers still came to life each evening under the flame of innumerable candles. It was then that I liked the flat best. It was then that its gilding and its shadows leapt and flickered most suggestively as the little pointed flames swayed in the draught, and that the golden floors lay like pools reflecting the daggers of the lights. It was then that I used to creep on stockinged feet to the end of the long vista, a scared adventurer in the hushed palace of Sleeping Beauty, and it was on such an evening that I saw my great-grandmother, as I most vividly remember her, coming towards me, from the length of that immeasurable distance, tiny, bent, and alone.

She was a rude, despotic old materialist, without an ounce of romance or fantasy in her body, but to me that night she was every malevolent fairy incarnate, more especially that disgruntled one who had so disastrously attended Sleeping Beauty's christening. I had often been frightened of her tongue; that night I was frightened of her magic. I stood transfixed, incapable of the retreat for which I still had ample time. I remember being wildly thankful that I had on, at least, a clean pinafore. Very slowly she advanced, propped upon her stick, all in black beneath the candles, pausing now and then to look about her, as though she welcomed this escape from the aged servants who usually attended her, or from the guests, deferential but inquisitive, who came, as she shrewdly knew, to boast afterwards of their admission into this almost legendary fastness. I realized that she had not yet caught sight of me, white blot though I must have been at the end of that shadowy aisle of rooms.

Very leisurely she was, savouring the wealth of her possessions, stealing out of her room when no one knew that she was abroad; as clandestine, really, as I myself—and suddenly I knew that on no account must she learn the presence of an eavesdropper. It was no longer fear that prompted me to slip behind the curtain looped across the last door; it was a desperate pity; pity of her age, I suppose, pity of her frailty, pity of her as the spirit of that house, stubborn in the preservation of what was already a thing of the past, whose life would go out with hers; it was her will alone that kept the house together, as it was her will alone that kept the breath fluttering in her body. What thoughts were hers as she lingered in her progress I cannot pretend to tell; I only know that to me she was a phantom, an evocation, a symbol, although, naturally, being but a child, I gave her no such name. To me, at the moment, she was simply a being so old and so fragile that I half expected her to crumble into dust at my feet.

She crossed the dining room and passed me, flattened against the wall and trying to cover the white of my pinafore with a fold of the curtain; so close she passed to me, that I observed the quiver of her fine hands on the knob of her stick and the transparency of the features beneath the shrouding mantilla of black lace. I wondered what her errand might be, as she stood, so bent and shrunken, beneath the immense height of the ballroom. But it was evident that errand she had none. She stood there quietly surveying, almost as though she took a protracted and contemplative farewell, all unaware of the eyes of youth that spied upon her. Her glance roamed round, with satisfaction, I thought, but whether with satisfaction at the beauty of the room, or at having kept off for so long the tides that threatened to invade it, I could not tell.

Then, as she stood there, the clocks in the room began to strike the hour. There were thirty clocks in the room—I had often counted them—big clocks, little clocks, wall clocks, table clocks, grandfather clocks, and even a clock with a musical box in its intestines; and it was a point of honour with Baptiste that they should all strike at the same moment. So now they began; first the deep note of the buhl clock in the corner, then the clear ring of a little Cupid hitting a hammer on a bell, then a rumble and a note like a mastiff baying, then a gay trill, then the first bars of a chime, then innumerable others all joining in, till the room was filled with the music of the passing hour, and my great-grandmother standing in the middle, listening, listening. . . . I could see her face, for her head was lifted, and her expression was a thing I shall never forget, so suddenly lighted up was it; so pleased; so gallant; so, even, amused. She had, I think, her private joke and understanding with the clocks. The little flames of the candles quivered in the vibration of the air, but as the last notes died away they steadied again, like a life which has

(117)

wavered for an instant, only to resume with a strengthened purpose. And as the silence fluttered down once more, my great-grandmother drooped from her strange, humorous ecstasy, and it was as a little figure bent and tired that I saw her retrace her steps down the long vista of the lighted rooms.

Lambert Orme

❦ SIR HAROLD NICOLSON ❧

Sir Harold Nicolson (1886–1961) was an English diplomat, historian and biographer and the husband of Victoria Sackeville-West. *Lambert Orme* is a chapter from *Some People* (1927), a collection of semi-fictional character studies of persons whom Nicolson knew in his childhood and early youth. The description of the central character is an exact portrait of Ronald Firbank, although the latter never went to Oxford. Nicolson met him in Madrid in 1910 and again in Constantinople. The incidents of the ride in Spain and of the sail up the Bosphorus are true. Firbank, however, did not have the love affair described, nor did he die in the war. The "untidy man" at the Bloomsbury party was Maynard Keynes, and the lady "whom, from a distance, I had so much admired," Lady Ottoline Morrell. The discussion of the two Tennyson books is funnier if one realizes that Nicolson was the author of the "other."

I

IT would be impossible, I feel, to actually be as decadent as Lambert looked. I split the infinitive deliberately, being in the first place no non-split diehard (oh, the admirable Mr. Fowler!), and desiring secondly to emphasise what was in fact the dominant and immediate consideration which Lambert evoked. I have met many men with wobbly walks, but I have never met a walk more wobbly than that of Lambert Orme. It was more than sinuous, it did more than undulate: it rippled. At each step a wave was started which passed upwards through his body, convexing his buttocks, concaving the small of his back, convexing again his slightly rounded shoulders, and working itself out in a backward swaying of the neck and head. This final movement passed off more rapidly than the initial undulations, with the resulting impression of a face upturned generally, but bowing at rhythmic intervals, as if a tired royalty or a camel slouching heavily along the road to Isfahan. At each inclination the lock of red-gold hair which shrouded the lowness of his brow would flop, and rise again, and then again would flop. He was a tall young man and he would bend his right knee laterally, his right foot resting upon an inward-pointing toe. He had retreating shoulders, a retreating fore-head, a retreating waist. The face itself was a curved face, a boneless face, a rather pink face, fleshy about the chin. His eyelashes were fair and fluttering; his lips were full. When he giggled, which he did with nervous frequency, his underlip would come to rest below his upper teeth. He held his cigarette between the index and the middle fingers, keeping them out-stretched together with the gesture of a male im-personator puffing at a cigar. His hands, rather damp on their inner side, gave the impression on their outer side of being double-jointed. He dressed simply, wearing an opal pin, and a velours hat tilted angularly. He had a peculiar way of speaking: his sentences came in little splashing pounces; and then from time to time he would hang on to a word as if to steady himself: he would say "Simplytooshatter-ing FOR words," the phrase being a slither with a wild clutch at the banister of "for." He was very shy.

I had not met nor noticed Lambert Orme during my first term at Oxford, but in the Easter vacation he came out to Madrid with a letter of introduction to my people. They asked him to luncheon. I eyed him with sullen disapproval. He stood for none of the things which I had learnt at Wellington. Clearly he was not my sort. He had the impudence to announce that he had resolved to devote himself to art, music and literature. "Before I am twenty-one," he said, "I shall have painted a good picture, written a novel, and composed a waltz." He pronounced it *valse*. My gorge rose within me. I refused during the whole course of luncheon to speak to Lambert Orme. And yet behind my indignation vibrated a little fibre of curiosity. Or was it more than curiosity? I hope that it was something more. Subsequently I was reproved by my mother for my behaviour. She said in the first place that I should have better manners. In the second place she said that I was little more than a Philistine. And in the third place she said that she was sure that poor boy wasn't very strong.

It interests me to recapture my own frame of mind at the time of this my first meeting with Lambert Orme. It amuses me to look back upon the block of intervening years in which I also aped æstheticism, toyed with the theory that I also could become an intellectual. Have I returned after all these garish wanderings to the mood which descended upon me that afternoon in the dark and damask dining-room at Madrid? No, I have not returned. It is true that some faint and tattered fibres of heartiness do still mingle with my ageing nerves. I *have* my Kipling side. But I can at least admit to-day that Orme was in several ways a serious person. And I have been told by people whose opinion I would not dare to disregard that such was indeed the case.

II

The immediate result of my mother's lecture was that I promised to take the fellow for a ride. At the back of my mind (but not I fear so very far at the back) was a desire to humiliate Lambert, a quite caddish desire on my part to show off. I sent the horses to the entrance of the Casa de Campo and drove down there with Lambert in a cab. He mounted his horse and remained there with surprising firmness, and, moreover, with an elegance which shamed the clumsiness of my own arrant style. His languid manner dropped from him; if his back curved slightly it was but with a hellenic curve, the forward-seat of some Panathenaic rider. I was at pains to readjust my conception of him to this altered angle. We rode out under the avenues to where the foot-hills look back to the façade of the palace chalk-white against the smoke above the town: in front, the ramparts of the Guadarrama were jagged with pinnacles of snow. The larks rose from clumps of broom and lavender: a thousand larks above us: a shrill overtone under the crisp spring sky; and from west to east a flock of April clouds trailed rapidly, pushing in front of them patches of scudding shade. The feeling of that afternoon is now upon me: I see no reason to become sentimental about it: even in our most intimate period

Lambert Orme possessed for me no emotional significance: yet I recognise that on that afternoon the sap began to mount within me. That, and the summer evening in Dr. Pollock's garden, are my first two dates.

Not that Lambert said very much. I feel indeed that he was actually unconscious of my existence. He was thinking probably of Albert Samain and of Henri de Régnier, of how pleasant it was, that spring day, among the uplands of Castille. I said: "Over there—you may see it if he sun strikes—is the Escorial." He said, "Yes, I see." I said, "And Aranjuez is over there," pointing vaguely towards Toledo. He turned his head in the direction indicated. "And Segovia?" he asked. I was not very certain about Segovia, but I nodded northwards. "La Granja," I added, "is quite close to it—really only a few miles." We turned our horses, and the wind and sun were behind us. The smoke of the town billowed into sharp layers, an upward layer of white smoke hanging against a sweep of grey smoke, in its turn backed by a crinkled curtain of black. The sun and snow-wind behind us lit and darkened this grisaille. "Oh!" I exclaimed, "what an El Greco sky!" It was an opening. He could have taken it had he wished. He merely said, "Does the King live in the palace? Is he there now?" I answered that he was.

We crossed the Manzanares, where there were women washing white sheets. They beat them against the boulders. The palace above us was turning pink against the sunset. Lambert asked me to tea. I gave my horse to the groom and walked round with him to the rooms he had taken near the Opera House. It was some sort of pension, and he had characteristically caused the walls to be distempered with a light buff wash, and had arranged the room with red silk, and walnut furniture, and two large gilt candelabra from a church. He was very rich. Upon his writing-table lay a ruled sheet of music-manuscript, and upon another table some paint-brushes and tubes of water-colour. He had painted a little picture of an infanta in what I now realise to have been the manner of Brabazon. It was rather good. There were a great many cushions and several French books. He became artificial again when he entered his rooms and his voice slithered and he ordered tea in highly irritating French. There was a sheet of vellum lying near the fireplace on which, in an upright scribble, Lambert had written: "Mon âme est une infante . . ." and then again "Mon âme est . . ." and then, very calligraphically, "en robe de parade." It was cold in his room and he lit the logs in the fire. He then threw incense on it, and a puff of scented smoke billowed beyond the grate. My antagonism returned to me.

Lambert thereafter became very foolish about the tea. He did hostess: his gestures were delicate: there was a tea-cloth which was obviously his own. I lit my pipe and said I must be going. He picked up a book at random: I really believe it was at random. He said, "Would you like to take this?" I said I would. It was the *Jardin de Bérénice*. I suppose that, really, is what dates the occasion.

·III

When I returned to Oxford I visited Lambert in his rooms at Magdalen, drawn by an attraction which I should have hesitated to admit. They were in the new buildings and looked out upon the deer park: as one sipped one's Malaga, one could hear the stags barking amorously underneath the trees. His sitting-room was exquisitely decorated. When I think of that room I am again convinced that there was something *cabotin* about Lambert Orme: people at the age of twenty should not have rooms like that. He had painted it a shiny black: there were grey sofas with petunia cushions: there was a Coromandel cabinet with blue china on the top and some hard-stone stuff inside. It was not in the least like the room of an undergraduate: it made me at first rather ashamed of my own room with its extracts from "the hundred best pictures," its photograph of the charioteer of Delphi, and its kettle-holder with the Balliol arms: it made me, in the end, like my own room very much indeed. And yet inevitably I was entranced by that little *gîte* (I use the correct word) at Magdalen: by the firelight flickering upon the yellow books: by the Manet reproductions, by the Sobranye cigarettes in their china box. Lambert possessed even in those days a collection of curious literature, and I would sit there after dinner reading *Justine,* or the novels of M. Achille d'Essebac, or even *Under the Hill.* All this, I feel sure, was admirable training. My early oats I find were singularly tame. But they were oats none the less. Lambert at the time was writing his novel *Désiré de St. Aldegonde.* He would read me passages which I

failed entirely to understand. They were in the style, curiously
enough, of M. Maeterlinck: a style which, in English, tastes like
bananas and cream. The book was published some time in 1910 by
the Bodley Head. It attracted no attention whatever. And when
Lambert, under the influence of M. Guillaume Appollinaire, came
to adopt his second manner, he bought up the remaining copies of
Désiré and burnt them on the rocks at Polperro.

It was all very pleasant and seductive my dropping down like that
to Magdalen; but it became a little awkward when Lambert, in his
velours hat, would climb the hill to visit me at Balliol. In any case, I
never learnt to cope with Balliol until after I had left it: my real
Oxford friends were only made when I met them again in after life.
The effect of Balliol upon my development was salutary and over-
powering. But it didn't work at the time. On looking back at Balliol
I realise that during those three years I was wholly abominable. That
Balliol should have shared this opinion indicates its admirable sense.
But although I had at that time but little conception of what Balliol
was thinking, yet I realised quite definitely that they would not, that
they did not, approve of Lambert at all. I cannot therefore say that I
relished his visits. My sitting-room with its grained wood walls looked
somewhat squalid at his entry: the rep sofa, the brass reading lamp
with its torn red shade, that other light hanging naked but for a glass
reflector: the inadequate books: Stubbs' charters, Smith's classical
dictionary, Liddell and Scott—none of that crystalline glitter of those
rooms at Magdalen. My scout would burst in with his cap on, and
bang the chipped plates beside the fire: the tin covers rattled. The
kettle also rattled internally when one poured it out. There was
always a little coal inside the kettle. The spout of the tea-pot spouted
diagonally owing to a slight abrasion. The cloth was stained and bore
in place of embroidery my name in marking ink. There were buttered
buns and anchovy toast. Lambert ate them gingerly.

"I wish," I said to him, being incensed by the refinement of his
attitude, "that you wouldn't wear a hat."

"But if I didn't," he giggled, "I might be taken for an undergraduate."

"But at least not that hat, and at least not at that angle."

"Now don't be tahsome."

There were moments when I hated Lambert. It is a mystery to me how Magdalen tolerated him for so long. The end came, as was inevitable, after a bumper supper. I never knew what they did to Lambert: I know only that he escaped in his Daimler never to return. I missed him for a bit, and then I was glad of his departure. I realised that I had been tarred a little by his brush. I mentioned the matter, rather tentatively, to Sligger Urquhart. He seemed to have no particular feeling for Lambert either for or against: he pouted for a moment, and then said that he had found him "absurdly childish." I do not suppose that that remark was intended to be very penetrating: I know only that it penetrated me like a lance. The angle from which I had begun to regard Lambert Orme was shifted suddenly: it ceased to be an ascending angle and became in the space of a few seconds a descending angle: I had begun, in a way, to look up to Lambert: I now, quite suddenly and in every way, found myself looking down. A few days later Sligger, most subtle of dons, presented me with a copy of *Marius the Epicurean*. I found it on my table when I came back from the river: there was a note inside saying, "I think you had better read this": and on the fly-leaf he had written "H.N. from F.F.U." By this homœopathic treatment I was quickly cured. And yet this false start, if it was a false start, left me troubled and uncertain. I remained uncertain for several months.

IV

As so often in such cases, my ensuing reaction against the eighteen-nineties took the form of a virulent loathing which I have never since been able to shake off. I am assured by reliable people that it was a serious movement of revolt and liberation: I can see for myself that the Yellow Book group were all extremely kind and made jokes which, at the time, were found amusing: I am prepared to respect, but I cannot like them. The whole business is too reminiscent of those puzzled and uncertain months at Oxford. It takes me straight back to that room at Magdalen: "Now listen to this, it's too too wonderful: it's really too much fun." I have a sense of many little wheels revolving brightly but devoid of cogs. I have a sense predominantly of the early Lambert Orme.

I did not see him again for some five years. He went round the world and sent me a postcard from Yokohama. He was immensely impressed by the beauty of American cities, and it was from them, I think, that he first learnt to see life as a system of correlated planes. It was several years, however, before his very real and original talent for association was able finally to cast the slough of symbolism. When I next met him he was still intensively concerned with the relation between things and himself: it was only in his final period that he became predominantly interested in the relation of things towards each other. His talent, which though singularly receptive was not very muscular, had failed to extract any interesting synthesis from the confrontation of the universe with his own twitching heart: he had tried, and he had failed, to interpret conscious cognition by a single simple emotion. But in his later period he did in fact succeed in conveying an original analysis, implicit rather than expressed, of the diversity and interrelation of external phenomena: he was able to suggest a mood of sub-conscious perplexity sensitive to unapparent affinities. The conception of life as a repetition of self-contained and finite entities can be integrated only by the pressure of a compelling imagination: Lambert's imagination though mobile was not compelling: I suspect indeed that less power is required to disintegrate such entities, to suggest a world of atoms fortuitously whirling into certain shapes, to indicate a tremendous unknown, quivering below the crust of our convention. His later poetry succeeded because of its reference to this unapparent reality. I am now assured that some of his later poems were very respectable.

Meanwhile, however, Lambert Orme continued to represent for me something "absurdly childish"; his attitude of mind struck me as undeveloped and out of date. He was obsessed by false claims. He was no longer, not in any sense, a guide: he was just someone who rather uninterestingly had wandered off. The circumstances of our meeting, five years after he had escaped from Magdalen, confirmed me in this opinion. It made me very angry with Lambert Orme, and when I think of it to-day I become angry again.

He came to Constantinople on his way back from Egypt. He left a note saying that he had "descended" at the Pera Palace and would like to see me. I was interested to hear from him again, and told him to come to the Embassy at 9.30 the next morning and I would take him sailing up the Bosphorus. I had a sailing boat in those days, a perilous little affair, which I called the *Elkovan*. I had bought it in a moment of optimism, imagining that I would sail daily out into the Marmora, and that on Sundays I would go for longer expeditions to Ismid and Eregli and the Gulf of Cyzikos. But in practice the thing became a bore. The current which streamed out from the Black Sea permitted no such liberty of movement. I ascertained that if I followed the current I should be unable, when the wind fell at sunset, to return. So I would tack painfully against the stream, gaining but a mile or so in as many hours, and then I would swing round and float back rapidly while the minarets showed their black pencils against the setting sun. This pastime became monotonous; it was only on those rare occasions when the south wind blew strongly that one derived the impression of sailing at all. The Sunday on which I had invited Lambert Orme to accompany me was one of these occasions. A spring day opened before me, enlivened by warm gusts of the Bithynian wind—the wind which the Byzantines to this day call *νότος*: I ordered a large and excellent luncheon; with luck we should get out beyond Kavak and into the Black Sea. We might bathe even. I looked forward to my day with pleasure.

I waited for Lambert Orme. At 10.0 a man brought me a note in his neat hellenic writing. "Today is too wonderful," he wrote, "it is the most wonderful day that ever happened: it would be too much for me: let us keep to-day as something marvellous that did not occur." I dashed furiously round to his hotel, but he had already left with his courier to visit the churches. I scribbled "Silly ass" on my card and left it for him. I then sailed up the Bosphorus indignant and alone. When I returned my servant met me with a grin: my sitting-room was banked with Madonna lilies. "C'est un Monsieur," he said, "qui vous a apporté tout ça." "Quel Monsieur?" "Un Monsieur qui porte le chapeau de travers."

V

I thereafter and for many years dismissed Lambert from my mind. As a person he really did not seem worth the bother, as an intellect he was absurdly childish—he represented the rotted roseleaves of the Yellow Book. I came to be more and more ashamed of the period when I also had dabbled in æstheticism, a feeling of nausea came over me when I thought of the Malaga and cigarettes in that expensive room at Magdalen. Lambert represented a lapse.

I do not to-day regard him as a lapse. He was inconvenient doubtless and did me external harm. But he represented my first contact with the literary mind. I see now that my untutored self required some such stimulant: that it should have been Grand Marnier and not some decent brandy is immaterial: he provided an impetus at the very moment when the wheels hesitated to revolve. Balliol was all very well, and Sligger Urquhart at least understood and assisted, but my palate was, in fact, too insensitive for so matured a vintage. I therefore look on Lambert, in retrospect, as a short cut. What I failed to realise was the possibility that Lambert also might grow up. His later method, that obtuse angle from which he came to regard life, would, had I realised it, have been an even shorter cut and to more interesting objectives. But once I had discarded him, I did so with no reservations. I thought that any resumption of his influence would entail a retrogression: I failed in my stupidity to see that he had once again sprung ahead of me: and while I dabbled in Bakst and Flecker, Lambert had already reached the van.

As I write of this period, its atmosphere of diffident uncertainty descends upon me. I wish to convey some sharp outline of Lambert Orme, but it all results in a fuzz of words. I am still quite unaware whether I regard Lambert as ridiculous, as tragic, or as something legendary. A section of me is prepared to take him seriously, to read with admiration those of his poems which I am told are good. Another, and less reputable section, wishes to deride Lambert, to hold him up to obloquy. And yet another section feels rather soppy about him, simply because he died in the war. Which is, of course, absurd. Physically he is definite enough. I can see him again, as at our next meeting, sinuously descending the steps of the National Gallery. A day in late October with the cement around the fountains glistening from the damp of fog. A stream of traffic past Morley's Hotel, another stream past the shop of Mr. Dent, a river of traffic down Whitehall. And in the centre, that ungainly polygon, doves and urchins and orange-peel, and a sense of uncloistered quiet. It was the autumn of 1913: he had abandoned his velours, which since our Oxford days had become the head-gear of the proletariate: he wore instead a black

Borsalino which he had purchased while studying baroque at Ancona. But still he wilted: he wilted when I accosted him: he entered the Café Royal with a peculiarly self-conscious undulation which made me shy.

He still employed the old vocabulary (he said that I had been "very tahsome" at Constantinople), but his whole angle had shifted. The former avid subjectivity was leaving him, he was far less excited: his interest in life was no less passionate but had come under some form of control: predominantly he was interested in the sort of things that had never interested him before. He was in love with the wife of the Rumanian Military Attaché at Brussels. He talked about it quite simply as if he had always been a sensualist. He had decided to live in Paris, and had, in fact, already bought a house at Neuilly: he would write and collect pictures, and see to his own education: once a month he would go to Brussels for love and inspiration. He had evolved a not uninteresting theory of the necessity of living in a mechanical framework: at Neuilly the externals of his life were to be organised according to the strictest time-table: every day was in all material respects to be identical with every other day: this rhythmic repetition would in the end produce a background of symmetry against which all new experience would acquire a more intense significance, would assume the proportions of a physical displacement. The eighteen-nineties and the nineteen hundreds (he spoke of them in a detached and objective manner) had failed because they dissipated their emotions: they were unable either to concentrate or to select. Their system of life was garish and dispersed: his own system, out at Neuilly, would be a monochrome and concentric: he would limit his emotions: he would achieve a pattern rather than an arabesque. I suggested that so artificial a system of detachment might in itself be limiting. He was unexpectedly sensible about it all: he said that he realised that his system could only be an experiment, that even if successful it might be suitable only for himself. But he was quite determined. And ten months later, in July of 1914, he published *Lay Figures,* which, with his book of war poems, places him in a perfectly definite position. There is something very mean in me which resents this position. I am not myself very convinced by it. But it is recognised by people whose judgment I am honestly quite unable to ignore.

VI

At moments, in the roar and rattle of the early stages of the war, I would reflect a little grimly on the collapse of Lambert's symmetry, on those cobweb time-tables swept aside unnoticed in the onrush of the maddened beast. He sent me a copy of *Lay Figures* which reached me in the early days of August and which remained unopened for many years. Until the spring of 1916 he stayed at Paris, justifying his existence by a little hospital-work, writing those poems which figure as "mes hôpitaux" in his war volume. And then in March he crossed over to England and joined the army. He came to see me before he left for France. He did not look as odd in his uniform as I had expected: he talked voraciously about the new movements in French literature and in a way which I failed entirely to understand: of his training down at Salisbury he said little, giggling feebly when I asked him about it, telling me "not to be morbid" when I pressed for details. I could see no signs of any alteration in his physique: a little fatter in the face, perhaps, a little more fleshy round the jaw; but he still wilted, and his walk was as self-conscious as ever. I asked him if he was afraid of Flanders, whether the prospect of the trenches, alarmed him as much as it alarmed me. He said that he dreaded the rats, and was afraid of mines. "You see," he said, "it is the evitable or the wholly unexpected that is horrible. The rest is largely mechanical. It becomes a question of masochism. I certainly shall not mind the rest." I thought at the time he was being optimistic, but I have since met a man in the Anglo-Persian Oil Company who was with Lambert both in France and Mesopotamia. "Oh, no," this man said to me, "he was a quiet sort of fellow, Orme. And he had a violent temper. But he was rather a good regimental officer: he put up a good show, I remember, at Sheikh Sa'ad. A very good show. We liked him on the whole."

Sheikh Sa'ad and Magdalen, that Coromandel cabinet, those bleached and ochre flats—Lambert himself would have savoured these contrasts: it was the sort of thing by which his rather dulled sense of humour would have been aroused. Was it aroused, I wondered, as he lay in the hospital ship at Basrah dying of dysentery? I like to think that it may perhaps have been aroused. He had dignity and courage: I expect he giggled slightly when they told him that he was unlikely to survive.

I heard of his death as I was running, late from luncheon, down the Duke of York's steps. I met a man coming up the steps who had been at Oxford with us. "You have heard," he said, "that Orme has died in Mesopotamia?" I walked on towards the Foreign Office feeling very unheroic, very small. I had no sense, at the moment, of wastage—that sorrow which oppresses us to-day when we think back upon the war. I had no sense of pity even, feeling, as I have said, that so startling an incongruity would have illumined Lambert's courage with a spasm of amusement. I merely felt exhausted by this further appeal to the emotions: a sense of blank despair that such announcements should have ceased to evoke any creditable emotional response: a sense of the injustice of my sheltered lot: a sense of numbed dissatisfaction: a revolting sense of relief that it hadn't been me.

VII

In the summer of 1925 I went to a party in Bloomsbury. I went with much diffidence, alarmed at entering the Areopagus of British culture. They treated me with distant but not unfriendly courtesy. The fact that, through no fault of my own, I was in evening dress increased the gulf between us. I sidled to the back of the room, hoping to remain unobserved. There was a curious picture on the wall which I studied attentively, trying to extract some meaning from its doubtless significant contours. My host came up to me. "What," I asked, "is that supposed to represent?" Had I been less unstrung I should not, of course, have asked that question. My host winced slightly and moved away. I turned towards the book-shelves, searching in vain for the friendly bindings of one of mine own books. They were all talking about a sculptor called Brancousi. I pulled out a copy of Hugh Faussett's *Tennyson* and began to read. An untidy man came up to me and glanced over my shoulder. He had eyes of great kindness and penetration, and he adopted towards me a manner which suggested that I either had said, or was about to say, something extremely interesting. I asked him whether he had read the book and

he answered that he had, and that he felt it was so far more intelligent than the other one that had been published simultaneously.
I agreed that it was, it was. He then moved away, and I put the
book back tidily in its place. On the shelf above it were some volumes
of poetry, and among them Lambert Orme's *Lay Figures* which I had
never read. I opened it with suddenly awakened interest, and began
to turn the pages. My eye was arrested by a heading: "Constantinople:
April 1912." I sat down on the floor at that, and began to read.
"Thera" I read:

> "Thera, if it indeed be you
> That are Santorin,
> There wander in,
> The furtive steamers of the Khedivial Mail Company,
> Rusted, barnacled,
> And from the bridge the second officer
> Shouts demotic to the Company's agent
> Bobbing alpaca in a shore boat.
>
> Thera, if it indeed be you,
> That are Santorin,
> You will fully understand
> This my cleansing—
> At which he leant forward and pulled a rope towards him,
> And the yacht sidled cross-ways,
> At an angle,
> 'That,' he said (he was a man of obtuse sensibilities)
> 'Is Bebek.' "

It went on like this through several stanzas, and conveyed in its
final effect a not unconvincing picture of the poet sailing somewhat
absent-mindedly up the Bosphorus in a little white boat, accompanied,
as he so often repeated, by a man of obtuse sensibilities. I was a little
wounded by this posthumous revelation, and put the book down for
a moment while I thought. After all, I thought, Lambert didn't
come. If he had come he mightn't have found me in the least obtuse.
I should never have said "That is Bebek." I should have waited till he
asked. And surely, coming back at sunset, and I so silent—surely if he

had come, the poem would have been a little less personal. My host was searching in the book-case behind me, and the rest of the room were in suspense about something, evidently waiting for him to illustrate his discourse. "I know," he said, "it's here somewhere—I was only reading it last night. They want to do a new edition of both books together—both *Lay Figures* and the *War Poems*." I held the book up to him and he took it from me, a little curtly perhaps, anxious to regain his seat and to continue the discussion. "You see," he continued, "there is no doubt that Orme was a real pioneer in his way. Of course his stuff was crude enough and he had little sense of balance. But take this, for instance——' He began to turn the pages. "Yes. Here it is. Now this is written in 1912. It describes him sailing up the river at Constantinople with some local bore: there's really something in it. There really is." At this he adjusted the light, behind him, jerked himself back into his cushion, and began. "Thera," he began,

> "Thera, if it indeed be you
> That are Santorin. . . ."

He read the whole poem, and when it was finished they made him read it again. They then discussed the thing with appreciation, but with that avoidance of superlatives which so distinguishes their culture. The untidy man leant forward and knocked his pipe against the grate. "Yes, there is no doubt," he said, "that Orme, had he lived, would have been important. It is a pity in a way. He must have been an interesting man. Did you ever meet him?" He was addressing my host: he was not addressing me.

"No," my host answered; "he lived in Paris I believe. I've never met anyone who knew him."

The lady, whom, from a distance, I had so much admired, was sitting in the chair in front of me. She turned round and, for the first time, spoke to me. "Mr. Nicholls," she said, "would you mind opening one of the windows? It is getting hot in here."

I did as I was told.

Incident in Azania

❧ EVELYN WAUGH ❧

EVELYN WAUGH (1903–1968) made his name in England in the early
1920s with his satires of post-World War I London society. In *Decline
and Fall* and *Vile Bodies* he depicted the hilarious, if at times terrifying
world of witty and charming aristocrats who have lost their old values
but who continue to honor the old forms for whatever snobbish satisfaction they may still offer. In 1930 Waugh became converted to Roman
Catholicism which brought a different and more serious preoccupation
to his still satirical fiction.

In his introductory paragraph to this story, Evelyn Waugh wrote:
"Azania is a large, imaginary island off the East Coast of Africa; in
character and history a combination of Zanzibar and Abyssinia. At the
end of *Black Mischief* the native administration was overthrown and a
joint protectorate established by the British and French. Several of the
characters in this story appeared in *Black Mischief*."

I

THE Union Club at Matodi was in marked contrast to the hillside, bungalow dwellings of the majority of its members. It stood
in the centre of the town, on the water front; a seventeenth-century
Arab mansion built of massive whitewashed walls round a small court;
latticed windows overhung the street from which, in former times,
the womenfolk of a great merchant had watched the passing traffic;
a heavy door, studded with brass bosses gave entrance to the dark
shade of the court, where a little fountain sprayed from the roots of
an enormous mango; and an open staircase of inlaid cedar-wood led
to the cool interior.

An Arab porter, clothed in a white gown scoured and starched like a Bishop's surplice, crimson sash and tarboosh, sat drowsily at the gate. He rose in reverence as Mr. Reppington, the magistrate, and Mr. Bretherton, the sanitary-inspector, proceeded splendidly to the bar.

In token of the cordiality of the Condominium, French officials were honorary members of the Club, and a photograph of a former French President ("We can't keep changing it," said Major Lepperidge, "every time the frogs care to have a shimozzle") hung in the smoking room opposite the portrait of the Prince of Wales; except on Gala nights, however, they rarely availed themselves of their privilege. The single French journal to which the Club subscribed was *La Vie Parisienne,* which, on this particular evening, was in the hands of a small man of plebeian appearance, sitting alone in a basket chair.

Reppington and Bretherton nodded their way forward. "Evening, Grainger." "Evening, Barker." "Evening, Jagger," and then in an audible undertone Bretherton inquired, "Who's the chap in the corner with *La Vie?*"

"Name of Brooks. Petrol or something."

"Ah."

"Pink Gin?"

"Ah."

"What sort of day?"

"Bad show, rather. Trouble about draining the cricket field. No subsoil."

"Ah. Bad show."

The Goan barman put their drinks before them. Bretherton signed the chit.

"Well, cheerioh."

"Cheerioh."

Mr. Brooks remained riveted upon *La Vie Parisienne.*

Presently Major Lepperidge came in, and the atmosphere stiffened a little. (He was O.C. of the native levy, seconded from India.)

"Evening, Major," from civilians. "Good evening, sir," from the military.

"Evening. Evening. Evening. Phew. Just had a very fast set of lawner with young Kentish. Hot service. Gin and lime. By the way, Bretherton, the cricket field is looking pretty seedy."

"I know. No subsoil."

"I say, that's a bad show. *No subsoil.* Well, do what you can, there's a good fellow. It looks terrible. Quite bare and a great lake in the middle."

The Major took his gin and lime and moved towards a chair; suddenly he saw Mr. Brooks, and his authoritative air softened to unaccustomed amiability. "Why, hallo, Brooks," he said. "How are you? Fine to see you back. Just had the pleasure of seeing your daughter at the tennis club. My missus wondered if you and she would care to come up and dine one evening. How about Thursday? Grand. She'll be delighted. Good-night you fellows. Got to get a shower."

The occurrence was sensational. Bretherton and Reppington looked at one another in shocked surprise.

Major Lepperidge, both in rank and personality, was the leading man in Matodi—in the whole of Azania indeed, with the single exception of the Chief Commissioner at Debra Dowa. It was inconceivable that Brooks should dine with Lepperidge. Bretherton himself had only dined there once and *he* was Government.

"Hullo, Brooks," said Reppington. "Didn't see you there behind your paper. Come and have one."

"Yes, Brooks," said Bretherton. "Didn't know you were back. Have a jolly leave? See any shows?"

"It's very kind of you, but I must be going. We arrived on Tuesday in the *Ngoma*. No, I didn't see any shows. You see, I was down at Bournemouth most of the time."

"One before you go."

"No really, thanks, I must get back. My daughter will be waiting. Thanks all the same. See you both later."

Daughter . . . ?

II

There were eight Englishwomen in Matodi, counting Mrs. Bretherton's two-year-old daughter; nine if you included Mrs. Macdonald (but no one *did* include Mrs. Macdonald who came from Bombay and betrayed symptoms of Asiatic blood. Besides, no one knew who Mr. Macdonald had been. Mrs. Macdonald kept an ill-frequented

pension on the outskirts of the town named "The Bougainvillea").
All who were of marriageable age were married; they led lives under
a mutual scrutiny too close and unremitting for romance. There were,
however, seven unmarried Englishmen, three in Government service,
three in commerce and one unemployed, who had fled to Matodi
from his creditors in Kenya. (He sometimes spoke vaguely of "plant-
ing" or "prospecting", but in the meantime drew a small remittance
each month and hung amiably about the Club and the tennis courts.)

Most of these bachelors were understood to have some girl at
home; they kept photographs in their rooms, wrote long letters regularly, and took their leave with hints that when they returned they
might not be alone. But they invariably were. Perhaps in precipitous
eagerness for sympathy they painted too dark a picture of Azanian
life; perhaps the Tropics made them a little addle-pated. . . .

Anyway, the arrival of Prunella Brooks sent a wave of excitement
through English society. Normally, as the daughter of Mr. Brooks,
oil company agent, her choice would have been properly confined to
the three commercial men—Mr. James, of the Eastern Exchange
Telegraph Company, and Messrs. Watson and Jagger, of the Bank—
but Prunella was a girl of such evident personal superiority, that in
her first afternoon at the tennis courts, as has been shown above, she
transgressed the shadow line effortlessly and indeed unconsciously,
and stepped straight into the inmost sanctuary, the Lepperidge bungalow.

She was small and unaffected, an iridescent blonde, with a fresh
skin, doubly intoxicating in contrast with the tanned and desiccated
tropical complexions around her; with rubbery, puppyish limbs and
a face which lit up with amusement at the most barren pleasantries;
an air of earnest interest in the opinions and experiences of all she
met; a natural *confidante*, with no disposition to make herself the
centre of a group, but rather to tackle her friends one by one, in their
own time, when they needed her; deferential and charming to the
married women; tender, friendly, and mildly flirtatious with the men;
keen on games but not so good as to shake masculine superiority; a
devoted daughter denying herself any pleasure that might impair the
smooth working of Mr. Brooks's home—"No, I *must* go now. I couldn't
let father come home from the Club and not find me there to greet
him"—in fact, just such a girl as would be a light and blessing in

any outpost of the Empire. It was very few days before all at Matodi were eloquent of their good fortune.

Of course, she had first of all to be examined and instructed by the matrons of the colony, but she submitted to her initiation with so pretty a grace that she might not have been aware of the dangers of the ordeal. Mrs. Lepperidge and Mrs. Reppington put her through it. Far away in the interior, in the sunless secret places, where a twisted stem across the jungle track, a rag fluttering to the bough of a tree, a fowl headless and full spread by an old stump marked the taboo where no man might cross, the Sakuya women chanted their primeval litany of initiation; here on the hillside the no less terrible ceremony was held over Mrs. Lepperidge's tea table. First the questions; disguised and delicate over the tea cake but quickening their pace as the tribal rhythm waxed high and the table was cleared of tray and kettle, falling faster and faster like ecstatic hands on the taut cow-hide, mounting and swelling with the first cigarette; a series of urgent, peremptory interrogations. To all this Prunella responded with docile simplicity. The whole of her life, upbringing and education were exposed, examined and found to be exemplary; her mother's death, the care of an aunt, a convent school in the suburbs which had left her with charming manners, a readiness to find the right man and to settle down with him whenever the Service should require it; her belief in a limited family and European education, the value of sport, kindness to animals, affectionate patronage of men.

Then, when she had proved herself worthy of it, came the instruction. Intimate details of health and hygiene, things every young girl should know, the general dangers of sex and its particular dangers in the Tropics; the proper treatment of the other inhabitants of Matodi, etiquette towards ladies of higher rank, the leaving of cards. . . . "Never shake hands with natives, however well educated they think themselves. Arabs are quite different, many of them very like gentlemen . . . no worse than a great many Italians, really . . . Indians, luckily, you won't have to meet . . . never allow native servants to see you in your dressing gown . . . and be very careful about curtains in the bathroom—natives peep . . . never walk in the side streets alone—in fact you have no business in them at all . . . never ride outside the compound alone. There have been several cases of bandits . . . an American missionary only last year, but he was some kind of non-Conformist . . . *We owe it to our men folk* to take no unnecessary risks . . . a band of brigands commanded by a Sakuya called Joab . . . the Major will soon clean him up when he gets the levy into better shape . . . they find their boots very uncomfortable at present . . . meanwhile it is a very safe rule to take a *man* with you *everywhere.* . . ."

III

And Prunella was never short of male escort. As the weeks passed it became clear to the watching colony that her choice had narrowed down to two—Mr. Kentish, assistant native commissioner, and Mr. Benson, second lieutenant in the native levy; not that she was not consistently charming to everyone else—even to the shady remittance man and the repulsive Mr. Jagger—but by various little acts of preference she made it known that Kentish and Benson were her favourites. And the study of their innocent romances gave a sudden new interest to the social life of the town. Until now there had been plenty of entertaining certainly—gymkhanas and tennis tournaments, dances and dinner parties, calling and gossiping, amateur opera and church bazaars—but it had been a joyless and dutiful affair. They knew what was expected of Englishmen abroad; they had to keep up appearances before the natives and their co-protectionists; they had to have something to write home about; so they sturdily went through the recurring recreations due to their station. But with Prunella's coming a new lightness was in the air; there were more parties and more dances and a point to everything. Mr. Brooks, who had never dined out before, found himself suddenly popular, and as his former exclusion had not worried him, he took his present vogue as a natural result of his daughter's charm, was pleased by it and mildly embarrassed. He realised that she would soon want to get married and faced with equanimity the prospect of his inevitable return to solitude.

Meanwhile Benson and Kentish ran neck and neck through the crowded Azanian spring and no one could say with confidence which was leading—betting was slightly in favour of Benson, who had supper dances with her at the Caledonian and the Polo Club Balls—

when there occurred the incident which shocked Azanian feeling to its core. Prunella Brooks was kidnapped.

The circumstances were obscure and a little shady. Prunella, who had never been known to infringe one jot or tittle of the local code, had been out riding alone in the hills. That was apparent from the first, and later, under cross-examination, her syce revealed that this had for some time been her practice, two or three times a week. The shock of her infidelity to rule was almost as great as the shock of her disappearance.

But worse was to follow. One evening at the Club, since Mr. Brooks was absent (his popularity had waned in the last few days and his presence made a painful restraint) the question of Prunella's secret rides was being freely debated, when a slightly fuddled voice broke into the conversation.

"It's bound to come out," said the remittance man from Kenya, "so I may as well tell you right away. Prunella used to ride with *me*. She didn't want us to get talked about, so we met on the Debra Dowa road by the Moslem Tombs. I shall miss those afternoons very much indeed," said the remittance man, a slight, alcoholic quaver in his voice, "and I blame myself to a great extent for all that has happened. You see, I must have had a little more to drink than was good for me that morning and it was very hot, so with one thing and another, when I went to change into riding breeches I fell asleep and did not wake up until after dinner time. And perhaps that is the last we shall ever see of her . . ." and two vast tears rolled down his cheeks.

This unmanly spectacle preserved the peace, for Benson and Kentish had already begun to advance upon the remittance man with a menacing air. But there is little satisfaction in castigating one who is already in the profound depths of self-pity and the stern tones of Major Lepperidge called them sharply to order. "Benson, Kentish, I don't say I don't sympathise with you boys and I know exactly what I'd do myself under the circumstances. The story we have just heard may or may not be the truth. In either case I think I know what we all feel about the teller. But that can wait. You'll have plenty of time to settle up when we've got Miss Brooks safe. That is our first duty."

Thus exhorted, public opinion again rallied to Prunella, and the urgency of her case was dramatically emphasised two days later by the arrival at the American Consulate of the Baptist missionary's right ear loosely done up in newspaper and string. The men of the colony—excluding, of course, the remittance man—got together in the Lepperidge bungalow and formed a committee of defence, first to protect the women who were still left to them and then to rescue Miss Brooks at whatever personal inconvenience or risk.

IV

The first demand for ransom came through the agency of Mr. Youkoumian. The little Armenian was already well known and, on the whole, well liked by the English community; it did them good to find a foreigner who so completely fulfilled their ideal of all that a foreigner should be. Two days after the foundation of the British Womanhood Protection Committee, he appeared at the major's orderly room asking for a private audience, a cheerful, rotund, self-abasing figure, in a shiny alpaca suit, skull cap and yellow, elastic-sided boots.

"Major Lepperidge," he said, "you know me; all the gentlemen in Matodi know me. The English are my favourite gentlemen and the natural protectors of the under races all same as the League of Nations. Listen, Major Lepperidge, I ear things. Everyone trusts me. It is a no good thing for these black men to abduct English ladies. I fix it O.K."

To the Major's questions, with infinite evasions and circumlocutions, Youkoumian explained that by the agency of various cousins of his wife he had formed contact with an Arab, one of whose wives was the sister of a Sakuya in Joab's band; that Miss Brooks was at present safe and that Joab was disposed to talk business. "Joab make very stiff price," he said. "He want one undred thousand dollars, an armoured car, two machine guns, a undred rifles, five thousand rounds of ammunition, fifty orses, fifty gold wrist watches, a wireless set, fifty cases of whisky, free pardon and the rank of honorary colonel in the Azanian levy."

"That, of course, is out of the question."

The little Armenian shrugged his shoulders. "Oh, well, then he cut off Miss Brooks's ears all same as the American clergyman. Listen, Major, this is one damn awful no good country. I live ere forty years,

I know. I been little man and I been big man in this country, all same rule for big and little. If native want anything you give it im quick, then work ell out of im and get it back later. Natives all damn fool men but very savage all same as animals. Listen, Major, I make best whisky in Matodi—Scotch, Irish, all brands I make im; I got very fine watches in my shop all same as gold, I got wireless set,—armoured car, orses, machine guns is for you to do. Then we clean up tidy bit fifty-fifty, no?"

V

Two days later Mr. Youkoumian appeared at Mr. Brooks's bungalow. "A letter from Miss Brooks," he said. "A Sakuya fellow brought it in. I give im a rupee."

It was an untidy scrawl on the back of an envelope.

Dearest Dad,
  I am safe at present and fairly well. On no account attempt to follow the messenger. Joab and the bandits would torture me to death. Please send gramophone and records. Do come to terms or I don't know what will happen.

  Prunella

It was the first of a series of notes which, from now on, arrived every two or three days through the agency of Mr. Youkoumian. They mostly contained requests for small personal possessions . . .

Dearest Dad,
  Not those records. The dance ones. . . . Please send face cream in pot in bathroom, also illustrated papers . . . the green silk pyjamas . . . Lucky Strike cigarettes . . . two light drill skirts and the sleeveless silk shirts . . .

The letters were all brought to the Club and read aloud, and as the days passed the sense of tension became less acute, giving way to a general feeling that the drama had become prosaic.

"They are bound to reduce their price. Meanwhile the girl is safe enough," pronounced Major Lepperidge, voicing authoritatively what had long been unspoken in the minds of the community.

The life of the town began to resume its normal aspect—administration, athletics, gossip; the American missionary's second ear arrived and attracted little notice, except from Mr. Youkoumian, who produced an ear trumpet which he attempted to sell to the mission headquarters. The ladies of the colony abandoned the cloistered life which they had adopted during the first scare; the men became less protective and stayed out late at the Club as heretofore.

Then something happened to revive interest in the captive. Sam Stebbing discovered the cypher.

He was a delicate young man of high academic distinction, lately arrived from Cambridge to work with Grainger in the immigration office. From the first he had shown a keener interest than most of his colleagues in the situation. For a fortnight of oppressive heat he had sat up late studying the texts of Prunella's messages; then he emerged with the startling assertion that there was a cypher. The system by which he had solved it was far from simple. He was ready enough to explain it, but his hearers invariably lost hold of the argument and contented themselves with the solution.

". . . you see you translate it into Latin, you make an anagram of the first and last words of the first message, the second and last but one of the third when you start counting from the centre onwards. I bet that puzzled the bandits . . ."

"Yes, old boy. Besides, none of them can read anyway . . ."

"Then in the fourth message you go back to the original system, taking the fourth word and the last but three . . ."

"Yes, yes, I see. Don't bother to explain any more. Just tell us what the message really says."

"It says, 'DAILY THREATENED WORSE THAN BREATH.'"

"Her system's at fault there, must mean 'death'; then there's a word I can't understand—PLZGF, no doubt the poor child was in great agitation when she wrote it, and after that TRUST IN MY KING."

This was generally voted a triumph. The husbands brought back the news to their wives.

". . . Jolly ingenious the way old Stebbing worked it out. I won't bother to explain it to you. You wouldn't understand. Anyway, the result is clear enough. Miss Brooks is in terrible danger. We must all do something."

"But who would have thought of little Prunella being so clever . . ."

"Ah, I always said that girl had brains."

VI

News of the discovery was circulated by the Press agencies throughout the civilised world. At first the affair had received wide attention. It had been front page, with portrait, for two days, then middle page with portrait, then middle page half way down without portrait, and finally page three of the *Excess* as the story became daily less alarming. The cypher gave the story a new lease on life. Stebbing, with portrait, appeared on the front page. Ten thousand pounds was offered by the paper towards the ransom, and a star journalist appeared from the skies in an aeroplane to conduct and report the negotiations.

He was a tough young man of Australian origin and from the moment of his arrival everything went with a swing. The colony sunk its habitual hostility to the Press, elected him to the Club, and filled his leisure with cocktail parties and tennis tournaments. He even usurped Lepperidge's position as authority on world topics.

But his stay was brief. On the first day he interviewed Mr. Brooks and everyone of importance in the town, and cabled back a moving "human" story of Prunella's position in the heart of the colony. From now onwards to three millions or so of readers Miss Brooks became Prunella. (There was only one local celebrity whom he was unable to meet. Poor Mr. Stebbing had "gone under" with the heat and had been shipped back to England on sick leave in a highly deranged condition of nerves and mind.)

On the second day he interviewed Mr. Youkoumian. They sat down together with a bottle of mastika at a little round table behind Mr. Youkoumian's counter at ten in the morning. It was three in the afternoon before the reporter stepped out into the white-dust heat, but he had won his way. Mr. Youkoumian had promised to conduct him to the bandits' camp. Both of them were pledged to secrecy. By sundown the whole of Matodi was discussing the coming expedition, but the journalist was not embarrassed by any inquiries; he was alone that evening, typing out an account of what he expected would happen next day.

He described the start at dawn . . . "grey light breaking over the bereaved township of Matodi . . . the camels snorting and straining at their reins . . . the many sorrowing Englishmen to whom the sun meant only the termination of one more night of hopeless watching . . . silver dawn breaking in the little room where Prunella's bed stood, the coverlet turned down as she had left it on the fatal afternoon . . ." He described the ascent into the hills——" . . . luxuriant tropical vegetation giving place to barren scrub and bare rock . . ." He described how the bandits' messenger blindfolded him and how he rode, swaying on his camel through darkness, into the unknown. Then, after what seemed an eternity, the halt; the bandage removed from his eyes . . . the bandits' camp. ". . . twenty pairs of remorseless eastern eyes glinting behind ugly-looking rifles . . ." here he took the paper from his machine and made a correction; the bandits' lair was to be in a cave ". . . littered with bone and skins." . . . Joab, the bandit chief, squatting in barbaric splendour, a jewelled sword across his knees. Then the climax of the story; Prunella bound. For some time he toyed with the idea of stripping her, and began to hammer out a vivid word-picture of her girlish frame shrinking in the shadows, Andromeda-like. But caution restrained him and he contented himself with ". . . her lovely, slim body marked by the hempen ropes that cut into her young limbs . . ." The concluding paragraphs related how despair suddenly melted to hope in her eyes as he stepped forward, handing over the ransom to the bandit chief and "in the name of the *Daily Excess* and the People of Great Britain restored her to her heritage of freedom."

It was late before he had finished, but he retired to bed with a sense of high accomplishment, and next morning deposited his manuscript with the Eastern Exchange Telegraph Company before setting out with Mr. Youkoumian for the hills.

The journey was in all respects totally unlike his narrative. They started, after a comfortable breakfast, surrounded by the well wishes of most of the British and many of the French colony, and instead of riding on camels they drove in Mr. Kentish's baby Austin. Nor did they even reach Joab's lair. They had not gone more than ten miles before a girl appeared walking alone on the track towards them. She was not very tidy, particularly about the hair, but, apart from this, showed every sign of robust well-being.

"Miss Brooks, I presume," said the journalist, unconsciously following a famous precedent. "But where are the bandits?"

Prunella looked inquiringly towards Mr. Youkoumian who, a few steps in the rear, was shaking his head with vigour. "This British newspaper writing gentleman," he explained, "e know all same Matodi gentlemen. E got the thousand pounds for Joab."

"Well, he'd better take care," said Miss Brooks, "the bandits are all round you. Oh you wouldn't see them, of course, but I don't mind betting that there are fifty rifles covering us at this moment from behind the boulders and bush and so on." She waved a bare, sun-tanned arm expansively towards the innocent-looking landscape. "I hope you've brought the money in gold."

"It's all here, in the back of the car, Miss Brooks."

"Splendid. Well, I'm afraid Joab won't allow you into his lair, so you and I will wait here, and Youkoumian shall drive into the hills and deliver it."

"But listen, Miss Brooks, my paper has put a lot of money into this story. I got to see that lair."

"I'll tell you all about it," said Prunella, and she did.

"There were three huts," she began, her eyes downcast, her hands folded, her voice precise and gentle as though she were repeating a lesson, "the smallest and the darkest was used as my dungeon."

The journalist shifted uncomfortably. "Huts," he said. "I had formed the impression that they were caves."

"So they were," said Prunella. "Hut is a local word for cave. Two lions were chained beside me night and day. Their eyes glared and I felt their foetid breath. The chains were of a length so that if I lay perfectly still I was out of their reach. If I had moved hand or foot . . ." She broke off with a little shudder . . .

By the time that Youkoumian returned, the journalist had material for another magnificent front page splash.

"Joab has given orders to withdraw the snipers," Prunella announced, after a whispered consultation with the Armenian. "It is safe for us to go."

So they climbed into the little car and drove unadventurously back to Matodi.

VII

Little remains of the story to be told. There was keen enthusiasm in the town when Prunella returned, and an official welcome was organised for her on the subsequent Tuesday. The journalist took many photographs, wrote up a scene of homecoming that stirred the British public to the depths of its heart, and soon flew away in his aeroplane to receive congratulation and promotion at the *Excess* office.

It was expected that Prunella would now make her final choice between Kentish and Benson, but this excitement was denied to the colony. Instead, came the distressing intelligence that she was returning to England. A light seemed to have been extinguished in Azanian life, and in spite of avowed good wishes there was a certain restraint on the eve of her departure—almost of resentment, as though Prunella were guilty of disloyalty in leaving. The *Excess* inserted a paragraph announcing her arrival, headed ECHO OF KIDNAPPING CASE, but otherwise she seemed to have slipped unobtrusively from public attention. Stebbing, poor fellow, was obliged to retire from the service. His mind seemed permanently disordered and from now on he passed his time, harmlessly but unprofitably, in a private nursing home, working out hidden messages in Bradshaw's Railway Guide. Even in Matodi the kidnapping was seldom discussed.

One day six months later Lepperidge and Bretherton were sitting in the Club drinking their evening glass of pink gin. Banditry was in the air at the moment for that morning the now memberless trunk of the American missionary had been found at the gates of the Baptist compound.

"It's one of the problems we shall have to tackle," said Lepperidge. "A case for action. I am going to make a report of the entire matter."

Mr. Brooks passed them on his way out to his lonely dinner table;

he was a rare visitor to the club now; the petrol agency was uniformly
prosperous and kept him late at his desk. He neither remembered nor
regretted his brief popularity, but Lepperidge maintained a guilty
cordiality towards him whenever they met.

"Evening, Brooks. Any news of Miss Prunella?"

"Yes, as a matter of fact I heard from her to-day. She's just been
married."

"Well I'm blessed . . . I hope you're glad. Anyone we know?"

"Yes, I am glad in a way, though of course I shall miss her. It's that
fellow from Kenya who stayed here once; remember him?"

"Ah, yes, him? Well, well . . . Give her my salaams when you
write."

Mr. Brooks went downstairs into the still and odorous evening.
Lepperidge and Bretherton were completely alone. The Major leant
forward and spoke in husky, confidential tones.

"I say, Bretherton," he said, "look here, there's something I've
often wondered, strictly between ourselves, I mean. Did you ever
think there was anything fishy about that kidnapping?"

"*Fishy,* sir?"

"Fishy."

"I think I know what you mean, sir. Well some of us *have* been
thinking, lately . . ."

"Exactly."

"Not of course anything definite. Just what you said yourself, sir,
fishy."

"Exactly . . . Look here, Bretherton, I think you might pass the
word round that it's not a thing to be spoken about, see what I mean?
The missus is putting it round to the women too . . ."

"Quite, sir. It's not a thing one wants talked about . . . Arabs, I
mean, and frogs."

"Exactly."

There was another long pause. At last Lepperidge rose to go. "I
blame myself," he said. "We made a great mistake over that girl. I
ought to have known better. After all, first and last when all's said
and done, Brooks *is* a commercial wallah."

Glory in the Daytime

✻ DOROTHY PARKER ✻

DOROTHY PARKER (1893–1967) started her literary career as drama
critic on *Vanity Fair* and later on *The New Yorker*. She spent many
years in Hollywood as a script writer. A few verses, a handful of short
stories and some quoted remarks have sufficed to make her America's
most famed and dreaded wit. *Glory in the Daytime* was published in
After Such Pleasures (1933).

M R. MURDOCK was one who carried no enthusiasm whatever
for plays and their players, and that was too bad, for they
meant so much to little Mrs. Murdock. Always she had been in a
state of devout excitement over the luminous, free, passionate elect
who serve the theater. And always she had done her wistful wor-
shiping, along with the multitudes, at the great public altars. It is
true that once, when she was a particularly little girl, love had im-
pelled her to write Miss Maude Adams a letter beginning "Dearest
Peter," and she had received from Miss Adams a miniature thimble
inscribed "A kiss from Peter Pan." (That was a day!) And once,
when her mother had taken her holiday shopping, a limousine door
was held open and there had passed her, as close as *that,* a wonder of
sable and violets and round red curls that seemed to tinkle on the
air; so, forever after, she was as good as certain that she had been not
a foot away from Miss Billie Burke. But until some three years after
her marriage, these had remained her only personal experiences with
the people of the lights and the glory.

Then it turned out that Miss Noyes, new come to little Mrs.
Murdock's own bridge club, knew an actress. She actually knew an

actress; the way you and I know collectors of recipes and members of garden clubs and amateurs of needlepoint.

The name of the actress was Lily Wynton, and it was famous. She was tall and slow and silvery; often she appeared in the role of a duchess, or of a Lady Pam or an Honorable Moira. Critics recurrently referred to her as "that great lady of our stage." Mrs. Murdock had attended, over years, matinee performances of the Wynton successes. And she had no more thought that she would one day have opportunity to meet Lily Wynton face to face than she had thought—well, than she had thought of flying!

Yet it was not astounding that Miss Noyes should walk at ease among the glamorous. Miss Noyes was full of depths and mystery, and she could talk with a cigarette still between her lips. She was always doing something difficult, like designing her own pajamas, or reading Proust, or modeling torsos in plasticine. She played excellent bridge. She liked little Mrs. Murdock. "Tiny one," she called her.

"How's for coming to tea tomorrow, tiny one? Lily Wynton's going to drop up," she said, at a therefore memorable meeting of the bridge club. "You might like to meet her."

The words fell so easily that she could not have realized their weight. Lily Wynton was coming to tea. Mrs. Murdock might like to meet her. Little Mrs. Murdock walked home through the early dark, and stars sang in the sky above her.

Mr. Murdock was already at home when she arrived. It required but a glance to tell that for him there had been no singing stars that evening in the heavens. He sat with his newspaper opened at the financial page, and bitterness had its way with his soul. It was not the time to cry happily to him of the impending hospitalities of Miss Noyes; not the time, that is, if one anticipated exclamatory sympathy. Mr. Murdock did not like Miss Noyes. When pressed for a reason, he replied that he just plain didn't like her. Occasionally he added, with a sweep that might have commanded a certain admiration, that all those women made him sick. Usually, when she told him of the temperate activities of the bridge club meetings, Mrs. Murdock kept any mention of Miss Noyes's name from the accounts. She had found that this omission made for a more agreeable evening. But now she was caught in such a sparkling swirl of excitement that she had scarcely kissed him before she was off on her story.

"Oh, Jim," she cried. "Oh, what do you think! Hallie Noyes asked me to tea tomorrow to meet Lily Wynton!"

"Who's Lily Wynton?" he said.

"Ah, Jim," she said. "Ah, really, Jim. Who's Lily Wynton! Who's Greta Garbo, I suppose!"

"She some actress or something?" he said.

Mrs. Murdock's shoulders sagged. "Yes, Jim," she said. "Yes. Lily Wynton's an actress."

She picked up her purse and started slowly toward the door. But before she had taken three steps, she was again caught up in her sparkling swirl. She turned to him, and her eyes were shining.

"Honestly," she said, "it was the funniest thing you ever heard in your life. We'd just finished the last rubber—oh, I forgot to tell you, I won three dollars, isn't that pretty good for me?—and Hallie Noyes said to me, 'Come on in to tea tomorrow. Lily Wynton's going to drop up,' she said. Just like that, she said it. Just as if it was anybody."

"Drop up?" he said. "How can you drop *up?*"

"Honestly, I don't know what I said when she asked me," Mrs. Murdock said. "I suppose I said I'd love to— I guess I must have. But I was so simply— Well, you know how I've always felt about Lily Wynton. Why, when I was a little girl, I used to collect her pictures. And I've seen her in, oh, everything she's ever been in, I should think, and I've read every word about her, and interviews and all. Really and truly, when I think of *meeting* her— Oh, I'll simply die. What on earth shall I say to her?"

"You might ask her how she'd like to try dropping down, for a change," Mr. Murdock said.

"All right, Jim," Mrs. Murdock said. "If that's the way you want to be."

Wearily she went toward the door, and this time she reached it before she turned to him. There were no lights in her eyes.

"It—it isn't so awfully nice," she said, "to spoil somebody's pleasure in something. I was so thrilled about this. You don't see what it is to me, to meet Lily Wynton. To meet somebody like that, and see what they're like, and hear what they say, and maybe get to know them. People like that mean—well, they mean something different to me. They're not like this. They're not like me. Who do I ever see? What do I ever hear? All my whole life, I've wanted to know—I've almost prayed that some day I could meet— Well. All right, Jim."

She went out, and on to her bedroom.

Mr. Murdock was left with only his newspaper and his bitterness for company. But he spoke aloud.

" 'Drop up!' " he said. " 'Drop *up*,' for God's sake!"

The Murdocks dined, not in silence, but in pronounced quiet. There was something straitened about Mr. Murdock's stillness; but little Mrs. Murdock's was the sweet, far quiet of one given over to dreams. She had forgotten her weary words to her husband, she had passed through her excitement and her disappointment. Luxuriously she floated on innocent visions of days after the morrow. She heard her own voice in future conversations. . . .

I saw Lily Wynton at Hallie's the other day, and she was telling me all about her new play—no, I'm terribly sorry, but it's a secret, I promised her I wouldn't tell anyone the name of it. . . . Lily Wynton dropped up to tea yesterday, and we just got to talking, and she told me the most interesting things about her life; she said she'd never dreamed of telling them to anyone else. . . . Why, I'd love to come, but I promised to have lunch with Lily Wynton. . . . I had a long, long letter from Lily Wynton. . . . Lily Wynton called me up this morning. . . . Whenever I feel blue, I just go and have a talk with Lily Wynton, and then I'm all right again. . . . Lily Wynton told me . . . Lily Wynton and I . . . "Lily," I said to her . . .

The next morning, Mr. Murdock had left for his office before Mrs. Murdock rose. This had happened several times before, but not often. Mrs. Murdock felt a little queer about it. Then she told herself that it was probably just as well. Then she forgot all about it, and gave her mind to the selection of a costume suitable to the afternoon's event. Deeply she felt that her small wardrobe included no dress adequate to the occasion; for, of course, such an occasion had never before arisen. She finally decided upon a frock of dark blue serge with fluted white muslin about the neck and wrists. It was her style, that was the most she could say for it. And that was all she could say for herself. Blue serge and little white ruffles—that was she.

The very becomingness of the dress lowered her spirits. A nobody's frock, worn by a nobody. She blushed and went hot when she recalled the dreams she had woven the night before, the mad visions of intimacy, of equality with Lily Wynton. Timidity turned her heart liquid, and she thought of telephoning Miss Noyes and saying she had a bad cold and could not come. She steadied, when she planned a course of conduct to pursue at teatime. She would not try to say anything; if she stayed silent, she could not sound foolish. She would listen and watch and worship and then come home, stronger, braver, better for an hour she would remember proudly all her life.

Miss Noyes's living-room was done in the early modern period. There were a great many oblique lines and acute angles, zigzags of aluminum and horizontal stretches of mirror. The color scheme was sawdust and steel. No seat was more than twelve inches above the floor, no table was made of wood. It was, as has been said of larger places, all right for a visit.

Little Mrs. Murdock was the first arrival. She was glad of that; no, maybe it would have been better to have come after Lily Wynton; no, maybe this was right. The maid motioned her toward the living-room, and Miss Noyes greeted her in the cool voice and the warm words that were her special combination. She wore black velvet trousers, a red cummerbund, and a white silk shirt, opened at the throat. A cigarette clung to her lower lip, and her eyes, as was her habit, were held narrow against its near smoke.

"Come in, come in, tiny one," she said. "Bless its little heart. Take off its little coat. Good Lord, you look easily eleven years old in that dress. Sit ye doon, here beside of me. There'll be a spot of tea in a jiff."

Mrs. Murdock sat down on the vast, perilously low divan, and, because she was never good at reclining among cushions, held her back straight. There was room for six like her, between herself and her hostess. Miss Noyes lay back with one ankle flung upon the other knee, and looked at her.

"I'm a wreck," Miss Noyes announced. "I was modeling like a mad thing, all night long. It's taken everything out of me. I was like a thing bewitched."

"Oh, what were you making?" cried Mrs. Murdock.

"Oh, Eve," Miss Noyes said. "I always do Eve. What else is there to do? You must come pose for me some time, tiny one. You'd be nice to do. Ye-es, you'd be very nice to do. My tiny one."

"Why, I—" Mrs. Murdock said, and stopped. "Thank you very much, though," she said.

"I wonder where Lily is," Mis Noyes said. "She said she'd be here early—well, she always says that. You'll adore her, tiny one. She's really rare. She's a real person. And she's been through perfect hell. God, what a time she's had!"

"Ah, what's been the matter?" said Mrs. Murdock.

"Men," Miss Noyes said. "Men. She never had a man that wasn't a louse." Gloomily she stared at the toe of her flat-heeled patent leather pump. "A pack of lice, always. All of them. Leave her for the first little floozie that comes along."

"But—" Mrs. Murdock began. No, she couldn't have heard right. How could it be right? Lily Wynton was a great actress. A great actress meant romance. Romance meant Grand Dukes and Crown Princes and diplomats touched with gray at the temples and lean, bronzed, reckless Younger Sons. It meant pearls and emeralds and chinchilla and rubies red as the blood that was shed for them. It meant a grim-faced boy sitting in the fearful Indian midnight, beneath the dreary whirring of the *punkahs,* writing a letter to the lady he had seen but once; writing his poor heart out, before he turned to the service revolver that lay beside him on the table. It meant a golden-locked poet, floating face downward in the sea, and in his pocket his last great sonnet to the lady of ivory. It meant brave, beautiful men, living and dying for the lady who was the pale bride of art, whose eyes and heart were soft with only compassion for them.

A pack of lice. Crawling after little floozies; whom Mrs. Murdock swiftly and hazily pictured as rather like ants.

"But—" said little Mrs. Murdock.

"She gave them all her money," Miss Noyes said. "She always did. Or if she didn't, they took it anyway. Took every cent she had, and then spat in her face. Well, maybe I'm teaching her a little bit of sense now. Oh, there's the bell—that'll be Lily. No, sit ye doon, tiny one. You belong there."

Miss Noyes rose and made for the archway that separated the living-room from the hall. As she passed Mrs. Murdock, she stooped suddenly, cupped her guest's round chin, and quickly, lightly kissed her mouth.

"Don't tell Lily," she murmured, very low.

Mrs. Murdock puzzled. Don't tell Lily what? Could Hallie Noyes think that she might babble to the Lily Wynton of these strange confidences about the actress's life? Or did she mean— But she had no more time for puzzling. Lily Wynton stood in the archway. There she stood, one hand resting on the wooden molding and her body swayed toward it, exactly as she stood for her third-act entrance of her latest play, and for a like half-minute.

You would have known her anywhere, Mrs. Murdock thought. Oh, yes, anywhere. Or at least you would have exclaimed, "That woman looks something like Lily Wynton." For she was somehow different in the daylight. Her figure looked heavier, thicker, and her face—there was so much of her face that the surplus sagged from the strong, fine bones. And her eyes, those famous dark, liquid eyes. They were dark, yes, and certainly liquid, but they were set in little hammocks of folded flesh, and seemed to be set but loosely, so readily did they roll. Their whites, that were visible all around the irises, were threaded with tiny scarlet veins.

"I suppose footlights are an awful strain on their eyes," thought little Mrs. Murdock.

Lily Wynton wore, just as she should have, black satin and sables, and long white gloves were wrinkled luxuriously about her wrists. But there were delicate streaks of grime in the folds of her gloves, and down the shining length of her gown there were small, irregularly shaped dull patches; bits of food or drops of drink, or perhaps both, sometime must have slipped their carriers and found brief sanctuary there. Her hat—oh, her hat. It was romance, it was mystery, it was strange, sweet sorrow; it was Lily Wynton's hat, of all the world, and no other could dare it. Black it was, and tilted, and a great, soft plume drooped from it to follow her cheek and curl across her throat. Beneath it, her hair had the various hues of neglected brass. But, oh, her hat.

"Darling!" cried Miss Noyes.

"Angel," said Lily Wynton. "My sweet."

It was that voice. It was that deep, soft, glowing voice. "Like purple velvet," someone had written. Mrs. Murdock's heart beat visibly.

Lily Wynton cast herself upon the steep bosom of her hostess, and murmured there. Across Miss Noyes's shoulder she caught sight of little Mrs. Murdock.

"And who is this?" she said. She disengaged herself.

"That's my tiny one," Miss Noyes said. "Mrs. Murdock."

"What a clever little face," said Lily Wynton. "Clever, clever little face. What does she do, sweet Hallie? I'm sure she writes, doesn't she? Yes, I can feel it. She writes beautiful, beautiful words. Don't you, child?"

"Oh, no, really I—" Mrs. Murdock said.

"And you must write me a play," said Lily Wynton. "A beautiful, beautiful play. And I will play in it, over and over the world, until I am a very, very old lady. And then I will die. But I will never be forgotten, because of the years I played in your beautiful, beautiful play."

She moved across the room. There was a slight hesitancy, a seeming insecurity, in her step, and when she would have sunk into a chair, she began to sink two inches, perhaps, to its right. But she swayed just in time in her descent, and was safe.

"To write," she said, smiling sadly at Mrs. Murdock, "to write. And such a little thing, for such a big gift. Oh, the privilege of it. But the anguish of it, too. The agony."

"But, you see, I—" said little Mrs. Murdock.

"Tiny one doesn't write, Lily," Miss Noyes said. She threw herself back upon the divan. "She's a museum piece. She's a devoted wife."

"A wife!" Lily Wynton said. "A wife. Your first marriage, child?"

"Oh, yes," said Mrs. Murdock.

"How sweet," Lily Wynton said. "How sweet, sweet, sweet. Tell me, child, do you love him very, very much?"

"Why, I—" said little Mrs. Murdock, and blushed. "I've been married for ages," she said.

"You love him," Lily Wynton said. "You love him. And is it sweet to go to bed with him?"

"Oh—" said Mrs. Murdock, and blushed till it hurt.

"The first marriage," Lily Wynton said. "Youth, youth. Yes, when I was your age I used to marry, too. Oh, treasure your love, child, guard it, live in it. Laugh and dance in the love of your man. Until you find out what he's really like."

There came a sudden visitation upon her. Her shoulders jerked upward, her cheeks puffed, her eyes sought to start from their hammocks. For a moment she sat thus, then slowly all subsided into place. She lay back in her chair, tenderly patting her chest. She shook her head sadly, and there was grieved wonder in the look with which she held Mrs. Murdock.

"Gas," said Lily Wynton, in the famous voice. "Gas. Nobody knows what I suffer from it."

"Oh, I'm so sorry," Mrs. Murdock said. "Is there anything——"

"Nothing," Lily Wynton said. "There is nothing. There is nothing that can be done for it. I've been everywhere."

"How's for a spot of tea, perhaps?" Miss Noyes said. "It might help." She turned her face toward the archway and lifted up her voice. "Mary! Where the hell's the tea?"

"You don't know," Lily Wynton said, with her grieved eyes fixed on Mrs. Murdock, "you don't know what stomach distress is. You can never, never know, unless you're a stomach sufferer yourself. I've been one for years. Years and years and years."

"I'm terribly sorry," Mrs. Murdock said.

"Nobody knows the anguish," Lily Wynton said. "The agony."

The maid appeared, bearing a triangular tray upon which was set an heroic-sized tea service of bright white china, each piece a hectagon. She set it down on a table within the long reach of Miss Noyes and retired, as she had come, bashfully.

"Sweet Hallie," Lily Wynton said, "my sweet. Tea—I adore it. I worship it. But my distress turns it to gall and wormwood in me. Gall and wormwood. For hours, I should have no peace. Let me have a little, tiny bit of your beautiful, beautiful brandy, instead."

"You really think you should, darling?" Miss Noyes said. "You know——"

"My angel," said Lily Wynton, "it's the only thing for acidity."

"Well," Miss Noyes said. "But do remember you've got a performance tonight." Again she hurled her voice at the archway. "Mary! Bring the brandy and a lot of soda and ice and things."

"Oh, no, my saint," Lily Wynton said. "No, no, sweet Hallie. Soda and ice are rank poison to me. Do you want to freeze my poor, weak stomach? Do you want to kill poor, poor Lily?"

"Mary!" roared Miss Noyes. "Just bring the brandy and a glass." She turned to little Mrs. Murdock. "How's for your tea, tiny one? Cream? Lemon?"

"Cream, if I may, please," Mrs. Murdock said. "And two lumps of sugar, please, if I may."

"Oh, youth, youth," Lily Wynton said. "Youth and love."

The maid returned with an octagonal tray supporting a decanter of brandy and a wide, squat, heavy glass. Her head twisted on her neck in a spasm of diffidence.

"Just pour it for me, will you, my dear?" said Lily Wynton. "Thank you. And leave the pretty, pretty decanter here, on this enchanting little table. Thank you. You're so good to me."

The maid vanished, fluttering. Lily Wynton lay back in her chair, holding in her gloved hand the wide, squat glass, colored brown to the brim. Little Mrs. Murdock lowered her eyes to her teacup, carefully carried it to her lips, sipped, and replaced it on its saucer. When she raised her eyes, Lily Wynton lay back in her chair, holding in her gloved hand the wide, squat, colorless glass.

"My life," Lily Wynton said, slowly, "is a mess. A stinking mess. It always has been, and it always will be. Until I am a very, very old lady. Ah, little Clever-Face, you writers don't know what struggle is."

"But really I'm not—" said Mrs. Murdock.

"To write," Lily Wynton said. "To write. To set one word beautifully beside another word. The privilege of it. The blessed, blessed peace of it. Oh, for quiet, for rest. But do you think those cheap bastards would close that play while it's doing a nickel's worth of business? Oh, no. Tired as I am, sick as I am, I must drag along. Oh, child, child, guard your precious gift. Give thanks for it. It is the greatest thing of all. It is the only thing. To write."

"Darling, I told you tiny one doesn't write," said Miss Noyes. "How's for making more sense? She's a wife."

"Ah, yes, she told me. She told me she had perfect, passionate love," Lily Wynton said. "Young love. It is the greatest thing. It is the only thing." She grasped the decanter; and again the squat glass was brown to the brim.

"What time did you start today, darling?" said Miss Noyes.

"Oh, don't scold me, sweet love," Lily Wynton said. "Lily hasn't been naughty. Her wuzzunt naughty dirl 't all. I didn't get up until late, late, late. And though I parched, though I burned, I didn't have a drink until after my breakfast. 'It is for Hallie,' I said." She raised the glass to her mouth, tilted it, and brought it away, colorless.

"Good Lord, Lily," Miss Noyes said. "Watch yourself. You've got to walk on that stage tonight, my girl."

"All the world's a stage," said Lily Wynton. "And all the men and women merely players. They have their entrance and their exitses, and each man in his time plays many parts, his act being seven ages. At first, the infant, mewling and puking——"

"How's the play doing?" Miss Noyes said.

"Oh, lousily," Lily Wynton said. "Lousily, lousily, lousily. But what isn't? What isn't, in this terrible, terrible world? Answer me that." She reached for the decanter.

"Lily, listen," said Miss Noyes. "Stop that. Do you hear?"

"Please, sweet Hallie," Lily Wynton said. "Pretty please. Poor, poor Lily."

"Do you want me to do what I had to do last time?" Miss Noyes said. "Do you want me to strike you, in front of tiny one, here?"

Lily Wynton drew herself high. "You do not realize," she said, icily, "what acidity is." She filled the glass and held it, regarding it as though through a lorgnon. Suddenly her manner changed, and she looked up and smiled at little Mrs. Murdock.

"You must let me read it," she said. "You mustn't be so modest."

"Read—?" said little Mrs. Murdock.

"Your play," Lily Wynton said. "Your beautiful, beautiful play. Don't think I am too busy. I always have time. I have time for everything. Oh, my God, I have to go to the dentist tomorrow. Oh, the suffering I have gone through with my teeth. Look!" She set down her glass, inserted a gloved forefinger in the corner of her mouth, and dragged it to the side. "Oogh!" she insisted. "Oogh!"

Mrs. Murdock craned her neck shyly, and caught a glimpse of shining gold.

"Oh, I'm so sorry," she said.

"As wah ee id a me ass ime," Lily Wynton said. She took away her forefinger and let her mouth resume its shape. "That's what he did to me last time," she repeated. "The anguish of it. The agony. Do you suffer with your teeth, little Clever-Face?"

"Why, I'm afraid I've been awfully lucky," Mrs. Murdock said. "I——"

"You don't know," Lily Wynton said. "Nobody knows what it is. You writers—you don't know." She took up her glass, sighed over it, and drained it.

"Well," Miss Noyes said. "Go ahead and pass out, then, darling. You'll have time for a sleep before the theater."

"To sleep," Lily Wynton said. "To sleep, perchance to dream. The privilege of it. Oh, Hallie, sweet, sweet Hallie, poor Lily feels so terrible. Rub my head for me, angel. Help me."

"I'll go get the Eau de Cologne," Miss Noyes said. She left the room, lightly patting Mrs. Murdock's knee as she passed her. Lily Wynton lay in her chair and closed her famous eyes.

"To sleep," she said. "To sleep, perchance to dream."

"I'm afraid," little Mrs. Murdock began. "I'm afraid," she said, "I really must be going home. I'm afraid I didn't realize how awfully late it was."

"Yes, go, child," Lily Wynton said. She did not open her eyes. "Go to him. Go to him, live in him, love him. Stay with him always. But when he starts bringing them into the house—get out."

"I'm afraid—I'm afraid I didn't quite understand," Mrs. Murdock said.

"When he starts bringing his fancy women into the house," Lily Wynton said. "You must have pride, then. You must go. I always did. But it was always too late then. They'd got all my money. That's all they want, marry them or not. They say it's love, but it isn't. Love is the only thing. Treasure your love, child. Go back to him. Go to bed with him. It's the only thing. And your beautiful, beautiful play."

"Oh, dear," said little Mrs. Murdock. "I—I'm afraid it's really terribly late."

There was only the sound of rhythmic breathing from the chair where Lily Wynton lay. The purple voice rolled along the air no longer.

Little Mrs. Murdock stole to the chair upon which she had left her coat. Carefully she smoothed her white muslin frills, so that they would be fresh beneath the jacket. She felt a tenderness for her frock; she wanted to protect it. Blue serge and little ruffles—they were her own.

When she reached the outer door of Miss Noyes's apartment, she stopped a moment and her manners conquered her. Bravely she called in the direction of Miss Noyes's bedroom.

"Good-by, Miss Noyes," she said. "I've simply got to run. I didn't realize it was so late. I had a lovely time—thank you ever so much."

"Oh, good-by, tiny one," Miss Noyes called. "Sorry Lily went by-by. Don't mind her—she's really a real person. I'll call you up, tiny one. I want to see you. Now where's that damned Cologne?"

"Thank you ever so much," Mrs. Murdock said. She let herself out of the apartment.

Little Mrs. Murdock walked homeward, through the clustering dark. Her mind was busy, but not with memories of Lily Wynton. She thought of Jim; Jim, who had left for his office before she had arisen that morning, Jim, whom she had not kissed good-by. Darling Jim. There were no others born like him. Funny Jim, stiff and cross and silent; but only because he knew so much. Only because he knew the silliness of seeking afar for the glamour and beauty and romance of living. When they were right at home all the time, she thought. Like the Blue Bird, thought little Mrs. Murdock.

Darling Jim. Mrs. Murdock turned in her course, and entered an enormous shop where the most delicate and esoteric of foods were sold for heavy sums. Jim liked red caviar. Mrs. Murdock bought a jar of the shiny, glutinous eggs. They would have cocktails that night, though they had no guests, and the red caviar would be served with them for a surprise, and it would be a little, secret party to celebrate her return to contentment with her Jim, a party to mark her happy renunciation of all the glory of the world. She bought, too, a large, foreign cheese. It would give a needed touch to dinner. Mrs. Murdock had not given much attention to ordering dinner, that morning. "Oh, anything you want, Signe," she had said to the maid. She did not want to think of that. She went on home with her packages.

Mr. Murdock was already there when she arrived. He was sitting with his newspaper opened to the financial page. Little Mrs. Murdock ran in to him with her eyes a-light. It is too bad that the light in a person's eyes is only the light in a person's eyes, and you cannot tell at a look what causes it. You do not know if it is excitement about you, or about something else. The evening before, Mrs. Murdock had run in to Mr. Murdock with her eyes a-light.

"Oh, hello," he said to her. He looked back at his paper, and kept his eyes there. "What did you do? Did you drop up to Hank Noyes's?"

Little Mrs. Murdock stopped right where she was.

"You know perfectly well, Jim," she said, "that Hallie Noyes's first name is Hallie."

"It's Hank to me," he said. "Hank or Bill. Did what's-her-name show up? I mean drop up. Pardon me."

"To whom are you referring?" said Mrs. Murdock, perfectly.

"What's-her-name," Mr. Murdock said. "The movie star."

"If you mean Lily Wynton," Mrs. Murdock said, "she is not a movie star. She is an actress. She is a great actress."

"Well, did she drop up?" he said.

Mrs. Murdock's shoulders sagged. "Yes," she said. "Yes, she was there, Jim."

"I suppose you're going on the stage now," he said.

"Ah, Jim," Mrs. Murdock said. "Ah, Jim, please. I'm not sorry at all I went to Hallie Noyes's today. It was—it was a real experience to meet Lily Wynton. Something I'll remember all my life."

"What did she do?" Mr. Murdock said. "Hang by her feet?"

"She did no such thing!" Mrs. Murdock said. "She recited Shakespeare, if you want to know."

"Oh, my God," Mr. Murdock said. "That must have been great."

"All right, Jim," Mrs. Murdock said. "If that's the way you want to be."

Wearily she left the room and went down the hall. She stopped at the pantry door, pushed it open, and spoke to the pleasant little maid.

"Oh, Signe," she said. "Oh, good evening, Signe. Put these things somewhere, will you? I got them on the way home. I thought we might have them some time."

Wearily little Mrs. Murdock went on down the hall to her bedroom.

The Eternal Moment

⚜ E. M. FORSTER ⚜

E. M. FORSTER (1879–1970) wrote five novels between 1905 and 1924, ending with the brilliant *A Passage to India,* a study of prejudice and misunderstanding among the British rulers of that country. Thereafter he abandoned fiction. *The Eternal Moment,* which was first published in a volume of short stories under that title in 1928, contains the essence of his message: "Only connect." He believed that the gap between ages, classes and nationalities could be bridged by the determined reaching out of imaginative and sensitive individuals.

I

"DO you see that mountain just behind Elizabeth's toque? A young man fell in love with me there so nicely twenty years ago. Bob your head a minute, would you, Elizabeth, kindly."

"Yes'm," said Elizabeth, falling forward on the box like an unstiffened doll. Colonel Leyland put on his pince-nez, and looked at the mountain where the young man had fallen in love.

"Was he a nice young man?" he asked, smiling, though he lowered his voice a little on account of the maid.

"I never knew. But it is a very gratifying incident to remember at my age. Thank you, Elizabeth."

"May one ask who he was?"

"A porter," answered Miss Raby in her usual tones. "Not even a certificated guide. A male person who was hired to carry the luggage, which he dropped."

"Well! well! What did you do?"

"What a young lady should. Screamed and thanked him not to

insult me. Ran, which was quite unnecessary, fell, sprained my ankle, screamed again; and he had to carry me half a mile, so penitent that I thought he would fling me over a precipice. In that state we reached a certain Mrs. Harbottle, at sight of whom I burst into tears. But she was so much stupider than I was, that I recovered quickly."

"Of course you said it was all your own fault?"

"I trust I did," she said more seriously. "Mrs. Harbottle, who, like most people, was always right, had warned me against him; we had had him for expeditions before."

"Ah! I see."

"I doubt whether you do. Hitherto he had known his place. But he was too cheap: he gave us more than our money's worth. That, as you know, is an ominous sign in a low-born person."

"But how was this your fault?"

"I encouraged him: I greatly preferred him to Mrs. Harbottle. He was handsome and what I call agreeable; and he wore beautiful clothes. We lagged behind, and he picked me flowers. I held out my hand for them—instead of which he seized it and delivered a love oration which he had prepared out of I Promessi Sposi."

"Ah! an Italian."

They were crossing the frontier at that moment. On a little bridge amid fir trees were two poles, one painted red, white and green, and the other black and yellow.

"He lived in Italia Irredenta," said Miss Raby. "But we were to fly to the Kingdom. I wonder what would have happened if we had."

"Good Lord!" said Colonel Leyland, in sudden disgust. On the box Elizabeth trembled.

"But it might have been a most successful match."

She was in the habit of talking in this mildly unconventional way. Colonel Leyland, who made allowances for her brilliancy, managed to exclaim: "Rather! yes, rather!"

She turned on him with: "Do you think I'm laughing at him?"

He looked a little bewildered, smiled, and did not reply. Their carriage was now crawling round the base of the notorious mountain. The road was built over the debris which had fallen and which still fell from its sides; and it had scarred the pine woods with devastating rivers of white stone. But farther up, Miss Raby remembered, on its gentler eastern slope, it possessed tranquil hollows, and flower-clad rocks, and a most tremendous view. She had not been quite as facetious as her companion supposed. The incident, certainly, had been ludicrous. But she was somehow able to laugh at it without laughing much at the actors or the stage.

"I had rather he made me a fool than that I thought he was one," she said, after a long pause.

"Here is the Custom House," said Colonel Leyland, changing the subject.

They had come to the land of *Ach* and *Ja*. Miss Raby sighed; for she loved the Latins, as every one must who is not pressed for time. But Colonel Leyland, a military man, respected Teutonia.

"They still talk Italian for seven miles," she said, comforting herself like a child.

"German is the coming language," answered Colonel Leyland. "All the important books on any subject are written in it."

"But all the books on any important subject are written in Italian. Elizabeth—tell me an important subject."

"Human Nature, ma'am," said the maid, half shy, half impertinent.

"Elizabeth is a novelist, like her mistress," said Colonel Leyland. He turned away to look at the scenery, for he did not like being entangled in a mixed conversation. He noted that the farms were more prosperous, that begging had stopped, that the women were uglier and the men more rotund, that more nourishing food was being eaten outside the wayside inns.

"Colonel Leyland, shall we go to the *Grand Hôtel des Alpes,* to the *Hôtel de Londres,* to the *Pension Liebig,* to the *Pension Atherley-Simon,* to the *Pension Belle Vue,* to the *Pension Old-England,* or to the *Albergo Biscione?*"

"I suppose you would prefer the *Biscione.*"

"I really shouldn't mind the *Grand Hôtel des Alpes.* The *Biscione* people own both, I hear. They have become quite rich."

"You should have a splendid reception—if such people know what gratitude is."

For Miss Raby's novel, "The Eternal Moment," which had made her reputation, had also made the reputation of Vorta.

"Oh, I was properly thanked. Signor Cantù wrote to me about three years after I had published. The letter struck me as a little pathetic, though it was very prosperous: I don't like transfiguring people's lives. I wonder whether they live in their old house or in the new one."

Colonel Leyland had come to Vorta to be with Miss Raby; but he was very willing that they should be in different hotels. She, indifferent to such subtleties, saw no reason why they should not stop under the same roof, just as she could not see why they should not travel in the same carriage. On the other hand, she hated anything smart. He had decided on the *Grand Hôtel des Alpes,* and she was drifting towards the *Biscione,* when the tiresome Elizabeth said: "My friend's lady is staying at the *Alpes.*"

"Oh! if Elizabeth's friend is there that settles it: we'll all go."

"Very well'm," said Elizabeth, studiously avoiding even the appearance of gratitude. Colonel Leyland's face grew severe over the want of discipline.

"You spoil her," he murmured, when they had all descended to walk up a hill.

"There speaks the military man."

"Certainly I have had too much to do with Tommies to enter into what you call 'human relations.' A little sentimentality, and the whole army would go to pieces."

"I know; but the whole world isn't an army. So why should I pretend I'm an officer. You remind me of my Anglo-Indian friends, who were so shocked when I would be pleasant to some natives. They proved, quite conclusively, that it would never do for them, and have never seen that the proof didn't apply. The unlucky people here are always trying to lead the lucky; and it must be stopped. You've been unlucky: all your life you've had to command men, and exact prompt obedience and other unprofitable virtues. I'm lucky: I needn't do the same—and I won't."

"Don't then," he said, smiling. "But take care that the world isn't an army after all. And take care, besides, that you aren't being unjust to the unlucky people: we're fairly kind to your beloved lower orders, for instance."

"Of course," she said dreamily, as if he had made her no concession. "It's becoming usual. But they see through it. They, like ourselves, know that only one thing in the world is worth having."

"Ah! yes," he sighed. "It's a commercial age."

"No!" exclaimed Miss Raby, so irritably that Elizabeth looked back to see what was wrong. "You are stupid. Kindness and money are both quite easy to part with. The only thing worth giving away is yourself. Did you ever give yourself away?"

"Frequently."

"I mean, did you ever, intentionally, make a fool of yourself before your inferiors?"

"Intentionally, never." He saw at last what she was driving at. It was her pleasure to pretend that such self-exposure was the only possible basis of true intercourse, the only gate in the spiritual barrier that divided class from class. One of her books had dealt with the subject; and very agreeable reading it made. "What about you?" he added playfully.

"I've never done it properly. Hitherto I've never felt a really big fool; but when I do, I hope I shall show it plainly."

"May I be there!"

"You might not like it," she replied. "I may feel it at any moment and in mixed company. Anything might set me off."

"Behold Vorta!" cried the driver, cutting short the sprightly conversation. He and Elizabeth and the carriage had reached the top of the hill. The black woods ceased; and they emerged into a valley whose sides were emerald lawns, rippling and doubling and merging each into each, yet always with an upward trend, so that it was 2000 feet to where the rock burst out of the grass and made great mountains, whose pinnacles were delicate in the purity of evening.

The driver, who had the gift of repetition, said: "Vorta! Vorta!"

Far up the valley was a large white village, tossing on undulating meadows like a ship in the sea, and at its prow, breasting a sharp incline, stood a majestic tower of new grey stone. As they looked at the tower it became vocal and spoke magnificently to the mountains, who replied.

They were again informed that this was Vorta, and that that was the new campanile—like the campanile of Venice, only finer—and that the sound was the sound of the campanile's new bell.

"Thank you; exactly," said Colonel Leyland, while Miss Raby rejoiced that the village had made such use of its prosperity. She had feared to return to the place she had once loved so well, lest she should find something new. It had never occurred to her that the new thing might be beautiful. The architect had indeed gone south for his inspiration, and the tower which stood among the mountains was akin to the tower which had once stood beside the lagoons. But the birthplace of the bell it was impossible to determine, for there is no nationality in sound.

They drove forward into the lovely scene, pleased and silent. Approving tourists took them for a well-matched couple. There was indeed nothing offensively literary in Miss Raby's kind angular face; and Colonel Leyland's profession had made him neat rather than aggressive. They did very well for a cultured and refined husband and wife, who had spent their lives admiring the beautiful things with which the world is filled.

As they approached, other churches, hitherto unnoticed, replied— tiny churches, ugly churches, churches painted pink with towers like pumpkins, churches painted white with shingle spires, churches hidden altogether in the glades of a wood or the folds of a meadow— till the evening air was full of little voices, with the great voice singing in their midst. Only the English church, lately built in the Early English style, kept chaste silence.

The bells ceased, and all the little churches receded into darkness. Instead, there was a sound of dressing-gongs, and a vision of tired tourists hurrying back for dinner. A landau, with *Pension Atherley-Simon* upon it, was trotting to meet the diligence, which was just due. A lady was talking to her mother about an evening dress. Young men with rackets were talking to young men with alpenstocks. Then, across the darkness, a fiery finger wrote *Grand Hôtel des Alpes*.

"Behold the electric light!" said the driver, hearing his passengers exclaim.

Pension Belle Vue started out against a pinewood, and from the brink of the river the *Hôtel de Londres* replied. *Pensions Liebig* and *Lorelei* were announced in green and amber respectively. The *Old-England* appeared in scarlet. The illuminations covered a large area, for the best hotels stood outside the village, in elevated or romantic situations. This display took place every evening in the season, but only while the diligence arrived. As soon as the last tourist was suited, the lights went out, and the hotel-keepers, cursing or rejoicing, retired to their cigars.

"Horrible!" said Miss Raby.

"Horrible people!" said Colonel Leyland.

The *Hôtel des Alpes* was an enormous building, which, being made of wood, suggested a distended chalet. But this impression was corrected by a costly and magnificent view terrace, the squared stones of which were visible for miles, and from which, as from some great reservoir, asphalt paths trickled over the adjacent country. Their carriage, having ascended a private drive, drew up under a vaulted portico of pitch-pine, which opened on to this terrace on one side, and into the covered lounge on the other. There was a whirl of officials— men with gold braid, smarter men with more gold braid, men smarter still with no gold braid. Elizabeth assumed an arrogant air, and carried a small straw basket with difficulty. Colonel Leyland became every inch a soldier. Miss Raby, whom, in spite of long experience, a large hotel always flustered, was hurried into an expensive bedroom, and advised to dress herself immediately if she wished to partake of table d'hôte.

As she came up the staircase, she had seen the dining-room filling with English and Americans and with rich, hungry Germans. She liked company, but tonight she was curiously depressed. She seemed to be confronted with an unpleasing vision, the outlines of which were still obscure.

"I will eat in my room," she told Elizabeth. "Go to your dinner: I'll do the unpacking."

She wandered round, looking at the list of rules, the list of prices, the list of excursions, the red plush sofa, the jugs and basins on which was lithographed a view of the mountains. Where amid such splendour was there a place for Signor Cantù with his china-bowled pipe, and for Signora Cantù with her snuff-coloured shawl?

When the waiter at last brought up her dinner, she asked after her host and hostess.

He replied, in cosmopolitan English, that they were both well.

"Do they live here, or at the *Biscione?*"

"Here, why yes. Only poor tourists go the *Biscione.*"

"Who lives there, then?"

"The mother of Signor Cantù. She is unconnected," he continued, like one who has learnt a lesson, "she is unconnected absolutely with us. Fifteen years back, yes. But now, where is the *Biscione?* I beg you contradict if we are spoken about together."

Miss Raby said quietly: "I have made a mistake. Would you kindly give notice that I shall not want my room, and say that the luggage is to be taken, immediately, to the *Biscione*."

"Certainly! certainly!" said the waiter, who was well trained. He added with a vicious snort, "You will have to pay."

"Undoubtedly," said Miss Raby.

The elaborate machinery which had so recently sucked her in began to disgorge her. The trunks were carried down, the vehicle in which she had arrived was recalled. Elizabeth, white with indignation, appeared in the hall. She paid for beds in which they had not slept, and for food which they had never eaten. Amidst the whirl of gold-laced officials, who hoped even in that space of time to have established a claim to be tipped, she moved towards the door. The guests in the lounge observed her with amusement, concluding that she had found the hotel too dear.

"What is it? Whatever is it? Are you not comfortable?" Colonel Leyland in his evening dress ran after her.

"Not that; I've made a mistake. This hotel belongs to the son; I must go to the *Biscione*. He's quarrelled with the old people: I think the father's dead."

"But really—if you are comfortable here——"

"I must find out tonight whether it is true. And I must also"—her voice quivered—"find out whether it is my fault."

"How in the name of goodness——"

"I shall bear it if it is," she continued gently. "I am too old to be a tragedy queen as well as an evil genius."

"What does she mean? Whatever does she mean?" he murmured, as he watched the carriage lights descending the hill. "What harm has she done? What harm is there for that matter? Hotel-keepers always quarrel: it's no business of ours." He ate a good dinner in silence. Then his thoughts were turned by the arrival of his letters from the post office.

Dearest Edwin,—It is with the greatest diffidence that I write to you, and I know you will believe me when I say that I do not write from curiosity. I only require an answer to one plain question. Are you engaged to Miss Raby or no? Fashions have altered even since my young days. But, for all that an engagement is still an engagement, and should be announced at once, to save all parties discom-

fort. Though your health has broken down and you have abandoned your profession, you can still protect the family honour.

"Drivel!" exclaimed Colonel Leyland. Acquaintance with Miss Raby had made his sight keener. He recognized in this part of his sister's letter nothing but an automatic conventionality. He was no more moved by its perusal than she had been by its composition.

As for the maid whom the Bannons mentioned to me, she is not a chaperone—nothing but a sop to throw in the eyes of the world. I am not saying a word against Miss Raby, whose books we always read. Literary people are always unpractical, and we are confident that she does not know. Perhaps I do not think her the wife for you; but that is another matter.

My babes, who all send love (so does Lionel), are at present an unmitigated joy. One's only anxiety is for the future, when the crushing expenses of good education will have to be taken into account.

Your loving Nelly.

How could he explain the peculiar charm of the relations between himself and Miss Raby? There had never been a word of marriage, and would probably never be a word of love. If, instead of seeing each other frequently, they should come to see each other always it would be as sage companions, familiar with life, not as egoistic lovers, craving for infinities of passion which they had no right to demand and no power to supply. Neither professed to be a virgin soul, or to be ignorant of the other's limitations and inconsistencies. They scarcely even made allowances for each other. Toleration implies reserve; and the greatest safeguard of unruffled intercourse is knowledge. Colonel Leyland had courage of no mean order: he cared little for the opinion of people whom he understood. Nelly and Lionel and their babes were welcome to be shocked or displeased. Miss Raby was an authoress, a kind of radical; he a soldier, a kind of aristocrat. But the time for their activities was passing; he was ceasing to fight, she to write. They could pleasantly spend together their autumn. Nor might they prove the worst companions for a winter.

He was too delicate to admit, even to himself, the desirability of

marrying two thousand a year. But it lent an unacknowledged per-
fume to his thoughts. He tore Nelly's letter into little pieces, and
dropped them into the darkness out of the bedroom window.

"Funny lady!" he murmured, as he looked towards Vorta, trying to
detect the campanile in the growing light of the moon. "Why have
you gone to be uncomfortable? Why will you interfere in the quarrels
of people who can't understand you, and whom you don't understand. How silly you are to think you've caused them. You think
you've written a book which has spoilt the place and made the inhabitants corrupt and sordid. I know just how you think. So you will
make yourself unhappy, and go about trying to put right what never
was right. Funny lady!"

Close below him he could now see the white fragments of his
sister's letter. In the valley the campanile appeared, rising out of
wisps of silvery vapour.

"Dear lady!" he whispered, making towards the village a little
movement with his hands.

II

Miss Raby's first novel, "The Eternal Moment," was written round
the idea that man does not live by time alone, that an evening gone
may become like a thousand ages in the courts of heaven—the idea
that was afterwards expounded more philosophically by Maeterlinck.
She herself now declared that it was a tiresome, affected book, and
that the title suggested the dentist's chair. But she had written it
when she was feeling young and happy; and that, rather than
maturity, is the hour in which to formulate a creed. As years pass, the
conception may become more solid, but the desire and the power to
impart it to others are alike weakened. It did not altogether displease
her that her earliest work had been her most ambitious.

By a strange fate, the book made a great sensation, especially in
unimaginative circles. Idle people interpreted it to mean that there
was no harm in wasting time, vulgar people that there was no harm in
being fickle, pious people interpreted it as an attack upon morality.
The authoress became well known in society, where her enthusiasm

for the lower classes only lent her an additional charm. That very year Lady Anstey, Mrs. Heriot, the Marquis of Bamburgh, and many others, penetrated to Vorta, where the scene of the book was laid. They returned enthusiastic. Lady Anstey exhibited her water-colour drawings; Mrs. Heriot, who photographed, wrote an article in *The Strand;* while *The Nineteenth Century* published a long description of the place by the Marquis of Bamburgh, entitled "The Modern Peasant, and his Relations with Roman Catholicism."

Thanks to these efforts, Vorta became a rising place, and people who liked being off the beaten track went there, and pointed out the way to others. Miss Raby, by a series of trivial accidents, had never returned to the village whose rise was so intimately connected with her own. She had heard from time to time of its progress. It had also been whispered that an inferior class of tourist was finding it out. and, fearing to find something spoilt, she had at last a certain diffidence in returning to scenes which once had given her so much pleasure. Colonel Leyland persuaded her; he wanted a cool healthy spot for the summer, where he could read and talk and find walks suitable for an athletic invalid. Their friends laughed; their acquaintances gossiped; their relatives were furious. But he was courageous and she was indifferent. They had accomplished the expedition under the scanty ægis of Elizabeth.

Her arrival was saddening. It displeased her to see the great hotels in a great circle, standing away from the village where all life should have centred. Their illuminated titles, branded on the tranquil evening slopes, still danced in her eyes. And the monstrous *Hôtel des Alpes* haunted her like a nightmare. In her dreams she recalled the portico, the ostentatious lounge, the polished walnut bureau, the vast rack for the bedroom keys, the panoramic bedroom crockery, the uniforms of the officials, and the smell of smart people—which is to some nostrils quite as depressing as the smell of poor ones. She was not enthusiastic over the progress of civilisation, knowing by Eastern experiences that civilisation rarely puts her best foot foremost, and is apt to make the barbarians immoral and vicious before her compensating qualities arrive. And here there was no question of progress: the world had more to learn from the village than the village from the world.

At the *Biscione,* indeed, she had found little change—only the pathos of a survival. The old landlord had died, and the old landlady was ill in bed, but the antique spirit had not yet departed. On the timbered front was still painted the dragon swallowing the child—the arms of the Milanese Visconti, from whom the Cantùs might well be descended. For there was something about the little hotel which compelled a sympathetic guest to believe, for the time at all events, in aristocracy. The great manner, only to be obtained without effort, ruled throughout. In each bedroom were three or four beautiful things —a little piece of silk tapestry, a fragment of rococo carving, some blue tiles, framed and hung upon the whitewashed wall. There were pictures in the sitting-rooms and on the stairs—eighteenth-century pictures in the style of Carlo Dolce and the Caracci—a blue-robed Mater Dolorosa, a fluttering saint, a magnanimous Alexander with a receding chin. A debased style—so the superior person and the textbooks say. Yet, at times, it may have more freshness and significance than a newly-purchased Fra Angelico. Miss Raby, who had visited dukes in their residences without a perceptible tremor, felt herself blatant and modern when she entered the *Albergo Biscione*. The most trivial things—the sofa cushions, the table cloths, the cases for the pillows —though they might be made of poor materials and be æsthetically incorrect, inspired her with reverence and humility. Through this cleanly, gracious dwelling there had once moved Signor Cantù with his china-bowled pipe, Signora Cantù in her snuff-coloured shawl, and Bartolommeo Cantù, now proprietor of the *Grand Hôtel des Alpes*.

She sat down to breakfast next morning in a mood which she tried to attribute to her bad night and her increasing age. Never, she thought, had she seen people more unattractive and more unworthy than her fellow-guests. A black-browed woman was holding forth on patriotism and the duty of English tourists to present an undivided front to foreign nations. Another woman kept up a feeble lament, like a dribbling tap which never gathers flow yet never quite ceases, complaining of the food, the charges, the noise, the clouds, the dust. She liked coming here herself, she said; but she hardly liked to recommend it to her friends: it was the kind of hotel one felt like that about. Males were rare, and in great demand; a young one was describing, amid fits of laughter, the steps he had taken to astonish the natives.

Miss Raby was sitting opposite the famous fresco, which formed the only decoration of the room. It had been discovered during some repairs; and, though the surface had been injured in places, the colours were still bright. Signora Cantu attributed it now to Titian, now to Giotto, and declared that no one could interpret its meaning; professors and artists had puzzled themselves in vain. This she said because it pleased her to say it; the meaning was perfectly clear, and had been frequently explained to her. Those four figures were sibyls, holding prophecies of the Nativity. It was uncertain for what original reason they had been painted high up in the mountains, at the extreme boundary of Italian art. Now, at all events, they were an invaluable source of conversation; and many an acquaintance had been opened, and argument averted, by their timely presence on the wall.

"Aren't those saints cunning!" said an American lady, following Miss Raby's glance.

The lady's father muttered something about superstition. They were a lugubrious couple, lately returned from the Holy Land, where they had been cheated shamefully, and their attitude towards religion had suffered in consequence.

Miss Raby said, rather sharply, that the saints were sibyls.

"But I don't recall sibyls," said the lady, "either in the N.T. or the O."

"Inventions of the priests to deceive the peasantry," said the father sadly. "Same as their churches; tinsel pretending to be gold, cotton pretending to be silk, stucco pretending to be marble; same as their processions, same as their—(he swore)—campaniles."

"My father," said the lady, bending forward, "he does suffer so from insomnia. Fancy a bell every morning at six!"

"Yes, ma'am; you profit. We've stopped it."

"Stopped the early bell ringing?" cried Miss Raby.

People looked up to see who she was. Some one whispered that she wrote.

He replied that he had come up all these feet for rest, and that if he did not get it he would move on to another centre. The English and American visitors had co-operated, and forced the hotel-keepers to take action. Now the priests rang a dinner bell, which was endurable. He believed that "corperation" would do anything: it had been the same with the peasants.

"How did the tourists interfere with the peasants?" asked Miss Raby, getting very hot, and trembling all over.

"We said the same; we had come for rest, and we would have it. Every week they got drunk and sang till two. Is that a proper way to go on, anyhow?"

"I remember," said Miss Raby, "that some of them did get drunk. But I also remember how they sang."

"Quite so. Till two," he retorted.

They parted in mutual irritation. She left him holding forth on the necessity of a new universal religion of the open air. Over his head stood the four sibyls, gracious for all their clumsiness and crudity, each proffering a tablet inscribed with concise promise of redemption. If the old religions had indeed become insufficient for humanity, it did not seem probable that an adequate substitute would be produced in America.

It was too early to pay her promised visit to Signora Cantù. Nor was Elizabeth, who had been rude overnight and was now tiresomely penitent, a possible companion. There were a few tables outside the inn, at which some women sat, drinking beer. Pollarded chestnuts shaded them; and a low wooden balustrade fenced them off from the village street. On this balustrade Miss Raby perched, for it gave her a view of the campanile. A critical eye could discover plenty of faults in its architecture. But she looked at it all with increasing pleasure, in which was mingled a certain gratitude.

The German waitress came out and suggested very civilly that she should find a more comfortable seat. This was the place where the lower classes ate; would she not go to the drawing-room?

"Thank you, no; for how many years have you classified your guests according to their birth?"

"For many years. It was necessary," replied the admirable woman. She returned to the house full of meat and common sense, one of the many signs that the Teuton was gaining on the Latin in this debatable valley.

A grey-haired lady came out next, shading her eyes from the sun, and crackling *The Morning Post*. She glanced at Miss Raby pleasantly, blew her nose, apologized for speaking, and spoke as follows:

"This evening, I wonder if you know, there is a concert in aid of the stained-glass window for the English Church. Might I persuade you to take tickets? As has been said, it is so important that English people should have a rallying point, is it not?"

"Most important," said Miss Raby; "but I wish the rallying point could be in England."

The grey-haired lady smiled. Then she looked puzzled. Then she realized that she had been insulted, and, crackling *The Morning Post,* departed.

"I have been rude," thought Miss Raby dejectedly. "Rude to a lady as silly and as grey-haired as myself. This is not a day on which I ought to talk to people."

Her life had been successful, and on the whole happy. She was unaccustomed to that mood, which is termed depressed, but which certainly gives visions of wider, if greyer, horizons. That morning her outlook altered. She walked through the village, scarcely noticing the mountains by which it was still surrounded, or the unaltered radiance of its sun. But she was fully conscious of something new; of the indefinable corruption which is produced by the passage of a large number of people.

Even at that time the air was heavy with meat and drink, to which were added dust and tobacco smoke and the smell of tired horses. Carriages were huddled against the church, and underneath the campanile a woman was guarding a stack of bicycles. The season had been bad for climbing; and groups of young men in smart Norfolk suits were idling up and down, waiting to be hired as guides. Two large inexpensive hotels stood opposite the post office; and in front of them innumerable little tables surged out into the street. Here, from an early hour in the morning, eating had gone on, and would continue till a late hour at night. The customers, chiefly German, re- freshed themselves with cries and with laughter, passing their arms round the waists of their wives. Then, rising heavily, they departed in single file towards some view-point, whereon a red flag indicated the possibility of another meal. The whole population was employed, even down to the little girls, who worried the guests to buy picture postcards and edelweiss. Vorta had taken to the tourist trade.

A village must have some trade; and this village had always been full of virility and power. Obscure and happy, its splendid energies had found employment in wresting a livelihood out of the earth, whence had come a certain dignity, and kindliness, and love for other men. Civilisation did not relax these energies, but it had diverted them; and all the precious qualities, which might have helped to heal the world, had been destroyed. The family affection, the affection for the commune, the sane pastoral virtues—all had perished while the campanile which was to embody them was being built. No villain had done this thing: it was the work of ladies and gentlemen who were good and rich and often clever—who, if they thought about the matter at all, thought that they were conferring a benefit, moral as well as commercial, on any place in which they chose to stop.

Never before had Miss Raby been conscious of such universal misdoing. She returned to the *Biscione* shattered and exhausted, remembering that terrible text in which there is much semblance of justice: "But woe to him through whom the offence cometh."

Signora Cantù, somewhat over-excited, was lying in a dark room on the ground floor. The walls were bare; for all the beautiful things were in the rooms of her guests whom she loved as a good queen might love her subjects—and the walls were dirty also, for this was Signora Cantù's own room. But no palace had so fair a ceiling; for from the wooden beams were suspended a whole dowry of copper vessels—pails, cauldrons, water pots, of every colour from lustrous black to the palest pink. It pleased the old lady to look up at these tokens of prosperity. An American lady had lately departed without them, more puzzled than angry.

The two women had little in common; for Signora Cantù was an inflexible aristocrat. Had she been a great lady of the great century, she would have gone speedily to the guillotine, and Miss Raby would have howled approval. Now, with her scanty hair in curl-papers, and the snuff-coloured shawl spread over her, she entertained the distinguished authoress with accounts of other distinguished people who had stopped, and might again stop, at the *Biscione*. At first her tone was dignified. But before long she proceeded to village news, and a certain bitterness began to show itself. She chronicled deaths with a kind of melancholy pride. Being old herself, she liked to meditate on the fairness of Fate, which had not spared her contemporaries, and often had not spared her juniors. Miss Raby was unaccustomed to extract such consolation. She too was growing old, but it would have pleased her better if others could have remained young. She remembered few of these people well, but deaths were symbolical, just as the death of a flower may symbolize the passing of all the spring.

Signora Cantù then went on to her own misfortunes, beginning with an account of a landslip, which had destroyed her little farm. A landslip, in that valley, never hurried. Under the green coat of turf water would collect, just as an abscess is formed under the skin. There would be a lump on the sloping meadow, then the lump would break and discharge a slowly-moving stream of mud and stones. Then the whole area seemed to be corrupted; on every side the grass cracked and doubled into fantastic creases, the trees grew awry, the barns and cottages collapsed, all the beauty turned gradually to indistinguishable pulp, which slid downwards till it was washed away by some stream.

From the farm they proceeded to other grievances, over which Miss Raby became almost too depressed to sympathize. It was a bad season; the guests did not understand the ways of the hotel; the servants did not understand the guests; she was told she ought to have a concierge. But what was the good of a concierge?

"I have no idea," said Miss Raby, feeling that no concierge would ever restore the fortunes of the *Biscione*.

"They say he would meet the diligence and entrap the new arrivals. What pleasure should I have from guests I entrapped?"

"The other hotels do it," said Miss Raby, sadly.

"Exactly. Every day a man comes down from the *Alpes*."

There was an awkward silence. Hitherto they had avoided mentioning that name.

"He takes them all," she continued, in a burst of passion. "My son takes all my guests. He has taken all the English nobility, and the best Americans, and all my old Milanese friends. He slanders me up and down the valley, saying that the drains are bad. The hotel-keepers will not recommend me; they send on their guests to him, because he pays them five per cent. for every one they send. He pays the drivers, he pays the porters, he pays the guides. He pays the band, so that it hardly ever plays down in the village. He even pays the little children to say my drains are bad. He and his wife and his concierge, they mean to ruin me, they would like to see me die."

"Don't—don't say these things, Signora Cantù." Miss Raby began to walk about the room, speaking, as was her habit, what was true rather than what was intelligible. "Try not to be so angry with your son. You don't know what he had to contend with. You don't know who led him into it. Some one else may be to blame. And whoever it may be—you will remember them in your prayers."

"Of course I am a Christian!" exclaimed the angry old lady. "But he will not ruin me. I seem poor, but he has borrowed—too much. That hotel will fail!"

"And perhaps," continued Miss Raby, "there is not much wicked-ness in the world. Most of the evil we see is the result of little faults —of stupidity or vanity."

"And I even know who led him into it—his wife, and the man who is now his concierge."

"This habit of talking, of self-expression—it seems so pleasant and necessary—yet it does harm——"

They were both interrupted by an uproar in the street. Miss Raby opened the window; and a cloud of dust, heavy with petrol, entered. A passing motor car had twitched over a table. Much beer had been spilt, and a little blood.

Signora Cantù sighed peevishly at the noise. Her ill-temper had ex-hausted her, and she lay motionless, with closed eyes. Over her head two copper vases clinked gently in the sudden gust of wind. Miss Raby had been on the point of a great dramatic confession, of a touching appeal for forgiveness. Her words were ready; her words always were ready. But she looked at those closed eyes, that suffering enfeebled frame, and she knew that she had no right to claim the luxury of pardon.

It seemed to her that with this interview her life had ended. She had done all that was possible. She had done much evil. It only re-mained for her to fold her hands and to wait, till her ugliness and her incompetence went the way of beauty and strength. Before her eyes there arose the pleasant face of Colonel Leyland, with whom she might harmlessly conclude her days. He would not be stimulating, but it did not seem desirable that she should be stimulated. It would be better if her faculties did close, if the senseless activity of her brain and her tongue were gradually numbed. For the first time in her life, she was tempted to become old.

Signora Cantù was still speaking of her son's wife and concierge;

of the vulgarity of the former and the ingratitude of the latter, whom she had been kind to long ago, when he first wandered up from Italy, an obscure boy. Now he had sided against her. Such was the reward of charity.

"And what is his name?" asked Miss Raby absently.

"Feo Ginori," she replied. "You would not remember him. He used to carry——"

From the new campanile there burst a flood of sound to which the copper vessels vibrated responsively. Miss Raby lifted her hands, not to her ears but to her eyes. In her enfeebled state, the throbbing note of the bell had the curious effect of blood returning into frozen veins.

"I remember that man perfectly," she said at last; "and I shall see him this afternoon."

III

Miss Raby and Elizabeth were seated together in the lounge of the *Hôtel des Alpes*. They had walked up from the *Biscione* to see Colonel Leyland. But he, apparently, had walked down there to see them, and the only thing to do was to wait, and to justify the wait by ordering some refreshment. So Miss Raby had afternoon tea, while Elizabeth behaved like a perfect lady over an ice, occasionally turning the spoon upside down in the mouth when she saw that no one was looking. The underwaiters were clearing cups and glasses off the marble-topped tables, and the gold-laced officials were rearranging the wicker chairs into seductive groups of three and two. Here and there the visitors lingered among their crumbs, and the Russian Prince had fallen asleep in a prominent and ungraceful position. But most people had started for a little walk before dinner, or had gone to play tennis, or had taken a book under a tree. The weather was delightful, and the sun had so far declined that its light had become spiritualized, suggesting new substance as well as new colour in everything on which it fell. From her seat Miss Raby could see the great precipices under which they had passed the day before; and beyond those precipices she could see Italy—the Val d'Aprile, the Val Senese and the mountains she had named "The Beasts of the South." All day those mountains were insignificant—distant chips of white or grey stone. But the evening sun transfigured them, and they would sit up like purple bears against the southern sky.

"It is a sin you should not be out, Elizabeth. Find your friend if you can, and make her go with you. If you see Colonel Leyland, tell him I am here."

"Is that all, ma'am?" Elizabeth was fond of her eccentric mistress, and her heart had been softened by the ice. She saw that Miss Raby did not look well. Possibly the course of love was running roughly. And indeed gentlemen must be treated with tact, especially when both parties are getting on.

"Don't give pennies to the children: that is the only other thing."

The guests had disappeared, and the number of officials visibly diminished. From the hall behind came the genteel sniggers of those two most vile creatures, a young lady behind the bureau and a young man in a frock coat who shows new arrivals to their rooms. Some of the porters joined them, standing at a suitable distance. At last only Miss Raby, the Russian Prince, and the concierge were left in the lounge.

The concierge was a competent European of forty or so, who spoke all languages fluently, and some well. He was still active, and had evidently once been muscular. But either his life or his time of life had been unkind to his figure: in a few years he would certainly be fat. His face was less easy to decipher. He was engaged in the unquestioning performance of his duty, and that is not a moment for self-revelation. He opened the windows, he filled the match-boxes, he flicked the little tables with a duster, always keeping an eye on the door in case any one arrived without luggage, or left without paying. He touched an electric bell, and a waiter flew up and cleared away Miss Raby's tea things. He touched another bell, and sent an underling to tidy up some fragments of paper which had fallen out of a bedroom window. Then "Excuse me, madam!" and he had picked up Miss Raby's handkerchief with a slight bow. He seemed to bear her no grudge for her abrupt departure of the preceding evening. Perhaps it was into his hand that she had dropped a tip. Perhaps he did not remember she had been there.

The gesture with which he returned the handkerchief troubled her with vague memories. Before she could thank him he was back in the doorway, standing sideways, so that the slight curve of his stomach was outlined against the view. He was speaking to a youth of athletic but melancholy appearance, who was fidgeting in the portico without. "I told you the percentage," she heard. "If you had agreed to it, I would have recommended you. Now it is too late. I have enough guides."

Our generosity benefits more people than we suppose. We tip the cabman, and something goes to the man who whistled for him. We tip the man who lights up the stalactite grotto with magnesium wire, and something goes to the boatman who brought us there. We tip the waiter in the restaurant, and something goes off the waiter's wages. A vast machinery, whose existence we seldom realize, promotes the distribution of our wealth. When the concierge returned, Miss Raby asked: "And what is the percentage?"

She asked with the definite intention of disconcerting him, not because she was unkind, but because she wished to discover what qualities, if any, lurked beneath that civil, efficient exterior. And the spirit of her inquiry was sentimental rather than scientific.

With an educated man she would have succeeded. In attempting to reply to her question, he would have revealed something. But the concierge had no reason to pay even lip service to logic. He replied: "Yes, madam! this is perfect weather, both for our visitors and for the hay," and hurried to help a bishop, who was selecting a picture postcard.

Miss Raby, instead of moralizing on the inferior resources of the lower classes, acknowledged a defeat. She watched the man spreading out the postcards, helpful yet not obtrusive, alert yet deferential. She watched him make the bishop buy more than he wanted. This was the man who had talked of love to her upon the mountain. But hitherto he had only revealed his identity by chance gestures bequeathed to him at birth. Intercourse with the gentle classes had required new qualities—civility, omniscience, imperturbability. It was the old answer: the gentle classes were responsible for him. It is inevitable, as well as desirable, that we should bear each other's burdens.

It was absurd to blame Feo for his worldliness—for his essential vulgarity. He had not made himself. It was even absurd to regret his transformation from an athlete: his greasy stoutness, his big black kiss-curl, his waxed moustache, his chin which was dividing and propagating itself like some primitive form of life. In England, nearly twenty years before, she had altered his figure as well as his character. He was one of the products of "The Eternal Moment."

A great tenderness overcame her—the sadness of an unskilful demiurge, who makes a world and beholds that it is bad. She desired to ask pardon of her creatures, even though they were too poorly formed to grant it. The longing to confess, which she had suppressed that morning beside the bed of Signora Cantù, broke out again with the violence of a physical desire. When the bishop had gone she renewed the conversation, though on different lines, saying: "Yes, it is beautiful weather. I have just been enjoying a walk up from the *Biscione*. I am stopping there!"

He saw that she was willing to talk, and replied pleasantly: "The *Biscione* must be a very nice hotel: many people speak well of it. The fresco is very beautiful." He was too shrewd to object to a little charity.

"What lots of new hotels there are!" She lowered her voice in order not to rouse the Prince, whose presence weighed on her curiously.

"Oh, madam! I should indeed think so. When I was a lad— Excuse me one moment."

An American girl, who was new to the country, came up with her hand full of coins, and asked him hopelessly "whatever they were worth." He explained, and gave her change: Miss Raby was not sure that he gave her right change.

"When I was a lad——" He was again interrupted, to speed two parting guests. One of them tipped him; he said, "Thank you." The other did not tip him; he said, "Thank you," all the same but not in the same way. Obviously he had as yet no recollections of Miss Raby.

"When I was a lad, Vorta was a poor little place."

"But a pleasant place?"

"Very pleasant, madam."

"Kouf!" said the Russian Prince, suddenly waking up and startling them both. He clapped on a felt hat, and departed at full speed for a constitutional. Miss Raby and Feo were left together.

It was then that she ceased to hesitate, and determined to remind him that they had met before. All day she had sought for a spark of life, and it might be summoned by pointing to that other fire which she discerned, far back in the travelled distance, high up in the mountains of youth. What he would do, if he also discerned it, she did not know; but she hoped that he would become alive, that he at all events would escape the general doom which she had prepared for the place and the people. And what she would do, during their joint contemplation, she did not even consider.

She would hardly have ventured if the sufferings of the day had not hardened her. After much pain, respectability becomes ludicrous. And she had only to overcome the difficulty of Feo's being a man, not the difficulty of his being a concierge. She had never observed that spiritual reticence towards social inferiors which is usual at the present day.

"This is my second visit," she said boldly. "I stayed at the *Biscione* twenty years ago."

He showed the first sign of emotion: *that* reference to the *Biscione* annoyed him.

"I was told I should find you up here," continued Miss Raby. "I remember you very well. You used to take us over the passes."

She watched his face intently. She did not expect it to relax into an expansive smile. "Ah!" he said, taking off his peaked cap, "I remember you perfectly, madam. What a pleasure, if I may say so, to meet you again!"

"I am pleased, too," said the lady, looking at him doubtfully.

"You and another lady, madam, was it not? Miss ——"

"Mrs. Harbottle."

"To be sure; I carried your luggage. I often remember your kindness."

She looked up. He was standing near an open window, and the whole of fairyland stretched behind him. Her sanity forsook her, and she said gently: "Will you misunderstand me, if I say that I have never forgotten your kindness either?"

He replied: "The kindness was yours, madam; I only did my duty."

"Duty?" she cried; "what about duty?"

"You and Miss Harbottle were such generous ladies. I well remember how grateful I was: you always paid me above the tariff fare——"

Then she realized that he had forgotten everything; forgotten her, forgotten what had happened, even forgotten what he was like when he was young.

"Stop being polite," she said coldly. "You were not polite when I saw you last."

"I am very sorry," he exclaimed, suddenly alarmed.

"Turn round. Look at the mountains."

"Yes, yes." His fishy eyes blinked nervously. He fiddled with his watch chain which lay in a furrow of his waistcoat. He ran away to warn some poorly dressed children off the view-terrace. When he returned she still insisted.

"I must tell you," she said, in calm, business-like tones. "Look at that great mountain, round which the road goes south. Look halfway up, on its eastern side—where the flowers are. It was there that you once gave yourself away."

He gaped at her in horror. He remembered. He was inexpressibly shocked.

It was at that moment that Colonel Leyland returned.

She walked up to him, saying, "This is the man I spoke of yesterday."

"Good afternoon; what man?" said Colonel Leyland fussily. He saw that she was flushed, and concluded that some one had been rude to her. Since their relations were somewhat anomalous, he was all the more particular that she should be treated with respect.

"The man who fell in love with me when I was young."

"It is untrue!" cried the wretched Feo, seeing at once the trap that had been laid for him. "The lady imagined it. I swear, sir—I meant nothing. I was a lad. It was before I learnt behaviour. I had even forgotten it. She reminded me. She has disturbed me."

"Good Lord!" said Colonel Leyland. "Good Lord!"

"I shall lose my place, sir; and I have a wife and children. I shall be ruined."

"Sufficient!" cried Colonel Leyland. "Whatever Miss Raby's intentions may be, she does not intend to ruin you."

"You have misunderstood me, Feo," said Miss Raby gently.

"How unlucky we have been missing each other," said Colonel Leyland, in trembling tones that were meant to be nonchalant. "Shall we go a little walk before dinner? I hope that you are stopping."

She did not attend. She was watching Feo. His alarm had subsided; and he revealed a new emotion, even less agreeable to her. His shoulders straightened, he developed an irresistible smile, and, when he saw that she was looking and that Colonel Leyland was not, he winked at her.

It was a ghastly sight, perhaps the most hopelessly depressing of all the things she had seen at Vorta. But its effect on her was memorable. It evoked a complete vision of that same man as he had been twenty years before. She could see him to the smallest detail of his clothes or his hair, the flowers in his hand, the graze on his wrist, the heavy bundle that he had loosed from his back, so that he might speak as a freeman. She could hear his voice, neither insolent nor diffident, never threatening, never apologizing, urging her first in the studied phrases he had learnt from books, then, as his passion grew, becoming incoherent, crying that she must believe him, that she must love him in return, that she must fly with him to Italy, where they would live for ever, always happy, always young. She had cried out then, as a young lady should, and had thanked him not to insult her. And now, in her middle age, she cried out again, because the sudden shock and the contrast had worked a revelation. "Don't think I'm in love with you now!" she cried.

For she realized that only now was she not in love with him: that the incident upon the mountain had been one of the great moments of her life—perhaps the greatest, certainly the most enduring: that she had drawn unacknowledged power and inspiration from it, just as trees draw vigour from a subterranean spring. Never again could she think of it as a half-humorous episode in her development. There was more reality in it than in all the years of success and varied achievement which had followed, and which it had rendered possible. For all her correct behaviour and lady-like display, she had been in love with Feo, and she had never loved so greatly again. A presumptuous boy had taken her to the gates of heaven; and, though she would not enter with him, the eternal remembrance of the vision had made life seem endurable and good.

Colonel Leyland, by her side, babbled respectabilities, trying to pass the situation off as normal. He was saving her, for he liked her very much, and it pained him when she was foolish. But her last remark to Feo had frightened him; and he began to feel that he must save himself. They were no longer alone. The bureau lady and the young gentleman were listening breathlessly, and the porters were tittering at the discomfiture of their superior. A French lady had spread amongst the guests the agreeable news that an Englishman had surprised his wife making love to the concierge. On the terrace outside, a mother waved away her daughters. The bishop was preparing, very leisurely, for a walk.

But Miss Raby was oblivious. "How little I know!" she said. "I never knew till now that I had loved him and that it was a mere chance—a little catch, a kink—that I never told him so."

It was her habit to speak out; and there was no present passion to disturb or prevent her. She was still detached, looking back at a fire upon the mountains, marvelling at its increased radiance, but too far off to feel its heat. And by speaking out she believed, pathetically enough, that she was making herself intelligible. He remark seemed inexpressibly coarse to Colonel Leyland.

"But these beautiful thoughts are a poor business, are they not?" she continued, addressing Feo, who was losing his gallant air, and becoming bewildered. "They're hardly enough to grow old on. I think I would give all my imagination, all my skill with words, if I could recapture one crude fact, if I could replace one single person whom I have broken."

"Quite so, madam," he responded, with downcast eyes.

"If only I could find some one here who would understand me, to whom I could confess, I think I should be happier. I have done so much harm in Vorta, dear Feo——"

Feo raised his eyes. Colonel Leyland struck his stick on the parquetry floor.

"—and at last I thought I would speak to you, in case you understood me. I remembered that you had once been very gracious to me —yes, gracious: there is no other word. But I have harmed you also: how could you understand?"

"Madam, I understand perfectly," said the concierge, who had recovered a little, and was determined to end the distressing scene, in which his reputation was endangered, and his vanity aroused only to be rebuffed. "It is you who are mistaken. You have done me no harm at all. You have benefited me."

"Precisely," said Colonel Leyland. "That is the conclusion of the whole matter. Miss Raby has been the making of Vorta."

"Exactly, sir. After the lady's book, foreigners come, hotels are built, we all grow richer. When I first came here, I was a common ignorant porter who carried luggage over the passes; I worked, I found opportunities, I was pleasing to the visitors—and now!" He checked himself suddenly. "Of course I am still but a poor man. My wife and children——"

"Children!" cried Miss Raby, suddenly seeing a path of salvation. "What children have you?"

"Three dear little boys," he replied, without enthusiasm.

"How old is the youngest?"

"Madam, five."

"Let me have that child," she said impressively, "and I will bring him up. He shall live among rich people. He shall see that they are not the vile creatures he supposes, always clamouring for respect and deference and trying to buy them with money. Rich people are good: they are capable of sympathy and love: they are fond of the truth; and when they are with each other they are clever. Your boy shall learn this, and he shall try to teach it to you. And when he grows up, if God is good to him he shall teach the rich: he shall teach them not to be stupid to the poor. I have tried myself, and people buy my books and say that they are good, and smile and lay them down. But I know this: so long as the stupidity exists, not only our charities and missions and schools, but the whole of our civilization, is vain."

It was painful for Colonel Leyland to listen to such phrases. He made one more effort to rescue Miss Raby. "Je vous prie de ne pas ——" he began gruffly, and then stopped, for he remembered that the concierge must know French. But Feo was not attending, nor, of course, had he attended to the lady's prophecies. He was wondering if he could persuade his wife to give up the little boy, and, if he did, how much they dare ask from Miss Raby without repulsing her.

"That will be my pardon," she continued, "if out of the place where I have done so much evil I bring some good. I am tired of memories, though they have been very beautiful. Now, Feo, I want you to give me something else: a living boy. I shall always puzzle you; and I cannot help it. I have changed so much since we met, and I have changed you also. We are both new people. Remember that; for I want to ask you one question before we part, and I cannot see why you shouldn't answer it. Feo! I want you to attend."

"I beg your pardon, madam," said the concierge, rousing himself from his calculations. "Is there anything I can do for you?"

"Answer 'yes' or 'no'; that day when you said you were in love with me—was it true?"

It was doubtful whether he could have answered, whether he had now any opinion about that day at all. But he did not make the attempt. He saw again that he was menaced by an ugly, withered, elderly woman, who was trying to destroy his reputation and his domestic peace. He shrank towards Colonel Leyland, and faltered: "Madam, you must excuse me, but I had rather you did not see my wife; she is so sharp. You are most kind about my little boy; but, madam, no, she would never permit it."

"You have insulted a lady!" shouted the colonel, and made a chivalrous movement of attack. From the hall behind came exclamations of horror and expectancy. Some one ran for the manager.

Miss Raby interposed, saying, "He will never think me respectable." She looked at the dishevelled Feo, fat, perspiring, and unattractive, and smiled sadly at her own stupidity, not at his. It was useless to speak to him again; her talk had scared away his competence and his civility, and scarcely anything was left. He was hardly more human than a frightened rabbit. "Poor man," she murmured, "I have only vexed him. But I wish he would have given me the boy. And I wish he would have answered my question, if only out of pity. He does not know the sort of thing that keeps me alive." She was looking at Colonel Leyland, and so discovered that he too was discomposed. It was her peculiarity that she could only attend to the person she was speaking with, and forgot the personality of the listeners. "I have been vexing you as well: I am very silly."

"It is a little late to think about me," said Colonel Leyland grimly.

She remembered their conversation of yesterday, and understood him at once. But for him she had no careful explanation, no tender pity. He was a man who was well born and well educated, who had all those things called advantages, who imagined himself full of insight and cultivation and knowledge of mankind. And he had proved himself to be at the exact spiritual level of the man who had no advantages, who was poor and had been made vulgar, whose early virtue had been destroyed by circumstance, whose manliness and simplicity had perished in serving the rich. If Colonel Leyland also believed that she was now in love with Feo, she would not exert herself to undeceive him. Nor indeed would she have found it possible.

From the darkening valley there rose up the first strong singing note of the campanile, and she turned from the men towards it with a motion of love. But that day was not to close without the frustration of every hope. The sound inspired Feo to make conversation and, as the mountains reverberated, he said: "Is it not unfortunate, sir? A gentleman went to see our fine new tower this morning and he believes that the land is slipping from underneath, and that it will fall. Of course it will not harm us up here."

His speech was successful. The stormy scene came to an abrupt and placid conclusion. Before they had realized it, she had taken up her *Baedeker* and left them, with no tragic gesture. In that moment of final failure, there had been vouchsafed to her a vision of herself, and she saw that she had lived worthily. She was conscious of a triumph over experience and earthly facts, a triumph magnificent, cold, hardly human, whose existence no one but herself would ever surmise. From the view-terrace she looked down on the perishing and perishable beauty of the valley, and though she loved it no less, it seemed to be infinitely distant, like a valley in a star. At that moment, if kind voices had called her from the hotel, she would not have returned. "I suppose this is old age," she thought. "It's not so very dreadful."

No one did call her. Colonel Leyland would have liked to do so; for he knew she must be unhappy. But she had hurt him too much; she had exposed her thoughts and desires to a man of another class. Not only she, but he himself and all their equals, were degraded by it. She had discovered their nakedness to the alien.

People came in to dress for dinner and for the concert. From the hall there pressed out a stream of excited servants, filling the lounge as an operatic chorus fills the stage, and announcing the approach of the manager. It was impossible to pretend that nothing had happened. The scandal would be immense, and must be diminished as it best might.

Much as Colonel Leyland disliked touching people he took Feo by the arm, and then quickly raised his finger to his forehead.

"Exactly, sir," whispered the concierge. "Of course we understand —— Oh, thank you, sir, thank you very much: thank you very much indeed!"

The Echo and the Nemesis

JEAN STAFFORD

Jean Stafford (b. 1915) was born in California, the daughter of a writer of westerns. She graduated from the University of Colorado and studied philology in Heidelberg. She has been married to the poet Robert Lowell and is the widow of A. J. Liebling. Her novels are *Boston Adventure, The Mountain Lion* and *The Catherine Wheel.* She won the Pulitzer Prize for fiction in 1970 for her collected short stories. *The Echo and the Nemesis* was first published in *The New Yorker* and later appeared in her collection *Children Are Bored on Sundays.*

SUE LEDBETTER and Ramona Dunn became friends through the commonplace accident of their sitting side by side in a philosophy lecture three afternoons a week. There were many other American students at Heidelberg University that winter—the last before the war—but neither Sue nor Ramona had taken up with them. Ramona had not because she scorned them; in her opinion, they were Philistines, concerned only with drinking beer, singing German songs, and making spectacles of themselves on their bicycles and in their little rented cars. And Sue had not because she was self-conscious and introverted and did not make friends easily. In Ramona's presence, she pretended to deplore her compatriots' escapades, which actually she envied desperately. Sometimes on Saturday nights she lay on her bed unable to read or daydream and in an agony of frustration as she listened to her fellow-lodgers at the Pension Kirchenheim laughing and teasing and sometimes bursting into song as they played bridge and Monopoly in the cozy veranda café downstairs.

Soon after the semester opened in October, the two girls fell into the habit of drinking their afternoon coffee together on the days they met in class. Neither of them especially enjoyed the other's company, but in their different ways they were lonely, and as Ramona once remarked, in her highfalutin way, "From time to time, I need a rest from the exercitation of my intellect." She was very vain of her intellect, which she had directed to the study of philology, to the exclusion of almost everything else in the world. Sue, while she had always taken her work seriously, longed also for beaux and parties, and conversation about them, and she was often bored by Ramona's talk, obscurely gossipy, of the vagaries of certain Old High Franconian verbs when they encountered the High German consonant shift, or of the variant readings of passages in Layamon's *Brut,* or the linguistic influence Eleanor of Aquitaine had exerted on the English court. But because she was well-mannered she listened politely and even appeared to follow Ramona's exuberant elucidation of Sanskrit "a"-stem declensions and her ardent plan to write a monograph on the word "ahoy." They drank their coffee in the Konditorei Luitpold, a very noisy café on a street bent like an elbow, down behind the cathedral. The din of its two small rooms was aggravated by the peripheral racket that came from the kitchen and from the outer shop, where the cakes were kept. The waiters, all of whom looked cross, hustled about at a great rate, slamming down trays and glasses and cups any which way before the many customers, who gabbled and rattled newspapers and pounded on the table for more of something. Over all the to-do was the blare of the radio, with its dial set permanently at a station that played nothing but stormy choruses from *Wilhelm Tell.* Ramona, an invincible expositor, had to shout, but shout she did as she traced words like "rope" and "calf" through dozens of languages back to their Indo-Germanic source. Sometimes Sue, befuddled by the uproar, wanted by turns to laugh and to cry with disappointment, for this was not at all the way she had imagined that she would live in Europe. Half incredulously and half irritably, she would stare at Ramona as if in some way she were to blame.

Ramona Dunn was fat to the point of parody. Her obesity fitted her badly, like extra clothing put on in the wintertime, for her embedded bones were very small and she was very short, and she had a foolish gait, which, however, was swift, as if she were a mechanical doll whose engine raced. Her face was rather pretty, but its features were so small that it was all but lost in its billowing surroundings, and it was covered by a thin, fair skin that was subject to disfiguring affections, now hives, now eczema, now impetigo, and the whole was framed by fine, pale hair that was abused once a week by a *Friseur* who baked it with an iron into dozens of horrid little snails. She habitually wore a crimson tam-o'-shanter with a sportive spray of artificial edelweiss pinned to the very top of it. For so determined a bluestocking, her eccentric and extensive wardrobe was a surprise; nothing was ever completely clean or completely whole, and nothing ever matched anything else, but it was apparent that all these odd and often ugly clothes had been expensive. She had a long, fur-lined cape, and men's tweed jackets with leather patches on the elbows, and flannel shirts designed for hunters in the state of Maine, and high-necked jerseys, and a waistcoat made of unborn gazelle, dyed Kelly green. She attended particularly to the dressing of her tiny hands and feet, and she had gloves and mittens of every color and every material, and innumerable pairs of extraordinary shoes, made for her by a Roman bootmaker. She always carried a pair of field glasses, in a brassbound leather case that hung over her shoulder by a plaited strap of rawhide; she looked through the wrong end of them, liking, for some reason that she did not disclose, to diminish the world she surveyed. Wherever she went, she took a locked pigskin satchel, in which she carried her grammars and lexicons and the many drafts of the many articles she was writing in the hope that they would be published in learned journals. One day in the café, soon after the girls became acquainted, she opened up the satchel, and Sue was shocked at the helter-skelter arrangement of the papers, all mussed and frayed, and stained with coffee and ink. But, even more, she was dumfounded to see a clear-green all-day sucker stuck like a bookmark between the pages of a glossary to *Beowulf*.

Sue knew that Ramona was rich, and that for the last ten years her family had lived in Italy, and that before that they had lived in New York. But this was all she knew about her friend; she did not even know where she lived in Heidelberg. She believed that Ramona, in her boundless erudition, was truly consecrated to her studies and that she truly had no other desire than to impress the subscribers to *Speculum* and the *Publications of the Modern Language Association*. She was the sort of person who seemed, at twenty-one, to have fought all her battles and survived to enjoy the quiet of her un-endangered ivory tower. She did not seem to mind at all that she was so absurd to look at, and Sue, who was afire with ambitions and sick with conflict, admired her arrogant self-possession.

The two girls had been going to the Konditorei Luitpold three times a week for a month or more, and all these meetings had been alike; Ramona had talked and Sue had contributed expressions of surprise (who would have dreamed that "bolster" and "poltroon" derived from the same parent?), or murmurs of acquiescence (she agreed there might be something in the discreet rumor that the Gothic language had been made up by nineteenth-century scholars to answer riddles that could not otherwise be solved), or laughter, when it seemed becoming. The meetings were neither rewarding nor entirely uninteresting to Sue, and she came to look upon them as a part of the week's schedule, like the philosophy lectures and the seminar in Schiller.

And then, one afternoon, just as the weary, mean-mouthed waiter set their cake down before them, the radio departed from its custom and over it came the "Minuet in G," so neat and winning and sur-prising that for a moment there was a general lull in the café, and even the misanthropic waiter paid the girls the honor, in his short-lived delight, of not slopping their coffee. As if they all shared the same memories that the little sentimental piece of music awoke in her, Sue glanced around smiling at her fellows and tried to believe that all of them—even the old men with Hindenburg mustaches and palsied wattles, and even the Brown Shirts fiercely playing chess—had been children like herself and had stumbled in buckled pumps through the simple steps of the minuet at the military command of a dancing teacher, Miss Conklin, who had bared her sinewy legs to the thigh. In some public presentation of Miss Conklin's class, Sue had worn a yellow bodice with a lacing of black velvet ribbon, a bouffant skirt of chintz covered all over with daffodils, and a cotton-batting wig that smelled of stale talcum powder. Even though her partner had been a sissy boy with nastily damp hands and white eyelashes, and though she had been grave with stage fright, she had had mo-ments of most thrilling expectation, as if this were only the dress rehearsal of the grown-up ball to come.

If she had expected all the strangers in the café to be transported by the "Minuet" to a sweet and distant time, she had not expected Ramona Dunn to be, and she was astonished and oddly frightened to see the fat girl gazing with a sad, reflective smile into her water glass. When the music stopped and the familiar hullabaloo was reestablished in the room, Ramona said, "Oh, I don't know of anything that makes me more nostalgic than that tinny little tune! It makes me think of Valentine parties before my sister Martha died."

It took Sue a minute to rearrange her family portrait of the Dunns, which heretofore had included, besides Ramona, only a mother and a father and three brothers. Because this was by far the simplest way, she had seen them in her mind's eye as five stout, scholarly extensions of Ramona, grouped together against the background of Vesuvius. She had imagined that they spent their time examining papyri and writing Latin verses, and she regretted admitting sorrow into their lives, as she had to do when she saw Ramona's eyes grow vague and saw her, quite unlike her naturally greedy self, push her cake aside, untouched. For a moment or two, the fat girl was still and blank, as if she were waiting for a pain to go away, and then she poured the milk into her coffee, replaced her cake, and began to talk about her family, who, it seemed, were not in the least as Sue had pictured them.

Ramona said that she alone of them was fat and ill-favored, and the worst of it was that Martha, the most beautiful girl who ever lived, had been her twin. Sue could not imagine, she declared, how frightfully good-looking all the Dunns were—except herself, of course: tall and dark-eyed and oval-faced, and tanned from the hours they spent on their father's boat, the *San Filippo*. And they were terribly gay and venturesome; they were the despair of the croupiers at the tables on the Riviera, the envy of the skiers at San Bernardino and of the yachtsmen on the Mediterranean. Their balls and their musicales and their dinner parties were famous. All the brothers had unusual artistic gifts, and there was so much money in the family that they did not have to do anything but work for their own pleasure in their studios. They were forever involved in scandals with their mistresses, who were either married noblewomen or notorious dancing girls, and forever turning over a new leaf and getting themselves engaged to lovely, convent-bred princesses, whom, however, they did not marry; the young ladies were too submissively Catholic, or too stupid, or their taste in painting was vulgar.

Of all this charming, carefree brood, Martha, five years dead, had been the most splendid, Ramona said, a creature so slight and delicate that one wanted to put her under a glass bell to protect her. Painters were captivated by the elegant shape of her head, around which she wore her chestnut hair in a coronet, and there were a dozen portraits of her, and hundreds of drawings hanging in the big bedroom where she had died and which now had been made into a sort of shrine for her. If the Dunns were odd in any way, it was in this devotion to their dead darling; twice a year Mrs. Dunn changed the nibs in Martha's pens, and in one garden there grew nothing but anemones, Martha's favorite flower. She had ailed from birth, pursued malevolently by the disease that had melted her away to the wick finally when she was sixteen. The family had come to Italy in the beginning of her mortal languor in the hope that the warmth and novelty would revive her, and for a while it did, but the wasting poison continued to devour her slowly, and for years she lay, a touching invalid, on a balcony overlooking the Bay of Naples. She lay on a blond satin chaise longue, in a quaint peignoir made of leaf-green velvet, and sometimes, as she regarded her prospect of sloops and valiant skiffs on the turbulent waves, the cypress trees, white villas in the midst of olive groves, and the intransigent smoldering of Vesuvius, she sang old English airs and Irish songs as she accompanied herself on a lute. If, in the erratic course of her illness, she got a little stronger, she asked for extra cushions at her back and half sat up at a small easel to paint in water-colors, liking the volcano as a subject, trite as it was, and the comic tourist boats that romped over the bay from Naples to Capri. If she was very unwell, she simply lay smiling while her parents and her sister and her brothers attended her, trying to seduce her back to health with their futile offerings of plums and tangerines and gilt-stemmed glasses of Rhine wine and nosegays bought from the urchins who bargained on the carriage roads.

When Martha died, Ramona's own grief was despair, because the death of a twin is a foretaste of one's own death, and for months she had been harried with premonitions and prophetic dreams, and often she awoke to find that she had strayed from her bed, for what awful purpose she did not know, and was walking barefoot, like a pilgrim, down the pitch-black road. But the acute phase of her mourning had passed, and now, although sorrow was always with her, like an alter ego, she had got over the worst of it.

She paused in her narrative and unexpectedly laughed. "What a gloom I'm being!" she said, and resumed her monologue at once but in a lighter tone, this time to recount the drubbing her brother Justin had given someone when he was defending the honor of a dishonorable soprano, and to suggest, in tantalizing innuendoes, that her parents were not faithful to each other.

Sue, whose dead father had been an upright, pessimistic clergyman and whose mother had never given voice to an impure thought, was bewitched by every word Ramona said. It occurred to her once to wonder why Ramona so frowned upon the frolics of the other American students when her beloved relatives were so worldly, but then she realized that the manners of the *haut monde* were one thing and those of undergraduates another. How queer, Sue thought, must seem this freakish bookworm in the midst of it all! And yet such was the ease with which Ramona talked, so exquisitely placed were her fillips of French, so intimate and casual her allusions to the rich and celebrated figures of international society, that Ramona changed before Sue's eyes; from the envelope of fat emerged a personality as *spirituelle* and knowing as any practicing sophisticate's. When, in the course of describing a distiller from Milan who was probably her mother's lover, she broke off and pressingly issued Sue an invitation to go with her a month from then, at the Christmas holiday, to San Bernardino to meet her brothers for a fortnight of skiing, Sue accepted immediately, not stopping to think, in the heady pleasure of the moment, that the proposal was unduly sudden, considering the sketchy nature of their friendship. "My brothers will adore you," she said, giving Sue a look of calm appraisal. "They are eclectic and they'll find your red hair and brown eyes irresistibly naïve." As if the plan had long been in her mind, Ramona named the date they would leave Heidelberg; she begged permission, in the most gracious and the subtlest possible way, to let Sue be her guest, even to the extent of supplying her with ski equipment. When the details were settled—a little urgently, she made Sue promise "on her word of honor" that she would not default—she again took up her report on Signor da Gama, the distiller, who was related by blood to the Pope and had other distinctions of breeding as well to recommend him to her mother, who was, she confessed, something of a snob. "Mama," she said, accenting the ultima, "thinks it is unnecessary for anyone to be badly born."

The Konditorei Luitpold was frequented by teachers from the Translators' Institute, and usually Ramona rejoiced in listening to them chattering and expostulating, in half a dozen European languages, for she prided herself on her gift of tongues. But today her heart was in Sorrento, and she paid no attention to them, not even to two vociferous young Russians at a table nearby. She disposed of the roué from Milan (Sue had read Catullus? Signor da Gama had a cottage at Sirmio not far from his reputed grave) and seemed to be on the point of disclosing her father's delinquencies when she was checked by a new mood, which made her lower her head, flush, and, through a long moment of silence, study the greasy hoops the rancid milk had made on the surface of her coffee.

Sue felt as if she had inadvertently stumbled upon a scene of deepest privacy, which, if she were not careful, she would violate, and, pretending that she had not observed the hiatus at all, she asked, conversationally, the names of Ramona's brothers besides Justin.

The two others were called Daniel and Robert, but it was not of them, or of her parents, or of Martha, that Ramona now wanted to speak but of herself, and haltingly she said that the "Minuet in G" had deranged her poise because it had made her think of the days of her childhood in New York, when she had been no bigger than her twin and they had danced the minuet together, Ramona taking the dandy's part. A friend of the family had predicted that though they were then almost identical, Ramona was going to be the prettier of the two. Now Sue was shocked, for she had thought that Ramona must always have been fat, and she was nearly moved to tears to know that the poor girl had been changed from a swan into an ugly duckling and that it was improbable, from the looks of her, that she would ever be changed back again. But Sue was so young and so badly equipped to console someone so beset that she could not utter a word, and she wished she could go home.

Ramona summoned the waiter and ordered her third piece of cake, saying nervously, after she had done so, "I'm sorry. When I get upset,

I have to eat to calm myself. I'm awful! I ought to kill myself for eating so much." She began to devour the cake obsessively, and when she had finished it down to the last crumb, and the last fragment of frosting, she said, with shimmering eyes, "Please let me tell you what it is that makes me the unhappiest girl in the world, and maybe you can help me." Did Sue have any idea what it was like to be ruled by food and half driven out of one's mind until one dreamed of it and had at last no other ambition but to eat incessantly with an appetite that grew and grew until one saw oneself, in nightmares, as nothing but an enormous mouth and a tongue, trembling lasciviously? Did she know the terror and the remorse that followed on the heels of it when one slyly sneaked the lion's share of buttered toast at tea? Had she ever desired the whole of a pudding meant for twelve and hated with all her heart the others at the dinner table? Sue could not hide her blushing face or put her fingers in her ears or close her eyes against the tortured countenance of that wretched butterball, who declared that she had often come within an ace of doing away with herself because she was so fat.

Leaning across the table, almost whispering, Ramona went on, "I didn't come to Heidelberg for its philologists—they don't know any more than I do. I have exiled myself. I would not any longer offend that long-suffering family of mine with the sight of me." It had been her aim to fast throughout this year, she continued, and return to them transformed, and she had hoped to be thinner by many pounds when she joined her brothers at Christmastime. But she had at once run into difficulties, because, since she was not altogether well (she did not specify her illness and Sue would not have asked its name for anything), she had to be under the supervision of a doctor. And the doctor in Heidelberg, like the doctor in Naples, would not take her seriously when she said her fatness was ruining her life; they had both gone so far as to say that she was *meant* to be like this and that it would be imprudent of her to diet. Who was bold enough to fly in the face of medical authority? Not she, certainly.

It appeared, did it not, to be a dilemma past solution, Ramona asked. And yet this afternoon she had begun to see a way out, if Sue would pledge herself to help. Sue did not reply at once, sensing an involvement, but then she thought of Ramona's brothers, whom she was going to please, and she said she would do what she could.

"You're not just saying that? You are my friend? You know, of course, that you'll be repaid a hundredfold." Ramona subjected Sue's sincerity to some minutes of investigation and then outlined her plan, which seemed very tame to Sue after all these preparations, for it consisted only of Ramona's defying Dr. Freudenburg and of Sue's becoming a sort of unofficial censor and confessor. Sue was to have lunch with her each day, at Ramona's expense, and was to remind her, by a nudge or a word now and again, not to eat more than was really necessary to keep alive. If at any time Sue suspected that she was eating between meals or late at night, she was to come out flatly with an accusation and so shame Ramona that it would never happen again. The weekends were particularly difficult, since there were no lectures to go to and it was tempting not to stir out of her room at all but to gorge throughout the day on delicacies out of tins and boxes that she had sent to herself from shops in Strasbourg and Berlin. And since, in addition to fasting, she needed exercise, she hoped that Sue would agree to go walking with her on Saturdays and Sundays, a routine that could be varied from time to time by a weekend trip to some neighboring town of interest.

When Sue protested mildly that Ramona had contradicted her earlier assertion that she would not dare dispute her doctor's word, Ramona grinned roguishly and said only, "Don't be nosy."

Ramona had found an old ladies' home, called the Gerstnerheim, which, being always in need of funds, welcomed paying guests at the midday meal, whom they fed for an unimaginably low price. Ramona did not patronize it out of miserliness, however, but because the food was nearly inedible. And it was here that the girls daily took their Spartan lunch. It was quite the worst food that Sue had ever eaten anywhere, for it was cooked to pallor and flaccidity and then was seasoned with unheard-of condiments, which sometimes made her sick. The bread was sour and the soup was full of pasty clots; the potatoes were waterlogged and the old red cabbage was boiled until it was blue. The dessert was always a basin of molded farina with a sauce of gray jelly that had a gray taste. The aged ladies sat at one enormously long table, preserving an institutional silence until the farina was handed around, and as if this were an alarm, all the withered lips began to move simultaneously and from them issued high squawks of protest against the dreary lot of being old and homeless and underfed. Sue could not help admiring Ramona, who ate her plate of eel and celeriac as if she really preferred it to tuna broiled with black olives and who talked all the while of things quite other than food—of Walther von der Vogelweide's eccentric syntax, of a new French novel that had come in the mail that morning, and of their trip to Switzerland.

Justin and Daniel and Robert were delighted that Sue was coming, Ramona said, and arrangements were being made in a voluminous correspondence through the air over the Alps. Sue had never been on skis in her life, but she did not allow this to deflate her high hopes. She thought only of evenings of lieder (needless to say, the accomplished Dunns sang splendidly) and hot spiced wine before a dancing fire, of late breakfasts in the white sun and brilliant conversation. And of what was coming afterward! The later holidays (Ramona called them *villeggiatura*), spent in Sorrento! The countesses' garden parties in Amalfi and the cruises on the Adriatic, the visits to Greece, the balls in the princely houses of Naples! Ramona could not decide which of her brothers Sue would elect to marry. Probably Robert, she thought, since he was the youngest and the most affectionate.

It was true that Sue did not quite believe all she was told, but she knew that the ways of the rich are strange, and while she did not allow her fantasies to invade the hours assigned to classes and study, she did not rebuff them when they came at moments of leisure. From time to time, she suddenly remembered that she was required to give something in return for Ramona's largess, and then she would say how proud she was of her friend's self-discipline or would ask her, like a frank and compassionate doctor, if she had strayed at all from her intention (she always had; she always immediately admitted it and Sue always put on a show of disappointment), and once in a while she said that Ramona was looking much thinner, although this was absolutely untrue. Sometimes they took the electric tram to Neckargemünd, where they split a bottle of sweet Greek wine. Occasionally they went to Mannheim, to the opera, but they never stayed for a full performance; Ramona said that later in the year Signor da Gama would invite them to his house in Milan and then they could go to La Scala every night. Once they went for a weekend to Rothenburg, where Ramona, in an uncontrollable holiday mood, ate twelve cherry tarts in a single day. She was tearful for a week afterward, and to show Sue how sorry she was, she ground out a cigarette on one of her downy wrists. This dreadful incident took place in the Luitpold and was witnessed by several patrons, who could not conceal their alarm. Sue thought to herself, Maybe she's cuckoo, and while she did not relinquish any of her daydreams of the festivities in Italy, she began to observe Ramona more closely.

She could feel the turmoil in her when they went past bakeshop windows full of cream puffs and cheesecake and petits fours. Ramona, furtively glancing at the goodies out of the corner of her eye, would begin a passionate and long-winded speech on the present-day use of Latin in Iceland. When, on a special occasion, they dined together at the Ritterhalle, she did not even look at the menu but lionheartedly ordered a single dropped egg and a cup of tea and resolutely kept her eyes away from Sue's boiled beef and fritters. When drinking cocktails in the American bar at the Europäischer Hof, she shook her head as the waiter passed a tray of canapés made of caviar, anchovy, lobster, foie gras, and Camembert, ranged fanwise around a little bowl of ivory almonds. But sometimes she did capitulate, with a piteous rationalization—that she had not eaten any breakfast or that she had barely touched her soup at the Gerstnerheim and that therefore there would be nothing wrong in her having two or perhaps three or four of these tiny little sandwiches. One time Sue saw her take several more than she had said she would and hide them under the rim of her plate.

As the date set for their departure for Switzerland drew nearer, Ramona grew unaccountable. Several times she failed to appear at lunch, and when Sue, in a friendly way, asked for an explanation, she snapped, "None of your business. What do you think you are? My nurse?" She was full of peevishness, complaining of the smell of senility in the Gerstnerheim, of students who sucked the shells of pistachio nuts in the library, of her landlady's young son, who she was sure rummaged through her bureau drawers when she was not at home. Once she and Sue had a fearful row when Sue, keeping up her end of the bargain, although she really did not care a pin, told her not to buy a bag of chestnuts from a vendor on a street corner. Ramona shouted, for all the world to hear, "You are sadly mistaken,

Miss Ledbetter, if you think you know more than Dr. Augustus Freudenburg, of the Otto-Ludwigs Clinic!" And a little after that she acquired the notion that people were staring at her, and she carried an umbrella, rain or shine, to hide herself from them. But, oddest of all, when the skis and boots and poles that she had ordered for Sue arrived, and Sue thanked her for them, she said, "I can't think what use they'll be. Obviously there never is any snow in this ghastly, godforsaken place."

There was an awful afternoon when Ramona was convinced that the waiter at the Luitpold had impugned her German, and Sue found herself in the unhappy role of intermediary in a preposterous altercation so bitter that it stopped just short of a bodily engagement. When the girls left the café—at the insistence of the management—they were silent all the way to the cathedral, which was the place where they usually took leave of each other to go their separate ways home. They paused a moment there in the growing dark, and suddenly Ramona said, "Look at me!" Sue looked at her. "I say!" said Ramona. "In this light you look exactly like my sister. How astonishing! Turn a little to the left, there's a dear." And when Sue had turned as she directed, a whole minute—but it seemed an hour to Sue —passed before Ramona broke from her trance to cry, "How blind I've been! My brothers would be shocked to death if they should see you. It would kill them!"

She put out her hands, on which she wore white leather mittens, and held Sue's face between them and studied it, half closing her eyes and murmuring her amazement, her delight, her perplexity at her failure until now to see this marvelous resemblance. Once, as her brown eyes nimbly catechized the face before her, she took off her right mitten and ran her index finger down Sue's nose, as if she had even learned her sister's bones by heart, while Sue, unable to speak, could only think in panic, What does she mean *if* they should see me?

Ramona carried on as if she were moon-struck, making fresh discoveries until not only were Sue's and Martha's faces identical but so were their voices and their carriage and the shape of their hands and feet. She said, "You must come to my room and see a picture of Martha right now. It's desperately weird."

Fascinated, Sue nodded, and they moved on through the quiet

street. Ramona paused to look at her each time they went under a street light, touched her hair, begged leave to take her arm, and called her Martha, Sister, Twin, and sometimes caught her breath in an abortive sob. They went past the lighted windows of the *Bier-stuben,* where the shadows of young men loomed and waved, and then turned at the Kornmarkt and began to climb the steep, moss-slick steps that led to the castle garden. As they went through the avenue of trees that lay between the casino and the castle, Ramona, peering at Sue through the spooky mist, said, "They would have been much quicker to see it than I," so Sue knew, miserably and for sure, that something had gone wrong with their plans to go to San Bernardino. And then Ramona laughed and broke away and took off her tam-o'-shanter, which she hurled toward the hedge of yew, where it rested tipsily.

"I could vomit," she said, standing absolutely still.

There was a long pause. Finally, Sue could no longer bear the suspense, and she asked Ramona if her brothers knew that she and Ramona were not coming.

"Of course they know. They've known for two weeks, but you're crazy if you think the reason we're not going is that you look like Martha. How beastly vain you are!" She was so angry and she trembled so with her rage that Sue did not dare say another word. "It was Freudenburg who said I couldn't go," she howled. "He has found out that I have lost ten pounds."

Sue had no conscious motive in asking her, idly and not really caring, where Dr. Freudenberg's office was; she had meant the guileless question to be no more than a show of noncommittal and courteous interest, and she was badly frightened when, in reply, Ramona turned on her and slapped her hard on either cheek, and then opened her mouth to emit one hideous, protracted scream. Sue started instinctively to run away, but Ramona seized and held her arms, and began to talk in a lunatic, fast monotone, threatening her with lawsuits and public exposure if she ever mentioned the name Freudenburg again *or* her brothers *or* her mother and father *or* Martha, that ghastly, puling, pampered hypochondriac who had totally wrecked her life.

Sue felt that the racket of her heart and her hot, prancing brain would drown out Ramona's voice, but it did nothing of the kind, and they stood there, rocking in their absurd attitude, while the fit continued. Sue was sure that the police and the townsfolk would come running at any moment and an alarm would be sounded and they would be arrested for disturbing the peace. But if anyone heard them, it was only the shades of the princes in the castle.

It was difficult for Sue to sort out the heroes and the villains in this diatribe. Sometimes it appeared that Ramona's brothers and her parents hated her, sometimes she thought they had been glad when Martha died; sometimes Dr. Freudenburg seemed to be the cause of everything. She had the impression that he was an alienist, and she wondered if now he would send his patient to an institution; at other times she thought the doctor did not exist at all. She did not know whom to hate or whom to trust, for the characters in this *Walpurgisnacht* changed shape by the minute and not a one was left out—not Signor da Gama or the ballet girls in Naples or the old ladies at the Gerstnerheim or the prehistoric figures of a sadistic nurse, a base German governess, and a nefarious boy cousin who had invited Ramona to misbehave when she was barely eight years old. Once she said that to escape Dr. Freudenburg she meant to order her father to take her cruising on the *San Filippo;* a minute later she said that that loathsome fool Justin had wrecked the boat on the coast of Yugoslavia. She would go home to the villa in Sorrento and be comforted by her brothers who had always preferred her to everyone else in the world—except that they hadn't! They had always despised her. Freudenburg would write to her father and he would come to fetch her back to that vulgar, parvenu house, and there, in spite of all her efforts to outwit them, they would make her eat and eat until she was the laughing stock of the entire world. What *were* they after? Did they want to indenture her to a sideshow?

She stopped, trailed off, turned loose Sue's arm, and stood crestfallen, like a child who realizes that no one is listening to his tantrum. Tears, terribly silent, streamed down her round cheeks.

Then, "It isn't true, you know. They aren't like that, they're good and kind. The only thing that's true is that I eat all the time," and softly, to herself, she repeated, "All the time." In a mixture of self-hatred and abstracted bravado, she said that she had supplemented all her lunches at the Gerstnerheim and had nibbled constantly, alone in her room; that Dr. Freudenburg's recommendation had been just the opposite of what she had been saying all along.

Unconsolable, Ramona moved on along the path, and Sue followed, honoring her tragedy but struck dumb by it. On the way through the courtyard and down the street, Ramona told her, in a restrained and rational voice, that her father was coming the next day to take her back to Italy, since the experiment of her being here alone had not worked. Her parents, at the counsel of Dr. Freudenburg, were prepared to take drastic measures, involving, if need be, a hospital, the very thought of which made her blood run cold. "Forgive me for that scene back there," she said. "You grow wild in loneliness like mine. It would have been lovely if it had all worked out the way I wanted and we had gone to Switzerland."

"Oh, that's all right," said Sue, whose heart was broken. "I don't know how to ski anyway."

"Really? What crust! I'd never have bought you all that gear if I had known." Ramona laughed lightly. They approached the garden gate of a tall yellow house, and she said, "This is where I live. Want to come in and have a glass of kirsch?"

Sue did not want the kirsch and she knew she should be on her way home if she were to get anything hot for supper, but she was curious to see the photograph of Martha, and since Ramona seemed herself again, she followed her down the path. Ramona had two little rooms, as clean and orderly as cells. In the one where she studied, there was no furniture except a long desk with deep drawers and a straight varnished chair and a listing bookcase. She had very few books, really, for one so learned—not more than fifty altogether —and every one of them was dull: grammars, dictionaries, readers, monographs reprinted from scholarly journals, and treatises on semantics, etymology and phonetics. Her pens and pencils lay straight in a lacquered tray, and a pile of notebooks sat neatly at the right of the blotter, and at the left there was a book open to a homily in Anglo-Saxon which, evidently, she had been translating. As soon as they had taken off their coats, Ramona went into the bedroom and closed the door; from beyond it Sue could hear drawers being opened and quickly closed, metal clashing, and paper rustling, and she imagined that the bureaus were stocked with contraband—with sweets and sausages and cheese. For the last time, she thought of Daniel and Justin and Robert, of whom she was to be forever deprived because their sister could not curb her brutish appetite.

She wandered around the room and presently her eye fell on a photograph in a silver frame standing in a half-empty shelf of the bookcase. It could only be Martha. The dead girl did not look in the least like Sue but was certainly as pretty as she had been described, and as Sue looked at the pensive eyes and the thoughtful lips, she was visited by a fugitive feeling that this was really Ramona's face at which she looked and that it had been refined and made immaculate by an artful photographer who did not scruple to help his clients deceive themselves. For Martha wore a look of lovely wonder and remoteness, as if she were all disconnected spirit, and it was the same as a look that sometimes came to Ramona's eyes and lips just as she lifted her binoculars to contemplate the world through the belittling lenses.

Sue turned the photograph around, and on the back she read the penned inscription "Martha Ramona Dunn at sixteen, Sorrento." She looked at the ethereal face again, and this time had no doubt that it had once belonged to Ramona. No wonder the loss of it had left her heartbroken! She sighed to think of her friend's desperate fabrication. In a sense, she supposed the Martha side of Ramona Dunn *was* dead, dead and buried under layers and layers of fat. Just as she guiltily returned the picture to its place, the door to the bedroom opened and Ramona, grandly gesturing toward her dressing table, cried, "Come in! Come in! Enter the banquet hall!" She had emptied the drawers of all their forbidden fruits, and arrayed on the dressing table, in front of her bottles of cologne and medicine, were cheeses and tinned fish and pickles and pressed meat and cakes, candies, nuts, olives, sausages, buns, apples, raisins, figs, prunes, dates, and jars of pâté and glasses of jelly and little pots of caviar, as black as ink. "Don't stint!" she shouted, and she bounded forward and began to eat as if she had not had a meal in weeks.

"All evidence must be removed by morning! What a close shave! What if my father had come without telling me and had found it all!" Shamelessly, she ranged up and down the table, cropping and lowing like a cow in a pasture. There were droplets of sweat on her forehead and her hands were shaking, but nothing else about her showed that she had gone to pieces earlier or that she was deep, deeper by far than anyone else Sue had ever known.

Sucking a rind of citron, Ramona said, "You must realize that our friendship is over, but not through any fault of yours. When I went off and turned on you that way, it had nothing to do with you at all, for of course you don't look any more like Martha than the man in the moon."

"It's all right, Ramona," said Sue politely. She stayed close to the door, although the food looked very good. "I'll still be your friend."

"Oh, no, no, there would be nothing in it for you," Ramona said, and her eyes narrowed ever so slightly. "Thank you just the same. I am exceptionally ill." She spoke with pride, as if she were really saying "I am exceptionally talented" or "I am exceptionally attractive."

"I didn't know you were," said Sue. "I'm sorry."

"*I'm* not sorry. It is for yourself that you should be sorry. You have such a trivial little life, poor girl. It's not your fault. Most people do."

"I'd better go," said Sue.

"Go! Go!" cried Ramona, with a gesture of grand benediction. "I weep not."

Sue's hand was on the knob of the outer door, but she hesitated to leave a scene so inconclusive. Ramona watched her as she lingered; her mouth was so full that her cheeks were stretched out as if in mumps, and through the food and through a devilish, mad grin she said, "Of *course* you could never know the divine joy of being twins, provincial one! Do you know what he said the last night when my name was Martha? The night he came into that room where the anemones were? He pretended that he was looking for a sheet of music. Specifically for a sonata for the harpsichord by Wilhelm Friedrich Bach."

But Sue did not wait to hear what he, whoever he was, had said; she ran down the brown-smelling stairs and out into the cold street with the feeling that Ramona was still standing there before the food, as if she were serving herself at an altar, still talking, though there was no one to listen. She wondered if she ought to summon Dr. Freudenburg, and then decided that, in the end, it was none of her business. She caught a trolley that took her near her pension, and was just in time to get some hot soup and a plate of cold meats and

salad before the kitchen closed. But when the food came, she found
that she had no appetite at all. "What's the matter?" asked Herr
Sachs, the fresh young waiter. "Are you afraid to get fat?" And he
looked absolutely flabbergasted when, at this, she fled from the café
without a word.

The Friend of the Family

❉ MARY McCARTHY ❉

MARY McCARTHY (b. 1912) made her initial literary reputation as the brilliant but severe drama critic of the *Partisan Review*. Encouraged to write fiction by her second husband, the critic Edmund Wilson, she produced a volume of short stories, *The Company She Keeps*, in 1942. This was followed by several widely successful satirical novels, all written in a limpid classical style unique in our fiction, including *The Oasis* (1949), *The Groves of Academe* (1952) and *The Group* (1963). Miss McCarthy has more recently become a famous champion of the dove cause in the Viet-Nam war. *The Friend of the Family* appeared in *Cast a Cold Eye* (1944).

HIS great qualification was that nobody liked him very much. That is, nobody liked him enough to make a point of him. Consequently, among the married couples he knew, he was universally popular. Since nobody cherished him, swore by him, quoted his jokes or his political prophecies, nobody else felt obliged to diminish him; on the contrary, the husbands or wives of his friends were always discovering in him virtues their partners had never noticed, and a husband who was notorious for detesting the whole imposing suite of his wife's acquaintance would make an enthusiasm of the obscure Francis Cleary, whom up to that time the wife had seldom thought about. In the long war of marriage, in the battle of the friends, Francis Cleary was an open city. Undefended, he remained immune, as though an inconspicuous white flag fluttered in his sharkskin lapel. The very mention of his name brought a certain kind of domestic argument to a dead stop. ("You don't like my friends." "I do too like your friends." "No, you don't, you hate them." "That's not true," and —triumphantly—"I like Francis Cleary.")

A symbol of tolerance, of the spirit of compromise, he came into his own whenever one of his friends married. A man who in his single state had lunched with Francis Cleary once or twice a year would discover to his astonishment, after two or three years of marriage, that Francis Cleary was now his closest friend: he was invited regularly for weekends, for dinner, for cocktail parties; he made the invariable fourth at bridge or tennis. Though he might never have been asked to the wedding ceremony (and in fact it was more usual for the wife to have him introduced to her quite by chance a few months later, in a restaurant, and to experience a kind of Aristotelian recognition—"Why hasn't Jack ever spoken of you? You must come to dinner next Thursday"), his azalea plant or cyclamen would be the first to arrive at the hospital when the baby was born.

If it was the wife who had originally been Francis Cleary's friend, the graph of intimacy would follow the same curve. A mild admirer who had always figured in the background of her life, imperceptibly he would have slid to the very center of the composition: he came to stay for two weeks in the summer, played chess with her husband, and took her to dinner when she was alone in town. He had become "your friend Francis Cleary," a walking advertisement of her husband's good nature. "How can you say I am jealous?" he would ask. "You had lunch with Francis Cleary only last week." Left by herself with this old friend, she would—as she had always done— get bored, play the phonograph, make excuses to go to the kitchen to see how the maid was getting along with the hollandaise. Yet at her husband's suggestion she would invite him again and again, because his presence in the house reassured her, told her that marriage had not really changed her, that she was still free to see her own friends, that her husband was a generous, fair-minded man who could not, naturally, be expected to share every one of her tastes. Moreover, it was so *easy* to have Francis Cleary. When her real friends came, something unpleasant usually happened—an argument, an ill-considered reference to the past—or if nothing actually happened, she suffered in the expectation of its happening, so that when they finally left she echoed her husband's "Thank God, that's over!" in the silence of her heart. A few awkward evenings, a weekend would serve, in most cases, to convince her that the love she felt for her friends was a positive obstacle to her happiness; and she would renounce it, though perhaps only provisionally (telling herself that surely, later on, in precisely the right circumstances Jim would come to see these people as she did—just as she was sure that sometime, next week or next year, Jim would come to like string beans, if she served them to him in a moment of intimacy and with precisely the right sauce). Meanwhile, however, it was certainly better to have Francis Cleary, who was after all a close friend of her real friends (had she not met him through them?), and as the years passed the distinction between her "real" friends and Francis Cleary would blur in her mind and she would imagine that he had always been one of her dearest associates.

His social mobility derived from the fact that he was capable of being used by other people as a symbol, and a symbol not only of an idea (e.g., tolerance) but of an actual person or persons. Thus a husband, drawing up a guest list for an evening party, might remark to his wife, "How about having the Caldwells?" (or the Muellers or the Kaplans). "Oh my God," his wife would shriek, "do we have to have *them*?" "I like them." "They're awful, and besides they won't know anybody." "They're old friends of mine. I owe them something." "Have them when I'm away then—you know they can't stand me." "Don't be silly. They'd be crazy about you if you'd give them half a chance." In desperation, the wife would cast about her. She saw her party, her charming, harmonious, mildly diversified party, heading straight for shipwreck on the rock of her husband's stubbornness. Then all at once an inspiration would seize her. "Look," she would say, in a more reasonable tone, "why don't you ask Francis Cleary instead? He'd get along very well with these other people. And he's your friend, just as much as Hugh Caldwell is. You're wrong if you think it's a matter of the Caldwells' being your friends. It's just that they wouldn't fit in." And the husband, reading the storm warnings as clearly as she, telling himself that if he insisted on the Caldwells his wife might treat them with impossible rudeness, and that even if she did not, she would make her concession an excuse for filling the house for months to come with her intolerable friends, that he might win the battle but lose the war, would reluctantly, grudgingly, consent. After all, Francis Cleary belonged to the circle of the detested Caldwells. To have him would be to have their spirit if not their substance, and, to be perfectly honest—he would say to himself —wasn't it the principle of the Caldwells rather than their persons that was the issue at stake?

Another hostess, on slightly better terms with the prospective host, or perhaps merely a better tactician, would begin differently. "Darling," she would say, looking up from the memorandum pad on which already a few names had been neatly aligned. "I have an idea. Why don't we ask Francis Cleary?" The air of discovery with which she brought forth this proposal would accord oddly with the fact that they always did have Francis Cleary at their parties, but the husband, who had been fearing something much worse (some old school friend or a marvelous singer she had met at a benefit), would in his relief not notice the anomaly. "All right," he would say, grateful to her for her interest in this rather dull old business associate, and before he had time to change his mind, she would have telephoned Francis Cleary and secured his acceptance. Then, when the question of the Caldwells was raised, she would pout slightly. "Oh," she would say, "don't you think that makes too much of the same thing? After all, we're having Francis Cleary, and I do think it's a mistake to have a bloc at a party." "I don't know." "Oh, darling, you remember the time we had all those Italians and they sat in the corner and talked to each other. . . ."

In either case, the outcome was the same. Francis Cleary would appear at the party, representing the absent, unassimilable Caldwells. He was their abstraction, their ghost. Unobtrusive, moderately well bred, he would come early and stay late. He made no particular social contribution, but the host, whenever he glanced in his direction, would feel a throb of solidarity with his own past, and at some point in the evening he and Francis Cleary would have a talk about the Caldwells and Francis would tell him all about Hugh Caldwell's latest adventure. Not ordinarily a brilliant talker, in this particular field Francis Cleary was unsurpassed. He was a master of the second-hand anecdote, the vicarious exploit. Hugh Caldwell, who suffered dreadfully from asthma and had a distressing habit of choking and gasping in the middle of his sentences, never could have done himself the justice Francis did. In fact, Hugh Caldwell, telling his own stories, interposed an obstacle, a distraction—himself, the living, asthmatic flesh—between the story and the audience. As the movies have supplanted the stage, and the radio the concert hall, so Francis Cleary in modern life tended to supplant his friend, Hugh Caldwell, and in supplanting him, he glorified him. He was the movie screen on which the aging actress, thanks to the magic of the camera and make-up man, appears young and radiant, purged of her wrinkles; he was the radio over which one hears a symphony without seeing the sweat of the first violinist.

And yet, like all canned entertainment, Francis Cleary produced, in the end, a melancholy effect. To listen to him too long was like going to the movies in the morning; it engendered a sense of alienation and distance. Eventually, the host would move away, his desire to see Caldwell killed, not quickened, by this ghostly reunion, as the appetite is killed by a snack before dinner, as the taste for van Gogh's paintings was killed by the reproductions of the "Sunflowers" and "L'Ar-lésienne" that used to symbolize cultural sympathies in the living rooms of Francis Cleary's friends. But as the lesson of "L'Arlésienne" prevented hardly anyone from making the same mistake with Picasso's "Lady in White," so the lesson of Hugh Caldwell never prevented the host from allowing Francis Cleary to substitute on some other occasion for another old friend who was distasteful to the hostess, and many parties would be composed exclusively of Francis Clearys, male and female, stand-ins, reasonable facsimiles, who could fraternize with each other under the Redon or the Rouault or the Renoir re-productions—ready with anecdote, quotation, and paraphrase, amiable and immune as seconds at a duel. Afterwards, the host and hostess, reviewing the situation, would be unable to decide why it was that though everybody stayed late, got drunk, and ate all the sandwiches, nobody had had a particularly good time. And the failure of the party, far from causing bitterness or recrimination, would actually draw them together. Murmuring criticisms of their guests, they would pull up the blankets and embrace, convinced that they preferred each other, or rather that they preferred themselves as a couple to anybody else they knew.

But what about Francis Cleary riding home in a taxi with his female equivalent? Sex was not for him; his given name disclosed this—it could be either masculine or feminine; nobody ever called him Frank. He might be a bachelor or a spinster; quite often, he was a couple, but a couple which functioned as an integer. If he had begun his Francis Cleary existence as a single man, it was unwise for him to marry, for a wife might define him too sharply, people might like her and then other people would dislike her; before he knew it, through her, he might become the issue rather than the solution of a dispute. To say that sex was not for him does not mean that he did not sometimes have girls, or, in his female aspect, men; he might even have been in love, but since nearly the whole area of his life was public and social, this one small reserved section which he kept for himself was private, intensely so. His romantic activities, if he had any, were extracurricular. They did not interfere with his social function, and it is impossible to tell which was cause and which effect: was it the fact that he had very early in life fallen in love with the married lady that placed his weekends and his evenings and his vacations at the disposal of his friends, or had he recognized from the very beginning that he was cast for the part of the professional friend and arranged his affairs accordingly, cultivating without real predilection sexual tastes so impossible that they must be forever gratified *sub rosa,* under assumed names, in Pullman cars, alleys, cheap hotel rooms, public parks? How was anybody to know? In some of his manifestations, it seemed quite plain that design was at the bottom of it, that love had been gladly foregone for the sound of the telephone bell. He would hint at a disastrous passion or a vice to each of his married friends when the intimacy reached a certain stage, like a stranger on a train who after a given amount of conversation produces a calling card, but these confessions had a faint air of fraudulence or at least of frivolity: how could anyone take very seriously a passion or a morbid inclination which left its victim free every day from five until midnight and all day Sundays and holidays? Nevertheless, his confessions were accepted, often with a kind of gratitude. They served to "explain" him to new acquaintances, who might have thought him peculiar if they had not been assured that he kept a truly horrible vice in his closet.

In other cases, there appeared to have been no calculation. He thought sporadically of marriage but kept looking for "the right person," who was assumed to exist somewhere just beyond the social horizon, like a soul waiting to be born. Yet whenever a living being materialized who wore the features of the right person, she was found to be already married or indifferent or tied to an aged mother or in some other way impossible. So the vigil continued, until time made it an absurdity, and at fifty Francis Cleary ceased to yearn, ascribed his fate to a geographical accident (everybody has his double and everybody has his complement, but not necessarily in New York or even in America), to an over-romantic temperament, or simply to the bad habit, contracted in adolescence and never overcome, of falling in love with married women, which made him regard every woman who lacked a husband as essentially incomplete. Putting love behind him, Francis Cleary would throw himself more actively than ever into the occupation of friendship, the life of visits, small gifts and favors exchanged, mild gossip, concern over illnesses, outings for the children, and would, quite often, experience a kind of late blooming which would inspire all his friends to hope that he was at last on the verge of marriage, while in reality it was the abandonment of the idea of marriage that had permitted his nature, finally, to express itself. In this aspect—the aspect of innocence—Francis Cleary was almost lovable. Certainly he commanded the affection if not the active preference of his friends, and those husbands and wives who had accepted him as the lesser evil grew to like him for himself. It is significant, nevertheless, that he was liked for goodness of heart, which does not provoke envy, rather than for talent, charm, or beauty, which do. And goodness of heart notwithstanding, it was still a chore to dine or take a walk with him alone, and if by chance in these *tête-à-têtes* a muted happiness was achieved, his companion could never quite get over it, referred to the occasion repeatedly in conversation ("You know, I had quite a good time with Francis Cleary the other day"), as though a miracle had been witnessed and virtue been its own reward.

Yet here perhaps there has been a confusion of identity. It is likely that the Francis Cleary we have just been speaking of, the good, bewildered, yearning Francis Cleary, was never the true Francis Cleary at all, but an uncle for whom the real one, the modern one, was named. Whenever they met the good Francis Cleary, his friends were struck by a certain anachronism in his character; they would say that he reminded them of their childhood, of a maiden aunt who did the mending, or a bachelor great-uncle who gave them a gold piece every Christmas morning and left his watch to them in his will when he died. The true Francis Cleary had no such overtones. He was as much a product of the age as nylon or plywood, and he could be distinguished from the others, those uncles and aunts of his who lingered on in a later period, by the fact that one did not pity him. One could not mourn for Francis, because he did not mourn for himself. He cast no shadow behind him of thwarted ambition, unconsummated desire, lost ideals. Indeed, one had only to set the word *frustration* beside him to see that the very conception of frustration was outmoded, hopelessly provincial—perhaps in the Middle West, in small towns, men still walked the streets restlessly at night, questioning their fate, wondering how it might have been otherwise, but in any advanced center of civilization, people, like sheets, came pre-shrunk; life held neither surprises nor disappointments for them.

And your true Francis Cleary was the perfect sanforized man, the ideal which others only approximated. He appeared to have no demands whatsoever—that was the beauty of him. Or rather, as in a correctly balanced equation, demands and possible satisfactions canceled out, so that the man himself, i.e., the problem, vanished. When an apartment door shut behind him, it was as if he had never been. Nobody discussed him in his absence, or if they did, it was only as a concession to convention. Once or twice a year, he had a small, official illness, and in his comfortable hotel apartment received flowers, books, and wine-flavored calf's-foot jelly from his friends. Like everything else about him, these illnesses had a symbolic character: they permitted his friends to bestow on him tokens of a concern they did not feel. Without these illnesses, his friends might have grown to think themselves monsters of insensibility—was it, after all, *natural* to have a close friend whom you never gave a thought to? Francis, farseeing, provident, took care that such questions should not arise. He could no more afford to be a thorn in the conscience, the subject of an inward argument, than to be the occasion of verbal debate. The true friend might languish in furnished rooms with pneumonia and only the girl across the hall to help, or fight delirium tremens in Bellevue, but Francis' sore throats were always well attended. In the same way, he would from time to time present his friends with some innocuous little problem (should he go to Maine or New Hampshire during his vacation?) with the air of a man who asks for help in the most serious crisis of his life. His friends would loyally come through with advice

and travel booklets, reminiscences of childhood summers, letters of
introduction, and feel, when Francis set off at last to the place where
he had intended to go originally, that they had stood by him through
thick and thin, that the demands of friendship had been handsomely
satisfied.

Once in a great while, when a friendship 'showed unmistakable
signs of limpness (when a husband and wife seemed to be falling in
love with each other again, or had reached the point of estrangement
where each saw his own friends, or began to cultivate the acquaintance
of another Francis Cleary, a competitor), Francis would go so far
as to borrow money from the husband. These loans were of course
mere temporary accommodations, and the warm glow of generosity
felt by the husband almost always served to restore the circulation of
the friendship. Still, during the short time he had the money (he
usually waited until the twenty-seventh to borrow and then paid it
back promptly the first of the next month), Francis was always very
nervous. Once or twice he thought he had seen fear in the husband's
eyes, fear that financial need would turn "that nice Francis Cleary,"
as the wives often called him, into another "poor old Frank." Was it
possible, he believed the husband was asking himself, that he could
have been deceived? Had importunity, cleverly disguised, always
lurked in this old, old acquaintance, and had it waited this long to
strike? The classic phrase of male disillusionment, *"I thought you
were different,"* trembled visibly on his lips, and Francis saw himself
slipping. The moment, of course, passed. Francis repaid the money,
and the husband, metaphorically wiping the sweat from his brow,
wondered how he could have doubted him. Certainly Francis was
different, had always been so. The friends who had been with him at
school or at college, and who could remember him at all, were absolutely at one on this point.

Even there, at the very beginning, importunity had been excluded
from his nature. The desire to excel, to shine, to be closest, best
friend, most liked, best dressed, funniest, had played no part with
him. He had been content simply to be there, to be along, the unnoticed eye-witness. Wherever he had gone to school, whether it was
Exeter or P. S. 12, whether Yale or Iowa or Carnegie Tech, the
Chicago Art Institute or Harvard Business, he was the man that
nobody could think of a quotation for when the yearbook was being

compiled; and if you opened the yearbook today you would find the editors' defeat commemorated by a blank below his photograph. Yet he had not been disliked, for there had been in him none of the burning hunger, the watchfulness, the covert shame (however carefully masked by studiousness, indifference to society, eccentricity, geological field trips, bird walks) that brand the true outsider for the vengeance of those inside. During the rushing period he had been neither too anxious nor too self-assured nor too indifferent, with the result that, in many cases, he was pledged to a slightly better fraternity than he might have expected to make; and in the cases where he was overlooked in the general excitement, the omission was always remedied—he was quietly taken in later on, in the junior year instead of the sophomore. And the welcome given him, whether tardy or prompt, never failed to create a small commotion among the outsiders, who knew themselves, correctly, to be more brilliant, better looking, richer, better scholars, better athletes, better drinkers, or whatever was considered valuable, than he. Inevitably, they construed the pledging of Francis Cleary as a calculated affront to themselves. Then and thereafter, forever and ever, the choice of Francis Cleary was not an affirmation of something, but a negation of something else.

Thus, in the family we were talking about, if Francis Cleary was for the husband a substitute for Hugh Caldwell, for the wife he was the flat denial of Hugh Caldwell. Mr. Caldwell, sitting in his lumpy armchair in the Village, might have been solacing himself for the fact that he was not invited to the Leightons with the idea that the wife was simply a bitch who would not let her husband see his rowdy old friends. But when Francis Cleary, another of John Leighton's friends of the same vintage, dropped in to see him, fresh from a cocktail party at the Leightons', Mr. Caldwell could no longer mistake her meaning. It was *he personally* who was being excluded, and if he stared at Francis Cleary and asked himself, "What in the name of God has this guy got that I haven't?" this was precisely the question Mrs. Leighton intended to leave with him.

At this point the reader may ask what possible motive Mrs. Leighton could have had. What drove her to persecute a man whom she hardly knew, who could not, even if he had wished it, have done her the slightest injury? The reply can best be put in the form of a further question. Let anyone to whom Mrs. Leighton's behavior seems inexplicable, or at any rate odd, ask himself why he does not like his wife's friends. Is it really—as he is always telling himself—that they are unattractive or that they bring out the worst in her, encourage her to spend too much money or to think about love affairs, or that they talk continually of things and people of whom he is ignorant, or that they borrow from her or take up too much of her time? Is it even, to be franker, that he is jealous of them? This explanation too is insufficient, for we can look around us and find husbands who will not allow their wives' friends or relations in the house but who display an amazing cordiality toward their wives' lovers, and we can find husbands who positively reject their wives' affection, who treat it as a bore and a nuisance, who yet will use every means to deprive their wives of what, from any sensible point of view, ought to be an outlet, a diversionary channel for that affection—the society of friends. Is not *envious,* rather, the word? Will the dubious reader acknowledge that his wife and her friends possess in common some quality that is absent from his own nature? It is this quality that attracted him to her in the first place, though by now he has probably succeeded in obliterating all traces of it from her character, just as the wife who marries the young poet because he is so different from all the other men she knows will soon succeed in getting him to go into the advertising business, or at the very least set up such a neurosis in him that he can only write one poem a year. What passes for love in our competitive society is frequently envy: the phlegmatic husband who marries a vivacious wife is in the same position as the businessman who buys up the stock of a rival corporation in order to kill it. The businessman may at the beginning delude himself with the idea that the rival company has certain patents which he very much wants to exploit, but it will shortly appear that these patents, once so heartily desired, are in competition with his own processes—they will have to be scrapped. We cannot, in the end, possess anything that is not ourselves. That vivacity, money, respectability, talent which we hoped to add to ourselves by marriage are, we discover to our surprise, unassimilable to our very natures. There is nothing we can do with them but destroy them, deaden the vivacity, spend the money, tarnish the respectability, maim the talent; and when we have finished this work of destruction we may even get angry—the wife of the poet may upbraid him because he no longer writes poems, or the dull husband of the gay girl may reproach her for her woodenness in company.

Yet now a distinction must be made. In some cases, it is our wife or our husband who is the direct object of our envy and our desire, and in these marriages the friends are mere accidental victims; we have nothing against them personally; if we hate them it is because we have seen them smiling with our wife. But there is another kind of marriage, where it is the partner who is the accidental victim: simply a hostage whom we have carried home from a raid on the enemy, that is, on the circle of the friends. We bear this person no actual ill-will; we may even pity him as we lop off an ear or a little finger in some nicety of reprisal. He himself is not the object of revenge, he is merely the symbol of our hostility, usually for some group, class, caste, sex, or race. Such cases are generally marked by a crude and striking disparity between the husband and the wife; observe the communist married to the banker's daughter, the anti-Semite who marries the beautiful Jewess, the businessman who marries an actress and makes her quit the stage. These marriages are exercises in metonymy: the part is taken for the whole, the symbol for the thing symbolized. One might think, in the case of the businessman and the actress, that he had taken leave of his senses—why marry an actress if not to sit in the front row at her first nights?—if one did not know that his college life had been poisoned by his failure to make the Thespian Society, and that his secret vendetta against the stage had already expressed itself in certain Times Square real estate operations, in investments in radio and movie companies, and, once, in an anonymous note addressed to the Commissioner of Licenses pointing out an indelicate passage in a current Broadway hit. The communist who subjects the banker's daughter to the petty squalor of life on Thirteenth Street—the unmade studio couch, the tin of evaporated milk flanking the rank brass ash tray on the breakfast table, the piles of dusty pamphlets, the late meetings, the cheap whiskey without soda, the hair done over the wash-basin with wave-set bought from a cut-rate druggist—this man may be actually repelled by the conditions in which he obliges her to live; but his home is a stage kept set for the call her horrified father will pay them. And the anti-Semite who marries a beautiful Jewess may imagine that he has been carried away by love, treat her with great kindness, and exempt her from the Jewish race by a kind of personal fiat, declaring over and over again to himself and possibly to her that he married her in spite of her relations, her mother, her sister, her hook-nosed uncles, while in reality he is bored with his wife (who actually does not seem very Jewish), and it is the yearly visit of his mother-in-law to which he looks forward with sadistic zest. Summer after summer, he may promise his wife that he will not use the word "kike" in the old lady's hearing again, but somehow it always slides out, the old lady goes upstairs in tears, and the marriage has once again been consummated.

This distinction must be noted for the sake of clarity, though to the friends and to the wives and the husbands it makes really very little difference whether they are disliked for themselves or for some more irrelevant reason. The child struck by a bomb is indifferent to the private motives of the bombardier. Thus, with the Leighton couple, to return to our original question, Mrs. Leighton may have detested Hugh Caldwell because he or someone like him had once run a crayon through her sketch at a night class at the Art Students League or because she was a stylist at Macy's and he a practicing nudist, or for any other reason that sprang from a divergence of interests. Or she may have found only one thing to disparage in Mr. Caldwell —his feeling of friendship for her husband. In either case, the result would be the same; whether from inclination or merely to spite her husband, Mrs. Leighton would see to it that Mr. Caldwell was not at home in her nice new house.

There are people who, whatever their good intentions, cannot renounce love, and there are people, a larger number, who cannot renounce victory. Thus, to take the second category first, a woman like Mrs. Leighton is not playing the game when she pretends to have sacrificed something by having only Francis Clearys at her parties; the jealousy and anger of the excluded Hugh Caldwell more than repay her for any superficial boredom she may have experienced during the evening. A still worse cheat is the anti-Semite who asks a Jewish Francis Cleary, a second cousin of his wife's, time after time to his house so that he may later express the most cruel and hair-raising opinions without being accused of bias. Most monstrous of all was the businessman already alluded to who married the actress and whose hatred of theatrical people stopped short of a young Francis Cleary, a radio actor with whom the wife had once played a season of summer stock. This man, whose name was Al, enacted for several months a pseudo-friendship with Francis. He invited him to lunch downtown, introduced him to radio magnates, listened to his morning broadcasts; the wife, the former actress, was at first bewildered and touched by these attentions, which she conceived to be overtures of love, and she began to look forward to the time when the house would be filled with her real friends, the playwrights, directors, and legitimate actors whom she missed so much in the country. It was not until her husband began to talk continually of the superiority of the verse drama of the air to the box-like drama of the stage that she perceived the malignancy of his design. Her answer was direct and militant. She treated Francis exactly as if he had been a genuine enthusiasm of her husband's—one night, without the slightest provocation, she turned him out of the house.

This shocking experience was crucial for the young actor Francis Cleary. It confirmed in him the sense, not yet quite solidified, of the perils of his position. For nearly two hours, as he paced the station platform, waiting for the train that would take him away from Fairfield County, away from important men who professed to admire Norman Corwin and were going to take him to lunch with the president of the Red Network, for this long-short intolerable time, he felt himself identified with the lot of humanity, with the mothers-in-law, sisters, true friends, ex-lovers for whom life is a series of indignities, with all those who, having attached themselves, are in a position to be dislodged. His heart cried out against the false husband who had not raised a hand to save him; it cried out and at length he hardened it. From this time on, Francis took the most energetic measures lest the taint of affection poison one of his friendships, and his reluctance to be identified with either partner to a marriage passed as devotion to the family, especially in doubtful cases like the Leightons', where to avoid the slightest appearance of partisanship, he concentrated his attention on the children and was always playing games with them on the floor or taking them out to the zoo or to holiday marionette shows—to the point that many of his friends kept remarking to each other that it was such a pity that Francis had never married because he was obviously mad about children. And though many of the children did not at all care for Francis and would even prefer sitting at a bar while their father drank with some dubious confederate to the most delightful outing Francis could offer them, others, more successfully educated by their parents, would take the name for the thing and being told that Francis adored them would docilely adore him back, to the limit, at any rate, of their capacities. But in either case, the mother, watching her child set out hand in hand with Francis to some accepted childish objective, was spared the slightest misgiving lest the child positively enjoy himself with Francis. Her own feelings about Francis assured her that there was no danger whatever that the child would get anything better than what he was used to at home.

In most instances, these precautionary measures were sufficient to keep Francis his status as friend. He watched, with professional amusement, the struggles of his younger counterparts to extricate themselves from the depths of a closer relation. He himself could never again be fooled when a husband or a wife, out of sheer malignance, would pretend to like him, seek out his company, complain that he was not asked to dinner often enough, lunch with him frequently alone, strike up a correspondence with him, till the other member of the couple would go nearly mad with exasperation and feelings of injustice, asking himself (if it were the husband) a hundred times a day how Dorothea could tolerate that lumpish little bore when she had a tantrum in the bedroom every time one of his real friends, one of his interesting friends, set a foot in the apartment. Francis could foretell, almost to the hour, the date of the inevitable rupture, and if it had not been for professional competition he might have warned his young namesake not to go to the Leightons on the night that John Leighton, *for absolutely no reason,* would break a highball glass over his head. He himself practiced such discretion in these matters that he occasionally resorted to flight when there was no real necessity for it. The smallest compliment paid him by a husband or a wife would make him suspect a danger, and he would scurry away to safety before the friendship had got half started, while the couple, who had been counting on him to replace the people they liked in their social life and had no morbid designs at all, would ask themselves what they could have done to offend that nice Mr. Cleary.

The night on the station platform had left him with its mark. Where formerly the desire to be loved, noticed, esteemed, had, if it ever feebly stirred in him, been repressed without a pang, now the *fear* of being loved became a positive obsession with him. He saw annihilation stare at him in any half-affectionate glance. Though his whole activity was given over to the manipulation of the symbols of devotion —presents, visits, solicitous inquiries, games, walks in the country— still the validation of a single one of these tokens would suffice to ruin him, just as, it is presumed, the introduction of a single five-dollar gold piece into the channels of our currency would upset our entire monetary system. The liking of a single human being would translate him into the realm of measures and values, the realm of comparisons. Someone had valued him, and the whole question of his value was opened. From being a zero, the dead point at which reckoning begins, he became a real number, if only the tiniest fraction, and thus entered the field of competition. Or to put it another way, he passed from being an x, an unknown and inestimable quantity which could be substituted for a known quantity (Hugh Caldwell) in any social equation, to being a known quantity himself, that is he passed from algebra into arithmetic. He no longer represented Hugh Caldwell, but existing now on the same plane was capable of being compared with him. However, his whole merit had consisted of the fact that nobody could possibly like him as much as Hugh Caldwell could be liked; and indeed if anybody liked him one-half, one-quarter, one-tenth as much, it was enough to finish him as the family friend.

A husband, hearing his wife's voice quicken as she answered Francis Cleary's telephone call, would be startled into asking himself the impermissible question: *Why do we see that fellow?* The light fervor of his wife's tone jarred on his sense of what was fitting; it breached some unspoken agreement—she was not playing fair. He felt as if he had been duped. From that moment on, he disliked Francis Cleary intensely, and his wife would have to fight to get him invited to a party, just as if he had been one of her own friends. If she were loyal in her attachments, she would soon find herself trying to see him when her husband was out of town or working late at the office; she would meet him between engagements in the bars of quiet hotels. But this illicit atmosphere was deeply uncongenial to Francis. Her affection, her fidelity, could not begin to make up to him for the fact that he was no longer asked to her house. Indeed he hated her for that affection, which, as he saw it, was responsible for all the trouble. Like the husband, he experienced a sense of outrage; he too had been betrayed by her. With her inordinate capacity for friendship, she had gulled them both. She, on her side, became aware that Francis was suffering from his exclusion. She imagined (this particular wife was rather stupid) that he missed his old friend, her husband; and to save Francis pain she began to lie. "Jerry misses you terribly," she would tell him, "but we see hardly anybody any more. Jerry hasn't been feeling well. We stay home and read detective stories. . . ." Francis, of course, knew better, and eventually it would happen that he met them when they were dining out with a large party of friends, and the poor wife's duplicity would be exposed. All her nudges and desperate, appealing glances went unanswered—Jerry would not invite Francis to sit down at their table. After that, Francis was always too busy to see her when she called. If anybody mentioned her name, he spoke of her with a rancor that was for him unusual, so that people assumed either that she had come between Francis and his old friend, her husband, or that she had tried to have an affair with Francis and failed. Of the husband he continued to speak in the highest terms, thus reinforcing both of these theories. And his admiration was not simulated. He respected Jerry for the contempt in which Jerry held him—it was an attitude they shared. As for the unfortunate wife, she could never make out what had gone wrong. In the end, she came to believe her husband when he told her, as he frequently did, that she had no talent for human relations.

Between the Scylla of an Al and the Charybdis of a Jerry's wife, Francis steers his uneasy course. Perhaps it is the vicissitudes of this life, the vigilance against the true and imaginary dangers, that are responsible for the change in Francis. Certainly it had been hard for him to be obliged, every year or so, to re-examine his premises. Francis had, it seemed to him, made a good bargain with the world. Yet whenever a Jerry's wife took a fancy to him, he questioned his own shrewdness. If she likes me, he would ask himself, why wouldn't others, and if likes, why not loves, and does she really and how much? It would be weeks, after such an experience, before Francis could silence these questions. Like a businessman, he feared that he had closed his deal with life too soon; the buyer might have paid much more. And as the businessman can only set his mind at rest by assuring himself that the property he disposed of was really good riddance of a negligible asset, so Francis' one recourse was to persuade himself once again that he had been perfectly correct in setting the zero, dejected yet triumphant, opposite his own name. But however successful as auditing, these midnight reckonings must have been painful, even to Francis; one night his anesthetized spirit must have awakened in rage and spite.

Or perhaps nature does abhor a vacuum; perhaps the wall of the sealed, sterile chamber that was Francis' nature collapsed from atmospheric pressure, and in rushed all the unattached emotions—that is, hatred, envy, fear, which, unlike love, do not cling to a definite object—that float, gaseous, over man's sphere. At any rate, Francis has been changing. Under our very eyes, he has been turning into everything that he, by definition, was not. If you have failed to notice the steps in this process, it is because you are so much in the habit of *not* thinking about Francis that he could transform himself into a snake on your parlor floor without attracting your attention. Your indifference has been a cloak of invisibility behind which he has been preparing for you some rather startling surprises. But now that your memory has been jogged on the point, you will recall that his manners, while never highly polished, were once more acceptable than they are today. There was a time, for example, when he left your cocktail parties promptly at seven-thirty, taking with him one of the more burdensome women guests for a *table-d'hôte* dinner in the Village. But in the course of years his leavetakings have been steadily retarded; soon your wife has been cooking scrambled eggs for him at nine o'clock; and now you are lucky if at midnight or two or three you do not have to make up a bed for him in the spare room or, at the very best, take him home in a taxi and open his door for him. Once it was the interesting guests who stayed, disputing, quoting poetry, playing the piano, singing; today the fascinating people have always somewhere else to go, and every party boils down to Francis Cleary; you do not question this, possibly, but accept it as an analogy to life.

Perhaps it is Francis' growing addiction to drink (he no longer waits for you to notice his empty glass but helps himself from the shaker or inquires boldly, "Did someone say something about another drink?") that keeps him late and is also responsible for the mounting truculence of his conversation. In the old days Francis was always prompt to shut off one of his anecdotes when his companion's interest slightly wavered away from him; indeed, much of his conversation seemed to be constructed around the interruption he awaited. Gradually, however, he has become more adhesive to his topics. He may be interrupted by the arrival of a newcomer, the host may excuse himself to fetch somebody's coat, or the hostess may go in to look at the baby—but Francis has put a bookmark in his story. "As I was saying," he resumes, when the distraction has passed. Furthermore, his opinions, which he used to modulate to suit the conversation, never taking up a position without preparing a retreat from it, have now become rigid and obtrusive. This is particularly true of him in his female aspect. Frances Cleary, once the indistinct listener, now arrives at a party with a single idea that haunts the conversation like a ghost. This idea is almost always regressive in character, the shade of a once-live controversy (abstract vs. representational art, progressive vs. classical education), but the female Frances treats it as though she personally were its relict; any change of subject she regards as irreverence to the dead. "Others may forget but I remember," her aggrieved expression declares. If the hostess is successful in deflecting her to some more personal topic, a single word overheard from across the room will be enough to send her train of ideas puffing out of the station once more. She has dedicated herself, say, to the defense of Raphael against the menace of Mondrian; momentarily silenced, she will instantly revive should one of the other guests be so careless as to remark, "She's as pretty as a picture." "You can talk about pictures all you want," Frances will begin. . . .

In the male Francis Cleary this belligerency is more likely to take a physical form. More and more often nowadays, Francis breaks glasses, ash trays, lamps. His elbow catches the maid's arm as she is serving the gravy, and the hostess's dress must go to the cleaners. All during an evening, he may have been his old undemanding self, but suddenly, at midnight, a sullenness will fall on him. "Oh, for Christ's sake," he will ejaculate when the talk goes over his head. Or he may grab someone else's hat and stumble savagely out, knocking over a table on his way.

As a couple, he does not drink too much. On the contrary, he quietly but firmly refuses the third and even the second drink. He arrives early, the two of him, and ensconces himself on the sofa (the Clearys of all numbers and genders have an affinity for the sofa, which they occupy as a symbol of possession). From this point of vantage, he, or shall we say for convenience' sake, they, overlook the proceedings with a kind of regal lumpishness. Though their position as friends of the family may be new and still insecure, they treat the very oldest and dearest members of the wife's or the husband's circle (the college roommate, the former lover) as candidates for their approval. They do not consider it necessary to talk in the ordinary way, but put sharp, inquisitorial questions to the people that are brought up to them ("Would you mind telling me the significance of that yellow necktie?" "Why do the characters in your novels have such a depressing sex life?"), or else they merely sit, demanding to be entertained.

Like the drinking Francis Cleary, they stay until the last guest has gone, and present a report of their findings to the host and hostess. Nothing has escaped them; they have noticed your former roommate's stammer and your lover's squint; they have counted the highballs of the heavy drinker and recorded the tremor of his hand; the woman you thought beautiful is, it turns out, bowlegged, and the lively Russian should have washed his hair. And they present these findings with absolute objectivity; they do not judge but merely report. Though each human being is, so to speak, a work of art, the Clearys are scientists, and take pride in disobeying the artist's commands. If the artist places a highlight at what he considers a central point of his personality, a highlight that says, "Look here," the Clearys instantly look elsewhere: the expressiveness of a man's eyes will never blind them to the weakness of his chin. And you and your wife, who have hitherto obeyed the laws of art and humanity and looked where you were told to look, are now utterly confounded by this clear, bleak view. Your friends whom you regarded as wholes are now assemblages of slightly damaged parts. You are plunged into despair, but you do not question the Clearys' right to conduct this survey, for their observations are given a peculiar authority and force by the fact that they refer to the other guests—whom they have just met—by their first names. "John drinks terribly, doesn't he?" they say, and it is useless for you to pretend that this particular evening was exceptional for your friend —that "John" asserts a familiarity with his habits that is greater, if anything, than your own. By the time they have finished their last glass ("Just a little cool water from the tap, please") and you have seen them to the door you and your wife are utterly drained of energy and belief. There is not even a quarrel left between you, for they have exposed your friends and hers with perfect impartiality. Your world has been depopulated. You have only each other and the Clearys.

Your sole escape from this intolerable situation is for one of you to blame the Clearys on the other. You can divide them up between you. If the husband, say, can be held responsible for Mr. and Mrs. Cleary ("*You* were the one who insisted on having them"), the wife can take Francis as her charge. You can treat them, that is, as friends, and this will immediately result in the exclusion of both factions. But now a super Francis Cleary must be found, a zero raised to a higher power, a negation of a negation. The search may be long, you may wander down false trails, but finally one night at a cocktail party you will find him, the ineffable blank, and you and your wife will seize him and drag him home with you to eat sandwiches and talk excitedly like lovers, of why you have never met before. Your difficulties are over, your wife smiles at you again, and when the two of you stand in the doorway to see him off, your arm falls affectionately across her shoulder.

But alas the same process is about to begin again, and the stakes have been raised. Your new nonentity is larger and emptier than your original little friend; naturally, he commands a higher price. Dozens of other couples are competing with you for this superb creation; he does not hold himself cheap. You realize very quickly from the envious glances your colleagues and neighbors cast toward him whenever you display him at a public gathering that if you want to hold on to him you will have to pay through the nose. Gone are the potted plants, the Christmas cheeses, the toys for the children that were regularly issued by the old Francis Cleary. The super friend gives nothing; he does not even try to make himself agreeable; he will not talk to old ladies or help with the dishes or go to the store for a loaf of bread. His company is all you will ever get of him, and the demands he makes on you will grow steadily more extortionate. If you want him around, his demeanor will tell you, you will have to give up your former friends, your work, your interests, your principles—the whole complex of idiosyncrasies that make up your nature—and your only reward for this terrible sacrifice is that your wife will have to make it too. Soon he will be bringing his own friends to your house, and these friends will be the other couples with whom you share him (did you imagine that he could confine himself to *you?*). Already he borrows your money, your books, and your whiskey.

He will stop at nothing, for he has always hated you and now he knows that he has got you where he wants you—you cannot live without him. Watching this monster as he sits at his ease on your sofa, your wife may look back with feelings of actual affection on your queer old friend, Hugh Caldwell; but now it is too late. Hugh Caldwell spits at the mention of your wife's name, and, quite possibly, at the mention of your own; and, anyway, you ask yourself, are you really sure that you want to see Hugh Caldwell again, especially if it would mean that your wife, in return, could see one of her old friends? No, you say to yourself, we cannot have *that*; there must be some compromise, some middle way—it is not necessary to go so far. Your mind beats on the door of the dilemma. Surely somewhere, you exclaim silently, somewhere in this great city, living quietly, perhaps, in a furnished room, there is a friend whom neither of us would have to feel so strongly about. . . . Some plain man or woman, some dowdy little couple of regular habits and indefinite tastes, some person utterly unobjectionable, unobtrusive, undefined. . . . With loving strokes, you complete the portrait of this ideal, and all the while there he sits, grinning at you, the lesser evil, but you do not recognize him.

After all, you say to yourself, my requirements are modest; I will give up anything for a little peace and quiet. You forget that it was in the name of peace and quiet that this despot was welcomed—just as the Jewish banker in the concentration camp forgets the donation he made to the Nazi party fund, back in 1931, when his great fear was communism; just as Benedetto Croce, antifascist philosopher, forgot in Naples the days when he supported Mussolini in the Senate at Rome, because order was certainly preferable to anarchy and Bolshevism was the real menace. You cannot believe, you will not ever believe, that your desire for peace and quiet, i.e., for the permanent stalemate, has logically resulted in the noisy oppressor on the sofa. On the contrary, his presence there seems to you a cruel and unaccountable accident.

You are not happy with your wife but you do not want change. In a more romantic period you might have dreamed of voluptuous blondes, fast women and low haunts; you might even have run off with the lady organist or the wife of the Methodist minister. But you are a man of peace and careful respectability. You do not ask adventure or the larger life. Though at one time, theoretically, you may have desired these things, you have perceived that adventure for one can readily be the excuse for adventure for all, and who knows but what your wife's or your neighbor's capacity for adventure might be greater than your own? If all men were created equal, programs for achieving equality would not exist. The industrialist would welcome the people's army into the gates of the factory, if he could be sure that nobody would be any better off than he. We do not want *more* than anyone else, though we may take more for fear of getting less. What we desire is absolute parity, and this can only be achieved by calculating in a downward direction, with zero as the ultimate, unattainable ideal. Our lives become a series of disarmament conferences: I will reduce my demands if you will reduce yours. With parity as our aim, it is impossible to calculate in an upward direction, for a nation will be allowed a navy which it has not the productive capacity to build, or a man may be granted freedoms which he has not the faculties to exercise, and gross inequalities will immediately result.

So long as you and I cannot accept the doctrine "From each according to his capacities, to each according to his needs," the totalitarian state will supply the answer to the difficulties of democracy and Francis Cleary will be the ideal friend. At this very moment, you are planning to overthrow the incumbent Cleary, who happens to be staying with you for the weekend. In a loud voice he has demanded something to eat, though he finished lunch only an hour ago. Your wife has rushed out to the kitchen to make him a chicken sandwich, and you sit watching him in uneasy silence. You are afraid to play the phonograph because he does not like music; you are afraid to initiate a topic of conversation because he resents any mention of persons he has not met or things he does not understand; you are afraid to pick up a newspaper lest he take it as a slight—and if you cross him he will pinch the baby.

The fires of resistance are lit in your heart as the sandwich comes in and he opens it with a blunt critical finger and asks for pickles and mayonnaise. Your pulse quickens in little throbs of solidarity with your unfortunate wife. You will make, you say to yourself, common cause with her and eject the tyrant. If she will do it *for* you, so much the better; but there can be no question whatever about the heartiness of your support. The danger is, of course, that in the warm fraternity of the revolt, the coziness of plans and preparations, the intimacy of secret meetings in lonely houses at night, with a reliable farmer standing guard (*Qui passe?*), certain illusions of your wife's may be revived. The whole question of friends may be opened again; a period of anarchy may even follow in which all the ghosts of both camps will meet once more in your living room and debate the old issues; tempers will rise and you will have to fling out of the house late at night and look for a room in a hotel. In the interests of peace, you say to yourself, would it not be wiser to select in advance some common friend and avoid the interregnum? Somewhere, only recently did you not meet a couple . . . ? In vain, you try to recall their faces and their name. Memory is obstinate but you do not despair. The very dimness of your impression convinces you that you are on the right track. They are the ones. If you meet them again, you will know them at once and rush forward to meet them with a glad cry of recognition. There is only one difficulty. Supposing they are already engaged . . . ?

Your only way out of this recurrent nightmare (not counting the humane one, which is hardly worth mentioning) is for you and your wife to take the logical next step, to become the Clearys, say, of Round Hill Road. Why should you shrink from it? What have you to lose? In what do you differ from the man on the sofa?

The Tillotson Banquet

❋ ALDOUS HUXLEY ❋

ALDOUS HUXLEY (1894–1963), a grandson of Thomas Huxley and a great-nephew of Matthew Arnold, was equally expert in science and literature. His early satiric novels, culminating in the classic *Point Counter-Point* portray English society in the 1920s with a distinct emphasis on decadence. *Brave New World*, his most famous book, is a survey of the future, with human beings reduced to automata by scientific progress. In the 1930s Huxley became concerned with the occult and experimented with drugs. In 1947 he moved to California to join the Ramakrishna Mission in Hollywood. *The Tillotson Banquet* appeared in *Collected Short Stories* (1957).

I

YOUNG Spode was not a snob; he was too intelligent for that, too fundamentally decent. Not a snob; but all the same he could not help feeling very well pleased at the thought that he was dining, alone and intimately, with Lord Badgery. It was a definite event in his life, a step forward, he felt, towards that final success, social, material, and literary, which he had come to London with a fixed intention of making. The conquest and capture of Badgery was an almost essential strategical move in the campaign.

Edmund, forty-seventh Baron Badgery, was a lineal descendant of that Edmund, surnamed Le Blayreau, who landed on English soil in the train of William the Conqueror. Ennobled by William Rufus, the Badgerys had been one of the very few baronial families to survive the Wars of the Roses and all the other changes and chances of English history. They were a sensible and philoprogenitive race. No

Badgery had ever fought in any war, no Badgery had ever engaged in any kind of politics. They had been content, to live and quietly to propagate their species in a huge machicolated Norman castle, surrounded by a triple moat, only sallying forth to cultivate their property and to collect their rents. In the eighteenth century, when life had become relatively secure, the Badgerys began to venture forth into civilized society. From boorish squires they blossomed into *grands seigneurs,* patrons of the arts, virtuosi. Their property was large, they were rich; and with the growth of industrialism their riches also grew. Villages on their estate turned into manufacturing towns, unsuspected coal was discovered beneath the surface of their barren moorlands. By the middle of the nineteenth century the Badgerys were among the richest of English noble families. The forty-seventh baron disposed of an income of at least two hundred thousand pounds a year. Following the great Badgery tradition, he had refused to have anything to do with politics or war. He occupied himself by collecting pictures; he took an interest in theatrical productions; he was the friend and patron of men of letters, of painters, and musicians. A personage, in a word, of considerable consequence in that particular world in which young Spode had elected to make his success.

Spode had only recently left the university. Simon Gollamy, the editor of the *World's Review* (the "Best of all possible Worlds"), had got to know him—he was always on the look out for youthful talent— had seen possibilities in the young man, and appointed him art critic of his paper. Gollamy liked to have young and teachable people about him. The possession of disciples flattered his vanity, and he found it easier, moreover, to run his paper with docile collaborators than with men grown obstinate and case-hardened with age. Spode had not done badly at his new job. At any rate, his articles had been intelligent enough to arouse the interest of Lord Badgery. It was, ultimately, to them that he owed the honour of sitting to-night in the dining-room of Badgery House.

Fortified by several varieties of wine and a glass of aged brandy, Spode felt more confident and at ease than he had done the whole evening. Badgery was rather a disquieting host. He had an alarming habit of changing the subject of any conversation that had lasted for more than two minutes. Spode had found it, for example, horribly mortifying when his host, cutting across what was, he prided himself, a particularly subtle and illuminating disquisition on baroque art, had turned a wandering eye about the room and asked him abruptly whether he liked parrots. He had flushed and glanced suspiciously towards him, fancying that the man was trying to be offensive. But no; Badgery's white, fleshy, Hanoverian face wore an expression of perfect good faith. There was no malice in his small greenish eyes. He evidently did genuinely want to know if Spode liked parrots. The young man swallowed his irritation and replied that he did. Badgery then told a good story about parrots. Spode was on the point of capping it with a better story, when his host began to talk about Beethoven. And so the game went on. Spode cut his conversation to suit his host's requirements. In the course of ten minutes he had made a more or less witty epigram on Benvenuto Cellini, Queen Victoria, sport, God, Stephen Phillips, and Moorish architecture. Lord Badgery thought him the most charming young man, and so intelligent.

"If you've quite finished your coffee," he said, rising to his feet as he spoke, "we'll go and look at the pictures."

Spode jumped up with alacrity, and only then realized that he had drunk just ever so little too much. He would have to be careful, talk deliberately, plant his feet consciously, one after the other.

"This house is quite cluttered up with pictures," Lord Badgery complained. "I had a whole wagon-load taken away to the country last week; but there are still far too many. My ancestors would have their portraits painted by Romney. Such a shocking artist, don't you think? Why couldn't they have chosen Gainsborough, or even Reynolds? I've had all the Romneys hung in the servants' hall now. It's such a comfort to know that one can never possibly see them again. I suppose you know all about the ancient Hittites?"

"Well . . ." the young man replied, with befitting modesty.

"Look at that, then." He indicated a large stone head which stood in a case near the dining-room door. "It's not Greek, or Egyptian, or Persian, or anything else; so if it isn't ancient Hittite, I don't know what it is. And that reminds me of that story about Lord George Sanger, the Circus King . . ." and, without giving Spode time to examine the Hittite relic, he led the way up the huge staircase, pausing every now and then in his anecdote to point out some new object of curiosity or beauty.

"I suppose you know Deburau's pantomimes?" Spode rapped out

as soon as the story was over. He was in an itch to let out his information about Deburau. Badgery had given him a perfect opening with his ridiculous Sanger. "What a perfect man, isn't he? He used to . . ."

"This is my main gallery," said Lord Badgery, throwing open one leaf of a tall folding door. "I must apologize for it. It looks like a roller-skating rink." He fumbled with the electric switches and there was suddenly light—light that revealed an enormous gallery, duly receding into distance according to all the laws of perspective. "I dare say you've heard of my poor father," Lord Badgery continued. "A little insane, you know; sort of mechanical genius with a screw loose. He used to have a toy railway in this room. No end of fun he had, crawling about the floor after his trains. And all the pictures were stacked in the cellars. I can't tell you what they were like when I found them: mushrooms growing out of the Botticellis. Now I'm rather proud of this Poussin; he painted it for Scarron."

"Exquisite!" Spode exclaimed, making with his hand a gesture as though he were modelling a pure form in the air. "How splendid the onrush of those trees and leaning figures is! And the way they're caught up, as it were, and stemmed by that single godlike form opposing them with his contrary movement! And the draperies . . ."

But Lord Badgery had moved on, and was standing in front of a little fifteenth-century Virgin of carved wood.

"School of Rheims," he explained.

They "did" the gallery at high speed. Badgery never permitted his guest to halt for more than forty seconds before any work of art. Spode would have liked to spend a few moments of recollection and tranquillity in front of some of these lovely things. But it was not permitted.

The gallery done, they passed into a little room leading out of it. At the sight of what the lights revealed, Spode gasped.

"It's like something out of Balzac," he exclaimed. "Un de ces salons dorés où se déploie un luxe insolent. You know."

"My nineteenth-century chamber," Badgery explained. "The best thing of its kind, I flatter myself, outside the State Apartments at Windsor."

Spode tiptoed round the room, peering with astonishment at all the objects in glass, in gilded bronze, in china, in feathers, in embroidered and painted silk, in beads, in wax, objects of the most fantastic shapes and colours, all the queer products of a decadent tradition, with which the room was crowded. There were paintings on the walls—a Martin, a Wilkie, an early Landseer, several Ettys, a big Haydon, a slight pretty water-colour of a girl by Wainewright, the pupil of Blake and arsenic poisoner, and a score of others. But the picture which arrested Spode's attention was a medium-sized canvas representing Troilus riding into Troy among the flowers and plaudits of an admiring crowd, and oblivious (you could see from his expression) of everything but the eyes of Cressida, who looked down at him from a window, with Pandarus smiling over her shoulder.

"What an absurd and enchanting picture!" Spode exclaimed.

"Ah, you've spotted my Troilus." Lord Badgery was pleased.

"What bright harmonious colours! Like Etty's, only stronger, not so obviously pretty. And there's an energy about it that reminds one of Haydon. Only Haydon could never have done anything so impeccable in taste. Who is it by?" Spode turned to his host inquiringly.

"You were right in detecting Haydon," Lord Badgery answered. "It's by his pupil, Tillotson. I wish I could get hold of more of his work. But nobody seems to know anything about him. And he seems to have done so little."

This time it was the younger man who interrupted.

"Tillotson, Tillotson . . ." He put his hand to his forehead. A frown incongruously distorted his round, floridly curved face. "No . . . . yes, I have it." He looked up triumphantly with serene and childish brows. "Tillotson, Walter Tillotson—the man's still alive."

Badgery smiled. "This picture was painted in 1846, you know."

"Well, that's all right. Say he was born in 1820, painted his masterpiece when he was twenty-six, and it's 1913 now; that's to say he's only ninety-three. Not as old as Titian yet."

"But he's not been heard of since 1860," Lord Badgery protested.

"Precisely. Your mention of his name reminded me of the discovery I made the other day when I was looking through the obituary notices in the archives of the World's Review. (One has to bring them up to date every year or so for fear of being caught napping if one of these old birds chooses to shuffle off suddenly.) Well there, among them— I remember my astonishment at the time—there I found Walter Tillotson's biography. Pretty full to 1860, and then a blank, except for a pencil note in the early nineteen hundreds to the effect that he had returned from the East. The obituary has never been used or added to. I draw the obvious conclusion: the old chap isn't dead yet. He's just been overlooked somehow."

"But this is extraordinary," Lord Badgery exclaimed. "You must find him, Spode—you must find him. I'll commission him to paint frescoes round this room. It's just what I've always vainly longed for —a real nineteenth-century artist to decorate this place for me. Oh, we must find him at once—at once."

Lord Badgery strode up and down in a state of great excitement.

"I can see how this room could be made quite perfect," he went on. "We'd clear away all these cases and have the whole of that wall filled by a heroic fresco of Hector and Andromache, or 'Distraining for Rent', or Fanny Kemble as Belvidera in 'Venice Preserved'— anything like that, provided it's in the grand manner of the 'thirties and 'forties. And here I'd have a landscape with lovely receding perspectives, or else something architectural and grand in the style of Belshazzar's feast. Then we'll have this Adam fireplace taken down and replaced by something Mauro-Gothic. And on these walls I'll have mirrors, or no! let me see . . ."

He sank into meditative silence, from which he finally roused himself to shout:

"The old man, the old man! Spode, we must find this astonishing old creature. And don't breathe a word to anybody. Tillotson shall be our secret. Oh, it's too perfect, it's incredible! Think of the frescoes."

Lord Badgery's face had become positively animated. He had talked of a single subject for nearly a quarter of an hour.

II

Three weeks later Lord Badgery was aroused from his usual after-luncheon somnolence by the arrival of a telegram. The message was a short one. "Found.—Spode." A look of pleasure and intelligence made human Lord Badgery's clayey face of surfeit. "No answer," he said. The footman padded away on noiseless feet.

Lord Badgery closed his eyes and began to contemplate. Found! What a room he would have! There would be nothing like it in the world. The frescoes, the fireplace, the mirrors, the ceiling. . . . And a small, shrivelled old man clambering about the scaffolding, agile and quick like one of those whiskered little monkeys at the Zoo, painting away, painting away. . . . Fanny Kemble as Belvidera, Hector and Andromache, or why not the Duke of Clarence in the Butt, the Duke of Malmsey, the Butt of Clarence. . . . Lord Badgery was asleep.

Spode did not lag long behind his telegram. He was at Badgery House by six o'clock. His lordship was in the nineteenth-century chamber, engaged in clearing away with his own hands the bric-à-brac. Spode found him looking hot and out of breath.

"Ah, there you are," said Lord Badgery. "You see me already preparing for the great man's coming. Now you must tell me all about him."

"He's older even than I thought," said Spode. "He's ninety-seven this year. Born in 1816. Incredible, isn't it! There, I'm beginning at the wrong end."

"Begin where you like," said Badgery genially.

"I won't tell you all the incidents of the hunt. You've no idea what a job I had to run him to earth. It was like a Sherlock Holmes story, immensely elaborate, too elaborate. I shall write a book about it some day. At any rate, I found him at last."

"Where?"

"In a sort of respectable slum in Holloway, older and poorer and lonelier than you could have believed possible. I found out how it was he came to be forgotten, how he came to drop out of life in the way he did. He took it into his head, somewhere about the 'sixties, to go to Palestine to get local colour for his religious pictures—scapegoats and things, you know. Well, he went to Jerusalem and then on to Mount Lebanon and on and on, and then, somewhere in the middle of Asia Minor, he got stuck. He got stuck for about forty years."

"But what did he do all that time?"

"Oh, he painted, and started a mission, and converted three Turks, and taught the local Pashas the rudiments of English, Latin, and perspective, and God knows what else. Then, in about 1904, it seems to have occurred to him that he was getting rather old and had been away from home for rather a long time. So he made his way back to England, only to find that everyone he had known was dead, that the dealers had never heard of him and wouldn't buy his pictures, that he was simply a ridiculous old figure of fun. So he got a job as a drawing-master in a girls' school in Holloway, and there he's been ever since, growing older and older, and feebler and feebler, and blinder and deafer, and generally more gaga, until finally the school has given him the sack. He had about ten pounds in the world when I found him. He lives in a kind of black hole in a basement full of beetles. When his ten pounds are spent, I suppose he'll just quietly die there."

Badgery held up a white hand. "No more, no more. I find literature quite depressing enough. I insist that life at least shall be a little gayer. Did you tell him I wanted him to paint my room?"

"But he can't paint. He's too blind and palsied."

"Can't paint?" Badgery exclaimed in horror. "Then what's the good of the old creature?"

"Well, if you put it like that . . ." Spode began.

"I shall never have my frescoes. Ring the bell, will you?"

Spode rang.

"What right had Tillotson to go on existing if he can't paint?" went on Lord Badgery petulantly. "After all, that was his only justification for occupying a place in the sun."

"He doesn't have much sun in his basement."

The footman appeared at the door.

"Get someone to put all these things back in their places," Lord Badgery commanded, indicating with a wave of the hand the ravaged cases, the confusion of glass and china with which he had littered the floor, the pictures unhooked. "We'll go to the library, Spode; it's more comfortable there."

He led the way through the long gallery and down the stairs.

"I'm sorry old Tillotson has been such a disappointment," said Spode sympathetically.

"Let us talk about something else; he ceases to interest me."

"But don't you think we ought to do something about him? He's only got ten pounds between him and the workhouse. And if you'd seen the blackbeetles in his basement!"

"Enough—enough. I'll do everything you think fitting."

"I thought we might get up a subscription amongst lovers of the arts."

"There aren't any," said Badgery.

"No; but there are plenty of people who will subscribe out of snobbism."

"Not unless you give them something for their money."

"That's true. I hadn't thought of that." Spode was silent for a moment. "We might have a dinner in his honour. The Great Tillotson Banquet. Doyen of British Art. A Link with the Past. Can't you see it in the papers? I'd make a stunt of it in the *World's Review*. That ought to bring in the snobs."

"And we'll invite a lot of artists and critics—all the ones who can't stand one another. It will be fun to see them squabbling." Badgery laughed. Then his face darkened once again. "Still," he added, "it'll be a very poor second best to my frescoes. You'll stay to dinner, of course."

"Well, since you suggest it. Thanks very much."

III

The Tillotson Banquet was fixed to take place about three weeks later. Spode, who had charge of the arrangements, proved himself an excellent organizer. He secured the big banqueting-room at the Café Bomba, and was successful in bullying and cajoling the manager into giving fifty persons dinner at twelve shillings a head, including wine. He sent out invitations and collected subscriptions. He wrote an article on Tillotson in the *World's Review*—one of those charming, witty articles, couched in the tone of amused patronage and contempt with which one speaks of the great men of 1840. Nor did he neglect Tillotson himself. He used to go to Holloway almost every day to listen to the old man's endless stories about Asia Minor and the Great Exhibition of '51 and Benjamin Robert Haydon. He was sincerely sorry for this relic of another age.

Mr Tillotson's room was about ten feet below the level of the soil of South Holloway. A little grey light percolated through the area bars, forced a difficult passage through panes opaque with dirt, and spent itself, like a drop of milk that falls into an inkpot, among the inveterate shadows of the dungeon. The place was haunted by the sour smell of damp plaster and of woodwork that has begun to moulder secretly at the heart. A little miscellaneous furniture, including a bed, a washstand and chest of drawers, a table and one or two chairs, lurked in the obscure corners of the den or ventured furtively out into the open. Hither Spode now came almost every day, bringing the old man news of the progress of the banquet scheme. Every day he found Mr Tillotson sitting in the same place under the window, bathing, as it were, in his tiny puddle of light. "The oldest man that ever wore grey hairs," Spode reflected as he looked at him. Only there were very few hairs left on that bald, unpolished head. At the sound of the visitor's knock Mr Tillotson would turn in his chair, stare in the direction of the door with blinking, uncertain eyes. He was always full of apologies for being so slow in recognizing who was there.

"No discourtesy meant," he would say, after asking. "It's not as if I had forgotten who you were. Only it's so dark and my sight isn't what it was."

After that he never failed to give a little laugh, and, pointing out of the window at the area railings, would say:

"Ah, this is the place for somebody with good sight. It's the place for looking at ankles. It's the grand stand."

It was the day before the great event. Spode came as usual, and Mr Tillotson punctually made his little joke about the ankles, and Spode as punctually laughed.

"Well, Mr Tillotson," he said, after the reverberation of the joke had died away, "to-morrow you make your re-entry into the world of art and fashion. You'll find some changes."

"I've always had such extraordinary luck," said Mr Tillotson, and Spode could see by his expression that he genuinely believed it, that he had forgotten the black hole and the blackbeetles and the almost exhausted ten pounds that stood between him and the workhouse. "What an amazing piece of good fortune, for instance, that you should have found me just when you did. Now, this dinner will bring me back to my place in the world. I shall have money, and in a little while—who knows?—I shall be able to see well enough to paint again. I believe my eyes are getting better, you know. Ah, the future is very rosy."

Mr Tillotson looked up, his face puckered into a smile, and nodded his head in affirmation of his words.

"You believe in the life to come?" said Spode, and immediately flushed for shame at the cruelty of the words.

But Mr Tillotson was in far too cheerful a mood to have caught their significance.

"Life to come," he repeated. "No, I don't believe in any of that stuff—not since 1859. The 'Origin of Species' changed my views, you know. No life to come for me, thank you! You don't remember the excitement, of course. You're very young, Mr Spode."

"Well, I'm not so old as I was," Spode replied. "You know how middle-aged one is as a schoolboy and undergraduate. Now I'm old enough to know I'm young."

Spode was about to develop this little paradox further, but he noticed that Mr Tillotson had not been listening. He made a note of the gambit for use in companies that were more appreciative of the subtleties.

"You were talking about the 'Origin of Species,' " he said.

"Was I?" said Mr Tillotson, waking from reverie.

"About its effect on your faith, Mr Tillotson."

"To be sure, yes. It shattered my faith. But I remember a fine thing by the Poet Laureate, something about there being more faith in honest doubt, believe me, than in all the . . . all the . . . I forget exactly what; but you see the train of thought. Oh, it was a bad time for religion. I am glad my master Haydon never lived to see it. He was a man of fervour. I remember him pacing up and down his studio in Lisson Grove, singing and shouting and praying all at once. It used almost to frighten me. Oh, but he was a wonderful man, a great man. Take him for all in all, we shall not look upon his like again. As usual, the Bard is right. But it was all very long ago, before your time, Mr Spode."

"Well, I'm not as old as I was," said Spode, in the hope of having his paradox appreciated this time. But Mr Tillotson went on without noticing the interruption.

"It's a very, very long time. And yet, when I look back on it, it all seems but a day or two ago. Strange that each day should seem so long and that many days added together should be less than an hour. How clearly I can see old Haydon pacing up and down! Much more clearly, indeed, than I see you, Mr Spode. The eyes of memory don't grow dim. But my sight is improving, I assure you; it's improving daily. I shall soon be able to see those ankles." He laughed, like a cracked bell—one of those little old bells, Spode fancied, that ring, with much rattling of wires, in the far-off servants' quarters of ancient houses. "And very soon," Mr Tillotson went on, "I shall be painting again. Ah, Mr Spode, my luck is extraordinary. I believe in it, I trust it. And after all, what is luck? Simply another name for Providence, in spite of the 'Origin of Species' and the rest of it. How right the Laureate was when he said that there was more faith in honest doubt, believe me, than in all the . . . er, the . . . er . . . well, you know. I regard you, Mr Spode, as the emissary of Providence. Your coming marked a turning-point in my life, and the beginning, for me, of happier days. Do you know, one of the first things I shall do when my fortunes are restored will be to buy a hedgehog."

"A hedgehog, Mr Tillotson?"

"For the blackbeetles. There's nothing like a hedgehog for beetles. It will eat blackbeetles till it's sick, till it dies of surfeit. That reminds me of the time when I told my poor great master Haydon—in joke, of course—that he ought to send in a cartoon of King John dying of a surfeit of lampreys for the frescoes in the new Houses of Parliament. As I told him, it's a most notable event in the annals of British liberty—the providential and exemplary removal of a tyrant."

Mr Tillotson laughed again—the little bell in the deserted house; a ghostly hand pulling the cord in the drawing-room, and phantom footmen responding to the thin, flawed note.

"I remember he laughed, laughed like a bull in his old grand manner. But oh, it was a terrible blow when they rejected his designs, a terrible blow! It was the first and fundamental cause of his suicide."

Mr Tillotson paused. There was a long silence. Spode felt strangely moved, he hardly knew why, in the presence of this man, so frail, so ancient, in body three parts dead, in the spirit so full of life and hopeful patience. He felt ashamed. What was the use of his own youth and cleverness? He saw himself suddenly as a boy with a rattle scaring birds—rattling his noisy cleverness, waving his arms in ceaseless and futile activity, never resting in his efforts to scare away the birds that were always trying to settle in his mind. And what birds! wide-winged and beautiful, all those serene thoughts and faiths and emotions that only visit minds that have humbled themselves to quiet. Those gracious visitants he was for ever using all his energies to drive away. But this old man, with his hedgehogs and his honest doubts and all the rest of it—his mind was like a field made beautiful by the free coming and going, the unafraid alightings of a multitude of white, bright-winged creatures. He felt ashamed. But then, was it possible to alter one's life? Wasn't it a little absurd to risk a conversion? Spode shrugged his shoulders.

"I'll get you a hedgehog at once," he said. "They're sure to have some at Whiteley's."

Before he left that evening Spode made an alarming discovery. Mr Tillotson did not possess a dress-suit. It was hopeless to think of getting one made at this short notice, and, besides, what an unnecessary expense!

"We shall have to borrow a suit, Mr Tillotson. I ought to have thought of that before."

"Dear me, dear me." Mr Tillotson was a little chagrined by this unlucky discovery. "Borrow a suit?"

Spode hurried away for counsel to Badgery House. Lord Badgery surprisingly rose to the occasion. "Ask Boreham to come and see me," he told the footman who answered his ring.

Boreham was one of those immemorial butlers who linger on, generation after generation, in the houses of the great. He was over eighty now, bent, dried up, shrivelled with age.

"All old men are about the same size," said Lord Badgery. It was a comforting theory. "Ah, here he is. Have you got a spare suit of evening clothes, Boreham?"

"I have an old suit, my lord, that I stopped wearing in—let me see —was it nineteen seven or eight?"

"That's the very thing. I should be most grateful, Boreham, if you could lend it to me for Mr Spode here for a day."

The old man went out, and soon reappeared carrying over his arm a very old black suit. He held up the coat and trousers for inspection. In the light of day they were deplorable.

"You've no idea, sir," said Boreham deprecatingly to Spode—"you've no idea how easy things get stained with grease and gravy and what not. However careful you are, sir—however careful."

"I should imagine so." Spode was sympathetic.

"However careful, sir."

"But in artificial light they'll look all right."

"Perfectly all right," Lord Badgery repeated. "Thank you, Boreham; you shall have them back on Thursday."

"You're welcome, my lord, I'm sure." And the old man bowed and disappeared.

On the afternoon of the great day Spode carried up to Holloway a parcel containing Boreham's retired evening-suit and all the necessary appurtenances in the way of shirts and collars. Owing to the darkness and his own feeble sight Mr Tillotson was happily unaware of the defects in the suit. He was in a state of extreme nervous agitation. It was with some difficulty that Spode could prevent him, although it was only three o'clock, from starting his toilet on the spot.

"Take it easy, Mr Tillotson, take it easy. We needn't start till half-past seven, you know."

Spode left an hour later, and as soon as he was safely out of the room Mr Tillotson began to prepare himself for the banquet. He lighted the gas and a couple of candles, and, blinking myopically at the image that fronted him in the tiny looking-glass that stood on his chest of drawers, he set to work, with all the ardour of a young girl preparing for her first ball. At six o'clock, when the last touches had been given, he was not unsatisfied.

He marched up and down his cellar, humming to himself the gay song which had been so popular in his middle years:

"Oh, oh, Anna Maria Jones!
Queen of the tambourine, the cymbals, and the bones!"

Spode arrived an hour later in Lord Badgery's second Rolls-Royce. Opening the door of the old man's dungeon, he stood for a moment, wide-eyed with astonishment, on the threshold. Mr Tillotson was standing by the empty grate, one elbow resting on the mantelpiece, one leg crossed over the other in a jaunty and gentlemanly attitude. The effect of the candlelight shining on his face was to deepen every line and wrinkle with intense black shadow; he looked immeasurably old. It was a noble and pathetic head. On the other hand, Boreham's outworn evening-suit was simply buffoonish. The coat was too long in the sleeves and the tail; the trousers bagged in elephantine creases about his ankles. Some of the grease-spots were visible even in candlelight. The white tie, over which Mr Tillotson had taken infinite pains and which he believed in his purblindness to be perfect, was fantastically lop-sided. He had buttoned up his waistcoat in such a fashion that one button was widowed of its hole and one hole of its button. Across his shirt front lay the broad green ribbon of some unknown Order.

"Queen of the tambourine, the cymbals, and the bones," Mr Tillotson concluded in a gnat-like voice before welcoming his visitor.

"Well, Spode, here you are. I'm dressed already, you see. The suit, I flatter myself, fits very well, almost as though it had been made for me. I am all gratitude to the gentleman who was kind enough to lend it to me; I shall take the greatest care of it. It's a dangerous thing to lend clothes. For loan oft loseth both itself and friend. The Bard is always right."

"Just one thing," said Spode. "A touch to your waistcoat." He unbuttoned the dissipated garment and did it up again more symmetrically.

Mr Tillotson was a little piqued at being found so absurdly in the wrong. "Thanks, thanks," he said protestingly, trying to edge away from his valet. "It's all right, you know; I can do it myself. Foolish oversight. I flatter myself the suit fits very well."

"And perhaps the tie might . . ." Spode began tentatively. But the old man would not hear of it.

"No, no. The tie's all right. I can tie a tie, Mr Spode. The tie's all right. Leave it as it is, I beg."

"I like your Order."

Mr Tillotson looked down complacently at his shirt front. "Ah, you've noticed my Order. It's a long time since I wore that. It was given me by the Grand Porte, you know, for services rendered in the Russo-Turkish War. It's the Order of Chastity, the second class. They only give the first class to crowned heads, you know—crowned heads and ambassadors. And only Pashas of the highest rank get the second. Mine's the second. They only give the first class to crowned heads . . ."

"Of course, of course," said Spode.

"Do you think I look all right, Mr Spode?" Mr Tillotson asked, a little anxiously.

"Splendid, Mr Tillotson—splendid. The Order's magnificent."

The old man's face brightened once more. "I flatter myself," he said, "that this borrowed suit fits me very well. But I don't like borrowing clothes. For loan oft loseth both itself and friend, you know. And the Bard is always right."

"Ugh, there's one of those horrible beetles!" Spode exclaimed.

Mr Tillotson bent down and stared at the floor. "I see it," he said, and stamped on a small piece of coal, which crunched to powder under his foot. "I shall certainly buy a hedgehog."

It was time for them to start. A crowd of little boys and girls had collected round Lord Badgery's enormous car. The chauffeur, who felt that honour and dignity were at stake, pretended not to notice the children, but sat gazing, like a statue, into eternity. At the sight of Spode and Mr Tillotson emerging from the house a yell of mingled awe and derision went up. It subsided to an astonished silence as they climbed into the car. "Bomba's," Spode directed. The Rolls-Royce gave a faintly stertorous sigh and began to move. The children yelled again, and ran along beside the car, waving their arms in a frenzy of excitement. It was then that Mr Tillotson, with an incomparably noble gesture, leaned forward and tossed among the seething crowd of urchins his three last coppers.

IV

In Bomba's big room the company was assembling. The long gilt-edged mirrors reflected a singular collection of people. Middle-aged Academicians shot suspicious glances at youths whom they suspected, only too correctly, of being iconoclasts, organizers of Post-Impressionist Exhibitions. Rival art critics, brought suddenly face to face, quivered with restrained hatred. Mrs Nobes, Mrs Cayman, and Mrs Mandragore, those indefatigable hunters of artistic big game, came on one another all unawares in this well-stored menagerie, where each had expected to hunt alone, and were filled with rage. Through this crowd of mutually repellent vanities Lord Badgery moved with a suavity that seemed unconscious of all the feuds and hatreds. He was enjoying himself immensely. Behind the heavy waxen mask of his face, ambushed behind the Hanoverian nose, the little lustreless pig's eyes, the pale thick lips, there lurked a small devil of happy malice that rocked with laughter.

"So nice of you to have come, Mrs Mandragore, to do honour to England's artistic past. And I'm so glad to see you've brought dear Mrs Cayman. And is that Mrs Nobes, too? So it is! I hadn't noticed her before. How delightful! I knew we could depend on your love of art."

And he hurried away to seize the opportunity of introducing that eminent sculptor, Sir Herbert Herne, to the bright young critic who had called him, in the public prints, a monumental mason.

A moment later the Maître d'Hotel came to the door of the gilded saloon and announced, loudly and impressively, "Mr Walter Tillotson." Guided from behind by young Spode, Mr Tillotson came into the room slowly and hesitatingly. In the glare of the lights his eyelids beat heavily, painfully, like the wings of an imprisoned moth, over his filmy eyes. Once inside the door he halted and drew himself up with a conscious assumption of dignity. Lord Badgery hurried forward and seized his hand.

"Welcome, Mr Tillotson—welcome in the name of English art!"

Mr Tillotson inclined his head in silence. He was too full of emotion to be able to reply.

"I should like to introduce you to a few of your younger colleagues, who have assembled here to do you honour."

Lord Badgery presented everyone in the room to the old painter, who bowed, shook hands, made little noises in his throat, but still found himself unable to speak. Mrs Nobes, Mrs Cayman, and Mrs Mandragore all said charming things.

Dinner was served; the party took their places. Lord Badgery sat at the head of the table, with Mr Tillotson on his right hand and Sir Herbert Herne on his left. Confronted with Bomba's succulent cooking and Bomba's wines, Mr Tillotson ate and drank a good deal. He had the appetite of one who has lived on greens and potatoes for ten years among the blackbeetles. After the second glass of wine he began to talk, suddenly and in a flood, as though a sluice had been pulled up.

"In Asia Minor," he began, "it is the custom, when one goes to dinner, to hiccough as a sign of appreciative fullness. *Eructavit cor meum*, as the Psalmist has it; he was an Oriental himself."

Spode had arranged to sit next to Mrs Cayman; he had designs upon her. She was an impossible woman, of course, but rich and useful; he wanted to bamboozle her into buying some of his young friend's pictures.

"In a cellar?" Mrs Cayman was saying, "with blackbeetles? Oh, how dreadful! Poor old man! And he's ninety-seven, didn't you say? Isn't that shocking! I only hope the subscription will be a large one. Of course, one wishes one could have given more oneself. But then, you know, one has so many expenses, and things are so difficult now."

"I know, I know," said Spode, with feeling.

"It's all because of Labour," Mrs Cayman explained. "Of course, I should simply love to have him in to dinner sometimes. But, then, I feel he's really too old, too *farouche* and *gâteux*; it would not be doing a kindness to him, would it? And so you are working with Mr Gollamy now? What a charming man, so talented, such conversation . . ."

"Eructavit cor meum," said Mr Tillotson for the third time. Lord Badgery tried to head him off the subject of Turkish etiquette, but in vain.

By half-past nine a kinder vinolent atmosphere had put to sleep the hatreds and suspicions of before dinner. Sir Herbert Herne had discovered that the young Cubist sitting next him was not insane and actually knew a surprising amount about the Old Masters. For their part these young men had realized that their elders were not at all malignant; they were just very stupid and pathetic. It was only in the bosoms of Mrs Nobes, Mrs Cayman, and Mrs Mandragore that hatred still reigned undiminished. Being ladies and old-fashioned, they had drunk almost no wine.

The moment for speech-making arrived. Lord Badgery rose to his feet, said what was expected of him, and called upon Sir Herbert to propose the toast of the evening. Sir Herbert coughed, smiled, and began. In the course of a speech that lasted twenty minutes he told anecdotes of Mr Gladstone, Lord Leighton, Sir Alma Tadema, and the late Bishop of Bombay; he made three puns, he quoted Shakespeare and Whittier, he was playful, he was eloquent, he was grave . . . At the end of his harangue Sir Herbert handed to Mr Tillotson a silk purse containing fifty-eight pounds ten shillings, the total amount of the subscription. The old man's health was drunk with acclamation.

Mr Tillotson rose with difficulty to his feet. The dry, snakelike skin of his face was flushed; his tie was more crooked than ever; the green ribbon of the Order of Chastity of the second class had somehow climbed up his crumpled and maculate shirt-front.

"My lord, ladies, and gentlemen," he began in a choking voice, and then broke down completely. It was a very painful and pathetic spectacle. A feeling of intense discomfort afflicted the minds of all who looked upon that trembling relic of a man, as he stood there weeping and stammering. It was as though a breath of the wind of death had blown suddenly through the room, lifting the vapours of wine and tobacco-smoke, quenching the laughter and the candle flames. Eyes floated uneasily, not knowing where to look. Lord Badgery, with great presence of mind, offered the old man a glass of wine. Mr Tillotson began to recover. The guests heard him murmur a few disconnected words.

"This great honour . . . overwhelmed with kindness . . . this magnificent banquet . . . not used to it . . . in Asia Minor . . . *eructavit cor meum.*"

At this point Lord Badgery plucked sharply at one of his long coat tails. Mr Tillotson paused, took another sip of wine, and then went on with a newly won coherence and energy.

"The life of the artist is a hard one. His work is unlike other men's work, which may be done mechanically, by rote and almost, as it were, in sleep. It demands from him a constant expense of spirit. He gives continually of his best life, and in return he receives much joy, it is true—much fame, it may be—but of material blessings, very few. It is eighty years since first I devoted my life to the service of art; eighty years, and almost every one of those years has brought me fresh and painful proof of what I have been saying: the artist's life is a hard one."

This unexpected deviation into sense increased the general feeling of discomfort. It became necessary to take the old man seriously, to regard him as a human being. Up till then he had been no more than an object of curiosity, a mummy in an absurd suit of evening-clothes with a green ribbon across the shirt front. People could not help wishing that they had subscribed a little more. Fifty-eight pounds ten —it wasn't enormous. But happily for the peace of mind of the company, Mr Tillotson paused to live up to his proper character by talking absurdly.

"When I consider the life of that great man, Benjamin Robert Haydon, one of the greatest men England has ever produced . . ." The audience heaved a sigh of relief; this was all as it should be. There was a burst of loud bravoing and clapping. Mr Tillotson turned his dim eyes round the room, and smiled gratefully at the misty figures he beheld. "That great man, Benjamin Robert Haydon," he continued, "whom I am proud to call my master and who, it rejoices my heart to see, still lives in your memory and esteem,—that great man, one of the greatest that England has ever produced, led a life so deplorable that I cannot think of it without a tear."

And with infinite repetitions and divagations, Mr Tillotson related the history of B. R. Haydon, his imprisonments for debt, his battle with the Academy, his triumphs, his failures, his despair, his suicide. Half-past ten struck. Mr Tillotson was declaiming against the stupid and prejudiced judges who had rejected Haydon's designs for the decoration of the new Houses of Parliament in favour of the paltriest German scribblings.

"That great man, one of the greatest England has ever produced, that great Benjamin Robert Haydon, whom I am proud to call my master and who, it rejoices me to see, still lives on in your memory and esteem—at that affront his great heart burst; it was the unkindest cut of all. He who had worked all his life for the recognition of the artist by the State, he who had petitioned every Prime Minister, including the Duke of Wellington, for thirty years, begging them to employ artists to decorate public buildings, he to whom the scheme for decorating the Houses of Parliament was undeniably due . . ." Mr Tillotson lost a grip on his syntax and began a new sentence. "It was the unkindest cut of all, it was the last straw. The artist's life is a hard one."

At eleven Mr Tillotson was talking about the pre-Raphaelites. At a quarter-past he had begun to tell the story of B. R. Haydon all over again. At twenty-five minutes to twelve he collapsed quite speechless into his chair. Most of the guests had already gone away; the few who remained made haste to depart. Lord Badgery led the old man to the door and packed him into the second Rolls-Royce. The Tillotson Banquet was over; it had been a pleasant evening, but a little too long.

Spode walked back to his rooms in Bloomsbury, whistling as he went. The arc lamps of Oxford Street reflected in the polished surface of the road: canals of dark bronze. He would have to bring that into an article some time. The Cayman woman had been very successfully nobbled. "Voi che sapete," he whistled—somewhat out of tune, but he could not hear that.

When Mr Tillotson's landlady came in to call him on the following morning, she found the old man lying fully dressed on his bed. He looked very ill and very, very old; Boreham's dress-suit was in a terrible state, and the green ribbon of the Order of Chastity was ruined. Mr Tillotson lay very still, but he was not asleep. Hearing the sound of footsteps, he opened his eyes a little and faintly groaned. His landlady looked down at him menacingly.

"Disgusting!" she said; "disgusting, I call it. At your age."

Mr Tillotson groaned again. Making a great effort, he drew out of his trouser pocket a large silk purse, opened it, and extracted a sovereign.

"The artist's life is a hard one, Mrs Green," he said, handing her the coin. "Would you mind sending for the doctor? I don't feel very well. And oh, what shall I do about these clothes? What shall I say to the gentleman who was kind enough to lend them to me? Loan oft loseth both itself and friend. The Bard is always right."

In the Absence of Angels

❀ HORTENSE CALISHER ❀

HORTENSE CALISHER (b. 1911) lives in New York and has appeared
frequently in *The New Yorker*. She is a graduate of Barnard and has
taught English at various universities. Among her works of fiction are
Extreme Magic, False Entry and *Textures of Life*.

BEFORE cockcrow tomorrow morning, I must remember everything I can about Hilda Kantrowitz. It is not at all strange that I
should use the word "cockcrow," for, like most of the others here, I
have only a literary knowledge of prisons. If someone among us were
to take a poll—that lax, almost laughable device of a world now past
—we would all come up with about the same stereotypes: Dickens'
Newgate, no doubt, full of those dropsical grotesques of his, under
which the sharp shape of liberty was almost lost; or, from the limp-
leather books of our teens, "The Ballad of Reading Gaol," that period
piece of a time when imprisonment could still be such a personal
affair. I myself recall, from a grade-school reader of thirty years ago, a
piece named "Piccola," called so after a flower that pushed its way up
through a crevice in a stone courtyard and solaced the man immured
there—a general, of God knows what political coloration.

Outside the window here, the only hedge is a long line of hydran-
geas, their swollen cones still the burnt, turned pink of autumn, still
at the stage when the housewives used to pick them and stand them
to dry on mantels, on pianos, to crisp and gather dust until they were
pushed, crackling, into the garbage, in the first, diluted sun of spring.

We here, women all of us, are in what until recently was a fashionable private school, located, I am fairly certain, somewhere in West-

chester County. There was no business about blindfolds from the guards on the trucks that brought us; rather, they let us sit and watch the flowing countryside, even comment upon it, looking at us with an indifference more chilling than if they had been on the alert, indicating as it did that a break from a particular truck into particular environs was of no import in a countryside that had become a cage. I recognized the Saw Mill River Parkway, its white marker lines a little worse for lack of upkeep, but its banks still neat, since they came in November, after the grass had stopped growing. Occasionally—at a reservoir, for instance—signposts in their language had been added, and there were concentrations of other trucks like ours. They keep the trains for troops.

This room was the kindergarten; it has been cleared, and the painted walls show clean squares where pictures used to be, for they have not yet covered them with their special brand of posters, full of fists and flags. Opposite me is their terse, typed bulletin, at which I have been looking for a long time. Built into the floor just beneath it, there is a small aquarium of colored tile, with a spigot for the water in which goldfish must have been kept, and beyond is the door that leads to our "latrine"—a little corridor of miniature basins and pygmy toilets and hooks about three and a half feet from the floor. In this room, which has been lined with full-size cots and stripped of everything but a certain innocent odor of crayon and chalk, it is possible to avoid imagining the flick of short braids, the brief toddle of a skirt. It is not possible in the latrine.

They ring the school bell to mark off the hours for us; it has exactly the same naïve, releasing trill (probably operated electrically by some thumb in what was the principal's office) as the bell that used to cue the end of Latin period and the beginning of math in the city high school where Hilda Kantrowitz and I were among the freshmen, twenty-five years ago. Within that school, Hilda and I, I see now, were from the first slated to fall into two covertly opposed groups of girls.

On the application we had all filled out for entrance, there was a line that said "Father's Business." On it I had put the word "manufacturer," which was what my father always called himself—which, stretching it only a little, is what I suppose he was. He had a small, staid leather-goods business that occupied two floors of an untidy building far downtown. When my mother and I went there after a shopping tour, the workers upstairs on the factory floor, who had banded together to give me a silver cup at my birth, would lean their stained hands on barrels and tease me jocularly about my growth; the new young girls at the cutting tables would not stop the astonishingly rapid, reflex routine of their hands but would smile at me diffidently, with inquisitive, sidelong glances. Downstairs, on the office-and-sales floor, where there was a staff of about ten, one or the other of my uncles would try to take me on his lap, groaning loudly, or Harry Davidson, the thin, henpecked cousin-by-marriage who was the book-keeper, would come out of the supply room, his paper cuffs scraping against a new, hard-covered ledger, which he would present to me with a mock show of furtiveness, for me to use for my poems, which were already a family joke.

The girls I went with, with whom I sat at lunch, or whom I rushed to meet after hours in the Greek soda parlor we favored, might too have been called, quite appositely, manufacturers' daughters, although not all of their fathers were in precisely that category. Helen's father was an insurance broker in an office as narrow as a knife blade, on a high floor of the most recent sky-scraper; Flora's father (of whom she was ashamed, in spite of his faultless clothes and handsome head, because he spoke bad English in his velvety Armenian voice) was a rug dealer; and Lotte's father, a German "banker," who did not seem to be connected with any bank, went off in his heavy Homburg to indefinite places downtown, where he "promoted," and made deals, coming home earlier than any of the others, in time for thick after-noon teas. What drew us together was a quality in our homes, all of which subscribed to exactly the same ideals of comfort.

We went home on the trolley or bus, Helen, Flora, Lotte, and I, to apartments or houses where the quality and taste of the bric-a-brac might vary but the linen closets were uniformly full, where the furniture covers sometimes went almost to the point of shabbiness but never beyond. Our mothers, often as not, were to be found in the kitchen, but though their hands kneaded dough, their knees rarely knew floors. Mostly, they were pleasantly favored women who had never worked before marriage, or tended to conceal it if they had, whose minds were not so much stupid as unaroused—women at whom the menopause or the defection of growing children struck suddenly in the soft depths of their inarticulateness, leaving them distraught, melancholy, even deranged, to make the rounds of the doctors until age came blessedly, turning them leathery but safe. And on us, their intransigent daughters, who wished to be poets, actresses, dancers, doctors—anything but merely teachers or wives—they looked with antagonism, secret pride, or dubious assent, as the case might be, but all of them nursing the sly prescience that marriage would almost certainly do for us, before we had quite done for ourselves.

This, then, was the group with which I began; in a curious way, which I must make clear to myself, as one makes a will, it is the group with which, perhaps tomorrow, somewhere outside this fading, post-humous room, I choose to end. Not because, as we clustered, by turns giggling, indecisive, and impassioned, in our soda parlors, we bore already that sad consanguinity of those women who were to refuse to stay in their traditional places either as wives, whom we identified with our mothers, or as teachers, whom we identified with lemon-faced aunts, lonely gas rings, and sexual despair. Hindsight gives us a more terrifying resemblance. Not as women but as people. Neither rich nor poor, we were among the last people to be—either by birth or, later, by conviction—in the middle.

For the rich, even while they spun in their baroque hysterias of possession, lived most intimately with the spectre of debacle. Like the poor, they were bred to the assumption that a man's thought does not go beyond his hunger, and like them, their images of ruin were ab-solute. When the spectre of violent change arose in our century, as it had in every century, this time with two mouths, one of which said "Need is common!," the other of which answered "Therefore let thought be common!," it was the very rich and the very poor who sub-scribed first—the rich transfixed in their fear, the poor transfixed in their hope. Curious (and yet not so curious, I see now) that from us in the middle, swinging insecurely in our little median troughs of satisfaction, never too sure of what we were or what we believed, was to rise that saving, gradient doubt that has shepherded us together, in entrenchments, in ambush, and in rooms like these.

Two cots away from mine sits a small, black-haired woman of the type the French call *mignonne*; one would never associate her with the strangely scored, unmelodic music, yawping but compelling, for which she was known. She is here for an odd reason, but we are all here for odd reasons. She is here because she will not write melody, as they conceive melody. Or, to be honest—and there is no time left here for anything but honesty—as most of us here would conceive melody. But we here, who do not understand her music, understand her reasons.

Down at the far end of the room, there is a gray, shadowy spinster who knows little of heresies concerning the diatonic scale. She is here because she believes in the probity of mice. All day long now, she sits on her bed in a trance of fear, but the story is that when they came to the college laboratory where for forty years she had bred mice and conclusions, she stood at first with her arm behind her, her hand, in its white sleeve, shaking a little on the knob of the closed door. Then she backed up against the door to push it inward, to invite them in, their committee, with the statement she was to sign. Past all the cages she led them, stopping at each to explain the lineage of the generation inside, until, tired of the interminable recital, they waved the paper under her nose. Then she led them to the filing cabinets, unlocked the drawers, and persuaded them to pore over page after page of her crisscrossed references, meanwhile intoning the monotonous record of her historic rodent dead. Not until then, until the paper had appeared a third time, did she say to them, with the queer cogency of those whose virtue is not usually in talk, "No. Perhaps I will end by lying for you. But the mice will not."

She, the shadowy, weak-voiced woman, and I are alike in one thing, although I am not here after any action such as hers. They came quite conventionally to my suburban cottage, flung open the door, and loaded me on the truck without a word, as they had previously come to another poet, Volk, on his island off the coast of Maine, to Peterson, the novelist, in his neat brick box at the far end of Queens, to all the other writers who were alive because of being away from the city on the day it went down. Quite simply, they, too, have read Plato, and they know that the writer is dangerous to them because he cannot help celebrating the uncommonness of people. For, no matter what epithalamiums they may extort from us, sooner or later the individuality will reappear. In the very poems we might carpenter for them to march to, in the midst of the sanitized theses, the decontaminate novels, sooner or later we will infect their pages with the subversive singularity of men.

She—the biologist—and I are alike because we are the only ones here who do not cry at night. Not because we are heroic but because we have no more hostages for which to weep. Her mice are scattered, or already docilely breeding new dogma under the careful guidance of one of the trainees brought over here from their closed, incredible, pragmatic world—someone born after 1917, perhaps, who, reared among the bent probities of hungry men, will not trouble himself about the subornation of mice.

And I, who would give anything if my son were with me here, even to be suborned, as they do already with children, can afford to sit and dream of old integrities only because I, too, no longer have a hostage—not since the day when, using a missile whose rhythm they had learned from us, they cracked the city to the reactive dirt from which it had sprung—the day when the third-grade class from the grammar school of a suburban town went on a field trip to the natural-history museum.

Anyone born in a city like that one, as I was, is a street urchin to the end of his days, whether he grew behind its plate glass and granite or in its ancient, urinous slums. And that last year, when it was said they were coming, I visited my city often, walking in the violet light that seeped between the buildings of its unearthly dusk, watching the multiform refractions of the crowd, telling myself "I do not care to survive this." But on the way up here, when, as if by intention, they routed our trucks through streets of fused slag and quagmire (which their men, tapping with divining rods, had declared safe), I sat there in one of the line of trucks looking dry-eyed at the dust of stone. Was it when the class was looking at the dinosaur, the *Archaeopteryx*, that the moment came? Was it while a voice, in soft, short syllables suited to his shortness, was telling him how a snake grew wings and became a bird, how a primate straightened its spine and became a man?

The room is quiet now, and dark, except for the moonlight that shows faintly outside on the hedge, faintly inside on the blurred harlequin tiles of the aquarium. Almost everyone is asleep here; even the person who rings the bell must be asleep, somewhere in one of the rooms in the wing they reserve for themselves. The little composer was one of the last who fell asleep; she cried for hours over the letter they brought her from her husband, also a musician, who wrote that

(261)

he was working for them, that there could be glory in it, that if she would only recant and work with him, they would release his mother, and the daughter, and the son. The letter was couched in their orotund, professional phrases, phrases that in their mouths have given the great words like "freedom" and "unity" a sick, blood-sour sound. But tomorrow she will agree, and there is no one here who will blame her. Only the gray woman at the other end of the room and I sit hunched, awake, on our cots—taking the long view, who have no other. I sit here trying to remember everything I can about Hilda Kantrowitz, who was my age, my generation, but who, according to their paper on the wall, will not be here with us. Perhaps the last justification for people like me is to remember people like Hilda, even now, with justice.

What I see clearest about Hilda now is her wrists. I am looking back, with some trouble, at a girl who was never, except once, very important to me, and with some effort I can see thick braids of a dullish, unwashed blond, stray wisps from the top of them falling over her forehead, as if she had slept so and had not taken time for a combing. I cannot see her face from the side at all, but from the front her nostrils are long and drawn upward, making the tip of her nose seem too close to the flat mouth, which looks larger than it is because its lines are not definite but fade into the face. The eyes I cannot see at all as yet. She is standing for recitation, holding the Latin book, and her wrists are painfully sharp and clear, as if they were in the center of a lens. They are red—chapped, I suppose—and their flat bones protrude a long way from the middy cuffs. She does not know the recitation—she almost never does—but she does not titter or flush or look smart-alecky, the way the rest of us do when this happens. She just stands there, her eyelids blinking rapidly, her long nostrils moving, and say nothing, swaying a little, like a dog who is about to fall asleep. Then she sits down. Later on, I learn that it may be true— she may never get enough sleep.

We find this out by inference, Lotte and I, when the two of us are walking home together on a winter afternoon. That day, Lotte and I, who live near one another, have made a pact to spend our carfare on eatables and walk all the way home together. We have nearly reached 110th Street and Cathedral Parkway, having dribbled pennies in a store here, a store there, amiably debating each piece of candy, each sack of Indian nuts. In the west, as we walk toward it, there is a great well of dying light fading to apple-green over the river, which we cannot as yet see. The faces of the people hurrying past us have something flowerlike and open about them as they bloom toward us and recede. We are tiring, feeling mournful and waif-like, with a delightful sadness that we breathe upon and foster, secure in the warm thought of home.

Down the block, there is a last, curving oasis of stores before the blank apartment houses begin. After that comes the long hill, with the church park and the hospital on the other side. Lotte has a last nickel. We walk slowly, peering into the stores. Next to a grill whose blind front is stencilled with lines of tangerine and false-blue light, there is one more store with a weak bulb shining. We press our faces against the glass of its door. It is a strange grocery store, if it is one, with no bakers' and bottlers' cardboard blurbs set in the window, no cherry brightness inside. Against its right-hand wall, galled wooden shelves hold a dark rummage of canned goods, with long, empty gaps between the brands. From a single line of cartons near the door on the lowest shelf, there is one hard, red glint of newness; these are packages of salt. Sprawled on the counter to the left, with her arms outflung between some box bottoms holding penny candy, there is a girl asleep. Her face, turned toward us, rests on a book whose thick, blunt shape we recognize almost as we do her. It is Hilda. Behind her, seen through the pane and the thin gruel of light, is the dim blotch of what looks like another room.

We confer, Lotte and I, in nudges, and finally Lotte pushes in ahead of me, her smothered giggle sounding above the rasp of a bell on the door. For a moment, it seems warmer inside—then not. A light is turned on in the back of the store, and we see that the second room is actually only a space that has been curtained off. The curtains are open. A woman comes forward and shakes Hilda angrily by the shoulder, with a flood of foreign words, then turns to us, speaking in a cringing voice. Candy? Crackers? How much money we got? Her face has a strong look to it, with good teeth and a mouth limned in blackish hair. In the half room behind her, on one of two day beds, a boy sits up, huddling in a man's thick sweater whose sleeves cover his hands. A smaller child clambers down from the other bed and runs to stand next to his mother. He is too young to have much hair, and the sight of his naked head, his meagre cotton shirt, and his wet diaper drooping between his legs makes me feel colder.

It becomes evident that Hilda and we know each other. I remember Hilda's cheekbones—sharp, and slowly red. The woman, all smiles now, moves toward us and lightly strokes Lotte's collar. That year, Lotte and I have made a fetish of dressing alike; we have on navy serge dresses with white collars pinned and identical silver bars.

"Little teachers!" the woman says. "Like little teachers!" She hovers over the counter a minute, then thrust a small box of crackers, the kind with marshmallow, into Lotte's hand. The baby sets up a cry and is pushed behind the woman's skirt. The boy on the bed stares at the box but says nothing. Confused, Lotte holds out her nickel. The woman hesitates, then shakes her head, refusing. Two fingers hover again over Lotte's collar but do not touch it. "Hilda will be teacher," the woman says. She makes a kind of genuflection of despair toward the place behind her, and we see that on a shelf there, in the midst of jumbled crockery and pans, is a man's picture, dark-bordered, in front of which a flame flickers, burning deep in a thick glass. She makes another gesture, as if she were pulling a cowl over her head, lets her hand fall against her skirt, and edges after us as we sidle toward the door. She bends over us. "Your mamas have what for me to sew, maybe? Or to clean?"

Hilda speaks, a short, guttural phrase in the language we do not understand. It is the only time she speaks. The woman steps back. Lotte still has the nickel in her open hand. Now Hilda is at the door. And now I see her mouth, the long lips pressed tight, turned down at the corners. She reaches out and takes Lotte's nickel. Then we are outside the door.

I do not remember anything about the rest of the walk home. But I remember that as I round the corner to my own street, alone, and am suddenly out of the wind, the air is like blue powder, and from the entrance to my house, as the doorman opens it and murmurs a greeting, the clean light scours the pavement. In the elevator, to my wind-smarting eyes the people look warmly blurry and gilded, and the elevator, rising perfectly, hums.

Lotte and I do not ever go back, of course, and we quickly forget the whole thing, for as the school year advances, the gap widens permanently between girls like us and those other unilluminated ones who are grinding seriously toward becoming teachers, for many of whose families the possession of a teacher daughter will be one of the bootstraps by which they will lift themselves to a feeling of security—that trust in education which is the dominant security in a country that prides itself on offering no other.

Then a bad time comes for me. My mother, after the birth of another child, late in life, is very ill and is sent away—to hunt for a warmer climate, it is said, although long afterward I know that it is a climate of the spirit for which she hunts. Once or twice during that time, she is brought home, able only to stand helplessly at the window, holding on to me, the tears running down her face. Then she is taken away again, for our windows are five flights up.

Business is bad, too, everywhere, and my father makes longer and longer sales trips away from home. We have a housekeeper, Mrs. Gallagher, who is really the baby's nurse, since we cannot afford a cook and a nurse, too. She does not wash my hair regularly or bother about my habits, and I grow dirty and unkempt. She is always whining after me to give up my favorite dresses to her own daughter, "a poor widow's child in a convent," after which, applying to my father for money, she buys me new dresses, probably with the daughter in mind, and my clothes become oddly tight and loud. Months later, after she is gone, it is found that she has drunk up a good part of my father's hoarded wines, but now no one knows this, and she is a good nurse, crooning, starched and fierce, over the basket that holds the baby, whom she possessively loves. Standing behind her, looking at the basket, which she keeps cloudy with dotted swiss and wreathed in rosy ribbon, I think to myself that the baby nestled there looks like a pink heart. Perhaps I think secretly, too, that I am the displaced heart.

So I begin to steal. Not at home, but at school. There I am now one of the lowest scholars. I have altogether lost track in Latin, and when I am sent to the board in geometry, I stand there desperately in front of the mazy diagram, the chalk in my slack hand, watching the teacher's long neck, in which the red impatience rises until it looks like a crane's leg. "Next!" she says, finally, and I walk back to my seat. At test time, I try frantically to copy, but the smart, safe ones ignore my pleading signal. And once the visiting nurse sends me home because there are nits in my bushy, tangled hair. Thereafter, when I follow on the heels of the crowd to the soda parlor—my hand guarding several days' saved-up carfare, in the hope of finding someone to treat—the sorority is closed.

So, day after day, I treat myself. For by now, although there is plenty of food at home and Mrs. Gallagher packs me thick sandwiches (mostly of cheese, which she buys conveniently in a big slab to last the week)—by now I am really hungry only and constantly for sweets. I live on the thought of them, for the suspended moment when the nugget is warm in my mouth or crammed, waiting, in my hidden hand. And the sweets that comfort me most are those bought secretly and eaten alone. It never occurs to me to ask Mrs. Gallagher for spending money. At noontime, habitually now, I slip into the dark coatroom, where the girls' coats are hung, one on top of another, and, sliding a hand from pocket to pocket, one can pretend to be looking for one's own. And there, once again, I meet Hilda.

We meet face to face in the lumpy shadows of the coatroom, each of us with a hand in the pocket of a coat that is not her own. We know this on the instant, recognition clamoring between us, two animals who touch each other's scent in the prowling dark. I inch my hand out of the gritty pocket and let it fall at my side. I do not see what Hilda does with her hand. But in that moment before we move, in the furry dusk of that windowless room, I see what is in her eyes. I do not give it a name. But I am the first to leave.

Even now, I cannot give it a name. It eludes me, as do the names of those whom, for layered reason upon reason, we cannot bear to remember. I have remembered as best I can.

The rest belongs to that amalgam called growing up, during which, like everyone else, I learn to stumble along somehow between truth and compromise. Shortly after that day, I fall ill of jaundice, and I am ill for a long while. During that time, my mother returns home, restored—or perhaps my illness is in part her restorative. Her housewifely shock at what she finds blows through our home like a cleansing wind, and her tonic scolding, severe and rational as of old, is like the bromide that disperses horror. When I go back to school, after months of absence, I have the transient prestige of one who has been seriously ill, and with my rehabilitated appearance this is almost enough to reinstate me. Then an English teacher discovers my poems, and although I am never again a sound student in any other class, I attain a certain eminence in hers, and I rise, with each display coaxed out of me, rung by rung, until I am safe. Meanwhile, Hilda has dropped out of school. I never ask, but she is gone, and I do not see her there again.

Once, some ten years later, I think I see her. During the year after I am married, but not yet a mother, or yet a widow, a friend takes me to a meeting for the Spanish resistance, at which a well-known woman poet speaks. On the fringes of the departing crowd outside the shabby hall, young men and women are distributing pamphlets, shaking canisters for contributions. I catch sight of one of them, a girl in a brown leather jacket, with cropped blond hair, a smudge of lipstick that conceals the shape of the mouth, but a smudge of excitement on cheekbones that are the same. I strain to look at her, to decide, but the crowd is pressing, the night is rainy, and I lose sight of her before I am sure. But now I have reason to be sure. Yes, it was she.

It was she—and I have remembered as best I can. While I have sat here, the moonlight, falling white on the cast-down figure of the other waker, slumped now in sleep, showing up each brilliant, signal detail of the room in a last, proffered perspective, has flooded in and waned. I hear the first crepitations of morning. I am alone with my life, and with the long view.

They will tell us this morning that we must come down off our pin point into the arena. But a pin point can become an arena.

They will tell us that while we, in our easy compassion, have carried the hunger of others in our minds, they have carried it on their backs. And this is true. For this, even when they say it corruptly, is their strength—and our indefensible shame.

They will tell us that we have been able to cherish values beyond hunger only because we have never known basic hunger ourselves— and this will be true also. But this is our paradox—and this is our stronghold, too.

They will tell us, finally, that there is no place for people like us, that the middle ground is for angels, not for men. But there is a place. For in the absence of angels and arbiters from a world of light, men and women must take their place.

Therefore, I am here, sitting opposite the white bulletin on the wall. For the last justification for people like us is to remember people like Hilda with justice. Therefore, in this room where there is no cockcrow except of conscience, I have remembered everything I can about Hilda Kantrowitz, who, this morning, is to be our prosecutor.

I will need to close my eyes when I have to enter the little latrine.

72⁻ 55700

... Edited and with an introd.
... rk. Scribner [1972]

... the Northmores, by H. James.—
...). Wilde.—Autres temps, by E.
... hen Braxton, by M. Beerbohm.—
... Sackeville-West.—Lambert Orme,
by H. N... ... ... E. Waugh.—Glory in the
daytime, by D. Parker.—The eternal moment, by E. M. Forster.—
The echo and the nemesis, by J. Stafford.—The friend of the family,
by M. Mc... ... ... quet, by A. Huxley.—In the
absence of angels, by H. Calisher.

1. Short stories, English. 2. Short stories, American.　　I. Title.

PZ1.A89Fab　　　　　　　　823'.01　　　　　　　73⁻37198
[PR1285]　　　　　　　　　　　　　　　　　　　　　　MARC
ISBN 0⁻684⁻12745⁻8